THE
AFRICAN
WITCH

JOYCE
CARY

The AFRICAN WITCH

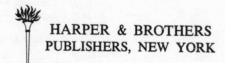

HARPER & BROTHERS
PUBLISHERS, NEW YORK

TO
ANTOINETTE FRANCES

I

An AWKWARD INCIDENT took place at Rimi races. Rimi races are always popular in Nigeria because the place is on the Niger river and not far from the railway. Great crowds of natives attend, and many white people. Sometimes there are thirty whites.

It is usual, for convenience, to reserve the paddock for invited guests, and in practice this arrangement excludes all natives except a few magnates like the Emir and his Ministers.

The Emir of Rimi has never attended the races, but he is always represented. On this occasion, three of his chief officers—dignified persons in blue and white robes, wearing large blue turbans—took up their places at one side of the enclosure, near the starting-post, before the first race, and remained there conversing among themselves for the rest of the day. They were an ornament to the occasion.

But when, just after the first race, the European spectators, turning away from the ropes, saw two negroes in European dress, one a very tall mulatto, one darker and shorter, strolling across the private ground, they felt strong surprise. This became indignation when it was known that the intruders had not been asked.

'Who are they?' everybody demanded.

The first was neatly dressed in dark blue, rather tight, with a stand-up collar and yellow boots; the other in a light grey flannel, with grey suede shoes and a grey felt hat. But this dandified perfection only increased the wrath of such as Honeywood, of the Rimi Hides Company, or Mrs. Pratt, who, pale and trembling with anger, exclaimed, 'They ought to be put down and beaten. That's the only way to teach such brutes!'

Just then the two young men laughed together at the remark made by one of them, and the spectacle of their nonchalance, their gaiety, infuriated the little white woman, so gentle and timid by nature that her life even in civilized Rimi was a nightmare to her. She wanted to strike the smiling faces—beat them down.

'Isn't anyone going to do anything?' she ejaculated.

'Look at the brutes, just showing off. Oh! where is Captain Rackham? He's the only man who really knows how to deal with such people. But I suppose he can't think of anything just now but his ladylove!'

The last word contained a mixture of expression only possible to Mrs. Pratt's flexible tongue and feelings; there was contempt for the lady, sympathy for Rackham, and yet a sentimental tenderness for them both.

11

The young girl who stood beside her—a new arrival, called Miss Honeywood—was quick to sympathize with her. 'I do hate people like that—they're so frightfully pushing, that kind of black man.'

Rackham, in fact, having ridden in the first race, had gone directly to find Miss Coote, to whom he had been engaged for the last six months. But she, too, had lately arrived in Africa, and his affection was eager. He was the assistant police commissioner at Rimi; an Irishman. He was a thin small man, dark and pale, with a small curled moustache and grey eyes. The grey eyes in the dark face gave him a penetrating look. He was a well-known amateur rider, and had the broad shoulders and stoop of a jockey; the narrow hips and slightly bowed legs. At the moment he was dressed like one, in a white silk shirt with red diagonal and a red cap; and in this dress he slightly exaggerated his stoop and jockey's roll. Even his legs seemed more bowed in their paper-thin boots.

Rackham was attractive to women because of his good looks, gaiety, and his love of women; because, too, of something feminine in his neatness, his fastidious dress. He had plenty of love-affairs, and it was generally agreed that at thirty-three he was inoculated against marriage. But on the voyage home, seven months before, he had found at the captain's table a little brown woman, with shortsighted brown eyes and a lame leg, who was introduced to him as Miss Judith Coote. She had been an Oxford don. Rackham, who liked pretty and amusing women, found himself condemned to sit beside this creature for a fortnight. He at once planned to remove from the table. He failed to do so on the first night; and a week later he was engaged.

The Service was astonished when they saw Miss Coote, who had no good features except her expression. Even the ship, who knew the lady, was surprised. They said that she had caught him.

But this was not true. Rackham had fallen in love. He had begun by finding Miss Coote extremely good company—better than anyone he had known—quick, light, and ready. This went far with Rackham, who was himself considered some of the best company in Nigeria.

He was one of those numerous young men whose lives were twisted by the war. He had been a scholar of his public school, meant for the Civil Service; but went direct from school to war, and afterwards, too restless and enervated to settle down again as a learner at the varsity, took the first job that offered him the open air and some polo.

He had enjoyed Africa, and Africa had enjoyed him. He had, like most Irishmen, a great power of enjoyment as well as a strong melancholy. But he had never enjoyed life so much as since his meeting with Miss Coote.

Mrs. Pratt said, 'He's fallen in love with her *brains*,' as if the man who did that must be a fool. But Rackham had not fallen in love with a mere brain, but with a whole woman just as passionate as himself, and perhaps rather more intelligent—certainly better trained. He had liked her at first because of her clear quick mind. Its judgment pleased all that was fastidious in his own. But he had soon loved the woman for the nature of the judgment, for her capacity to love him, and, at last, for her looks too.

Now it seemed to him that the brown face with the rather long nose and small chin; the light brown eyes, almost gold; the smooth straight hair, coiled in a Victorian bun; the thin round throat, the minute hands and feet, were of a most distinguished and fascinating beauty. She was like Lopokova, like a brown Queen Victoria in her first vivacity. He was disappointed when he failed to make her wear a cameo on her brown-spotted cotton blouses. But he insisted on a lace collar.

Miss Coote was ready to wear anything he chose, except the cameo, which made holes in her favourite blouses. She adored her handsome popular man with an innocent frankness which, in a sophisticated and even learned woman, was rather absurd.

Rackham was still looking for his Judy among the crowd when Mrs. Pratt and Miss Honeywood pounced on him, exclaiming, 'Have you seen them? Can't you turn them out?' At first he did not know what they were talking about. But when, by standing on tiptoe, he managed to catch sight of the two intruders, he turned white with anger. Indeed, he resembled for a moment, with the sharpening of his face, Mrs. Pratt herself.

The two negroes, finding themselves stared at, had lost their self-confidence. They looked uneasily round them—the mulatto with an arrogant glassy stare, the other nervously. But he, too, gave his hat a cock over one eye; struck an arrogant pose.

This enraged the watchers. A voice near Rackham called out—loud enough to be heard by the offenders—'Kick them out.' Two young bankers from the north, and a soldier, stood planted opposite them, like dogs about to spring.

Rackham, too, wanted to do something violent—to inflict public humiliation on the pair. He said bitterly, 'Something like this was bound to happen—I told the Resident, but he wouldn't let me put the police on the ropes.'

'Where is the Resident?' cried Mrs. Pratt.

Several people were asking for the Resident, but he was nowhere to be seen. None of the political officers could be found. This was noticed at last; and Mrs. Pratt said, 'Of course, they're dodging it. They're afraid. Oh! these politicals.'

Mrs. Pratt's husband was a doctor.

13

Mrs. Pratt was quite right. Burwash, the Resident, was hiding behind the temporary straw hut erected as a cloakroom and weighing-room; his assistant, Fisk, a young man arrived from Oxford less than six weeks before, had slipped into the crowd of natives standing outside the ropes.

The reason was that they had recognized both the mulatto and his companion. The former was called Coker. He was a local revivalist and agitator who had already given trouble. The other was a youth who claimed to be the next heir to the Rimi Emirate. He had already put in a formal claim, drawn up in the most Johnsonian prose. There were at least forty claimants to the Rimi throne, which had belonged to four different lines in the last sixty years; so that this young man had not been taken seriously. The Resident could not even remember his name, though he recollected clearly that he had been educated in England.

He was, however, extremely anxious not to have, to use his own phrase, any unfortunate incidents in his station. He knew that they would not be liked at headquarters. He was, therefore, almost apoplectic when Fisk found him.

Burwash's face at once became calm and smooth. He was a large dignified man who never allowed himself to appear ruffled. He smiled at Fisk, and said, 'I thought I'd get a little shade.'

'It's all right, sir,' said Fisk.

Burwash remembered to say, 'What's all right?' but he walked out of the hut and looked across the course.

'I meant about Aladai, sir,' said Fisk, who never forgot names.

'Ah, yes! The claimant.'

The two negroes were in conversation with Miss Coote. There was no doubt about the lady's enjoyment of their company. She was waving her hands, turning up her chin towards them. Her teeth flashed in a laugh. Her eyes, as usual when she laughed, almost disappeared, and she swayed with laughter. Then she took Aladai by the forearm, and raising her left-hand palm upwards in the air, bending her head towards her left shoulder, in the very attitude of the coquettish young woman who says, 'Do come along,' she turned him round towards the river. All three—the white woman limping, chattering, in the midst, the two blacks on each side of her, leaning inwards as if attracted by the powerful influence of her race and sex—walked off the course and out of the enclosure.

Nothing else was discussed for the rest of the meeting. At least a hundred times Mrs. Pratt screamed: 'The little fool!—but I always knew she'd do something impossible. I believe she's a Socialist. Most of these Oxford girls are, really'; and Miss Honeywood explained:

14

'She knew him at Oxford. She recognized him when she put on her spectacles.'

Rackham, who stayed close to Miss Honeywood, common friend of both parties, appeared much amused by the incident. He said, 'It's a regular old chestnut, isn't it?—the cannibal chief in the Balliol blazer.' He added that Miss Coote had been taken by surprise and didn't quite gather what was happening.

He repeated this apology almost as often as Mrs. Pratt her charges; and, as it was unknown for Rackham to repeat himself, the apology drew more notice to Miss Coote's conduct than her own indiscretion.

Meanwhile Judy Coote was gazing from right to left; and exclaiming, 'But, Louis, I'd no idea you really were a prince. How exciting it must be!'

The long rows of the crowd threw themselves on their faces beside the river road. The men rumbled like a long subdued roll of kettle-drums; the women, kneeling with their faces turned away from the great man upon whom they were not worthy to look, uttered long shrill screams, like piccolos.

'You should have told me.' She peered again. She had taken off her spectacles as soon as she recognized her friend, because she did not think that spectacles suited her. Miss Coote was not vain, but she made the best of herself. This was true even about her dress. For her bad dressing was not due to indifference or bad taste, but to lack of system and thought. She invariably found herself in the wrong garments, which she herself detested, because, for some reason, she had nothing else to wear.

'I did not quite realize it myself,' said the boy, in an uncertain voice.

'You seem to be a popular prince.'

Judy confined herself to exclamations because she knew that her young friend was still agitated. He was breathing fast, and a light sweat glistened on his high black forehead and pointed cheeks. His swaggering walk—all his movements were still a little exaggerated. He was in the condition of a nervous boy who has just passed through a critical test.

'There are many Rimi princes,' he said.

The other man, the tall mulatto, who had been presented to Judy as the Rev. Selah Coker, said solemnly, in careful English. 'You muss not believe him, mees. It is true he is our prince. Already the people call him Galadima. By Christ's help, he soon be our king.'

Mr. Coker was very tall and thin, had a long tobacco-coloured face, deeply pitted by smallpox. His features were European, and would have been handsome had it not been for the vertical elongation. His expression was now sad and somewhat sleepy—as if the man were exhausted. He obviously considered himself as, in some kind, an aide-de-camp to

Aladai. He carried his hat in his hand; and now, suddenly stretching his mouth, which was not large, to an immense oblong opening, and turning it towards the crowd, he bellowed a salutation in Rimi.

Judy jumped, and Aladai said sharply, 'Please don't do that.'

'I greet the people for you,' said Coker, and having uttered another roar, during which he turned completely round, like a patent foghorn with iron funnel and clockwork machinery, became sleepy and small-mouthed again. He said, in his flat clipped voice, 'De people come to hail you. You muss greet dem. You are prince of Rimi. Soon you be king. All people wan you for king. Rimi people wan Christian king, Mees Coote. They love Christ. Dat's the difference between Rimi people and white people. Rimi people love Christ, but white people hate Christ. African people have good hearts: when they hear about Christ, they are sad for Him—they love Him. African people are poor, mees, but they think better to be good and loving than rich and proud like white people.'

This pointed speech was given with force; the man's voice seemed to wake up, and even his face showed expression.

Judy liked his sincerity, and answered politely that in America, too, the negroes showed religious ardour.

She looked up at her other companion, to see if he could smile at this, but found him still preoccupied.

Judy Coote had last seen Louis Aladai in a north Oxford drawing-room. She had come in late, heard from the door a light, but sensitive, tenor sing Schubert's 'Ständchen,' and congratulated the hostess on her singer. The woman then presented her to Aladai.

She liked, at first sight, the handsome black with his magnificent carriage. The even colour of the black skin was an attraction to her—like that of a statue. But she was surprised to find this black statue, whose features were like those of a Greek bronze head slightly worn and roughed by the gentle movement of a Mediterranean current on a sandy bottom, animated by a quick and ingenuous mind. They talked with mutual enjoyment. Miss Coote, it is true, did not hear anything new or striking from a boy of twenty with a limited experience of life and thought. Perhaps, if Louis had been white, she would not have been so much impressed by his intelligence, or amused by long serious discussions about such stock subjects as English poetry, German music, French art, English politics, and primitive religion. But, even if he had been white, she would have been delighted by his quick sympathy, his instant response to shades of meaning and feeling. She found in him the real capacity for friendship, which is sympathy of mind—as sympathy of heart is that of love. She had enjoyed giving him, at his own request, special coaching on modern political history.

16

Rimi stands on the Niger. Its waterfront extends for a couple of miles along the right bank of the river, which is, at this point, twice as wide as the Thames at Tower Bridge. The town, within its mud walls, now greatly diminished in height by rain, forms a semi-circle, which runs half a mile up the slope of Rimi hill. Town and station are on the same hill; but the hill is concave towards the curve of the river, so that each seems to overlook the other. The Emir looks down upon the Residency bungalow and fort; and, from the fort, it is possible, with glasses, to see the ladies of the harem beating corn and scratching each other's heads within the most private courts of the royal palace.

The waterfront is broken by the wall which divides the huts, hards, and boats of the town from the stores and wharves of the trading companies and the marine.

A port seen from above is always a fine spectacle. It provides the right contrast of bold form, strong lines, and fine detail, of weight and delicacy. It turns the rough beauty of wild water into a jewel, set among formal pattern.

Judy Coote, who was staying on the waterfront, in the bungalow of the Hides Company, and who seldom came up the hill except in the evening, knew how much beauty was spread out in front of her; and, screwing up her eyes at it, exclaimed, 'How lovely it is!'

She longed to put on her spectacles, and for the moment wished that she might be alone to do so. But she thought, 'One can't have everything.'

Aladai said gravely, 'Yes, it is a country to be proud of. I have found that one can love it, too.'

'Why, too, Louis?'

'How many Africans feel any love for Africa—or Africans either?'

Judy was struck by the change in the boy's voice. She knew that he could be enthusiastic about things—even history or municipal government, as well as music or poetry. He had the African's sensitive temperament—more quick and responsive than a Sicilian's, and perhaps more moody. But she had not before heard any patriotic sentiments.

'Are you a nationalist?' she asked cautiously.

'I don't know,' he answered; and then, speaking with force, 'I think I am—if that means standing up for one's own people.'

Judy heard the tremor of excitement in the boy's voice, and remembered his swaggering uneasiness in the racecourse. She was glad to change the subject.

They had come near the town wall, but, instead of turning towards the gate, took the path along the ditch which leads to the river outside the wall.

'Aren't we going into the town?' she cried, disappointed.

'No, I live at Makurdi's.'

'Whose?'

'He is my uncle. Here he is, coming to receive us.'

17

She peered, with raised eyebrows, at the group of brightly-coloured figures advancing towards them from a large native compound on the waterside.

The foremost and largest of the group, now advanced two paces beyond the rest, wore a white linen coat. But below the coat a dark blue cloth descended to his feet.

'That is Uncle Makurdi,' said Aladai. 'He is my guardian.'

Uncle Makurdi, now less than five yards away, grew larger as he approached. He was a man of about six foot four in height and twenty-three stone weight. His shape was that of an enormous frog, swollen in the belly to the size of a dining-table. His eyes, fixed near the top of his shining and pointed head, projected so far that they seemed ready to pop out of it. His immense mouth was stretched so widely by his grin of welcome that his chin was hidden.

As he waddled forward, labouring with short thick arms, turning out his immense splay-feet, his stomach jumped, his knees knocked, his shoulders heaved, his pyramidal head rolled and jerked, so that Judy, in pity and anxiety, exclaimed, 'But the poor man; in this heat!' and hurried forward to receive his greeting. Makurdi did not take the hand until he had bowed so far forward that the whole shining top of his head was displayed to his guest.

Aladai made the presentation. Coker, turning towards the watchful crowd, shutting his eyes and opening his elastic mouth, bellowed, 'The white princess, friend of the King of England, greets Makurdi.'

Makurdi, having shaken hands, bowed again. He was speaking all the time, but partly from breathlessness, partly from agitation, he could not articulate any single word. The effect was like broken prayers uttered by a few badly trained choir-boys.

The rest of his party, consisting of gaily-dressed young girls and some children, formed a semi-circle round the visitor. Outside them the crowd pressed in, staring in silence.

Makurdi struck himself on the chest, made a powerful effort, and piped, in a thin high voice, 'Oh! how shall I say my pleasure. It is an important day for me.'

'Come, uncle, shall we go in out of the sun?'

'Yes, yes. But, pardon, all is not ready. Only just this minute, some boy come tell me Galadima bring lady from Oxford.'

Makurdi's compound consisted of a mass of buildings in mud, wood, and brick, some thatched, some covered with tin, huddled together behind a ruinous landing-stage. The store was an oblong wooden house with a tin roof, facing the water. One end of the store was Makurdi's private quarters, opening on to a large verandah, projecting beyond the front of the store almost to the water's edge.

Here Judy was presented to the members of his household—two men in European dress; a girl in a cotton frock; an old woman, in a black silk, who said nothing. Makurdi had meanwhile caused certain piles of goods, children, and canoe poles to be removed from the verandah, and a table and chairs to be brought out to it. Aladai and Judy took their seats; some of the brightly-dressed girls came hurrying with plates, with a teapot, with numerous pots of jam. One of them, placing a tin on the table, opened it, turned it upside down, and shook out, with a triumphant smile, a currant cake, which, grasping in her small strong hand, she placed in the lid of the tin—for plate. Makurdi begged to be excused from sitting down with his guests. He said, perspiring, that he was not fit.

For a few minutes he hovered behind their chairs, then suddenly disappeared into the house.

Judy, seeing the young man still thoughtful, began to praise the view of the river and Makurdi's hospitality. He got up to look at the river, as if he had not seen it before; and then remained in the middle of the verandah, gazing dreamily outwards.

'Your tea's getting cold, Louis.'

He turned suddenly towards her, and said, 'Ought I to have gone into the enclosure?'

'It didn't matter a bit—but I believe one is supposed to have an invitation.'

'Coker said that I wouldn't need one, as a Rimi prince.'

'Perhaps you don't. I'm sure you wouldn't. No, of course not. I'm sure if you ask the Resident——'

'But people thought I was pushing myself in——'

'They didn't understand that you had a right to be there.'

The young man walked up and down with quick nervous steps. Then, unexpectedly, he smiled at his friend, and said, 'If I had put on a turban, and three or four Hausa gowns, they'd have been delighted to see me.'

'Oh! I don't know about that.'

'Yes, yes—that is what is so strange.' He stopped and stared at her, as if she, being English, was part of the strangeness. 'Why do they not like me to wear their clothes—isn't it a compliment? But, of course, it looks as if I wanted to put myself on a level with them.'

Judy interrupted quickly, 'But you know it's not that——'

'What is it, then?'

'I think it's because we are such nationalists ourselves—we like to see people keeping old customs and their own dress. You know, Louis, that we are a very sentimental people, especially about old customs and picturesque dresses and views.'

But the boy was not attending to her. He was too much excited, and

19

his quick, leopard's walk up and down the verandah seemed to increase his excitement.

'I can't understand it,' he burst out. 'Such a great people—a great civilization! And they see that I love it. Think of how I felt when I began to read English books and to hear what civilization could mean—it was like growing up thousands of years in a few months.'

'But, Louis, Rimi has a civilization of its own.'

He made a quick gesture, only short of impatience by a little politeness. 'Rimi civilization! You know that it is a joke. Can you compare it with yours?—and that means all Europe. Think of the richness of the European peoples—the poetry, the music, the—the'—he waved his hand in the air—'the greatness of every kind.' He turned on her again. 'Rimi civilization! Do you know what it is?—*ju-ju*.'

'Not all of it, Louis.'

But he was not in a mood for argument. 'It is soaked with *ju-ju*. You may say a body is not blood—but if you took the blood out, what would be left? The blood of what you call Rimi civilization is *ju-ju*—so crude and stupid—you do not know what they can do. My own sister—but I mustn't tell you. It was three years ago, and she won't do it again.'

Judy pushed his cup slightly towards him. She did not interrupt him by saying, 'Your tea is cold'—her glance and gesture reminded him, but so gently that he was permitted to overlook it if he chose.

He broke off, and stared at the cup with the expression of a crystal-gazer. His lips continued to tremble a little, but his breathing became quieter, as if his excitement, like the noise of his voice, was flowing away into the sudden quiet.

'I didn't give you any sugar.'

He suddenly smiled at her and sat down. 'Two lumps, please. You think I am rather silly to be so excited?'

'No, no, Louis. What did your sister do?' Judy coloured a little, as she often did when she asked an indiscreet question out of curiosity. She was extremely curious—like all real women.

The boy made a gesture driving away the memory. 'Do you know what a witch trial is?—but I won't tell you now. It's too horrible a thing. And I stopped it. I told her I would go to the judge, and she was frightened.'

'What happens to witches here?'

'Just what happened to yours in Europe—they kill them.'

'Yes, we can't boast.'

'Yes, you can boast,' the boy exclaimed. 'You have stopped it—you have escaped from it—by your English civilization. And then you refuse it to us, in Rimi.'

'Your friend Mr. Coker went to some school out here, I suppose?'

Aladai raised his brows and looked sharply at her. Then he smiled, and she, too, smiled. It was an exchange like a wink. The boy suddenly gave a loud laugh like a crow—a Rimi laugh. In an instant he had passed from one kind of excitement to another, equally exuberant. 'I had forgotten how you could do that!' he exclaimed.

'Do what, Louis?'

'When somebody is full of hot air, you just—put a'—making a poking gesture with finger and thumb—'a little pin into the balloon.'

'Which balloon?'

'Of course, Coker is *ju-ju* too—it is what you call primitive religious *ju-ju*. But you can't say that it is so bad as Rimi *ju-ju*. And, besides, I shall not let Coker do any nonsense in Rimi.'

He paused, and corrected himself: 'Make any nonsense—what is the word?—play any tricks. If he starts any watch-tower tricks or spirit-women games here, I shall stop him—I shall smash him to pieces.'

'Off with his head,' said Judy, who thought that the young man was again growing too enthusiastic; and also that his autocratic airs were a little exaggerated. But he did not notice the interruption. He waved his hand—'If Coker becomes a danger, if he brought in this other *ju-ju* of blood, I should put him out of Rimi.'

Judy did not protest again. It struck her suddenly that she was not discussing politics now, but taking part in them. This boy was not a pupil to be amused by ideas, but a prince who expected to rule half a million people, and who already felt the weight of a real responsibility.

'They must see it,' he exclaimed.

'What, about the *ju-ju?*'

'That Rimi has a right to schools. Oh, I know some boys do go to schools—chiefs' sons to the Government school at Bauchi, and little pagan boys to the mission schools to learn their hymns—but how many do you think they all come to.'

'I've no idea.'

'About five hundred—in a million—I don't count the Mohammedans, their schools are a joke.'

Judy was surprised. It had never struck her that no one in Rimi went to school.

'But they have an education,' she said.

'In *ju-ju*, and the proper way to dig yams. Oh, yes, and some folksongs.' He paused again, and looked at Judy with an excited face. 'They must see it.' He jumped up, and began to walk about again; then suddenly laughed. 'It's too absurd—a million without schools—and Rimi civilization! Rimi! No, I love Rimi, and it is because I love it that I want to give it something worth calling a civilization.'

'But why not do it in Rimi's own language, Louis? You can always translate from English—and then your people can say that they understand Shakespeare better than we do.'

21

'But then——' He had once understood and laughed at this joke; he did not notice it now. He asked, seriously and anxiously, why she was opposed to English teaching.

'Because to take another people's language and literature directly may give them a feeling of inferiority, and it often takes a nation five hundred years to get over that feeling.'

'But, Miss Coote'—he sat down, puzzled—'I don't quite see.'

They began to argue the point.

Through the open windows Makurdi's voice came in a yell that caused Judy to look round in astonishment, but Aladai laughed.

'What are they talking about?' she asked.

'I fancy it's the same thing as we are talking about—politics.'

'It sounds like murder.'

'My uncle is a serious politician. Have some more tea?' He was in high spirits. He said again: 'They must see—they can't help it.'

It was quite true that Makurdi was talking politics. For the last few months he had talked nothing else. Makurdi's dream for twenty years had been to see his nephew Emir of Rimi. He knew better than anyone in the country what could be done with Rimi and Rimi trade by an intelligent emir guided by a business man of his experience.

Rimi was one of the best-placed ports of the Niger. The whole river trade passed its wharves, and, though that trade was declining, it was still great. The internal trade had also been bad, but Makurdi was sure that more could be made out of it. Rimi had thirty thousand people, and it was the capital of a province holding a million. Nothing but the incompetence of the old Emir, the ignorant greed of his market officials, and the conservatism of his village heads prevented every adult in that million from putting at least five shillings a year into the Treasury. Ten thousand pounds could be obtained from the dried-fish trade alone— by centralizing the market, releasing the principal dealers from dues, and licensing retailers.

The beer-sellers would willingly pay double to limit their numbers and get rid of competition. A licence system on the English model would accomplish this, and could also be represented as a temperance measure. The Resident would like it very much.

But first Aladai had to be made emir. This had seemed to both Makurdi and Aladai a small part of their difficulties—Aladai's claims, his character and intelligence, compared with those of any other candidate, made opposition seem contemptible.

The only other man who had ever had a popular following was Salé, who represented the Mohammedans. But Salé was of an inferior branch of the family; and, besides, the Emir hated him, and had forbidden him to enter Rimi.

22

Now, however, alarmed by Aladai's reception in the town—the very reception which Makurdi had organized and paid for—he had also forbidden Aladai to enter it.

Nobody cared, of course, for the Emir's hostility. It was almost an advantage—because of the nature of white officials, who always suspect jealousy in emirs, and use it as an indication of merit in the criticized. But it was a great handicap to be kept out of Rimi.

The Rimi ward heads, the feudal chiefs who kept their town houses in Rimi, and their countless dependants, would all be consulted in the choice of a new chief. The people themselves would be consulted, because that was another habit of residents. Taught by several rebellions they tried to pick a popular candidate. But how could Aladai make himself popular in Rimi if he was barred the town? The difficulties in Makurdi's way, now that they were close to him, seemed large and dangerous. The Court opposition, the Resident's silence, the unexpected hostility of the white traders, the intrigues of Salé's friends, frightened Makurdi so much that he could not sleep, and all day long he shouted and sweated, arguing, plotting.

Judy's visit at once suggested to him a new scheme. The appearance of any white person in any native house, like that of an official visitor in a slum, at once gives hopes of advantage, and an occasion to be seized for it.

He called a girl, and sent her for his niece Elizabeth. He gave orders to the girl to bring her at all costs. Meanwhile he could not even sit down in his impatience. He was in terror lest Aladai and the visitor should come to the end of their meal and go away; at every moment he thought of some new device for keeping them.

'Jamesu, go to store and get dem sardines. Get two tin.'

The sardines were opened, and sent in to Aladai and Miss Coote, who laughed a great deal, and took out one each. But Makurdi did not mind if they laughed. 'Jamesu, go to store and get one tin cold chicken.'

'Dem cold chicken very old, fader. Dey go swell up.'

Makurdi beat himself on the head in his distraction. 'Oh, you Jamesu, how you talk—why you no do what I tell you? Go get dem tin chicken.'

Jamesu could not find the chicken. He brought bacon. But ham is not a tea dish in Nigeria. Makurdi threw it at the boy, and called for sausages—not, of course, Oxford, which are for breakfast, but German sausages.

23

Elizabeth Aladai had a *ju-ju* house in the third ward of Rimi town, close to the market-place called the women's market.

It was next the main street, in a winding alley, or rather ditch—a dry one in winter, a watercourse in summer—and it was surrounded by a mass of crookeder narrower ditches, leading to compounds so crowded together, rotten, and ruinous that the ward head himself could not find his way through them. This part of Rimi was an African rookery.

Burwash's predecessors replanned Rimi on paper as long ago as 1922; the plan in the office showed a broad street, in dotted lines, where the *ju-ju* house was.

Makurdi's messenger, after hopping along the dry ditch of the main street, from one water-worn hole to another, for a hundred yards, turned the last corner, and found her way blocked by a crowd. Men, women, and children were sitting patiently on the ground.

'What is it?' she asked.

Several turned up their eyes at her, and said, 'A trial.'

They were country people. The whole inhabitants of a village had come to attend the trial, and, like country people, they were not to be moved out of their places.

These places were, however, no good to them, for they could not see into the *ju-ju* compound, or even approach the door, which was guarded, in the porch, by an impudent-looking girl in a blue cloth, smoking a cigarette.

In front of this porch, a young man, wearing nothing but a porter's loin-cloth, was walking up and down with a stick over his shoulder, and, as soon as the messenger caught sight of this youth, she began to shout and wave at him. But he paid no attention to her.

This young man was called Akande Tom, and he was said to be the latest favourite of the *ju-ju* woman Elizabeth. A *ju-ju* woman can choose her own man, and Elizabeth had had several husbands—all of them fine and young. Akande Tom had arrived in Rimi about a month before, with a gang of carriers, and since then Elizabeth's former husband had suddenly disappeared from Rimi. It was given out that he had gone away upon her *ju-ju* business; most people believed that she had turned him into a rat or a fish, and that he had been caught and destroyed in that shape. But he had been a conceited, drunken fool, who asked bribes from everyone coming to the *ju-ju* house, and nobody regretted him.

Akande Tom was a younger and handsomer man. He was about twenty, in his prime, over six foot tall, and to the neck his proportions were perfect—not in the Greek, but the African, manner. His lines were baroque rather than classical; his shoulders a little exaggerated in their flare, their indented cape, of muscle; the muscles of his flanks and thighs too exuberant. But these were not faults, they were the virtues of his native style. His faults were too-thin legs, which, being thin, therefore seemed a little crooked, and huge ugly feet. His neck also was too short for his immense shoulders and his head too small. But it was a fine head in the pure negro forms. Its huge everted lips, broad-ended flat nose, long powerful jaw, deep eyes, were each perfect in their type, modelled as if by an African sculptor, whose inspiration, like the palm sap of the jungle, made him drunk with life, so that his work was a dance of the hand.

Akande Tom was well aware of his own beauty. He swaggered up and down, in the short space in front of the *ju-ju* porch, with a strut and a swing which would have been ridiculous in anybody less entitled to vanity. He stepped like a cock who appears to say, as he quickly and proudly lifts each claw, 'Vile ground, how dare you touch me!' He swung up his head at each turn, so that only his broad crooked nostrils were presented at the crowd, as if to aim contempt at them; and the jerk of his left elbow dismissed them from his presence.

Makurdi's messenger, a young girl who had spent all her life on the waterside, put her fingers in the bag which hung from her neck, drew out a bright nickel halfpenny, and held it up so that her fingers covered the hole in the middle—all but the rim. It might have been a shilling.

Akande Tom did not seem to notice it. He made two more turns; then suddenly, instead of turning, he waved his stick, and shouted, 'What are you doing, rascals? Don't you see the messenger from the great judge to the Chief Lisbet Aladai?'—Lisbet was Elizabeth's native name.

The crowd did not move from their places. They cowered and swayed a little while Tom planted his huge feet on their ankles and thighs, trampling till he could reach a hand to the messenger.

When the halfpenny touched his hand, he dropped it at once, and shouted, 'No one can come in, I tell you. It's an order.'

The messenger quickly brought out sixpence. Tom did not seem to notice it. He swelled up till he appeared at least seven feet high, and shouted, 'If you have a message to the Lady Lisbet, you can tell it to me. No one else can go in now.'

The messenger took her bag and emptied it into her palm beside the sixpence. It contained one other halfpenny, three nickel anini (tenths), seven cowries, and a safety-pin. Tom cupped his hand at the level of his stomach. The messenger turned hers over upon it. Tom turned round and shouted, 'Make way, there, you country lumps—the messenger is from persons of the highest importance to the great and distinguished holy woman, Lisbet Aladai.'

The country people swayed, and cast upward angry, imploring glances, as Tom's feet crashed upon them. The messenger, inserting her toes here and there into the crannies and holes already pressed out and made anæsthetic by Tom's weight, safely reached the open ground.

She dived at the door. The impudent girl at once held out a hand. 'What are you doing?'

'I want to come in.'

'You can't.'

'But I haven't anything left.'

'He's taken your money, has he?'

Tom began to shout at her, 'I said she could go in.'

'Who are you?' replied the impudent girl.

'I'll tell Lisbet about you.'

'I'll tell her you've been taking presents.'

At this, Tom seemed to shrink. He was actually bending at the shoulders and knees. He said, in a low and modest voice, 'Come, my dear girl, I didn't do anything.'

Makurdi's messenger ducked her head and flew through the porch. The impudent girl was too lazy and bored to pursue her. She said only, 'That's your affair, Tom. If there's trouble, it's yours. I think it's time you had a whipping.'

'My dear girl, what are you saying?' Tom uttered a faint cackle of laughter, like a man who acknowledges the joke of a dentist.

'Lisbet knows how to whip, too. She's better than the Emir's own whipper—she takes the flesh off the bone. What do you mean—"I didn't do anything"? That doesn't matter. Lisbet eats all her men—all.'

The messenger dashed through an inner porch and stood in the main yard.

Although the people, crowded into the road, had been sitting with a patient look, those within the yard were still on their feet, pushing for places, chattering.

The plaintiffs could be seen standing near the high mud wall on the left, surrounding the women's *ju-ju* house, which is barred to men. They were a country family from a down-river pagan village—a father, three sons, and a group of their wives. Two young children stood among their legs, a girl and a boy.

They were talking earnestly, and all together, in bursts of excitement and gesticulation. But when the father, who stood above all the rest, a man with the head of a black Pharaoh, spoke, they were silent at once, listening to him with respectful politeness. The old man spoke in a forcible murmur, nodding his head, and moving his right hand as if to say, 'That, at least, is certain.'

The youngest of the wives, a young girl lately married, was conspicuous by her new clothes. She was like a child in church, trying to be serious, but so much excited by the crowd, by her own new cloth, of bright blue plush, wrapped round her firm maiden's breasts, by the glances cast at her, and the sudden importance of her family, that she could not manage to be so for more than half a minute at a time.

She was a pretty girl. Her skin was the colour of milk chocolate, with the matt sheen of a tulip's underside; her nose was broad, smooth, and flat, with perfectly even-flared nostrils; her lips full and curled, but not turned out; her throat round, strong, and thick. The shape of her face was like a shield; it broadened on an even full curve from her little pointed chin to her broad low forehead. Her ears were flat, very small, and curled like a shell. Her shoulders were broad, her flanks strong and bony. Her body had as little waist as the classical Venus. Her legs were straight, and had powerful ankles. The calf came lower than a white woman's, and avoided the ugly forms of a pegtop. Her feet were arched, deep through the instep, short in the toe, but too long in the heel. Her hands, stained red with henna, were small and broad in the palm, with short, quickly tapered fingers.

The smallpox had treated her kindly. She had but one noticeable depression—in the middle of her left cheek, so placed that it was a beauty spot.

This girl—Osi—was a well-known beauty; she was sixteen years old, and she had been married two months to the boy who stood beside her—Ojo—a powerful young man of eighteen, with an extremely ugly but good-natured face. Ojo was very black, and smallpox had left his skin as rough as old weather-worn rock. One nostril had been partly eaten away.

Whenever the father spoke, Osi turned up her shining eyes towards him and looked grave; but, even before he had finished, she had caught some passing eye, noticed a wrinkle in her cloth, and at once she was preening herself, moving her lips self-consciously, wriggling her shoulders, peeping over her shoulder. Once she smiled at a friend, showing all her brilliant teeth, her childish delight.

But she did not move from her husband's presence—an aura which seemed to extend about six inches from him in every direction. When he moved, she moved, not touching him, but keeping as much of herself as possible within that aura. Even when she was looking another way, she moved with him, as if she could feel his presence like a magnetic charge, whose strength informed her of his distance.

But suddenly the noise of excited voices died; the crowd fell into a

27

pattern caused by the different groups turning towards the *ju-ju* house, and at the same time shrinking back from it, so that they were pressed against the yard wall. The door in the mud wall opened, and Elizabeth was seen in the opening.

She almost filled the opening, which framed her with the sunlight streaming into the yard behind. She was a woman who seemed, in her height and proportions, bigger than the largest and most powerful men. In fact she was probably about five foot ten in height, and fifteen or sixteen stone in weight—not of fat, but of bone and muscle.

In feature she was like her brother Louis, but more negro, energetic, and sensual. She had the typical negro lips, rolled back until the red lining of the mouth could be seen; her jaw was immensely long, so that her whole face inclined backwards from the chin and the flat surface of the out-turned lips to the high tapering polished forehead.

She wore a black velvet cloth tightly wrapped round her below the armpits, and almost touching the ground. This cloth made her seem like a moving pillar. Its dead black, which appeared greenish in the sun, contrasted with living tints of the black flesh, which changed at each motion, flashing copper, golden, blue-brown in different angles of light.

The woman was far gone with child, but this, in her slow movement, added to her monumental dignity.

Her face was streaked with white paint on cheeks and forehead; and pieces of carved wood and bone, little bags of medicine, hung from her neck and arms, thick and firm as a man's leg.

Her hands were supported by two girls, her eyes closed, or apparently closed. She moved forward with a slow gliding movement; the girls, walking sideways as they held up her hands in both of theirs, advanced by awkward side steps, which contrasted with the smooth movement of the priestess.

As she approached the people, their faces, confident, lively a moment before, became rigid with terror. They knew that they were not witches, but the terror of the *ju-ju* woman's presence turned their bones to water.

A woman, following closely behind, carried a sick baby in her hands. The baby was visibly dying. It was no bigger than a skinned rabbit—a skeleton in a dry, stretched membrane. It was too feeble to move its arms and legs; but it cried ceaselessly, uttering a wail like a mouse's squeal, prolonged.

This woman had lost three children in the last month, and now her baby was dying. She had come to find the witch who had killed her children, and to save the baby. She seemed, however, too much broken by her wretchedness to take much interest in the witch hunt. She looked all the time at the baby, moving its huge cap to shade its shrivelled face. No doubt, too, she had every confidence in Elizabeth.

28

Elizabeth had been a *ju-ju* priestess for four years. She had succeeded an uncle on account of her special aptitude. In Africa, a *ju-ju* priest has a power of life and death which resides in him personally. He has knowledge and training; he has to be initiated, like priests elsewhere, but he must also have a quality which marks him off from others—the quality of power. A woman may have the quality as well as a man, and then she may become a priestess. The power is real, and so no one would dream of setting it aside by artificial rules limiting priestcraft to one sex or caste.

But Elizabeth was greater than her uncle, because she had been trained for the women's *ju-ju* as well as inheriting the men's. Also, she was an organizer. She had great power in Rimi. It was only limited by the modern scepticism, infecting some of the townspeople, and by the Mohammedan and Christian preachers.

She had found this a difficult case. The criminal is often obvious to the *ju-ju* priest. He proceeds on the same principles as a police detective looking for a murderer. He asks, 'Who has a grudge against the victim, or who stands to profit by his death?'

Perhaps some *ju-ju* priests act solely on deduction, but it is not the usual thing, for it would mean that the priest did not believe in his own magical powers; and not only priests, but almost every human being, black and white, believe that they have such powers. In Europe a woman talks of her intuition, a man of his luck; gardeners have a growing hand, and salesmen personality. A *ju-ju* priest is a medium and has the same temperament. He may commit frauds, but that does not prevent his believing in himself.

But Elizabeth had every reason to believe in her own powers, for she saw the visible effects of them. Every day women blessed her for making them bear, for bringing them good trade, good husbands, and men thanked her for curing their sore throats.

All morning she had been sitting in the outer yard, listening to evidence. She knew not only all the village gossip, but the characters of almost everyone connected with the victim and her family. She knew that the old father had quarrelled with his second son, father of the dead children, about a hoe. She knew that the mother had been a quarrelsome daughter-in-law; that she was jealous of Osi, the newest bride in the household, and a pet to the old father. She knew that she had humiliated the girl by putting her to dirty work and saying she was good for nothing else.

A mass of small quarrels and jealousies had accumulated in her memory during three hours' talk and argument, but she had not discovered any clue. No one seemed to bear a grudge against the plaintiff, and no one could profit by the children's deaths.

29

Osi, by all reports, had shown perfect good humour under provocation. The old father had taken trouble to make that plain. 'She was a good girl,' he said. 'Good wife, good daughter.'

Of course good-natured conduct is no proof of innocence in a witch. Witches are always cunning in disguising themselves. Pretty girls, too, excite hatred in older women, especially when they attract their husbands; and they are apt to be spoilt, to resent any kind of rudeness. But Elizabeth did not argue from this, 'Osi must be the witch,' because the evidence was quite insufficient; and, besides, her magical powers might indicate somebody else. Some enemy in the village.

These powers sometimes pick out the most unexpected persons. But their judgment is always confirmed at the witch trial.

Elizabeth had now no conscious will. She put from her mind all the evidence that she had heard. She had placed herself under control of the *ju-ju* spirit, and now she felt that spirit swelling and spreading through her whole body. She released her muscles—her arms hung like bags of lead on the aching hands of the girls—she softened her legs, bending them at the knees, making her flesh soft for the penetration of the spirit.

She was not conscious of her direction. Yet the girls felt her turn them this way and that, by a slow pressure, as she glided through the rigid, breathless crowd.

For half an hour she sought. Then, as she was passing close by the plaintiff's group, her hand jerked suddenly out, as if worked by a string, and gripped Osi by the wrist.

She continued to hold the girl, who stood staring at her with an expression of foolish wonder. Her husband, father-in-law, the whole of her family, had already shrunk back from her. Osi's tongue appeared between her trembling lips; she looked round and smiled, as if to say, 'This is silly.'

But in looking round she found herself alone, and the smile disappeared. She licked her lips again, and murmured something.

Elizabeth, meanwhile, stood still in her trance. She shivered and uttered a deep sigh; her eyes opened slowly. She looked at Osi, and appeared as much surprised as the girl herself.

'You, Osi,' she cried.

The girl tried again to speak, and then shook her head; her face was wet with sweat; her eyes and head were not still for an instant, as she looked about her, already shamefaced and guilty.

Her sister-in-law flew at her, screaming, hooking her clawed hand in the air. She would have gouged her eyes out had not her husband dragged her backwards, in terror lest she should anger the witch.

Osi, shrinking from her, suddenly began to babble. She said, over

30

and over again, 'I haven't—I don't understand—I didn't do anything—I can't.'

The two girls had caught her by the arm; she began to scream in her terror. But she was silent at once when Elizabeth said to her, 'Give up your medicine.'

The witch did not understand. But when they made her understand, at last, that she was asked to give up to Elizabeth the *ju-jus* with which she had destroyed the children, she answered that she had not got any.

'If you do not give them up, we will kill you,' said Elizabeth.

The girl tried to throw herself on the yard and catch Elizabeth's feet. She was now hysterical with fear, and could not form even a single word. Her speeches of appeal and denial came out so quickly and urgently that they overran each other and sounded like gibberish.

'Hear the witch talk,' said the crowd. 'She is trying to bewitch Lisbet too.'

They pressed away from her; her brothers were pushing the old father back towards the farthest corner of the yard.

Obstinacy and stupidity are things that tend to annoy quick-minded and intelligent people. They irritated Elizabeth. She said to her assistants, 'Take her away, and put the fire to her.'

The two girls dragged Osi away through the door of the *ju-ju* wall; they literally dragged her over the rough clay, because she herself, either on account of her fear or desperation, had fallen down and lay like a sack. But she had not fainted. She was still screeching her gibberish, faster, more confused, more urgent every minute.

The inner yard of the *ju-ju* house, like the outer, was filled with buildings of different shapes and sizes, scattered without regular plan. One row of square flat-topped huts, three together, at the far end of the yard, held the *ju-jus* themselves. This group stood apart. But the other three sides of the enclosure were crowded with huts, of all types and sizes; new and ruinous, round and square.

Osi was dragged into one of these, stripped, tied head and foot, and thrown against the wall. The assistants brought embers and lit a fire.

However, it was usual for Elizabeth to be present while a witch was being examined, because, if she should confess, it needed an expert to know whether the confession could be accepted as true. But when the girls had the fire ready, and sent for Elizabeth, they were told that she could not come then. They were to put off trial until her return.

Elizabeth had just received the message from Makurdi, and this was why Osi escaped from the fire.

When Makurdi saw his niece, calm and cool as if she had been brought on a hammock, he gave a kind of squawk of relief, indignation, and joy. The indignation was for the agony and suspense which her

31

absence had made him suffer. Grinning, panting, sweating like a squeezed sponge, he rushed at her, and began to explain, not his scheme, but the circumstances—the white woman's visit. He prepared the ground. 'She is his friend—you understand?—a friend from England.' Makurdi spoke Rimi to Elizabeth.

'Why not?' Elizabeth asked.

Makurdi, who, with all his study, was no diplomat, burst out, 'Ask her to your *ju-ju* house.'

'Why?'

'But don't you see? She will have to go into the town—Louis will go with her. The Emir's men dare not stop a white woman. She won't let them stop Louis. Thus Louis will get into the town, and the people will welcome him.'

Elizabeth's expression changed. Her eyes opened widely; her lips parted, showing her middle teeth. Then she suddenly broke into voluble animated speech.

Elizabeth had objections to every suggestion, but the fact that she urged them showed that she was ready to be convinced. She was conservative, like most women, but intelligent, and therefore, like intelligent women, she would act upon reason shown. But, though she never decided anything except by her own judgment, she liked to hear persuasion. When Makurdi had repeated his arguments three times, she nodded her head, and said, 'It is possible.'

She then unfolded the top layer of her cloth, gave it a vigorous tug, and retucked it under her armpits. This meant that she was about to undertake a journey.

Elizabeth was as eager as Makurdi to see Aladai emir, but for a different reason. She disliked Mohammedans almost as much as Christians, and Salé had already threatened the *ju-ju*.

It was true that Aladai said rude things about the *ju-ju*, but he was a fool boy. She could manage Aladai at any time. It was Salé and Coker whom she feared as enemies.

She was not half-way to the door before Coker walked in at it. He was always on the watch. He did not allow any council to be held without him. And he seemed to have that faculty of the born politician to know, through brick walls and great distances, exactly when and where a council was being held.

'What is it?' he asked Elizabeth. 'Where are you going?'

Elizabeth did not reply, or even look at the man whom she despised. But Makurdi, who knew Coker's influence in the town, explained his scheme.

'Not the *ju-ju* house,' said Coker calmly. 'That won't do.'

Makurdi grinned, sweated, caressed the man with his enormous swollen paw. 'But, my dear boy, this is the whole thing. It must be

32

Elizabeth who asks her. What else can Elizabeth show her but the women's *ju-ju?*'

'No, no. I know why you want her to go to the women's *ju-ju*. It is to make the women stronger. To make Elizabeth stronger. But the women's *ju-ju* is a bad thing. I don't agree with it.'

'But then you are a bastard,' said Elizabeth without heat.

'Oh, no, no, no,' cried Makurdi, waving his hands. 'No rude talk——'

'And you are a witch,' said Coker, equally calm and dignified.

'Oh, no, no. This is too important.'

'White man!'

'Baby-eater!'

'Oh, no, I beg you, I pray you, my son, my daughter——'

'Dung!' said Elizabeth, looking at the river.

'Bitch!'

Elizabeth said nothing, but the curve of her mouth easily surpassed verbal insult.

'For God's sake, my darlings, be calm. Do not get excited. The matter is so important. Everything depends on us.'

Makurdi was twirling this way and that, flapping his hands, throwing off, from nose, lips, chin, drops of sweat; and his voice was the shrill scream which had caused Judy in the next room to turn away from the consideration of proportional representation.

At the same moment another yell was heard. An old pagan stood in the doorway. Shaking both fists at Makurdi, she screeched in English, 'You tink you stop me spik white missy, I go big judge. Yaas. I tell him why dey call you Makurdi. I tell him where you catch gin. I tell him, you tief man.' And turning her face towards the window, through which Judy's startled face could be seen, she raised her voice still another power and frequency. 'You tief man, Makurdi. I tell em——'

Makurdi's wail of appeal changed to a shriek of rage. He flew at the woman, with his huge fist drawn back to smash her.

Coker glided coolly between them. The old woman, who had not seen the mulatto, stopped in the middle of another screech with open mouth; then suddenly turned and hobbled away.

When Makurdi turned back, Elizabeth was already in the outer room, and Judy, looking up at her with an expression of delighted curiosity, was in the act of saying, 'But how nice! I should love it. I do hope it's not too much trouble.'

She spoke, however, doubtfully, and looked at Aladai; for she saw his embarrassment. Perhaps he was still on bad terms with this magnificent sister.

But she longed to see a real *ju-ju* house. She murmured, 'I should love it'; and then, with a glance at Aladai, 'If there's time.' Aladai

33

understood her, and slightly moved his shoulders. He murmured, 'There's nothing there—the usual nonsense.'

'But I should like to see a real *ju-ju* house.'

'It is quite new, you know. Only five years in Rimi—this is not the bad *ju-ju*. The real bad *ju-jus* are hidden in the bush.'

Judy glanced at Elizabeth to see how she liked her *ju-ju* slighted; but the big woman's expression showed no change at all. It was still fixed in a magnificent and imperial calmness, mixed with a little disdain.

'If you want to go, Miss Coote,' said Aladai, in a disappointed tone.

'I really should rather like to see it.'

'I can't go with you, you know.'

'Oh, but why, Louis? I want you to explain things.'

Aladai had turned to Elizabeth. He said in Rimi, 'But you know I can't come.'

'You must,' said Elizabeth. 'She can't go alone.'

'Whose plan is this?' he said angrily.

Elizabeth, majestically turning from him, said to Judy, in very bad English, 'Missy, you come now—we go—he come after.'

Judy glanced again at Aladai, who stood uncertain and angry. Makurdi turned upon him.

'But of course you must go, Louis,' he said. 'You cannot let the white woman go alone. What would she think of you? It's not safe for her to-day, with all these strangers in town.'

'But the Emir's guard will stop me. And we don't want trouble with the Emir.'

'Nonsense! Stupid! But don't you see the Emir's your enemy? You have nothing to get from him; and how should they dare to stop you when you are in charge of this white woman?'

'In charge?'

'Yes, yes, you are in charge.' Makurdi put his huge fat hands against the boy, and thrust him towards the wharf. 'You must look after her. Let the people see that she is in your care. And who else should take charge but the Galadima? Isn't it your own town?'

Aladai still hung back. But now Judy, understanding that some difficulty had arisen, was looking at him with raised eyebrows.

Aladai was a young man, and his nerves were still quivering with the excitement of a princely ovation and a woman's homage. In England, Judy's friendship had meant little to him. Prettier and more distinguished women had received him. But in Africa already, as if the political atmosphere were a real aerial fluid affecting its inhabitants by mere absorption, he felt towards her the respect, gratitude, and admiring affection due to a princess by one whom she has deeply obliged.

It was not so much that he did not care to admit his barring out of the town, but that he could not bear to deprive himself of the pleasure

34

of continuing in Judy's company, that now he took up his hat, and said to her, 'The trouble is, that I'm not supposed to go into the town.'

'Why on earth not?'

'It's the old Emir. It seems that he doesn't like me. But I should like to come, if you don't mind risking it.'

'It's not my risk—it's yours.'

Makurdi's scheme worked perfectly. The *dogarai* at the gate, seeing Aladai with Judy, advanced, retreated, argued among themselves with so much ludicrous perplexity, that both Judy and Aladai laughed at them.

Aladai then explained, very politely, that he was going with his friend, the English lady, as far as the first pagan ward. The men muttered, and the party went by.

The visit to the *ju-ju* house crowned all Makurdi's expectation. As soon as the people knew that Aladai was in town, with a white princess straight from the English Court, they poured in from all sides—from the races, from the outer wards and the Hausa settlement outside the walls.

Judy, having passed through a labyrinth of narrow hollow streets, overhung by the tottering rotten mats which formed the walls of the native compounds, found herself alone with Elizabeth, and half a dozen other negro women, in just such a compound. She looked round with surprise at half a dozen round huts of the usual type, a few wooden mortars.

'Is this the *ju-ju* house?'

'Dis him,' said Elizabeth, whose English was weak. She waved her hand towards one of the round huts.

Judy ducked low through the door, and found herself in a smoke-blackened porch. The porter, a young and handsome girl in a bright blue cloth, at a word from Elizabeth opened the inner door, and at once closed it behind them.

This inner yard had a high wall. At the far end were three *zaurés* or flat-topped houses, joined together, with one door to the middle one. Two breasts were modelled in the wall, one above the other, on the left side of the door.

Elizabeth opened the door and walked in. She made no bow, and showed no reverence. Judy repressed her own desire to do reverence before a holy place.

She looked with surprise at a small room, a ten-foot cube, dimly lighted from holes near its mud ceiling. From this ceiling, and from wooden pegs stuck in the wall, hung bundles of herbs, pieces of dried leather, mysterious objects resembling mummified animals tied up in string. A bundle of sticks, with rounded and painted knobs, stood in a corner. At the far end of the room, slightly to one side, there was a stone column, rounded at the top, and polished black with dirt; and, beside it, what looked like a small cannon, sunk to the trunnions. It projected, slightly on one side, about two feet. The column was a few inches taller.

The cannon seemed to be made of rough iron, brown with old rust; but, when Judy looked closely at it, she saw that it was brass. The brown covering was a crust. It had been scraped off for a few inches at the back, close to the mouth.

'Are these the *ju-jus?*' Judy asked.

'Yaas. Dis are *ju-ju*.' Elizabeth touched the column. 'Dis very big *ju-ju*.' She put her hand on the cannon with the same careless familiarity. And dis where I make medicine. Blood very strong medicine.' She touched the scraped surface.

The brown crust was blood. Judy, much interested, said, 'You sacrifice here?'

'Chickens and goats,' said Elizabeth. 'One time, many people—not now. Judges no gree we give people.'

'Goats are just as good, aren't they? Better.'

Elizabeth shook her head and wrinkled her nose. '*Ju-ju* like people better. Women live for Rimi no catch children no more—no catch chop no more—*ju-ju* angry.'

'How many women belong to the *ju-ju?*'

'All Rimi people belong for *ju-ju*.'

'Men too?'

'All people—but women *ju-ju* live for dar.' She pointed at a low door in the wall behind.

Judy went to open the door, but Elizabeth at once stood in her path. 'You no fit go dar—*ju-ju* kill you, you go dar.'

'What's in there?'

Elizabeth shook her head. 'You go dar, you die.'

'But how does it help women?'

'If *ju-ju* gree for women—she go lookum—she catch baby.'

'Suppose a man went in?'

'He die one time.'

'I hope you don't help him to die!'

Elizabeth understood this very well. She smiled, and pointed to an object hanging from the ceiling. 'Dat man's wife tell him what she see for *ju-ju*. She die and he die.'

The object was a bag. Judy did not ask to see the contents.

There was a bad air in the *ju-ju* house; not a strong smell, but some essence, penetrating and active, which, unlike a smell, grew stronger in

36

its effects with time. Judy suddenly began to feel sick. She thanked Elizabeth, and turned quickly towards the door.

Elizabeth, following her to the yard, said, 'You sick now?'

'I did feel rather faint.'

'Dat de *ju-ju*,' said Elizabeth, with complacency. 'Very strong *ju-ju*. You stay there—he make you fall down. Perhaps you die.'

'And what about you?'

'Me? I catch strong *ju-ju* too. *Ju-ju* no fit do me any harm. He gree for me, *ju-ju*.'

Aladai's voice was heard outside, calling, 'Miss Judy.'

Elizabeth, suddenly agitated, rushed to the yard door, stretching out her huge arms, shouting, 'You no fit come here, you Aladai.'

He, having come up against her strong hands, said, 'You and your *ju-jus:* it's all nonsense, you know, Elizabeth.'

He looked at Judy over Elizabeth's shoulder, and smiled as if to say, 'You and I know that it's all nonsense.' But the smile was puzzled—a little suspicious.

Elizabeth was angry. She continued to push, shouting, 'Don't talk so—you want *ju-ju* hear you? Go away, you fool boy—you want he kill you?'

Aladai gave way backwards. He said contemptuously, 'But does your *ju-ju* understand English?'

'You fool boy, you white man; don't speak so.' She pushed him back by main force. '*Ju-ju* for English too—all tongues, all people.'

Aladai consented to be pushed into the porch. Outside, a huge crowd could be seen; and from behind the crowd shouts and shuffling could be heard, as if a fight were going on.

'I called you, Miss Judy, because I thought it was time we went back. Some of Salé's people are making trouble. Salé is one of my rivals.'

'Where is he?' The little woman peered anxiously across the square.

Aladai laughed. 'I'm afraid you won't see Salé here—he doesn't appear in town. His people do the riots for him—I expect they are pretty expensive, because they are often quite big. Listen to that.'

That was a loud and sudden scream, which made Judy jump. She looked round, and said, 'But it sounded quite close.'

Elizabeth became urgent; she threw out her arms. 'You fit to go now, miss? Go now, Louis. I got plenty work to do here.'

III

Rackham had been asked, unexpectedly, to ride again by the O.C. troops, Captain Rubin. At first he refused, but Miss Honeywood urged him to accept. She said that she wanted to see him win a race. This was true, but, also, she could see that the man was troubled about Judy, and she wanted to distract him.

Rackham agreed to ride. Rubin's horse was The Kraken, a celebrated sprinter and man-killer. He was a big bay stallion with German blood in him, probably Pomeranian. He was descended from one of the German pedigree sires looted from the Cameroons during the war. He was called The Kraken because he had a habit of whirling round until he had unseated his rider, and then jumping on him, biting him, kicking him, or even rolling on him.

Rackham usually enjoyed riding The Kraken. It was a thrill, and he was a highly-strung little man. But even while he was weighing in, shaking with nervousness so that the tip of his cutting whip vibrated like a tuning-fork, he was thinking about Judy, and feeling an unpleasant emotion about her. It was not anger. He could not be angry with the woman for refusing to cut an inconvenient friend. What he loved in Judy made it impossible for her to do so mean a thing. But he felt as if he had suffered a misfortune. He had not done so, but he felt so, and he resented the feeling. He was indignant, not, of course, with Judy, but with something else, larger and vaguer—fate perhaps; and seeing The Kraken sidling across the paddock, ears back, eyes rolling to show half the whites, a couple of terrified grooms hanging to the bridle, he walked up to the brute and gave him a kick in the belly.

This was a reasonable precaution. The Kraken was fond of blowing himself out when he was saddled, so that the girths, pulled tight one moment, hung in loops the next; and the rider, having mounted and taken a strong grip for the inevitable kicking and bucking, found himself, at the first twist, under the man-killer's belly and among his feet.

The Kraken tried to kick two spectators standing four yards behind him—not a safe distance from The Kraken, who could, when he meant murder, stretch himself out behind like lazy tongs. He then reared, lifting one groom off his feet.

Rackham mounted him in this position—he was used to it: This art was, having made sure of a tight saddle, to grip the pommel. When he was up, clinging like a monkey on a stick, he stooped forward, jerked the reins—which were reinforced with chain at the rings—out of the brute's teeth, and gave him a cut under the belly.

This made him kick and attempt to bolt. But Rackham had him by the head, and, when the brute went up again, gave him another cut behind.

This process, mixed with five or six whirls, was repeated half a dozen times. But The Kraken, after the first furious lashing-out, was not in earnest. When he had Rackham on his back, he knew that he had no chance of savaging him until the man got off again. Then, indeed, he might be able to catch him unawares. He had smashed his hat once, with a fore-hoof.

Now, still sidling, fighting, but only for the fun of the thing and out of natural vivacity, he went to the post so tamely that many of the spectators were disappointed.

He ran perfectly. Like other man-killers, he seemed to be built of steel and gut. Moreover he liked winning. Probably, if it had been necessary, The Kraken would have galloped himself to death rather than be beaten by another horse. He hated horses quite as much as men.

Rackham won for Rubin by six lengths; and dismounting with a leap which took him two yards beyond The Kraken's teeth, snapping behind him, he pushed his way, with some rudeness, through the congratulatory crowd, to be weighed. He was shaking so much that strangers remarked upon it. It was a peculiarity of Rackham that he continued to shake for some time after the reason had gone—as if, having been screwed up, he remained at tension, vibrating.

Dryas Honeywood, blushing with delight and excitement, was waiting for him outside the judge's hut. 'I thought you would be killed,' she said. 'I never saw anything like it since the rodeo.'

Rackham looked dark and set; it was obvious that he had not forgotten Judy. He said to her, 'Look here—what about some tennis?'

'Tennis—now?'

'I hear you're a star at home.'

'But aren't you riding again?'

'No; and this mob is rather getting on my nerves. But don't let me take you away.'

The girl, good-natured as usual, said that she, too, was sick of the crowd. They went to their several quarters to change; and in half an hour they met again on the tennis court, in the middle of the deserted station.

The girl beat the man very easily. Rackham was enchanted by her strokes. Enchanted is a true word. He had the feeling of an artist for what is perfect in its own kind of beauty, and as he shouted, 'Good *shot!* Oh, but you're the player,' talking Irish in his pleasure, he was

39

rejoicing not only in the girl's style, the beauty and strength of her movements, perfectly accorded to their function and her own powers, but in all that her grace and accomplishment stood for—a kind of world in which everyone and everything had the same quality. Such a world did not exist, but there were more and closer approximations to be found in Britain than Africa. Judy belonged to it.

When the warmth of his surprise and pleasure in Dryas's tennis had passed into the general body of their mutual sympathy, and they were walking, at about a quarter to six, towards the Residency for the evening drinks, they talked of Judy.

Rackham, now in high spirits, and therefore voluble and incapable of hiding any of the movements of his mind, explained just how he felt about Judy's indiscretion of the afternoon. It was fine of her, but it was a pity. 'You see, Dryas, it's always a ticklish affair running a country where the people are just coming out of being savages. There's nobody can be a bigger danger to himself and everyone else than the half-educated nigger—or white man, for that matter. Look at the ballyhoo in England itself. Every boy that can read the winners in the stop-press thinks he could do better than the Prime Minister.'

'I really rather hate black men, I'm afraid. They give me the grues.'

Rackham laughed, and looked at her with approval. She was a pretty girl, he thought now; though no more than pretty. Her face was too broad; her nose too thick. It was not a snub, but you expected it to be so from its front aspect. Her eyes were dark grey, far apart and long-shaped, with dark thick lashes which sharply outlined them, and gave that quality of still depth to the iris which a winter wood gives to water. The pupils were small, which made her glance seem more penetrating than sympathetic.

She had thick dark eyebrows, very slightly arched and dipping quickly towards the inner side. Her forehead was low, but broad. The whole upper part of the face was too broad for the small firm chin. Her mouth was neither large nor small, thick nor thin. The corners of the lips were sharply pointed. They closed in an unusually straight line, and their expression was calm and confident. Her hair was beautiful, dark red-brown, and glossy as a chestnut fresh from its rind. She had one large freckle on the broad wing of her left nostril.

She carried her head upright, rather tilted backwards, upon a round strong neck, hollowing her back and throwing forward her chin. Although she was not taller than Rackham—about five foot seven—this carriage, by enabling her to look down on people, made her seem, at first meeting, arrogant. But this appearance was contradicted by the friendly curiosity of her look and her questions. She had no pose or self-consciousness except in her body. She blushed easily.

But it was something in her quality that was charming to Rackham—

not merely her youth, because he did not at all admire some of the qualities of youth; not mere freshness and enjoyment of things, but her simplicity, her friendliness, which was still disinterested.

'I mustn't say that,' he said, 'and, in fact, I like my rascals of policemen. But you know what I mean about this afternoon.'

'Oh, yes. Though of course, Judy is rather special—and what else could she do?'

'She couldn't do anything else, and that's the truth of it. But she oughtn't to have been put in such a position. I told the Resident that yellow baboon Coker would be giving him trouble if he didn't look out—but, of course, he wouldn't heed a policeman. And then your political is always in a blue funk of the trousered ape. You can count on that.'

'Yes, indeed. But it's so queer; they're supposed to be so keen on the people—the real poor people—and then they sacrifice them to please a few who aren't really natives at all, just bad copies of English agitators on the make.'

'True for you. Bad copies.' But Rackham did not really believe that the copies were all bad. His objection was deeper. He did not examine it. Instead, he found pleasure in the company of a pretty and sympathetic girl who could beat him at tennis.

They had reached the Residency, a two-storey bungalow rather more than half-way up the hill. The Resident lived in the upper storey; the lower was the provincial office.

Rimi has a Scotch club—that is to say, a club open to all the station, to which each member brings his own chair, drinks, and anything else he may need. But on great days it was the custom for the Scotch club to be invited to one of the bungalows, whose owner would provide savouries to go with the drinks: fried yam, sardines on toast—any of the small dishes included under the head of small chop. On race night, the Scotch club and all its visitors were always asked to the Residency.

At least thirty people were gathered in the open space before the bungalow when Rackham and Miss Honeywood.arrived. These were chiefly visitors. The old members of the club—officials, two or three traders—had already formed their usual circle round a fire near the outer edge of the compound. In this circle there was a domestic air of familiar lassitude. The eight or nine pairs of legs, stretched out on foot-rests, were directed inwards; and the noses belonging to them seldom deviated from the same line. One man spoke at a time, and nobody interrupted him.

But the visitors were moving over the whole ground talking all together, laughing, hurrying eagerly from one group to another.

The Resident, looking, as usual on such occasions, two or three stone heavier than his real weight, stood in the midst of them, smiling at this

41

man, raising his hand to this other, and talking to a third, all at the same moment, and with such a genial art that each believed himself the most favoured.

When he had finished his speech, he would slowly throw himself back, until his head had receded up the slope of his white-coated belly, to an immense distance; and, at this distance, it would slowly turn in a new direction, and start in recognition of some new arrival. During this whole process, its features still wore the look of interest and esteem belonging to the recent conversation, and excited by the interlocutor. And this remained even after the Resident's start had warned the latter that some other thing or some other person had caught his notice. Then as he suddenly moved away—or, better, floated away—he would again turn downwards this smile, only a trifle faded, as if completing and sealing a private intimacy in the moment of departure.

This was Burwash's method of breaking off conversations—when his A.D.O. was not at hand to do it for him.

It acted well. Nobody, even if cut off in the middle of the most important communication, felt aggrieved or snubbed. Yet Burwash, unlike some Residents, did not pretend to be summoned away by a duty, by any kind of necessity. He made no secret of the fact that he was simply passing from one guest to another. Rackham's theory was that his success in the art of shunting depended entirely on that long straightening action which withdrew his face out of immediate intimacy, and in the gliding sideways motion with which he suddenly departed, even in the middle of a sentence.

'It all depends on the action,' he said. But Judy had answered, 'People like the Resident because he's friendly.'

Miss Honeywood had joined the station circle. Her brother, manager of Rimi Hides for the Rimi district, had left a place for her chair, and Rackham had to be content with the opposite side of the circle. He could not see any more of the girl, from this point, but the soles of mosquito-boots, partly obscured by wood smoke.

The man next him, whom he did not recognize, said to him, 'What did you think of those niggers at the races to-day?'

'I haven't thought of them.'

'And that girl going off with them! What I say is, that somebody ought to have stopped her. But they say she's one of these nigger worshippers.'

'Is that so?'

'Mind you, I'm not against the nigger in his proper place. But what I say is, what's the good of making him think he's equal to a white man when he isn't? It only makes trouble for everybody.'

'There's something in that.'

Rackham got up, and walked round the fire to speak to Dick

Honeywood. As he did so, he glanced at the girl lying in her chair. Her whole body was in shadow. It was not possible even to make out its outlines. But it stood before the eyes of Rackham's memory so firmly and clearly that he could have drawn it, even in its new attitude.

'Hullo, Dick. Had a good day?' he said to Honeywood, to explain his visit.

Honeywood, a tall, very handsome, young man, strongly resembling his sister, sat up and began to explain, in great detail, how cleverly he had made his bets. And also how lucky he had been. He took even more merit from the luck than the prescience.

'Ten pounds up on the day,' said Rackham. 'That's not bad.' He had taken two empty beer bottles from the chop-box which served Honeywood for table, and was now tossing them up and catching them. Each bottle turned three somersaults in the air and fell back, neck first, into his hand.

Rackham was a good conjuror and juggler. He had spent many hours a day acquiring the necessary control of his hands and material.

The circle, accustomed to Rackham's tricks, looked on calmly. The doctor, Pratt, from the other side of the fire, said, brusquely and impatiently, 'You ought to go on the stage, Jock.'

Rackham paid no attention to them. His narrow jaw was thrust up; his grey eyes were fixed on the glittering, jumping, bottles.

Miss Honeywood put down her feet, sat up on the leg-rest of her chair. Her eyes followed the bottles with a smile of delight.

Suddenly she laughed, poking down her head, raising her shoulders—a schoolgirl laugh, as if tickled by somebody. She wriggled her whole body inside her clothes.

Rackham picked up a third bottle. He had never before attempted, in public, to keep three bottles jumping at once. He could manage three balls, but he was not sure of three bottles. His body became tense, his eyes fixed; his cheeks were hollow.

Miss Honeywood, having recovered from her laugh, which had left her with a flushed and rather severe expression, frowned at the bottles, and said, 'I must try that.'

Sangster's voice, coming out of the darkness behind the fire-lit chairs, called 'Rackham!' Rackham continued to toss the bottles.

Sangster was the district officer in charge of the pagan division of Rimi province, in the hills behind Rimi. But his capital was close to Rimi, and he spent much time there because the Resident, short-handed and obliged to act as district officer of the headquarters division, liked his assistance, especially with the town pagans.

He was a short, hollow-chested man, with a hollow pale face, a very large twisted nose, and a small mouth. His manners were curt and his prejudices strong, but he was a famous pagan man and bush-fighter, a man of great courage and long experience. Also he could tell a good story.

His pale spoon-like face, shadowed in a crooked line by the twisted nose, now appeared as if suspended in the shadow behind Honeywood's chair, just above its owner's full rosy cheeks, perspiring beer.

'You're wanted, Jock,' he said, using Rackham's nickname, shortened from jockey.

'I told the sergeant about your tax money,' said Rackham, tossing the bottles with perfect regularity. A little muscle was jumping in his taut cheek.

'It's not the money. Come along. There's no time to waste.'

Rackham caught a bottle in his left hand, two in the right. They struck together with a loud clink, which caused him, for a moment, to look at them furiously, as if they had betrayed him. Then, with a wooden face, he put them down and stepped out of the circle. Miss Honeywood clapped her hands, and cried, 'Encore,' but he paid no attention to her. Nevertheless he was triumphant, quivering with joyful excitement. He had mastered the three bottles and his own nerves.

Sangster, who was wearing a long black overcoat, drew him aside, and said, 'Look here, that girl's not back.'

'She's probably gone straight home.'

'She hasn't. Mr. Bloody Aladai took her into the town, and she's there now, in the middle of a very promising riot. You and I have got to get her out.'

'Can I take the police into the town?'

'You'd better.'

'But what if it came to shooting?'

'That's your funeral.'

'Not a bit of it. I want to know where I stand.'

'Well, you can ask Burwash.'

He walked off. Rackham went to the Resident, whom he found in a very irritable and anxious state of mind. He asked several times: 'What is Miss Coote doing in the town at this hour?' To this, Rackham had no answer.

Burwash finally said, 'Certainly, you must take police. But it's very important to avoid anything like provocation. The people are in a very excited state.'

'Can I shoot, if necessary?'

'Shoot? My dear Rackham, things can't be as bad as that. At least, I most seriously hope not. Meanwhile we're wasting valuable time. You'd better get a move on.'

Rackham turned round and walked off. In twenty minutes he was on the way to the town with ten constables, armed with carbines and ten

44

rounds a man. Sangster, carrying a walking-stick, ambled beside him. He said, with unexpected kindness, 'Don't jump on the girl. It's not her fault.'

What had happened in Rimi was that Salé's Mohemmedan followers, enraged and frightened by the mob of Aladai's pagans and fishermen, had tried to prevent their passage through the east ward.

Coker, who was the leader of Aladai's town party, chiefly Christians and foreigners, led them into this ward, because, he said, it offered the shortest route to the waterside. But his real motive was probably to beat up the Mohammedan party. Coker's motives were always obscure because though he had a reason for everything he did, and seemed to believe it himself, it was seldom the true one. Now, for instance, leading the van of the fishermen armed with barge-poles, he was bellowing at the top of his voice, in Rimi, 'For the love of Jesus.' But as he danced in front of the crowd in his tight blue suit, with high stiff collar and long bright yellow boots, sometimes forwards, sometimes for many yards backwards, with his eyes shut, foam dripping from his lips, he flourished in one hand a torch of burning straw and in the other a machete, or bush knife, two feet long. His speech shrieked and bellowed from him like the steam blasts from a labouring engine—a phrase in English, a phrase in Rimi, thus: 'For the love of Jesus—no more rich man, no more poor man—white man love black man for the blood of Jesus— wicked men do not love—they go to hell—the rich man do not love— for blood of Jesus—they die, go to hell—they die—all wicked men die— all rich men die—all white men die—for the love of Jesus. If they no repent we kill wicked men—we fight for Jesus—all men love—white men, black men—all same to Jesus—all be same.'

Coker had been born in the Cameroons of a Syrian and a Yoruba, and brought up by a local American mission. He had entered the railway service, but his lack of English stopped his promotion. He had, however, made a small fortune by selling to the illiterate native travellers who asked for tickets to distant places, either forgeries of his own, or tickets to the next station. The profit was often 5,000 per cent. A tip to the station policeman secured the arrest of anyone who, having been thrown out of the train for overrunning his ticket, took the trouble to walk back and complain. But in the end a political officer from the distant bush, whose pagans had been swindled, laid a trap for him.

This did the political officer no good. The State railway department did not like to be deprived of a valuable public official. Clerks were then scarce. But Coker was sent to gaol by another political officer.

This was not a serious disaster. Coker knew that there would always be a job for him on the railway. Government departments are good to

45

their servants, who are also citizens. His job was ready for him when he came out of the gaol.

But he did not like the confined life of a booking-office. He became a preacher instead.

Coker had always been devout. For a time, he was a deacon in the African church at Pawa. But he had quarrelled with its negro parson on various points of theology as well as policy, and he found now that his personal creed did not fit any of the local churches. He therefore set up his own church in Rimi. Coker had soon gathered a congregation because he was visited, almost at will, by a powerful spirit. This was his own explanation. It was his way of using the phrase, 'Power of the spirit.' All Coker's religious phrases had a local twist—like Catholicism in Italy, France, America, or the English Church service in Kent, Ulster, Wales.

Coker gave himself to his powerful spirit by speech. When he began to speak, he would be apathetic, feeble. He would repeat long, almost meaningless, sentences three or four times. But, as he continued, he soon felt the spirit rise within him. It always responded to the mechanical wording of his speech. It rosé within him like a geyser or hot spring, and broke out of him in panting shouts which excited himself and the people to religious ecstasy. Under the influence of his sermons, Coker often beat his fists on the mud walls of his church hut till his hands poured blood. The people imitated him. An old woman had once cut herself with a knife so severely that she had lost the use of her left hand.

His key word was blood, but it appeared in different connections: blood of Jesus—blood of sacrifice—blood of the wicked man—blood of the sinner—the baptism of blood. He preached equality. He was not a Communist and reprobated the Communists as anti-Christ. But the geyser, as it burst out of him, uttered pure original Communism, the brotherhood of the pack and the herd, expressed in fraternal love for the like, in hatred of the unlike, sealed in the magical properties of blood.

Blood-love, blood-hatred, were the ethics of Coker's religion; its theology was the geyser, the hot fountain shot out of primæval mud.

Makurdi was one of the most devoted of his congregation; and, when he screamed for the blood of the rich to be poured out in repentance, it was Makurdi who shouted most loudly and groaned most deeply, sweating in his thrilling terror.

Makurdi had easily secured Coker for Aladai's party by offering a site for his church on the main street, and a remission of taxes on the poor. Coker was no hypocrite. He was ready to die for his religion, for he knew that it was true. Its truth was proved to him by its source. It came to him from óutside—from God—and, by its effect, it filled him with the rage of blood, it drove him mad.

Aladai and Judy were thirty yards away, closely surrounded by the notables of the pagan wards and Aladai's own uncles and cousins to the tenth degree; and, outside this smiling decorous group, the crowd cheered so loudly that the screams of Coker did not reach them at all.

Judy was therefore greatly surprised when all the smiles disappeared, and several round native bricks, five or six inches in diameter, of solid dry clay as hard as iron and almost as heavy, fell through the air. One struck the ground and burst like a shell. Another hit an old man standing within a yard of her. He fell like a bullock with the axe in his brain. Blood poured from a deep tear in his head.

Judy knelt down to staunch the blood with her handkerchief. She knew nothing about first aid, except that it was good to loosen the collars of fainters. But this old black man, whose face was fixed in a look of sleepy amazement, his mouth wide open, his eyes half closed, was bare to the waist.

She looked round for Aladai, and found herself alone with her patient. The respectable persons of her escort had bolted, and a strong force of the enemy were breaking through a mat wall just in front of her, in rear of Coker's fishermen. The construction of a native compound is ideal for war. It affords cover in every direction, but no serious obstacle to flank marches. The mud huts are bullet-proof, the mat walls hide development or flight. Contestants do not fight from street to street as is usual in Europe, but from compound to compound.

Immediately she was knocked off her feet by a pagan party from behind, and a furious battle took place over her head—or, as she afterwards declared, over her hat, which was trampled into pieces.

She was not frightened, because she did not believe, within herself, that these amusing and interesting black men would hurt her. Nevertheless she was enraged by the indignity of being rolled in the dirt, when somebody caught her by the wrist, lifted her, and set her on her feet. She was about to expostulate, with her usual sharpness, when she recognized Aladai.

He did not wait to apologize; he said: 'Follow me close; don't get cut off.' He then walked slowly through what appeared like a crowd of lunatics, prancing, rolling their eyes, uttering loud senseless shrieks, baring their teeth like animals. All faced Aladai. Judy was astonished by this odd behaviour until she saw that these people, though they parted in front of Aladai, were not his friends, but his enemies. Their lunatic appearance was due to this fact. Their rage and their antics had no sense, because their springs of fury carried them backwards instead of forwards. They were controlled by a force superseding their own intelligent will. At every minute Aladai was faced, at two yards' distance by raised clubs, aimed spears, men screaming their hatred at him, but he walked on evenly as a man strolling along an empty pavement. Perhaps it was for this reason that the spearmen and club-wavers, without lowering their weapons, literally fell backwards, suddenly throwing their weight on the crowd as he stepped up to them.

They closed again behind. The clubs just behind Judy were even closer than those in front. She did now realize danger. She kept so close to Aladai that her shoulder touched his coat. She was glad now of her small size, which made Aladai in front of her seem like a wall of defence.

Her hand once or twice came towards his coat-tail, but she did not take it. She felt that this would be undignified, and perhaps unwise. Almost *lèse-majesté*!

They reached a narrow recessed doorway between heavy pillars projecting three feet from a long yellow wall. Aladai called, and the door, instantly, and unexpectedly, was opened an inch or two, with slow caution. It was instantly flung back by a rush of the mob which also carried Aladai's party into the large porch or guard-room within.

And while half a dozen frightened house-slaves were battling to close the door again, a process not so hard as it seemed, because the construction of the doorway, in its recess, allowed only two or three attackers to push at one time, excited old men and two or three young ones in European dress, surrounded Aladai, not with applause but cries of fright and a storm of questions.

One shouted, 'Dey go burn de church'; another, 'Dey kill Mistah Coker.'

Aladai answered, 'Keep quiet, and stay here. They daren't come in here'; and, turning to Judy, he said, 'Miss Coote, this is my town house. You'll be safe here. But perhaps you wouldn't mind staying here, for a few minutes, until things are quieter? There's no danger of fire, because the roof is mud.'

'Of course, Louis. And thanks frightfully——'

Aladai was in too much of a hurry for thanks. 'And if you wouldn't mind my leaving you here for the present—I'm afraid of my poor people getting themselves into trouble.'

He went through the porch into the house. Judy was left even more delighted. 'What a royal phrase,' she thought. 'To keep my people from getting themselves into trouble! And how naturally it came up. I suppose it's in the blood. No, of course it isn't! It's the way he's learnt to think. But how good to hear that kind of thing—history speaking. Real history.'

Nobody in the hut paid any attention to her. They were too busy arguing with each other, and bewailing the situation.

She looked round for escape, or at least air, and saw, high up in the wall, a small window, about a foot square, and a stool not far from it.

She mounted the stool, and put her head out from the foul sweltering air of the porch. In front of her, to her joy, was the full spread of the market-place—now a battlefield upon which half a dozen contests were proceeding at the same time. Eagerly and anxiously she sought her spectacles; thank heaven they were not broken! The Emir's palace stood opposite—a huge yellow castle. Its four towers—forty feet high, joined by a curtain wall about ten feet lower—and the wall itself, were not pierced by any opening except the small arch of the main gate between the middle towers, which was closed by a heavy door of palm planks sewn together with iron strips.

Walls and towers were crenellated like a twelfth-century fortress, with high pointed cones of mud, painted white to prevent erosion. Turbans and spear-points, seen between the embrasures, showed that the walls were guarded, but otherwise the huge block might have been empty—a tomb or a deserted shell. The Court plainly considered itself besieged.

Outside on the bare flat earth, perhaps a hundred yards square, gently sloping towards the right in the direction of the waterside, the different battles seemed to be growing into one. Parties ran to help each other, recruits were pouring in from the wards. Bricks and sticks were flying, and now arrows were seen, flowing through the air, which was growing dark, like the silent dart of hawks with closed wings.

Judy was pulled from her stool. An excited old man wanted her to leave the window. He screamed at her in English, 'Dey kill—dey shoot. You come for in.'

Judy indignantly explained that she wanted to see. The old man, now supported by the whole company, screamed that she would be killed. One youth, foaming at the mouth, his eyes bulging like door-knobs, laid hold of her arm. 'If dey kill you, Galadima he kill us.'

'Mr. Aladai wouldn't kill anybody.'

'Yaas, yaas. He angry—he make us die.'

A long argument followed. Luckily some new message of woe caused the party to run out of the porch towards the back of the compound. Judy leapt upon her stool. But the battle had come to a disappointing end. Both sides were in retreat—running away from each other in a most ludicrous fashion. Judy laughed, thinking, 'How childish!'

But just then she perceived a kind of whirlpool close to the backward edge of that party which was retreating, at a careful comparison, rather more rapidly. This whirlpool increased in violence, widened, and showed a bare space of ground. But something was revolving round it—a horse. It broke at one side, and a man cantered easily in the open—Aladai, on a tall bay horse. It was a policeman's horse, with native bit and saddle.

Aladai was carrying a native cross-handled sword, which contrasted oddly with his neat suit of grey flannel. But he rode well. He cantered

49

now towards the other mob, flying uphill, and began to circle into them, performing over and over again the same manœuvre. He rode inwards a little way, wheeled to the right and circled again into the open, making a series of turns along the whole edge of the crowd.

Judy could not understand the motive of these tactics until she saw the panic and confusion of the rioters, who were continually broken and scattered. The horse, darkened with foam, panting after the continual checking and turning, stood now close to the palace wall. Aladai patted it, rested it a moment, and then cantered slowly towards a detached group, which, cut off by one of his circles, had taken it into its heads to run towards the houses at the side of the square—Aladai's own house. He did not hurry as he followed and wheeled to cut them off. Judy admired his seat in the barrel-like saddle, but she deplored his clothes. 'Really,' she thought, 'he ought to be in chain mail. And look at his trousers! What bad luck.'

Aladai's trousers had worked up his ankles, showing six inches of bright blue sock and the clasp of his suspender. Even a piece of black leg appeared as Aladai, now rounding up the fugitives, wheeled his horse across their front. Judy burst out laughing. 'It's a shame! But what a pity,' she said. 'Royalty ought to avoid such *contretemps*. But I suppose,' she reflected, 'natives don't see it like that at all. He looks quite terribly august to them. Oh!'

The 'Oh!' was caused by a sudden change in the scene. Aladai's horse had shied violently. It reared sideways, with starting white-ringed eyes, and flaring idiot nostrils. The shy was the sudden leap of real terror which unseats anybody but a good or lucky rider. Aladai was nearly thrown. He lost a stirrup, fell back on his rein. The cruel native curb cut into the jaw of the lunatic beast, which stood straight up and seemed about to fall backwards.

Aladai, holding by the mane, with both stirrups gone, one foot half-way round the edge of the saddle-cloth, seemed like a lost man. A voice close to Judy said, in English, 'It sees the blood—it's the blood.'

His voice was full of awe; and now Judy heard a murmur rise from the people, and it seemed to her that there was the same awe in the sound. No doubt they, too, were saying, in Rimi, 'It's the blood.'

The strong spirit still remaining in the spilt blood had frightened the horse, which no doubt, like all animals, could see it. The blood of the old man was wrestling with Aladai, throwing him.

But the horse, having whirled round, stood still, trembling. Aladai, who had not fallen, began to scramble back into his saddle.

The little group of tormented scuttlers, which he had been pursuing, had stopped to take breath, turned towards him. Now, just when Aladai was in this undignified posture, half on and half off, with his coat collar up to his ears behind, and his tie against his chin in front, a little dried-up old man, almost naked, darted out of this group. He carried a long stalking-spear, and in an instant he had thrust it straight into Aladai's body.

There was a pause—not a silence, but a perceptible drop in the volume of noise. The embrasures of the Emir's walls were suddenly crowded with faces, staring down. In the two retreating crowds—who had almost stopped retreating as soon as Aladai left them—hundreds stood, faced towards him, staring and motionless.

The little old man was seen running like a hare across the open. He carried his head down, and one hand in the air, crooked above his neck. His legs worked like released clockwork, going too fast.

A groan or sigh—the kind of sound that rises from the first stress of the ground in an earthquake—rose from the shadows at the sides of the square. Aladai, now firm in the saddle, looked round and his teeth were seen to flash. He was smiling. He looked down; hundreds of eyes followed his glance. They could not distinguish the spear lying there on the ground in the dark, but they thought that they did.

The spearman had disappeared. Three men in flowing gowns were still running, flopping like terrified old women; the rest were lying on their faces, throwing dust on their heads, and wailing, 'We repent, we repent! Oh, lord, we repent! King, chief, owner of the land!'

Aladai dismounted, called one of them, and handed over the horse. Then he picked up the spear, and walked slowly towards the right-hand section of the crowd. One trouser leg had come down, but the other had caught in his suspender. Judy was furious. 'Oh, that's not fair. That's *bad* luck. That's simply disgusting. Why doesn't someone tell him? But of course—he mustn't even be aware of such things. Even the idea of absurdity must not occur to a real royalty—by right divine.'

But the people were lying on their faces; the whole upper end of the market-place was paved with the large black and white cobbles, formed by their heads and buttocks.

Aladai walked through them, and, as he passed, they jumped up and followed, chattering, laughing.

It was now past six. The sun had set, and the market-place was hidden by darkness which seemed to rise from the ground—as if Africa had begun to breathe again in the cool, and its breath was black.

Judy, who now perceived that her leg was aching, sat down on her stool. She thought, 'Now we shan't be long.'

Aladai had said a few minutes. She knew that in Rimi a few minutes was the next larger division of time than an hour. But it was nine o'clock before the people in the house, suddenly returning to the porch, still more excited, if possible, than before, threw open the door and ejected her into the square. They did not actually use violence, but their gestures and looks desired her to go, and go quickly, with an urgency that made

51

her feet, when she found herself on the other side of the door, already closed behind her, that she had been thrown out.

Rackham was standing in front of her, about ten yards away. Further off she could see Sangster, and a police detachment, standing at ease.

Her indignation was instantly succeeded by joy. She hurried towards Rackham, even forgetting her spectacles on her nose in her eagerness to share her latest experience. He turned towards her with the stiff right-about of parade, and said, 'So there you are. What exactly have you been playing at?'

'Jerry, it's been the most thrilling day—really terrific!'

'It's a pity that more people weren't killed to give you a real show.'

He did not speak roughly; and Judy answered, 'But, Jerry, has anyone been killed? And, you know, I didn't kill them! They more nearly killed me.'

'Didn't you know that your nigger friend had no business in the town? You've nearly wrecked it between you.'

'But, Jerry, he was absolutely splendid. He saved the town, and he saved me too. He was magnificent.' Judy, in spite of herself, remembered the trousers, and gave a little laugh; but she ended with a loyal outburst, 'He was simply glorious!'

'He's been making a fool of you, Judy. But I suppose you don't mind that!'

Judy felt that he was angry with her, and that he was justified. But, because he was angry, she could not apologize. She said gaily, 'You're not cross, Jerry?'

'I might be, but I'm not. You're just irresponsible.'

'But, Jerry, I tell you, I didn't know anything about this rule. Besides, he came to look after me.'

This phrase, 'to look after me,' suddenly made Rackham angry. Judy might have spoken so of himself. He exclaimed, 'You haven't done your nigger friend much good, Judy. I should think this evening will about finish him. Didn't you know he wasn't allowed in town?'

'No. I only knew he was going to be Emir of it. And I hope he will be. I think he's born for the job. Really and honestly I do!'

'You don't make that kind of trousered ape into a chief out here. The people wouldn't thank us if we did.'

Judy had a quick temper, and she could never control it with Rackham—because she loved the man; because she never ceased to wonder at her luck in getting him, his anger always frightened her, and fear seized her, commanded her, made her fly at him.

'I see. It depends on trousers,' she said. 'It's what you call a respectable objection, at least. The man is not a savage, so he's not fit to be a ruler. But do you really think that you can always keep this country in the Middle Ages, as a kind of museum for anthropologists?'

Rackham said nothing. He hated quarrels as much as he loathed dirt, muddles, and, before Judy could say any more, Sangster, who had been strolling up and down the square, waving his walking-stick at the fugitives, uttering short sharp barks, like a dog herding sheep, came to join them. At once Judy was gay and polite. She apologized in just the right manner for giving him this trouble; explained how she had been caught in the town, and made one or two jokes, exactly suited to Sangster's tastes, about her adventures. 'They missed me with all the bricks. It was most considerate of them.'

Sangster did not laugh—he was never seen to laugh—but his small mouth unpuckered slightly, and he answered that he would have the building material charged to the town.

Sangster was annoyed with the woman. But, before they had walked fifty yards, she was chaffing him about his official uniform—blue pyjamas covered by an old black overcoat; and he, with visible pleasure, was twisting his little eyes at her, and saying, 'I got it out for your funeral.'

'Mr. Sangster, I really am ashamed of myself.'

'Don't do it again, that's all!'

'I should think not—never again!'

'You gave us a fright.'

'I'm not worth it.'

'No, you're not.'

A particular remark, so near flirting that it was a high compliment from Sangster and made Judy, even in her preoccupation with Rackham, feel a minute's pleasure. She liked Sangster. 'It's very good of you to say so,' she answered, and obtained another twist of the eyes and half-grin.

But when they reached the intersection of the town and main station road, called Oxford Circus, Sangster said, 'Good night,' and turned up the hill to his bungalow. At once Judy's control of herself and the situation, her power, was gone. She turned to the silent Rackham, meaning to apologize to him as she had apologized to Sangster. She had prepared her speech. But, instead of the tactful sensible speech, the following totally unexpected and frightening words came from her mouth:

'Now I think you'd better apologize.'

It was as though with Rackham she lived in a special realm or state with its own laws, which were not those of sense or even good nature, but of instinct and passion; and in that state neither he nor she had control over themselves.

Rackham answered, in an angry tone, 'I think you'd better go to bed,' and turned to shout an order to his sergeant. The man came running. Judy hurried away to the waterside.

But immediately an orderly was beside her with the lantern. Her dignity would not allow her to refuse this escort.

IV

WHEN ELIZABETH was summoned to Makurdi's, her two assistants cut Osi's leg-rope and pushed her into another hut, used as a prison. From outside, this hut seemed like any other, with small deep windows high up, and a thatched roof, old and rotten. But its walls were three feet thick, and it had a built ceiling of thick mud. It was a box of dried clay.

The cell was in twilight, like that of early evening. Osi could examine every part of it within a second or two of her entry. She saw the strong walls and the ceiling, the filth heaped on the floor, the remains of a stocks made out of clay at one side of the floor.

Clay stocks are made for each prisoner, whose legs are built into the wet clay, which, when it is hard, cannot be broken except with hammers.

A girl of about ten, quite naked, sat crouched against the wall behind these stocks, with her knees up to her nose and her hands clasped between her thighs. Her round, terrified eyes stared over the bony knees and across the broken stocks like a rabbit's from the bag end of its hole at an approaching stoat; and her whole body—legs, arms, all except her head—was shivering in a ceaseless vibration. It was not an even shake. Every few seconds there was a spasm which made her head shake too, her teeth chatter, her knees knock, and her stuck-out elbows flutter like the wings of a shot bird; but at once she would press down her arms, her back, her feet, squeeze her thighs together; clench her teeth, so that the spasm was controlled; and she sat again, clenched like the hand of a tortured person, and shaking only so much as she could not help.

But at the sight of Osi the spasms became more violent, closer together; the teeth chattered as loudly as a witch-rattle. Osi herself was panic-stricken. She had never seen this child before, but she knew that she must be a witch; and her flesh quivered as she pressed back from the staring eyes into the opposite wall. She trod upon something soft and looked down. Under her feet another child lay, a boy of ten or twelve, naked and dying. He seemed to be dying of thirst. His mouth hung open and his swollen tongue protruded from it. His body seemed already dead, a mummy; only his eyes were alive as they stared up at Osi from the dark of the floor. They too were full of terror, but a more helpless terror than the girl's.

Osi knew the boy. He was a Rimi boy of the third ward; but his case had been discussed in the markets. He was a very bad witch. He had burnt a rag containing some of his sister's blood, with the result that she had wasted and died. The boy, who had been apparently devoted to this sister, had sworn that he believed the brown stains on the rag to be chicken's blood. But the fact remained that he had killed his sister by witchcraft. Another sister who had defended him so strongly that she had herself since been accused of witchcraft, and was now awaiting trial, had maintained that the burning of the blood had been an accident, that the boy had no intention of doing harm.

But this was a bad plea. Obvious intention was not needed to kill by witchcraft. So-called accidents are always happening by which some child, perhaps a baby just able to walk, injures an object connected by sympathy with some person, who thereupon becomes ill or crippled. But the damage has been done, and therefore it is certain that a bad spirit has prompted the child. Spirits are always at work. Nothing happens by accident in Africa. Babies, even new-born, are a favourite disguise of the most dangerous spirits. Therefore the baby must die, preferably without letting out any of its dangerous blood. Bury it alive, so that no one need be near when the wicked spirit, full of rage, rushes out of it; or shut it up to starve.

The boy was found guilty at once. It had been unnecessary to torture him, because the method of his witchcraft was known. He had no secrets or *ju-ju* objects hidden. He had been put into the cell and left there to die. He had been there eight days.

But his eyes were still alive, and as they gazed at Osi she felt such fear that she could not stand. She fell sideways against the wall, and, turning, dropped on all fours. Then, with her face almost on the floor, she crawled away until, striking her shoulder against the stocks and looking up, she saw the trembling girl, and remembered the other witch. She flattened herself then against the floor, and cried out for help; gibbering her husband's name, her brother's, sister's.

Osi was taken back for examination as soon as Elizabeth had got rid of her visitors. But the girl would not confess how she had killed her sister-in-law's children. She only shrieked and gibbered when they burnt her legs.

Now, Elizabeth was a conscientious priestess. That was one of the reasons for her great prestige. Many *ju-ju* priests are satisfied with a confession and the delivering up of some object said to have caused the injury. They will even suggest this course, asking the victim, 'Did you use an image? Did you use a club—or crossed sticks?'—and so on.

But Elizabeth was more anxious to protect the people than to enlarge her own reputation as a witch-finder. She therefore did not give Osi leading questions. She wanted to get the truth out of her, and, seeing now that she could not do so while the girl was mad with fright and pain, she stopped the examination, saying to the assistants, 'It's no good to-day. The fool can't understand anything. She's not used to it yet. But to-morrow she will catch more sense. At least we will try then again.'

Osi was therefore put back in the cell. But the spoiled, loved girl, who had been surrounded with affection all her life, was in fact temporarily mad with bewilderment and agony. When they pushed her into the cell again, she dashed herself against the walls, screaming.

The windows—tapering holes not six inches in diameter on the outside of the thick walls—were too small even for a child's passage. But the African prisoner always looks for escape by the roof. That is the weak point in an African house.

Osi leapt at the ceiling, which was full of cracks, aiming her tied hands at them, trying to break the clay. She aimed at one spot near the middle, and soon her nails were broken away, her finger-tips torn and bleeding. She had made no impression. But she continued with a madwoman's strength and persistence. Suddenly a crack widened; a flake of mud bulged downwards. At a fourth leap, she caught it and brought it down; a triangular hole about an inch across had appeared in the ceiling. She aimed now at this hole; for a long time it seemed only to tear the sides of her fingers as well as the tops. But the clay powdered away. At last the hole was big enough to admit a hand. A higher, more desperate leap enabled her to crook her fingers through it, and her weight brought down a square yard of the mud. The palm-wood beams were exposed; and, behind that, through the rotten thatch, stars.

She lay where she had fallen sideways among the broken mud, supported on her swollen forearms and bleeding hands, and stared upwards. The beams had been laid in an unusual pattern—in two layers, crossed. The square between them was not two hands' length. She knew that she could not escape that way.

Outside there was the noise of fighting; screams, shouts; the glare of a house on fire shone through the window-holes and lighted the cell, shooting its yellow bars through the white pillar of the moonlight descending from the roof.

The sight of the fire made Osi scramble to her feet and leap at the bars. She pulled herself up to them again and again. But, even if she had had the strength and skill to swing herself up from the full stretch of her arms, she could not have put even a shoulder between the bars.

Suddenly, as she stood panting, sweating, gibbering, she noticed the little girl behind the stocks. Her position had not changed. Her eyes still stared as if they had never blinked; her body still shook in quick spasms. Osi rushed at her and caught her round the body. The child uttered a

56

scream of astonishing loudness and fought like a powerful dog; striking out, arching her back, biting at Osi's arm.

Osi pushed her upwards towards the bars and screamed, 'That way—that way.' Osi had not thought what she was going to do when she escaped. But now she screamed, 'The judge—the judge go to the white man—the judge.'

She did not know where this suggestion had come from. Her family had spoken of the white man only with anger, as a dangerous person who interfered with local customs and robbed the poor with taxes; but now she knew that only the judge could help her.

The little girl continued to fight; but her head was within a few inches of the bars; to escape from Osi she grabbed them. Osi pushed her from behind, shrieking still, 'Go to judge—the judge—say Osi here.' The rioters outside were yelling so loudly that she was obliged to shriek in order to make the child hear her.

The little girl was now half-way through the bars, hitched by her stomach. Osi leapt up and gave her a strong push. She kicked furiously, wriggled her hips through the square, and crawled away out of sight.

'Through the straw,' Osi shrieked at her. 'To the judge—the judge.'

She heard and saw nothing more. For a few moments she lay still. Then again the violence of her terror came upon her. What would that witch child do even if she did escape? Witches often went to the judge for help—but only to help themselves. Once more she began to leap at the bars, trying to splinter the timbers four inches thick and harder than iron, with the broken pulp of her finger-tips.

The little girl was called Ibu. She came from a downriver village. Two days before, she had been the family pet. The Rimi love and spoil children. But one afternoon, when she was amusing herself by beating corn in a toy mortar, with a pestle specially made for her, an angry man came up to her and shouted that she had made his mother sick.

The man's mother was at least seventy years old. Ibu knew her well, and had often watched her doddering through the village street. She was surprised to hear that she was ill. The man's anger frightened her. She burst into tears and called for her mama. Mama came running out, and in a fury flew at the man; but when he had told her, 'She's a witch—she's killing my mother,' she ran back again and left Ibu with him.

Ibu's father, uncles, and aunts now came out on one side and the man's relations on the other. They shouted at each other for an hour or more, while he stood in the middle, gripping Ibu by the arm, shaking her and saying, 'Stop your wickedness, you witch, or I'll kill you—I'll kill you now.'

Ibu continued to weep. But then the *ju-ju* man came. He was a young man. She knew him well. He had given her sweets and played with her.

She called out to him as soon as she saw him, 'Come and stop him! Come and stop the other man from hurting me.'

But the *ju-ju* man took her, beat her, told her that unless she stopped killing the old woman he would kill her.

She didn't know what he was talking about. She said so. So he beat her and brought her up to Rimi, to the *ju-ju* house, where he beat her again, out of annoyance with her screaming and shaking, and put her in the cell where Osi found her. She had been afraid to scream any more, but she had not been able to stop herself from shaking. She could not understand anything. But she knew that she had offended some power which now had complete control of everything that happened to her, and she only knew one power that could do that—a witch's. All these people were working for the witch; they were witch's people—the boy who lay panting and stared at her; the screaming woman who came and danced, breaking the ceiling. Only a witch would tear down a witch ceiling.

When the witch caught her and thrust her through the roof, she was sure that she was now going to be killed, as the *ju-ju* man had said.

But by great good luck she escaped from the witch, for the roof turned out to be rotten. It was full of holes at the eaves, and, when struggling to escape, she pushed her head at one of the holes, it opened sideways and let her through so easily that she dived head first into the air. She fell suddenly into the glare of fire and down upon flesh—the heads and shoulders of a crowd watching the burning of a compound on the opposite side of the lane from the *ju-ju* house.

A woman screamed angrily in her ear; she felt herself rolling between a fat, greasy back and the mat wall of the *ju-ju* compound, whose elastic spring seemed to catch and hold her.

She landed in a corridor formed by the legs of a row of people standing on the bank outside the wall and the inward bulge of the mats at the bottom. She felt no injury. The mats had broken her fall. She scuttled away on hands and knees through the dog-run opened before her; and even when the legs became fewer, and the run broadened until it was as wide as the bank of the street, she flew on. She had no objective. She did not dream of going to any white man. But her whole body and mind wanted to escape.

At last she was alone. Even the houses had stopped. But she was not in the bush. She looked round her in wonder at strange broken slopes, little mountains covered with thorn scrub. They frightened her by their strangeness under the moonlight, and she crept into the nearest dark hole, where she sat crouched, trembling, until she slept.

V

JUDY SHARED A ROOM with Dryas Honeywood in the upper storey of the Hides bungalow, which is the easternmost building on the waterfront. Next, westerly, lies the Hides store; the Niger Company Wharf; the Marine; two small stores and the station fishmarket. Then comes the market road, and beyond that the native stores—Makurdi's and a dozen others—crowded together in a triangle of ground between the road and the town ditch. Makurdi's is half a mile from Hides. But the waterfront—sometimes planked wharf, sometimes hard mud—extends the whole way.

This was a favourite walk of the two girls, who loved, especially Judy, the glittering river, the boats, the boatmen, the business of the waterside.

On the night of her quarrel with Rackham, Judy could not sleep. She felt, as usual after such quarrels, ill. Her heart beat violently, her head ached; she was feverish, thirsty, restless, She felt bewildered, as if this first quarrel was extraordinary—something which no one could have expected.

She turned all night under her net, which seemed to stifle her, and at dawn, unable to bear the confinement any longer, silently got up, gathered up her clothes, and slipped down to the office below.

No one was yet stirring. Even the fishermen were not awake. The sun was still three parts below the horizon; and the exposed upper rim gave no more direct light than red-hot metal on which a few brighter sparks of burning coal have stuck here and there. This red-hot crescent was rising behind the trees on the flat ground beyond the foot of Rimi hill, and made them as black as fire-bars.

The light in the sky and on the water did not seem to rise from this sun. It was a cool, all-pervading grey light, the colour of water in a glass; and in this light the bungalows with their red roofs, the stores, the grey tin roofs of Makurdi's, the native huts like small beehives set at all angles, seemed, on a vast scale, like those toys sealed up in globes of water with a little Father Christmas; which, shaken, produce a snow-storm. But the scale was immense. There was no feeling of inclusion.

The pink glow of the sun fell upon this grey, clear light like a coloured substance soaking into water; it did not reach far into the air. The river was paler, and seemed brighter than the sky; it was like greenish glass, glistening where the film of the thinner liquid rested upon its surface. It was like the bottom of the enormous transparent globe in which nothing moved but a minute lame insect.

It was cold. Judy shivered in her dressing-gown. But she was full of triumph and a masterful exhilaration. She limped to and fro, whirling herself round on her good leg, staring round her, peering at the sky, so that to any observer from outside it would have seemed that the insect had suddenly formed some wild plan of escape from its toy prison world.

Suddenly she darted into the bungalow, and a moment later came out in a bathing-dress. She shivered now in every muscle; crossing her arms over her breasts, walking on tiptoe as if to touch as little as possible of the cold earth. Her nose and brown knees were pink, her ankles blue. But she grinned with delight at her own enterprise.

She dived in skilfully, and swam rapidly and powerfully outwards. The Niger terrified her with its crocodiles, its currents, its banks, its sudden floods; she rejoiced in the treacherous river which she compelled and used with her hands. She turned over on her back and kicked up a fountain, kicking the water like a conquered giant.

Suddenly she heard a voice calling her; turned over on her breast, whirled round, and looked towards the shore. Already the sun had mounted another inch, and the pink stain had reached the upper sky. It was as light as day. She could see a tall figure standing at the corner of the Hides Wharf, and thought with vexed surprise, 'What on earth brings Dick out of bed at six in the morning?'

She made a vigorous gesture, meaning, 'Go away.' She thought, 'He'll think I haven't anything on.'

Judy did not like to be seen in a bathing-dress, on account of her short leg.

But now she saw that the watcher had a black face. She made a still more vigorous gesture; and the man understood her and walked briskly towards the town. She hastily swam ashore and ran into the office.

She dressed quickly, her teeth chattering, her fingers white and weak with cold, so that they refused to obey her. But she was humming with pleasure. The humming and the chattering teeth combined in such odd sounds as made her laugh.

As soon as she was dressed she sat down and wrote with an office pen, on African Hides stationery:

My Darling,—Why do we fight? It's because we're so terribly in love. I knew you had every reason to blow me up, and so I just shut my eyes and hit out. May I come to breakfast? Or will you come to breakfast with me? I'll give you a much better breakfast. It would really be a noble act on your part to eat my eggs after yesterday, and it will show that I'm forgiven.

I am, sir,
Your obedient servant,
Judith Coote

60

She read this over and, after consideration, changed 'we're' in the first line to 'I'm.' For she knew perfectly well that Rackham's affection for her was quite different from hers for him. He could not be described as 'terribly in love,' and now, after her bathe, she felt extremely, even passionately, honest.

Judy had natural passion, which had found an opening even in history, making her a poor historian but a very good coach. Her imagination was more creative than penetrating.

Judy folded this note into a cocked hat, taking particular care to make each fold exactly equal, to meet the critical eye of her lover, addressed the brim to Captain Rackham, M.C., and put it in the messenger's box.

As she came into the verandah, to mount the outside stairs towards the bedrooms, she was startled to see a man sitting on the edge of the steps. He jumped up. It was Aladai. He greeted her gravely, and said, 'I came to tell you how sorry I was for last night.'

'It was you on the quay?'

'I knew you sometimes went swimming in the morning.'

'You weren't watching all the time?'

'Oh, no. I saw you from uncle's, when you dived in. I knew it must be you or Miss Honeywood,'

'You were up very early.'

'I wanted to catch you. I couldn't come back last night because I had to get Coker away before he made any trouble. I am most frightfully sorry that you——'

'But I haven't enjoyed anything so much for years. You were splendid, Louis. I had no idea——' She stopped, a little embarrassed.

Aladai smiled and said, 'You had no idea what?'

'I was going to say that I'd no idea you could handle a crowd like that.' The boy could not hide his pleasure; but he imitated the proper nonchalance: 'That was nothing. They are sheep.'

'But the spear——'

'Oh, yes, that spear.' He laughed.

'How did you dodge it? I was sure it had hit you.'

'It did.' He turned and pointed to his coat over the right breast. There was a short cut in the cloth.

'Do you wear armour?'

With another dramatic gesture he took out of his pocket a worn, leather-covered book and handed it to Judy. It was a prayer-book. In one corner, towards the upper right-hand corner, there was a deep, broad cut. It penetrated into the leaves. Judy opened the book and found that it had gone more than two-thirds through the book. Page 163 was dented and thinned, but not broken.

Judy said, 'How lucky you had it on you—really providential.'

'I always have it on me.'

'Isn't it rather bulky?'

'It would annoy my tailor very much.'

'I never knew you felt like that, Louis.'

'I don't. But my uncle and the ladies of my family would not allow me to go out without that book. Whatever coat I wear, it is sewn into the pocket.'

'Sewn?'

'Yes; when I put on the coat, there it is. The pocket is stitched at the top.'

'Like a *ju-ju*.'

'That's what the ladies think,' said Louis with a smile, replacing the book, 'and they have to be considered.'

'Now they can say that it saved your life.'

'They do say it. They have said it already a thousand times.'

'And they have not sewn it to-day. They know you will carry it.'

'They sewed it, and I unsewed it to show you.'

'They might have mended your coat at the same time.'

'No, no.' Aladai smiled at her. 'They won't do that. No one will mend the coat now.'

'Why not?'

Another dramatic flourish.

'With this coat I will defeat the power of Satan.'

Judy looked at him as if to say, 'Now what *exactly* do you mean?'

'It is a miracle.' He laughed.

'But, Louis——'

'Don't you see—I have a great *ju-ju* now, and so I can beat the other *ju-ju*—the Devil's *ju-ju*. Don't smile at me, Miss Coote. You don't know what *ju-ju* is—what still happens in some of our villages; poor creatures accused and their whole lives spoilt. Perhaps they kill themselves. It is the Devil's *ju-ju*—the *ju-ju* of fear and ignorance and spite; that is why I am so glad of my new big *ju-ju*.' He held up the prayer-book.

Judy looked doubtfully at the book; and Aladai instantly knew what she was thinking. He put it back in his pocket, smiled at her, and said, 'You think I am reverting—isn't that the word?'

Judy slightly blushed. 'No, no, Louis; but, of course, it was a piece of pure luck, wasn't it?'

'Very lucky indeed for me—my only luck yesterday. Miss Coote, I wanted to ask you something. Are you doing anything now?'

'Only being hungry. I was looking for a biscuit.'

'I was wondering—if I could ask a favour—a very great favour.'

'I suppose a king may speak to a cat.'

Louis laughed, but at once became grave again. 'You know it was Elizabeth and not I who took you into the town last night. But I'm afraid Mr. Burwash won't believe that. I was wondering if you would mind explaining to him.'

'Of course I will.'

'He's in his office now.'

'You mean now?'

'It would be the best time—for me too. Before the Waziri comes to report. Goodness knows what lies he'll tell about me.'

'Oh, I see. You think we ought to go together?' Involuntarily she glanced up the hill towards the station.

It was now seven o'clock. Some carriers could be seen on the station road, arriving from the bush. They were finishing the day's march. A gang of chained convicts, in charge of a red-turbaned native policeman, clanked out of the town gates. They carried latrine buckets on their heads. Boys in white singlets were moving in the station compounds on the hill, and Captain Rubin's horse-boys could be seen riding towards the polo-ground on the tall Kraken and the two polo-ponies.

The offices were now busy. Outside the Residency two white-robed messengers, plump and fussy as bees, were making threatening gestures at a thin little black insect—some pagan with a grievance. He waved a spear, but retreated.

Aladai walked up and down in the sun while he waited. The sun was a finger's width clear of the eastern edge of Rimi hill, and already turning pale at the upper edge, as if cooling. The air was cool, and the light itself struck upon objects with a cool yellow, like the yellow of a flower petal. It felt warm only on the cheek; as Aladai each time turned his face towards it he smiled involuntarily, as if greeting the African sun, from which he had been exiled for three years.

Only the consciousness of Miss Coote's nearness, which was like that of a tutor, and of his English clothes, prevented him from laughing, cracking his fingers, singing. He caught himself humming 'Heiden-röslein,' a tune that seemed to have been invented at that moment by his feelings, to express their confidence and exhilaration.

He laughed when he thought of Miss Coote's serious look when he spoke of *ju-ju*—the glance of the tutor. She was a dear friend, but still the tutor. He should not have used the word to her. It was not safe with any white people, even white friends; they were always ready to think, 'How typically negro.' Luck was the word. It was also the truth. What a stroke of luck! It had transformed his position in a moment. There was no doubt about his election now. All Rimi would talk of him to-day, and his *ju-ju*. Already Elizabeth, that shrewd woman, had said to him, 'You are chosen by the *ju-ju* itself.'

'Röslein auf der Heiden,' he sang, and turned on his rising toe as if making a dance step. Miss Coote came down the bungalow steps in a green-and-white spotted cotton frock; and he bit off his song, stiffened his walk. But she too was smiling; and her jump off the last step, in spite of her leg, had the spring of joy in it, like a child's. Happiness made her a pretty woman. He was charmed by her, and said, 'What a pretty dress you have, and the sunshade to match.'

He had meant to please her in his gratitude; and he was very successful. Miss Coote blushed again, turned her bright eyes towards him, and said, 'Do you really like it?'

'Very much indeed. It's a beautiful dress.'

Miss Coote smiled broadly, showing her small, even teeth. She said in a grave tone, as if dealing with an important matter, 'It's a new one, just come. I think it *is* rather nice.'

'Where did you get it?' he asked, as they turned up the hill.

'Out of a catalogue. But it's just right.' She put up her sunshade—a frilly Victorian sunshade. It was quite unneeded to protect her at this hour, but obviously she felt the need of expressing her enjoyment in the frock, the morning, and the sunshade itself.

'You too have good luck.'

'Yes, in some things I do'; and her eyes turned towards Rackham's bungalow, but he was not to be seen. 'Yes, really I suppose I am a lucky person—very lucky. But I shouldn't like to risk spears in a summer suiting. You mustn't trust luck too far, Aladai.'

'I don't. It's done all it could for me already in sending me to Oxford.'

'You think that was lucky? Yes, of course it was.'

'I am the only Rimi man who's ever been in England—who's ever had any real education at all—one out of a million.'

'Don't despise your Rimi education too much; it seems to be very good as far as it goes.'

'I don't; but what should I be if it was all I had—rubbing my nose in the dirt in front of Elizabeth's *ju-ju?* Don't be sentimental about our Rimi education, Miss Coote.'

'No, I mustn't be. I really mustn't be.'

The Resident admitted them at once. He was sitting behind a large kitchen table piled with paper trays. He jumped up to give Judy a chair, but himself remained standing. In this way he avoided offering Aladai a seat.

She had barely uttered four words of apology before he cut her short with, 'But it was not your fault. Good gracious, Miss Coote, it is we who must apologize to you.'

'And I asked Mr. Aladai to go with me because he knew the town and would explain things to me.'

'Quite, quite'—straightening himself and looking down at Aladai from the distant summit. 'Oh, perfectly.' He coughed and glanced out of the window.

Aladai, bending forward, began to say that he had of course not intended to enter the town again, after the Emir's prohibition, but that under the circumstances he had thought it better to go with Miss Coote, as the town was full of strangers, and the pagan ward unaccustomed to visitors.

'Perfectly, perfectly,' said Burwash. 'Shall we say'—he stooped forward with his most genial smile; an expression which seemed to add a positive radiance to the natural polish of his broad cheeks—'shall we say, "All's well that ends well"?'

'It is very kind of you'—from Judy.

'On the contrary, Miss Coote.'

'You are most good'—from Aladai.

'Not at all, Mister—ah—Aladai. And may I thank you for your letter of—ah—last week, I think—about a school for Rimi? I've just been looking at it. I am very interested in that question myself. No one can exaggerate the importance of the education question. But I think you will agree that education, even in the northern provinces, is showing very promising development. Slow, no doubt, but sure.' And then he made a little speech about the difficulty and danger of educating a primitive community in a hurry; and the great importance of inculcating character; 'or guts—if Miss Coote will excuse me. I believe that they are absolutely right in Katsina in their emphasis on guts.'

'So do I, sir, but I thought that, as there was no Government school at all in Rimi, no real education——'

'Ah!' Burwash shook his head. 'What can we do? Rimi is poor.'

'But, sir——' The young man, who must have been holding his breath ever since the Resident had uttered the word education, and was now at high pressure, appeared, to Judy's great alarm, about to burst. She broke in quickly:

'You're busy.'

'Not at all, Miss Coote—but perhaps if Mr. Aladai would call some time, and go into the whole situation——'

'I should wish that very much.' Aladai, in his gratitude, felt an impulse of warm affection towards the Resident. Unconsciously he bent forward, smiling; his eyes turned slightly upward.

The Resident smiled upon him. 'Yes, we must have a real good talk about Rimi.'

'I should be delighted, sir. That is most kind. But I am sure I cannot tell you anything about Rimi; oh, no, it is I who must learn.'

'Well, well.' Once more the Resident threw back his body and diminished towards the ceiling. His head turned away towards the window and he murmured: 'Ah! I believe I see——'

Judy understood. 'Good-bye, Mr. Burwash. Thank you so much.'

'Not at all, Miss Coote.'

'Thank you awfully, sir. You are truly, in the words of my own country, "a father and a mother." '

Burwash, without answering, shook hands warmly with Aladai, and with the same gesture moved the hand gently towards the door.

But Aladai walked out backwards; or, if not exactly backwards, sideways. As he rejoined Judy in the compound, she said to him thoughtfully, 'Don't be too hopeful, Louis. You heard what Mr. Burwash said—"slow and sure." It really is a rule out here.'

'I felt like going down on my nose to him.'

'Well, he was friendly, of course, but——'

'He was decently polite to me, and I do think he's interested.'

Judy was silent and did not look at her friend. She feared that some of the emotion in his voice might appear in his too expressive features, and that her look would increase it.

'You think I was too obsequious?'

'No, no, Louis.'

'Do you know, I was not conscious of being that at all. I simply felt love for him, real love. You think that is sentimental?'

'That isn't sentimental. If it is genuine feeling, it can't be sentimental.'

'Emotional, then. It is a Rimi fault. We show our feelings too much, and especially our affectionate feelings.'

'Is that a fault? Isn't it rather our fault that we hide them?'

'How good you are at finding the right thing to say.'

Sangster was approaching in full uniform. He was accompanied by a woman in a dark grey dress, who was speaking to him very earnestly.

She was a woman of about sixty, tall and thin, with excessively narrow shoulders. Her nose was Roman; but its resolution did not agree with the receding, formless chin. This was Mrs. Vowls, the Resident's sister-in-law; a widow described by Rackham with great disgust as a crank. Rackham hated cranks. Crankiness was a subject upon which he and Judy had agreed to differ. For Judy thought that the name had been applied at one time or another to all the most interesting and important people in the world.

But she could not like Mrs. Vowls, whose crankiness took the common form, among her type, of sentimental anarchism. She called herself a Liberal; and she had been brought up by her papa, a Liberal member of Parliament, somewhere in the 'sixties, to revere Mill. But somehow, she had kept of that teaching only the notion that all the evils of the world were due to its Governments.

Mrs. Vowls had just returned from a visit to Kifi Mission, about thirty miles from Rimi. Judy, who wanted to know about the mission, greeted her warmly, asked her how she had liked Kifi.

The woman did not answer; she was always rude to Judy. She feebly dropped her hand, and looked round for Sangster. But that officer had disappeared as if into space. Aladai stood, hat in hand; now, as Mrs. Vowls again turned her foolish blue eyes, full of sadness and the confusion of her timid mind, towards Judy, he bowed.

She paid no attention to him. She was rude to everybody whom she feared, including all strangers, but especially black ones. Aladai bowed again, but his smile was growing fixed and embarrassed.

Judy, pushing up her chin and turning her head sideways, using her most polite voice—a kind of fluting sound, like that of a bird charmer—and at the same time making what Rackham called her hostess gesture—a motion of the left hand, held loosely, palm upwards, at the level of the breast—said, 'Mrs. Vowls, let me introduce Mr. Louis Aladai,' and then fluting at Aladai, and slightly shaking the fingers of the left hand: 'Should I say the Galadima Aladai?'

She turned once more to the lady. 'Mr. Aladai is heir-presumptive to the Sarauta of Rimi.'

Judy was in terror that this woman, who plainly took little stock of the graces of life, whether in dress or manner, would insult her friend. Even so much rudeness as she had shown already to herself would be an insult to Aladai in his position. She fluted and smiled, therefore, to the utmost of her power, seeking with all her will to persuade Mrs. Vowls to behave with reasonable politeness.

Mrs. Vowls stared at Aladai, who now, with a most wretched air, performed a third lower bow, almost a cringe.

'He will be Emir, you understand,' said Judy, her voice trembling with urgency.

Mrs. Vowls gave a little jump, causing her hat also to give a little jump, and held out her hand. She smiled not merely graciously, but even tenderly. 'Of course, yes,' she murmured, as if to herself. 'I heard my brother—how do you do—I am glad—but you will have a hard fight.'

Aladai said that he hoped not.

'You have many enemies,' said Mrs. Vowls; and now, in her earnestness, she seemed a person of consideration. 'We are your worst enemies. But you know that yourself.'

Aladai said pleasantly that he had many friends among white people, and he did not find them hostile. Mrs. Vowls shook her head vigorously. 'Don't you believe it, Mister—Mister——'

'Aladai.'

'They only pretend to be friendly. How can they be friendly to you when they have stolen your country and made slaves of your people?'

'There are very few slaves left in Rimi, and they could have their freedom if they chose to take it.'

But Mrs. Vowls, if she listened to him, did not pay any attention. She continued with vigour: 'They hate you, because they have robbed you'; and suddenly she asked Aladai, 'Did they receive you at the races?'

'I visited the races,' said the boy, but his smile had again become artificial, his expression was false.

'They will hate you more than the rest,' said Mrs. Vowls, 'because you are as good as they are—in education. I mean—you are better in every other way——'

Aladai smiled, and said that he could not claim any superiority.

But Mrs. Vowls insisted that all races were superior to the English, who were simply grabbers and robbers. 'You have only to look at the map.'

'I do not think Mr. Burwash is a grabber,' said Aladai politely.

'My brother. H'm! You were at Oxford, weren't you?'

'Yes, for two years. I could not wait to take my degree because of the situation in Rimi. But perhaps I shall be able to go back again.'

'Tell me about Oxford.' She wanted to know, of course, if Oxford was in a degenerate condition; if it was true that the undergraduates were drunken, irreligious wasters and Communists.

Aladai, who had been asked this question a hundred times, answered that he could not tell. Among three thousand undergraduates there were different kinds of people.

Meanwhile Judy had discovered what Sangster meant by the show. The Vizier, who had passed some time before, now reappeared in the compound and, turning towards the town, crouched down to touch the earth with his right hand. This was his own simplified obeisance, a degenerate prostration. Simultaneously a blast of trumpets, out of tune, sounded from the town road; and, turning that way, Judy saw, emerging from behind the A.D.O. bungalow, four or five horsemen, in red turbans and red-striped robes like bed-ticking, and crusaders' saddles. They were members of the royal guard—mounted *dogarai*. They were armed with cross-handled swords and long spears. They advanced in a succession of leaps, making their horses prance and rear, so that their progress, though picturesque, was extremely slow.

They were followed by a crowd of mounted officials, courtiers, townsmen anxious to display their loyalty and their horses. In a few moments the compound was full of horses, circling and throwing their heads. Their riders were shouting at the tops of their voices, 'Hail, King of the World.'

A huge black stallion was now to be seen in the opening, fighting with his bit. He reared at every third pace, catching on his chest the foam that slavered from his mouth. Then suddenly he made half a dozen leaps forward, each of them an attempt to bolt. The rider, a billowing mass of white, out of which a single bird-claw of a hand projected, was seen to sway violently in the saddle. Then the claw twisted and the horse checked, stood straight up, its lower jaw wrenched back, its fore-hooves in the air. Two huge *dogarai* rushed forward to catch his head. The courtiers dismounted in a flutter of blue-and-white gowns, shouting at their servants, struggling with their swords, clothes, reins, all apparently in a desperate hurry. Their hasty, impatient gestures and anxious cries were like those of competitors in an obstacle race. The reason appeared when the first to reach the ground darted towards the Emir. It was a race of which the winner had the prize of service to the master. But, although the first-comer alone had room in the front row, all had time to assemble before the chief had been dismounted. This operation was long and complicated, so much obscured from the watchers by the crowd of attendants, the long waving spears, the raised sleeves and arms that Judy did not realize what was happening till she asked Aladai, who answered, 'They're taking the old man off his horse. It's always a long job.'

'I noticed the horse was rather big.'

'It's his age. They say he's got to be strapped on.'

Just then the crowd divided, and sank down, with the rustling sound of scraping feet and stiff robes, in two long billows glittering with white and blue. Loud cries of greeting broke out. At the end of this lane three figures were seen: a giant in a red turban carrying an eight-foot um-brella, which he twirled rapidly between his hands; a mountain of indigo blue out of which, as through a little black window, peeped two red sparks—the Master of the Horse; and in front of them, under the umbrella, a little creature in pure gleaming white. He was like a pillow balanced on its bottom edge and carrying on its other a smaller, rounder pillow. Between the two a little black crescent, three inches long and two wide, could be seen. This was his eyes and the bridge of his nose—all that was left uncovered of the royal face.

'Oh, the poor little thing!' said Dryas's voice, causing Judy and Aladai to turn to their left with surprise and amusement.

The young woman's expression was quite changed. Rackham, who stood beside her, in uniform, and who had also turned to look, smiled at this unexpected change of feature. It was obvious that she was longing to pick up the little Emir, to console the poor little mite.

'You'd like to play with him?' said Rackham.

Dryas paid no attention. 'You don't mean they really *tie* him on the horse?' she exclaimed with indignation. Rackham, still smiling at her, received a glance that was full of disgust and surprise.

'They have got to,' said Aladai. 'He's very old, you know—at least eighty.'

'Eighty!' cried the girl. The indignation was replaced by blankness, the no-meaning of a dissolving view; and then again by a very clear expression—one of disgust. 'Eighty,' she murmured, raising her eyebrows and looking at the little Emir in a manner which said clearly, 'How horrible! Why is he allowed out?'

Rackham laughed loudly, with a note of delight. The little creature began to move forward, but in jerks and starts, like rusty clockwork. Now it stopped; now it ran tottering, as if about to fall on its nose, recovered itself, made ten stately paces, then dipped, wavered sideways. What seemed strange for a moment to Judy was the solemnity with which the whole gathering of important, serious persons in their best clothes watched the little creature in its ludicrous head-dress go through its solitary performance. She wanted to laugh. But then at once, seeing the grave faces all about her, she perceived that she was making a mistake. She, too, became serious, and felt the importance of the occasion. She felt it keenly. The Emir approached. The scrape of his slippers, the harsh, loud rattle of his breathing, like the final gasps of an old mine-engine, could be heard; his little face, resembling one of those dried heads from the Pacific which one sees in museums—heads from which all the bones have been extracted till they are shrunk to the size of a potato—had no expression. Only the buried eyes, glittering, darting from side to side defiant glances, like those of a stoat caught in the middle of a pack, showed the life of the hidden, obscured creature within the bundle of clothes and the mummified body. To judge by the expression of its eyes, that creature was not yet sorry for itself.

The Resident now appeared at the door of his office. He had put on his white uniform coat, with his medals, and stood with great dignity, yet not stiffly. Burwash had mastered the art of appearing genial even in full-dress uniform.

He bowed; the Emir staggered; their hands touched and were laid upon their breasts. Again a bow, a stagger; the pair, looking like the giant and the dwarf at a circus, entered the office.

A boy in a red felt cap, with a look of agony on his face, scuttled across the compound with a large rug in his hands. It flapped against his legs, nearly throwing him over. Two courtiers snatched it from him, glared at each other; the huge Sarkin Dawaki, Master of the Horse, tore it out of their hands and turned towards the office door. The monkey-like Waziri, suddenly popping out of the door with surprising agility, uttered three scolding words to the Master of the Horse, gathered the rug from him, plunged back again. His actions were without dignity. He was like a flustered nanny fetching the baby's mat to cover the wet grass. But in an old-fashioned Court, where the master's favour, the favour of an autocrat, is really efficacious, contempt for personal dignity is the highest kind of flattery.

The Vizier with his own hands spread his master's carpet in front of the Resident's table, going down on his knees to smooth out the folds.

The Emir with one tremendous stagger reached the centre of the rug, and collapsed. That is to say, the turban sank down until it seemed that it would fall clean through the flimsy material beneath to the floor.

But it stopped and jerked backwards, the little black crescent which was the Emir's eyes and the bridge of his nose was again seen, and the chicken-claw made a wavering gesture in the air.

No one had heard a sound; but the Waziri, who was squatting beside his master—not, of course, on the rug, but the floor—at once exclaimed in a loud, harsh, indifferent voice: 'The King of the World salutes the judge and says that he is angry, very angry.'

This was obvious already to all in the room, for the Emir left his mouth covered.

To speak to Burwash without uncovering his mouth was an insult, a defiance. The natives in the room were already looking at the Resident with those wooden faces which express in them the highest degree of watchfulness and apprehension. No one moved an eyelash.

Burwash, who had been till this minute smiling with even more than his usual benignity, now looked grave, deeply sympathetic. He said that he was extremely sorry to hear this bad news. The claw made another wavering gesture. The Vizier, half closing his eyes and singing out his words like a town crier repeating from memory, declared that the Emir had been insulted and abused. His orders had not been obeyed, and he was prevented from making them obeyed; and he asked was he Aliu, the Emir, or was Rimi to be ruled by criminals like Aladai and Salé? For if he was ruler, he demanded that Aladai should be brought to trial for his crimes and Salé sent away out of the country; and, if not, he would like to know it.

Burwash, having listened with a respectful and attentive air, now leant back in his chair and made quite a long speech. But there was no appearance of dictation. He avoided carefully the manner and tone of superiority, or even instruction. He spoke as in conversation, lightly, sometimes playing with his pen, raising his eyebrows, smiling suddenly, nodding, leaning forward in his chair to ask a question. He asked many questions. This was his favourite manner of avoiding the brusqueness of statement. Didn't the Emir think, he asked, that possibly some of the difficulties of his administration were due to the uncertainty of the succession? Of course, this was only a suggestion. But in other countries it had been found that a doubt about the succession had made trouble. Of course (raising his eyebrows and voice together), the system of Rimi was strictly hereditary. It was also elective. This was its great beauty. It was in this respect superior to many in the towns of the *turawa* (whites). But the Emir would remember that they had often discussed the value of the elective principle in Rimi.

The Emir, the Vizier, the whole roomful of negroes, stared at the man with unblinking eyes; sharp, conscious, and at the same time hopeless. What was the fellow driving at? they asked. Of course, they understood his words. Rimi are intelligent people, and every man in the room was self made. All had risen from the ranks by ability. The Vizier had been a slave. The Treasurer had been a foundling. The Master of the Horse had started as a soldier in the Niger Company. The Chief Justice was a village boy who had learnt to write from a rich pilgrim. The Emir himself had been born to the slave concubine of a younger son of the royal house—a farmer too poor and obscure to excite his brother's jealousy. He had gone to his first war on foot, since his father had the only horse in the family.

An oriental Court is always revolutionary; like that of a dictator or usurper, made up of careerists. It does not suffer from lack of ability, but of honesty and principle. So all these men understood very well the Resident's meaning. What they could not make out was his object; and that was what they wanted to know.

Burwash then gave a little talk upon democratic principles, and the importance of allowing people to have a voice in their own government, and ended by enquiring if the Emir would not, perhaps, agree that the people should be consulted about the succession. He was not, of course, suggesting (leaning forward and speaking very earnestly) that the Emir was to be bound by anybody's suggestions. But did he not think that a consultation of public wishes might throw a light on a difficult problem?

He stopped; the sleeve of the Emir's gown was slightly agitated and the Vizier sang: 'The King says what is the judge going to do?'

Burwash smiled affectionately. 'Oh, you think that the time has not come for making such an advance?'

The Emir's sleeve moved an inch or two, and the Vizier leant towards him. This time, in the deep silence of the office, a faint whispering could be heard behind the mouth-veil, like the quick rustling of dry leaves. The Vizier declaimed: 'The King says that if Aladai is permitted to remain free in Rimi, and Salé not sent away, he will himself go away.'

Burwash's look changed slightly. He still looked benevolent, elder brotherly; but his expression had no longer a natural appearance. It was like the polite mask of a host who goes on smiling and greeting his guests when he has just been told that the bailiffs are in the study.

The Emir's threat was a serious one. For an Emir to go into voluntary exile means confusion in the country, disturbance of trade, and loss of tax moneys; possibly civil war; and certainly an enquiry from the Governor. Downing Street would hear about it, and the Secretary of State for the Colonial Department might feel obliged, on his own account, to censure somebody and exculpate someone else; apportioning praise and blame according to some private system quite incomprehensible by the victims but understood to be forced upon him (as he may sometimes hint verbally to the victim's influential friends, if any at hand) by the policy of the Government; otherwise, by a complex of party politics, Press ballyhoo, his personal character and situation, the Prime Minister's character and situation, and the political philosophy of the permanent head, who took a first-class from Balliol in the year 1890.

Burwash was greatly disturbed. He smiled gaily and said, 'But the Emir must have misunderstood. There is no difference of opinion between us.'

The Emir collapsed. The effect was startling. It was as though the man had fallen into dust, leaving only a bundle of clothes which, as the wind escaped from them, slowly fell in upon themselves. The turban rolled down towards the floor.

But suddenly it was checked and began to swing towards the right. The gown was violently agitated. The Vizier scrambled to his feet. The Emir was about to rise. They surrounded the carpet, hiding him completely. When, a moment later, they fell back, their master was seen once more upright. the pillow-case was balanced miraculously on its edge.

It made a stagger; Burwash, who had also risen, hastened forward and held out his hand. But the Emir did not take the hand; he made another stagger, which, turning to the left, carried him right out of the office, and down the three steps of the stoop. At each step he fell, and recovered himself by striking on the next step; the last fall continued for three yards, when the creature, by another astounding effort, brought himself up all standing, and proceeded for four or five paces with the traditional duck-waddle appropriate to a great chief. This brought him to his horse; the Court surrounded him; the three trumpeters blew a new and unexpected discord; an excited old man, with his eyes and teeth standing out of his head, fired off a tower musket, which kicked him, visibly, a yard backwards; and the black stallion was seen standing on its hindlegs, with the little white bundle firmly secured between the cantles of its huge saddle, and its crimson twisted reins dangling loosely in the parrot-claw. The horse gave a tremendous leap, scattering the courtiers, who flew to mount their own.

Burwash, on the stoop of the office, continued to smile affably until the last ragamuffin had run after the last horse, and even then, turning to the A.D.O. Fisk, did not cease to look genial.

'Do you think he means it, sir?' Fisk asked him.

'What, to go away? Of course not. Just bluff. But old Aliu is really very difficult. Most unreasonable. I was wondering if there was anything behind all this.'

'He doesn't like Aladai's popularity in the town.'

'No, but I mean behind it. There was some talk about putting up the old man's allowance. Paxton turned it down. I wonder has it rankled? I don't really see why he shouldn't get another ten or twenty pounds a month. The Treasury could afford it.'

He reflected. Fisk, a fair-haired young man, very thickset, with blue eyes and a broad, square-ended nose, stood waiting with an expectant and ready air, as if the Resident had only to say, 'Now I want you to go to the North Pole,' for him to answer, 'Right, sir,' and set off at once.

Fisk always had this manner. This was his first post in the service, and he had arrived only six weeks before. His attitude to Burwash was that of a keen young fag to the captain of the eleven whom he has fortunately secured as a master.

Burwash, on the other hand, treated his A.D.O. as a personal friend, and discussed everything with him. He was fond of the boy, and sometimes complained of his official manner. But it was difficult to find fault with a manner in which there was as little servility as familiarity; only a brisk politeness and ready obedience.

'You know, Fisk, if this Aladai had any sense, he'd go away by himself for a bit on his own—run up to the mission, for instance. They've been expecting him there for a week. It would do him a lot more good than stirring up trouble in the town.'

'Do you think so, sir?' Fisk was doubtful. 'It would prove that he had some sense of responsibility. But I gather he thinks that he ought to be on the spot to——'

'A pity someone doesn't put it to him,' Burwash interrupted.

Fisk began to understand, and said briskly, 'I get my kerosene from Makurdi.'

'Not personally, I suppose.'

'No, but I could pass that way—it would look quite casual.'

'Don't suggest it, of course. We mustn't interfere. That would be fatal.'

Fisk, who now understood perfectly, answered that he would take great care to be neutral. He then marched off, full of resolute cunning.

VI

THE MOUNTAINS under which Ibu spent the night were rubbish
heaps lying between the third and fourth wards—about four acres of
land formed like a miniature Dartmoor. Its crags were ruins of old
clay walls; its swelling moors heaps of dirt and mud, baked hard and
covered with dry scrub; its mosses deep brick holes full of shifting and
rotting dirt. Spaces like these are often found in African towns. They
may be unknown to anyone but their neighbours, because they are often
entirely surrounded by compounds and have no entrance at all from
any street.

This space in Rimi, one of seven or eight in the close-packed town,
was the largest and also the oldest. It was maintained as waste by the
hatred between the two wards. The Mohammedans would not let the
pagans encroach upon it, and the pagans burnt out the only Mohammedan who had dared to push out his mat walls three or four yards
towards their side.

The ruins upon it, like the older, smoothed heaps, belonged to ancient
times—that is to say, fifty, five hundred, to two thousand years ago.
No one knows within a thousand years or so how old Rimi is. The
margin of error is at least ninety per cent. These waste lands in Rimi are
playgrounds for any children who can, and dare, get to them; each has
its gangs, who drive off all intruders.

There were three chief gangs in the third ward borderland—two
pagan and one Mohammedan—keeping usually to their own ward
sides; but there was a fourth gang, nominally Mohammedan, which
would sometimes seize and range over the whole country. This was a
palace gang, rightly feared by all nice little Rimi boys. The leader was a
Hausa boy called Musa. He was about twelve years old, but extremely
small for his age; neither was he strong nor in possession of that wiry
health supposed to be necessary to small heroes. He was a miserable
weed, with limbs like sticks, of which the left leg was crooked, a long
scraggy neck, a face all mouth and eye-sockets, with a nose consisting
only of nostrils. His right eye had been destroyed by ophthalmia, and
he suffered miseries from various kinds of skin diseases—there were
always three or four open and vigorous sores on his thin wretched
carcass.

But Musa was the unquestioned leader of his gang, sometimes of
twenty or thirty boys. Although many of them were diseased, half

crippled, and stunted like himself, he was probably the weakest of them; yet if any newcomer dared to set his voice or hand against Musa, he would be crushed by the whole gang. Musa was not loved, except by one or two intimates and his wife, but he was acknowledged a leader. He did not live in the hearts of his people, but in their nervous systems. When he came out from the back parts of the palace, in the early morning, his one eye red from firesmoke and lack of sleep, his legs bleeding from the scratching of his nails, covered with dirt and wood ash, and sometimes worse filth picked up where he had last curled himself for a few minutes' rest, he would begin at once to scream and yell, brag and bully, and continue to do so all day. He was always tired and sick, but his furious spirit, all that his friends and enemies meant by Musa, never ceased from the most violent and purposeful activity.

He would scream at the first boy he met, 'Come on, you bastard, we're going to have a hunt. Have you got a bow? Why haven't you, you fool? Go and get one. . . . Then make one. Don't you know how? Oh, you son of a lump! You Rimi fool! I suppose I must teach you, then.'

He was ready to teach anybody anything. Not that he was skilful or full of practical knowledge. On the contrary, he knew very little, much less than the Rimi pagans, whom he despised, and who had their fathers and their chiefs to look after their education. Musa was a waif who knew nothing exactly, except dirty stories and a great many lies. But he believed that he knew everything, and his confidence made others supply his deficiency by the unusual energy he provoked in them.

Musa's gang had the best bows, spears, shields, toy-guns, traps of any other in Rimi; because Musa was always shouting at them, 'Oh, you fool! What's that? A spear! It's just a stick. Crooked too. Go away. You're not a hunter. You're a bastard! Go away, Rimi fool!'

Musa had a wife called Oya, a girl of nine or ten, pretty but stupid. She was, however, a devoted wife, and faithful to him in spite of very good offers.

Musa called Oya his wife, but she was really his betrothed. Among the Rimi, like many Hausa clans, children are betrothed very young, and, after the age of eight, live together, and sleep together, like brothers and sisters, until marriage. This produces, often, a relationship of feeling which explains at once the devotion and the lack of sentiment among Hausa and Rimi couples. They are like brothers and sisters and married people at the same time. They take and express the most unsentimental views of each other's character, and they are so bound together in their lives that if one dies the other cannot live any longer.

Musa and Oya, having lived together, day and night, for three years,

76

already had a very close relationship. Wherever Musa went, Oya followed him, carrying their child on her back, secured by a string. This child was a short thick piece of wood with a rag tied round it, two holes for eyes, and a burnt streak for mouth. But Oya nursed it carefully, and when the sun was hot she put a piece of calabash on its head just as a careful mother should do.

On the morning after the Aladai riot, Musa's gang was exhausted. It had spent most of the night rushing from one battle to another. Musa himself had been at all fires and in the centre of all battles, including the attack on a beerhouse at the waterside, where he got very drunk. Oya could not get him home, so she spent the night with him in a dug-out on the river-bank, lying upon him to keep him warm, and clinging to him to keep herself warm. In the morning they were turned out by the boatmen who gave them breakfast and some warm gruel to drink.

Musa made the boatmen laugh by his description of the old beer woman's attempts to defend her property. He played the old woman to perfection, screaming, bending his back, wriggling his buttocks, shaking his fists; and then, springing upright, he cried, 'The old fool! Why didn't she take a spear to the *wofis?* Now, if I had a beerhouse, I'd like to see anyone touching my beer! I'd just go up to them, and say, "You bastards; do you know who I am? I am Musa, son of the King of the World, and the Lord of Rimi. I am the friend of the Emir of Kano and the Sultan of England. Repent, bastards, oh, fools of Rimi dogs! Down on your noses, offal, while I put this whip to your backs!" '

The boatmen gave him two anini, together worth less than a farthing, which he exchanged in the women's market for thirty cowries. These he gave to Oya to keep for the family purse; the rest he spent on honey cakes, which were equally divided between the couple.

It was now about eight o'clock, and the streets were filling. He set a donkey running in the wrong direction by a skilful prod, and, when the donkeyman rushed at him with a stick, he stood his ground and finally screamed the man to shame. 'What are you doing, fool? I didn't touch your decaying beast. You dare to touch me and I'll kill you. Do you know who I am? I am the son of the Lord of the World,' etc., etc. In the middle of this, three white men—the big judge, the doctor, and the captain of the police—came by, and the Emir's guard, clearing a path for them, pushed the donkeyman to the wall. But Musa, and Oya close behind, holding to one of his rags, would not give way. When the white men drew near, he gave them a soldier's salute, and screamed in Rimi, 'Hail, great lords of the muck-heap—a thousand thousand salutations with dung! God damn you for ever and ever,' turning all the usual greetings into something rude or worse. The people were horrified by such conduct. Several voices behind Musa called out, 'Silence. Knock him down—it's one of those palace rats,' but Musa did not wait to be cuffed, and perhaps whipped, by the respectable citizens of the ward. He followed the white men, and, when the orderly turned to drive him away, set up such cries that they turned round.

At once he made a polite curtsey—'Lords—lions—I did nothing.'

'Let the children alone,' the judge said, to the orderly.

Musa followed, therefore, in triumph, with Oya close behind, part of the procession; and afterwards, while the white men were examining the site of the fire in the third ward, opposite the *ju-ju* house, he pushed forward and explained to them how the people had shouted, 'Burn the town—burn the whole town.'

This was a lie. All Musa's news came straight out of his fancy, which was romantic. He saw himself burning a whole town, and so he declared that the crowd had wanted to do so.

The white men were discussing a plan for making the streets wider. They thought that if they prevented the burnt houses from being rebuilt, and pulled down the *ju-ju* house, they would be able to make a new wide road from the central market to the women's market, and so to the waterside.

The plan had been proposed often. All the townspeople were opposed to such a senseless scheme, which reduced even further the small space left for their crowded compounds. They fought against it now.

The ward head, an old man, explained that the *ju-ju* house was a sacred place—especially the women's part of it—and that the people would not like it to be pulled down.

The judge answered gravely, 'But why can it not be moved? It is a new place. It is the old mosque in front that troubles me. I don't want to touch that.'

The mosque was a ruin, unused for a long time—since the first and last Mohammedan Emir of Rimi had been killed thirty years before.

'But the *ju-ju* house is new, lord,' said the old ward chief.

'So I say, and therefore it can be moved.'

'But the mosque is old, lord; it is the *ju-ju* house which is new.'

'Yes, yes, chief. I understand. And I say I wish to preserve your mosque, but in that case the *ju-ju* house will have to go.'

'Master, King of the World, it is the *ju-ju* house we must keep; it is new—the *ju-ju* house is the new building, just finished, only five years. It is the mosque which is——'

'Yes, yes, chief,' said the judge, and then, puzzled by the man's excitement, he turned to the crowd, and asked, 'He means that the mosque is old, the *ju-ju* house new?'

The crowd looked confused. They perceived that there was some-thing mysterious in this question. Musa, however, who thought it was time to assert himself again, jumped forward, and shouted, 'Don't you believe them, lord. They're all liars in this ward—a lot of murderers. They wanted to burn the whole town—I heard them.'

But this did not succeed well. The judge looked displeased. He had begun to say, again, that if the *ju-ju* house was new, it could be moved. A *dogarai* took Musa by the ear, drew him through the crowd, with Oya still coupled to him, like a tender, put his foot against him, and shot him ten yards down the lane, where he crashed against a wall. Oya, still attached to the rag, also whirled with him and crashed.

Musa would have gone back to kill the *dogarai*, or, at least, to shame him, if he had not been partly stunned. Oya wept with surprise and alarm. She said to Musa, 'It's your own fault for going with the white men.'

'Shut up, woman,' Musa gasped, holding his head with both hands. 'What do you understand? Nothing.'

'There's always trouble with white men.'

'Shut up, you fool. Women are fools.'

'I want to go home.'

'I'll beat you in a minute.'

Oya began to cry, and Musa, though he could hardly stand, rose up and beat her until she began to retaliate. She was much the stronger of the two, and Musa always stopped beating her as soon as she began to beat him. 'All right,' he said, staggering away, 'I'll let you off now. I don't want to kill you. Ask my pardon and it's yours. But if you don't, you won't come with me to-day; and we're going to have a good game—oh, such a good game! I've got a new game for to-day.'

Oya ceased to thump him, and asked what the game was to be.

'I won't tell you. What do you expect? How could a man tell a woman what he was going to do? That would spoil everything.'

Oya begged his pardon, and was allowed again to take hold of the rag—one of Musa's rags seldom lasted Oya more than a day.

Musa's game proved to be an old one—a rat hunt in the waste land of the third ward. But his screams of excitement made it seem attractive to each member of the gang in turn. Though they were all found in the same languid and bilious state, red-eyed and sleepy, within twenty minutes nine of them had assembled, with spears, bows, slings, shields, and even a stalking-mask, in a compound adjoining their hunting-ground.

This compound, belonging to a Hausa merchant who sold cosmetics to the palace women, was always open to Musa, and formed the gang's entrance, by the back of the latrine, to the waste land.

Musa was now in a condition of excitement which would have seemed lunatic to anyone who had not observed its continuous purpose. He rushed to and fro without cease, giving orders, contradicting them, showing, by demonstration, how to drive or stalk the game, how to shoot, how to use a spear, how to throw from a sling, and shrieking the whole time a stream of encouragement and abuse.

'Call that a sling—it's a rag! Get a bigger stone. Go over there, you fool!—where the wind is blowing from. Look here, bastard, this is how a rat goes.' Musa, now taking the part of a rat, went down on all fours, and ran up and down, sniffing the air. He even attempted to wriggle his nose, but, as he had no nose, he wriggled his lips and eyebrows instead.

'He smells the wind, you fool! Go and let him smell you, so he will run this way. Go away, Oya! Go away, woman! Curse you! Do you want to spoil me?' He flew at Oya. And now, when Oya tried to fight him, the gang at once set upon her and knocked her head over heels. She ran off, weeping and cursing. Musa, compunctious, bawled after her, 'Don't you understand, fool? You can't have women at a hunt, or nothing would happen. A hunter mustn't have anything to do with women. Women make men weak. Now, hunters, I'm the *ju-ju* man. Come here, and I'll tell you if this is a good day to hunt. Come and get your medicine for hunting. What do you want to kill? Come on, fool! I'm asking you. Don't you know? Is it an elephant? Call it an elephant, curse you! Of course it's an elephant. Very well. Your name is Elephant-Killer, and this is your elephant medicine.' He picked up a fragment of dirt and wrapped it in a leaf. 'Hang this on your neck. Now you will find elephants whenever you want to, and your arrows will kill them dead. Here is your arrow poison.' He gave the boy another leaf. 'Be careful not to prick yourself with your own arrow, or you will die in pain—yes, very quick, like this.' Musa opened his mouth, goggled his eye, fell backwards, and uttered a death-rattle. But he did not fall right down. He had no time for that. He had not fallen six inches, or rattled for more than ten seconds, before another idea had flashed into his mind. 'And when you kill each elephant, the right foreleg is my leg, the king's leg; the left foreleg is the *ju-ju's* leg; and the right hindleg is the hunter's leg; and the left hindleg is the town's leg; and the heart is the women's; and the rest of the body belongs to the poor and the beasts of the forest; and the teeth are mine, the king. You shall bring to me—— Listen, you fool! Are you listening? No, you are not, you bastard! I say, the teeth are mine, but if they are good long teeth, as long as this'—stretching out his arms—'I'll give you one back. And you'—turning to the next boy—'what do you want to kill—a leopard? Quick, fool! What? A lion? Yes, a lion. Here is your medicine. You shall kill a big big lion. Your name is Killer of a Thousand Lions. But wait a minute! The skin of the lion belongs to the king, and—wait a minute, curse you!—when you kill this lion, see that the lion's wife does not catch sight of you, or the medicine will be no good, and you will die like this'—falling back, goggling his eye, choking. 'Die, quick, quick, but in terrible pain, like this'—clasping his throat and writhing. 'Go away, woman, curse you!'

He had caught Oya in the act of reaching for the rag. She had been approaching for some time—still full of resentment and bitterness, still enraged against Musa. But her feet had carried her to his back, and her hand had searched for the rag. When Oya had been for a second time beaten and thrown into a thorn-bush, Musa distributed his hunters in a circle, to advance on a certain heap, close by the walls of the third ward, where new rubbish had lately been piled.

Musa himself was stationed in the post of honour—that is to say, the highest and most conspicuous. He had claimed for himself the stalking-mask, made out of a crooked branch and some feathers and two pieces of string. The branch with feathers tied to it was supposed to resemble the head of a marabou stork; the string was used to tie it to Musa's head.

It was not a good mask, even for a toy. But to Musa its attraction was not in its own quality, but in what he could do with it. He advanced now over the skyline—with a long pointed stick in his hand, a bundle of leaves hung from his neck, and the crooked branch hanging sideways above his forehead—nodding his head, high-stepping, and sometimes fluttering his arms. He had forgotten that he was a hunter. He was a marabou stork. He jerked up one leg and sank his chin on his breast, wriggled his behind, and then, suddenly stooping, pushing out his lips to make a beak, he pecked towards the ground.

Oya could be seen a few yards behind him. She was still crying, but her hand was already raised in the rag-grasping position.

The rest of the gang were still hunters. They were stalking the mound, rushing forward six steps, crouching, starting, shading their eyes as if to gaze into the distance, looking round with a warning gesture.

Just as Oya reached the rag, the elephant- and lion-killers charged together, and were seen stabbing at a hole with their spears.

For a moment Musa was distracted by Oya. His anger was great, for she had destroyed a work of genius—a representation of the marabou stork which, Musa felt, though he did not think about it at all, was even better than a real marabou.

He struck Oya with his spear, whereupon she took it from him and beat him with it. The marabou head fell over his one eye and blinded him; he tripped, and struck his nose, or, rather, the middle of his face, on a heap of earth.

Three hunters came to his rescue. Oya ran for her life, screaming. Musa was lifted to his feet and consoled. He was, after all, the smallest boy there. His face was bleeding, and his eye was watering. He was breathless and giddy. But his first audible word was a curse, and then he exclaimed, 'Stop it, fools! You're spoiling everything. I am the king. Where are my elephant's teeth and the lion's skin?'

The elephant- and lion-killers had stopped driving their spears into the hole, and now stood looking into it with perplexed faces.

Musa, seeing their faces, said, 'Why, there really is something there— or is it a real rat?' In a frenzy of excitement, he rushed towards them. 'Ooee, wait for me! I want to see!'

However, the two killers had begun already to use their spears again, though in a mechanical and routine manner, without the proper yells and flourishes.

Musa, breathless, scrambled down the heap, and found that they were prodding a girl, who sat in the hole, looking up at them with round fixed eyes. She held her hands tightly clasped between her thighs, and her whole body was quivering, like a bird's when it is caught and held in the hand.

'It's a girl,' said one killer.

'Have you killed her?'

'Yes, but she won't die.'

'She won't do anything.'

'She's a fool.'

'She's frightened,' said Oya, suddenly reappearing. 'Send her away. We don't want her in our game.'

'What's your name?' Musa asked.

Ibu stared at him. She did not feel quite sure that she had a name any longer, since she had been driven away by her mother and father. They had said she was somebody else—somebody wicked. She did not feel like the Ibu any longer. Ibu had a home, a villager a mother, and her own private toys. The lion-killer said, 'I asked her before, but she won't say anything.'

'She's a fool,' said Musa. 'Look how she shakes. She's a duiker—like this.' Musa went down on his hands, and jerked his head about, made a little skip, put down his head towards the ground, and then suddenly threw it up again and ran for a few yards. All the time he wriggled, especially his behind, as if wagging a short tail.

To the admiring gang this seemed a wonderful representation of a duiker, the smallest of the deer, as it goes trembling on its thin legs through the bush, stopping every moment to turn its large eyes about, darting off in a panic.

82

'She's a duiker; kill her again,' Musa shouted, once more the hunter. 'Not too hard, you fool! Can't you see she's frightened?'

The killers prodded Ibu again, more gently; while Musa, stooping down, shouted at her, 'You're dead now. Fool, don't you understand? It's a game. We're catching slaves. You're sick, and we're killing you. Die now. Lie down, you fool, and die—like this.' Musa lay down, stretched out his arms, twisted himself, moaned, heaved, jumped bodily from the ground, uttered a shriek, and went into convulsions, which ended after a full minute, in the middle of the enchanted gang, in a slow painful death.

He had by now forgotten the girl. He was also hungry. He jumped up, and shouted, 'Now I am the Emir of Kano coming back from war, and you are my banner-men. Go on, now. Where's the singer? You there, fool! Sing then. And the drummers. You must drum. Hit your shield with a spear.' The procession marched off; but when it was passing through the Hausas' compound, Oya said, 'That girl's coming with us—I knew she would. I'll go and drive her.'

'Yes, go and drive her.'

Oya went and chased the girl away. Ibu ran faster than Oya.

But when they reached the big market, she was following again, ten yards behind the last of the gang, who, the stupidest of all, had been given the duty of white men. Musa, like most of the palace dwellers, had a low opinion of the whites.

In the market-place the gang began to melt. One boy turned off to his mother's stall, to beg a cake; another was captured by a Mohammedan uncle, who wanted to know why he was not at school, learning his Koran. Others went home to breakfast. When Musa entered the narrow stinking alley, or sewer ditch, which runs down both sides of the palace from the big market, he was preceded only by one drummer, one trumpeter, blowing through his hands, and followed only by Oya and his Prime Minister, who had also to carry the State umbrella, made of a broad banana leaf stuck on a wooden spear.

Oya turned and saw Ibu staring after them down the mouth of the alley. She darted back, cursing, and drove her headlong across the market. But when she and Musa and the three remaining members of the gang were within a few yards of the postern gate, leading into the back parts of the palace, the child was again on their heels. Oya flew at her, but now she did not run. She allowed herself to be beaten, scratched in the face, punched. At last Musa shouted, 'Let her alone, the fool!'

Musa began to think that he had made a conquest. The girl kept looking at him. She was a pretty girl.

'But we don't want her,' screamed Oya.

'Why shouldn't she walk after us, if she wants to? Let her alone.'

Oya punched the little girl in the face so that she fell; her lips were bleeding. Musa and the trumpeter set upon Oya, and punched her also in the face. Musa was angry.

Oya was driven away. The trumpeter, the Prime Minister, the drummer, re-formed to conduct the king into his palace—a real palace. As he took his place of honour in the procession, he turned to Ibu, and said to her, with a grand air, 'This is my palace. You can come in, if you like. Don't mind that wife of mine. She's a fool.'

Ibu, though stupid with terror, confusion of mind, misery, cold, and hunger, was an intelligent child. This quality had probably been her ruin. All intelligent, good-looking persons are exposed to jealousy, and jealousy is the subconscious source of the hatred which produces injuries—from injuries, fear; and from fear, an accusation of witchcraft. In this way Africa has destroyed, every year for some millions of years, a large proportion of its more intelligent and handsome children.

Ibu was a clever little girl, and she did not believe Musa when he told her that he was taking her into the King's palace. She knew the palace. It was the large wall and towers on the big market which she had just left behind her—the biggest and most wonderful building in the world. But Musa was going through a broken doorway in a tumbledown mud wall, half washed away and patched with old mats.

Ibu ran after Musa, because he was now her world—that is to say, the feel of things which gave her confidence to live. His invitation was something that had happened to her before. She understood it, as she had recognized the boy's game. With Musa and these children she was among familiar things, and she dared not lose them again.

She darted through the broken door close on the heels of the Prime Minister. She kept closer still when she looked round her and saw what was behind the door.

She had expected a compound—a yard surrounded by huts, with two or three mortars in it, a few water-pots, and perhaps some women beating corn. She seemed to be in the slums of Rimi over again, but dirtier, more confused, and crowded. The riverside wards of Rimi were at any rate in compounds, and each compound had its women's side, its men's side, its porch and inner porch, and latrine; but here there were no arrangements and no order. Everywhere one saw heaps of rubbish, lounging dirty men and women, smoking cigarettes and scratching themselves; chickens, dogs, even horses, at which Ibu stared in wonder and awe. She had not seen many horses, and only then when prancing under some chief—for which reason she supposed them to be fierce and dangerous.

But the people frightened her as well as the horses. She understood at once, in her nerves, that they were not like village people, even bad village people, or the townspeople in the markets. They were different in every way—the ones who laughed at Musa's procession, and the ones who abused him; those who stared at her, and the women who made jokes about her as she ran after the boys—all seemed frightening to her sedate village nerves.

But she could not go back. She was lost in what seemed like a town composed entirely of these disorderly broken compounds; some without any huts at all, others full of ruins; little triangular corners behind houses occupied by a single old leper, rotting in the shade; dark and stinking corridors where horses snorted and stamped, turning their huge terrifying eyes towards the trumpeter, the drummer, the Prime Minister, shouting, 'Make way for the King of the Sudan, blood brother to the King of England,' and herself, edging her way along the dirty walls.

In some of the compounds children, who seemed as wild and strange as Musa himself, threw dung at his procession; in another they were attacked by an angry old man, at whom they screamed abuse for five minutes.

Ibu, taught to be respectful to all old people, hid from this scene. It was not the boys who frightened her, but the scene. It made her shake.

The old man finally called out; a *dogarai* appeared with a huge iron-bound club. The boys ran, laughing and shrieking curses and jokes. Ibu was cut off; she cowered back in her corner, her eyes starting, her muscles trembling in a spasm. But, as the Prime Minister's yellow heels disappeared round the door, she held her breath, and projected herself straight at the *dogarai* in the doorway. He made a sweeping blow at her, but she ducked under his arm and fell through the doorway.

She almost bumped against a fat old woman, approaching the doorway from the other side. She dodged her only just in time. The fat old woman was abusing the *dogarai*. She shouted, 'What are you doing to the boy? You let the children alone, you latrine bucket!'

Whether the *dogarai* had been a prisoner and worked in the scavenger's chain gang or not, this term annoyed him, and he answered by calling the old woman a whore.

But she easily defeated him in the succeeding argument. He was essentially thick-headed and slow-tongued. She ended on a high note: 'And when I tell my Lord what you said to me, he'll skin you, you leprous rat—and poison the hyenas with what the worms haven't eaten of your objectionable guts. Go away, you ill-mannered Rimi cur; you make me ashamed.'

Ibu had slipped away into a shadow. She concealed herself behind a water-pot, and looked round for Musa. She could not see him or any of his party. But she saw many other children. The yard was plainly a women's yard—it was full of women and children of all ages up to twelve and thirteen. Ibu was glad to see a women's yard again. It assured her that this strange town had at least one usual compound in it. But she did not like the women any more than the lounging men in the other parts of the town—the leper in his corner, the angry old man. The women, like the men, seemed to have nothing to do. They were sitting and lying about in the shade, smoking cigarettes, and laughing at the fat woman.

'Good, Fanta. That was a good one.'

'Fanta, you make me laugh.'

'Fanta is as good as a fish dance.'

They were all dressed in their best clothes, and Ibu did not like that either. The women she knew at home wore a single rag in the morning, or nothing at all, and none of them had time to laugh or chaff. They were gloomy and bad-tempered, hurrying to work. She crouched further into her corner.

Fanta continued to shout abuse long after the *dogarai* had slunk away. She then suddenly burst into shrieks of laughter, which made her soft body and round cheeks shake like porridge in a calabash. The women took up the laugh. Most of them shrieked with laughter. Fanta then waddled round the yard, repeating again all her best remarks to the *dogarai*, and describing the man's face and feelings as he had retreated. She had not seen his face, because it was turned away, but she described it, and her description caused her to laugh again, until she could hardly speak—'Like a—a—a—monkey's behind. Allah! I'm dying.'

And the women also screamed with laughter and cried to Allah.

Fanta was a very black Hausa. Ibu knew that she was a Hausa, by her name. She had painted her eyes until they seemed to be set in moulded lead; her hands were the colour of fresh-sawn mahogany. A huge stud of pink coral was thrust through her right nostril, and her neck, arms, and ankles were hung with so many necklaces and huge silver rings, an inch thick, that at every step she clanked and rattled like a convict.

She frightened Ibu more than all the other women, because she seemed to be the richest.

A voice above Ibu exclaimed, 'Who are you, child?'

It was a girl come to dip a calabash full of water. She was looking over the pot at Ibu.

Ibu said nothing. Her knees began to shake. The girl turned round, and cried out, 'Here's another of those kids come here to steal the cigarettes.'

The women paid no attention. But the girl, a young girl of about fourteen, was righteously indignant. She had her standards. She insisted the women should hear and attend. She went on screaming till Fanta came over to the water-pot. She stared down at Ibu, and said, just like Oya, 'She's frightened.'

Then she said, 'But I don't know her. Who is she? Who are you, child?'

Ibu licked her dry lips, but did not answer.

'And where did you come from?'

Ibu could not answer. She began to shake again, violently. Fanta gazed at her. 'She's frightened. Why, the poor little thing, she's trembling. Look at her. I expect that bastard of a *dogarai* frightened her. There now, what's your name? It's all right.' She picked up Ibu, and consoled her. 'Would you like a sweetie? Of course you would.' The other women now began to take an interest in Ibu. They surrounded her, and agreed that she was a pretty child, very well made. She would make a good match.

'My lord would like her,' said Fanta. 'He likes pretty children. What's your name, sweetie? Are you dumb?'

Ibu shook her head, but said nothing.

'She's afraid,' said Fanta. 'That's it. Oh, the poor thing!' She took Ibu into her hut, and gave her sweets. This was the child's first food for twenty-four hours. It was still a long time before she dared ask for a drink. But meanwhile she had a name. Musa, coming to buy cigarettes, shouted, 'I found her in the hunting-ground. She's a deer woman—the one that shakes. How do you like my palace, shaker? Plenty chop— plenty cigarettes—perhaps I'll take you for a wife.'

Oya, who was in close attendance, also with a cigarette in her mouth, now gave Ibu a sly push that knocked her down. Fanta drove them both out of the hut. She wanted to play with her new toy. In an hour Ibu was dressed, painted, with bangles on her wrists, and even a ring on her finger. She knew herself again; she was Shaker.

She had now twenty mothers instead of one, and she knew in her feelings that all these women were children-spoilers.

But she was not happy. She could not be at peace. She could not even sleep without twitching and starting up every twenty minutes. However, the habit which, above all, is most likely to make a child un-popular did not do so for Ibu, because no one noticed it. She did not cry out in her fright. She was too much afraid. For she was surrounded by difference. Even the noises in this place were different—not the beating of mortars, but murmuring of voices and laughter; not the noise of her grandfather adzing a canoe, but the sudden scream of a mare, the shouts of a quarrel rising from one of the box-like cells in which these strange people lived.

But she had discovered already that Musa had not been telling all lies. He was not the son of the king—he was apparently nobody. This was the effect on Ibu's mind of Fanta's statement that Musa had no family, no mother, but simply 'lived here.'

But it was true that this was the Emir's palace. The great walls which she could still see from the women's compound, and which she had called the palace, were only the Emir's own house and fort. Here, behind, were the compounds of his slaves, dependants, wives, servants.

Ibu had been a chatterer at home. She did not utter a word now; and she did not even want to ask questions. She liked to be near these people, but not among them. Her favourite place was still the back of the water-pot, where she often sat all day, as still as the pot itself, jumping only into life when someone noticed her. When she jumped, she began also to shake, and this made the women pity her and love her.

Soft fearful people like the timid and the weak simply because they are weak and timid—partly from sympathy, partly because they do not fear them. Fanta especially took a fancy to her, and would often take her from her refuge and make her sit between her knees, while she lounged with a cigarette and a cup of gin, chaffing her, stroking her head, new-frizzed and shaved by the royal barber, and saying, 'Little silly one, what are you afraid of now? Isn't this a good place to be in? You're a lucky girl. This is the finest house in the world, and it has more people in it than any other house. My lord is the greatest being in the world, and he has the greatest family. To anybody who comes, he says, "I am your father. Here is food for you." My lord is the greatest war chief that ever was. He conquered the whole world, including the Emir of Bida. He ate a hundred towns every day, and a thousand slaves. He had many captains to fight for him, and now, when they are old and sick and the wars are stopped, they come and say to my lord, "Lord, I die"; and he says to them, "Here is food and rest and honour."

'Yes,' said Fanta with vigour, 'he gives them horses too. They don't get horses in Kano and Bida. But my lord is, of course, superior to those mean ones. He is the King of the Sudan.'

The King of the Sudan is a title belonging to the late Emir of Kontagora, a great war chief in his day. But most of the old war chiefs claimed it at one time or another. Aliu of Rimi was the last.

VII

THE RESIDENT wanted Rackham for his account of the riot, and kept him to breakfast. Afterwards he took him to town to inspect the native gaol. His real purpose was to sound the native gaol governor about the political situation in the town. Rackham, who spoke Rimi, was to interpret.

He did not return to the station till four o'clock, when he found this note: 'I'm at Captain Rubin's for tea. Old engagement. Can't get out of it. But I *must* see you before polo.'

'Isn't that typical of Judy!' he thought. 'That *must*. And I suppose she's almost as intelligent as they're grown!'

But he was glad. Rackham hated quarrels so much that he found it extremely difficult to make them up. He liked to pretend that they hadn't happened. He had been glad that Burwash had saved him, all day, from the need of a reconciliation. Just as a man who awaits an operation feels relief at a postponement, so he was pleased that it was forced upon him—like the same man with the peace of a decision.

Rackham and Rubin were friends. The two men, it seemed, had little in common, for though Rubin loved horses and horse-talk, and Rackham was a jockey, they did not talk horses. Rackham took little interest in horses except as vehicles, and did not find them amusing subjects of conversation. This did not prevent Rubin talking horses to Rackham. He was one of those men who cannot suit their conversation to others. Rackham had said of him, 'Rubin's brain is like Irish stew, it goes on bubbling and you take what comes—chiefly scrag-end'—but this was before he came to like the man.

This afternoon he strolled over to Rubin at a little past four o'clock. It was a polo day. His excuse for the visit was to arrange sides with Rubin, who was president of polo. He met Rubin in his compound. He was inspecting a pony.

Rubin was not a big man, but he seemed taller than he was because of his backward-leaning carriage. He had a round belly, which he carried a long way in front of him. He had a very red face, a large red beak, much pitted, like a piece of old cast-iron exposed for many years to the weather; and under the beak, divided into two equal curls by its depressed tip, a reddish-brown moustache. The moustache curled fiercely upwards at the points. This moustache had been compared, also by Rackham, to twin-bow waves of Niger water in a muddy reach, under the nose of a palæolithic dug-out.

His chin was short but prominent, shaped like a heel, cleft, and supported by another chin below, which joined an enormous neck not much paler than a turkey's.

Like other fat men whose legs are not too short, he had natural dignity, but, at the moment—one large freckled hand posed on his hip, and in his other a walking-staff five feet long, made of a polo-stick without the head—with one foot forward in the old stand-at-ease position and his nose high in the air, he was an impressive figure.

It was true that his hat, thrust well forward over his eyes, was a ruin, and that he was wearing a boot on one foot and a slipper on the other, but the station was accustomed to see him in odd get-up. He could never bear to buy hats, and he was frequently seized with a new idea in the middle of a change of clothes.

He had been seen going to his subaltern's house, at six in the morning, dressed only in short pants, socks and slippers, with a hairbrush in one hand, and one of those patent folding boot-jacks which agents sell to tenderfeet in the other. He had just thought of an improvement in the jack which would enable it to take off boots.

He greeted Rackham with a slight lift or throw of the clin, native style, and said, 'You're just in time.'

'What for?'

'Look at that pony.'

Rackham looked. The pony was about twelve two, jet black, deep in the barrel, very thick in the crest, rather short-legged. Its tail almost touched the ground, and its forelock came nearly to the tip of its nose.

'It seems to have four legs,' said Rackham, 'from this distance.'

'That's an Azben,' said Rubin impressively. 'A pure Azben. Look at that head. Arab in every line. It's like a stag's. And its little ears. And that barrel. And, mind you, this *wofi*'—indicating a wretched-looking boy who was leading the horse by the halter—'says it belongs to the Treasury clerk. I just happened to look up, or I wouldn't have seen it.'

'Scandalous. Very lucky.'

'Buy him, Jock.'

'I don't want any ponies. Why don't you buy him?'

'I've got too many as it is. I wonder would what's-his-name—Fisk—buy him?'

'I thought you approved of clerks having ponies?' said Rackham. 'Didn't you make one of them play polo?'

'Yes, just look at him. Look at his coat, look at his nose and tail.' Rubin, approaching the pony with majestic strides, passed his hand over the dusty coat, and locked his fingers in the tangled hair. He looked severely at the horse-boy, and said, 'You no fit have *doki* like this. This *doki* fit for king.'

He turned suddenly, and shouted, 'Auta!'

A Hausa horse-boy, with a sulky face, came ambling from the back.

'Auta, take this pony and clean him proper.'

Auta stared. Rubin's boys-had all been with him for fifteen years and more. They did as little as they chose; and only when they liked.

'See here, Auta. Azben pony,' said Rubin; and, breaking into bad Hausa, he exclaimed, 'Beautiful horse—a king—see how they treat him like a donkey.'

Auta, grumbling, jerked the rope from the wretched horse-boy and led the pony away. Rubin gazed after him with an earnest expression, then suddenly put both hands on his knees, stooped, and shut one eye.

'Got a pain?' said Rackham.

'Marvellous action.'

'You'll have a marvellous action if you get a jigger in your right foot.'

Rubin took him by the arm. 'Come in and have something. As a matter of fact I've got a friend coming.'

Rackham said nothing. They went into the house. Rubin, pointing to a table laid for three, said, 'I've got a friend of yours to tea.'

'What, Judy?'

'You're spoiling a nice little party. A deep-laid scheme.'

'You're lucky to get your guest. You heard about last night?'

'Mrs. Pratt told me she'd eloped with the Black Prince. Boy, bring boot. But I forgot. The ladies. Perhaps I'd better change. What d'ye think, Jock?'

'Why, you're all right.'

'It wasn't the right thing, in my young days, to wear boots in the drawing-room.'

'Judy won't know, and if she did she wouldn't mind.'

'She's a sensible woman that,' said Rubin warmly. 'They told me she was clever, but you wouldn't know it to meet her. A real nice girl.'

'A bit of a handful at times. Look at yesterday.'

'It's on your mind, yesterday. Bring me the hooks, boy. You know I always want 'em on the right boot. Funny thing.' he murmured, 'that your right leg is fatter than the left. You don't use it more. I wonder, is it usual?'

'How would you like your girl going off like that—with a nigger? And the trouble is—she likes him.'

'That's a problem. I haven't got a girl. Poof!' The last was a tremendous explosion of breath, let out, like steam from a high-pressure cylinder, after a successful pull at the right boot.

'You wouldn't take it so coolly if you had.'

'I daresay not. No. That's very likely. I shouldn't. Not at all. No, no. Poof!' He stamped heavily, driving his heel home, and put the boot-hooks on the tea-table. Rackham picked them up, and beckoned with them to the boy, who took them away.

'All the same,' said Rubin, 'old Sergeant Musa is a white man to the backbone.' And, suddenly growing animated, he told a long story about Sergeant Musa, who had saved somebody's life in the war, and who now kept a friend's old parents in the town.

In the middle of the story Judy arrived, and Rubin, now full of enthusiasm, repeated it from the beginning—'Not his own parents, mind you, but a friend's. Chap that died of wounds after the scrap at Mora mountain.'

Judy, whose eyes now and then turned anxiously towards Rackham, causing him to look extremely stiff and to assume a cold, bored expression, said that the Rimi had a genius for friendship—'I love to see the way two old fishermen will walk hand in hand.'

'You should try it,' said Rackham.

'Two lumps?' said Rubin, who did his own pouring out.

'Jerry thinks I'm too fond of black men,' said Judy. 'What do you think, Captain Rubin?'

'Some of them are better than others,' said Rubin, 'and some worse. My first house-boy tried to poison me—to get the cook into trouble; but it was pure affection on his part. He was jealous. It was my first tour, and I was rather struck.'

'It was hitting below the belt.'

'I was struck by the whole affair,' said Rubin, with dignity. He was more than usually dignified when relating his own discoveries. 'I said to myself, "Why should this black fellow take such a fancy to me for a pound a month and two shillings a week chop money?"'

'Why, indeed,' said Rackham.

'Because it was his nature, Jock. That's it—nature!'

'That's what I say,' said Judy. 'They're very affectionate—all these people are.'

Rackham answered that this was a characteristic of animals, too, and, seeing that Judy did not like the comparison, he said drily, 'I am not trying to depreciate your friends.'

'You've got a complex, Jock,' said Rubin.

'I didn't know you'd been reading Freud.'

'I haven't, but that's what you've got. You don't like black men because they're black. What do you think, Miss Coote?'

'I've heard that some black people feel like that about the whites.'

'They do—some of them. I had a corporal who couldn't stick the look of a white man. Never got over it. When his time was up he went and took a job with an Emir somewhere. But he hated leaving the army.'

'It's not as though they come off on the tablecloth,' said Judy. 'Don't you eat anything at tea, Captain Rubin?'

'No, thanks.' He murmured at once. 'The more waist, the less feed.' He gave a short loud chuckle, and, since neither Judy nor Rackham, preoccupied with themselves, smiled, he murmured, 'Not too bad, old boy!'

Rackham suddenly made a little speech, neatly phrased and spaced, in which he declared that he had no irrational dislike, or, if Rubin chose to use the word, complex, about coloured people. It was obviously absurd to divide people by colour. He objected to exactly the same things in whites as blacks, and he liked the same things. No doubt in the future world-state, which Judy liked to talk about, there would be no distinction by colour.

'I shouldn't think there'll be much intermarriage,' Judy put in; but Rackham paid no attention to her, and went on, 'But at present I think you've got to consider the political situation. The blacks out here are not fit to run their own show, and it will be a long time before they learn. Meanwhile we've got to keep the machine running, and the only peaceful way of doing that is to support white prestige.'

'Hear, hear,' said Rubin. 'Have some more tea.'

'Meaning, that I ought to cut my friends,' said Judy.

'No, I don't mean that. I only mean that you ought to be careful about getting mixed up in town rows.'

'He's quite right, Miss Coote,' said Rubin, with immense weight. 'It's good advice. Leave all that to the political department. Mind you, I'm not saying that I like all their ideas, but that's the way they're educated nowadays. They pick it up at the varsities and trot it out on the coast. Personally, I think Socialism is a great mistake. Nobody wants it. Though, of course, poor Henry Winter was a Socialist—as Red as you make 'em. You remember Henry, Jock?' So he told a long story about the excellent Harry Winter, concluding, 'So, you see, there's something to be said for Socialism. It cured poor Harry of D.T.'s'; and, as his guests were leaving, he added, 'One's got to remember that it takes more than one swallow to make a mess night.'

Rackham was now in good spirits. He had exactly the same feeling as if he had just mastered a new trick with the bottles. He took Judy to his bungalow while he changed for polo, and they laughed so much together that the boy, disgusted, as always, by the thought of a mistress, would not answer when he was called. But Judy fetched the boots from the back verandah.

'You mustn't wait on me.'

'Why not, if I like it?'

'You'll spoil me. Never spoil a husband.'

'There's ways and ways of that,' said Judy, imitating his Irish accent. 'And I'm not sure if you wouldn't be the worse of Mrs. Pratt.'

'Heavens, yes! I'd kill that woman. Yet there's no harm in her. She's a good-hearted little thing enough.'

'She's ambitious for him. That's why she never leaves him alone.'

'A big ambition—to be M.O. at Kano or Kaduna instead of Rimi.'

'I suppose it's a good thing,' said Judy.

Rackham, who knew that Judy considered him lacking in ambition, twisted up his nose, and said, 'A good thing, Judy! Look at your aspiring friends: Burwash wants the C.M.G.—Call Me Governor. Rubin wants a wife to keep his rheumatism warm. Carphew wants to see his photograph in the *Tatler*, between the Countess of Snob and the Earl of Contango. Little Fisk wants to bear the white man's burden; and Sangster's whole dream is to be the fadder and mudder of a bush ape and keep him from the contamination of soap.'

'And what is your ambition, Jerry?'

'To win the Irish Sweep, and retire.'

'That's a noble aim, anyhow.'

'What about yours? To win the winner?'

'A sweep, indeed!'

Rackham uttered his snort of laughter, which only Judy could strike out of him, and exclaimed, in broad Ulster, 'Ah! To hell with ye! Wait till ye're ringed. I'll give ye wonderland.'

'Is that the same as *Tir nan oge?*'

'For a British heavyweight, it is'; and he gave another shout of laughter, put up his fists, and danced round her. Judy, always wanting exact information, continued to seek it. 'Where exactly is the place for a knock-out?'

Which caused Rackham to laugh so much that he could hardly stand. He answered at last, 'Here, and you're it.'

Already his nerves were tingling with the influence of polo. His muscles jumped under tension. His eyes sparkled, and as he talked, darting from one subject to another, he poured out puns and allusions, as if his mind, like his body, was acrobatic.

But all this display was for Judy—or, rather, it would not have taken place had it not been for the clearness of the air between them.

Polo at Rimi was a serious game, although it was usually played three a side, in five-minute chukkers.

Rubin and Rackham, meeting on the ground, withdrew to one side to choose their teams. This usually took some time, and caused discussion, because though Rubin, as president and founder of the club, claimed and used the right, for the sake of peace and fair play, as he put it, to arrange the teams, his arrangement did not always please the opposing captain.

It was because the criticism of players, as chosen, was sometimes free that the two captains went aside to pick them; while they, on the touchline (there are no boards at Rimi), innocently showed off their boots and breeches to the spectators, and especially the ladies.

Rubin, adjusting his extraordinary hat, began, as always, by saying, 'Well now, Jock, who do you want?' and then, without a pause, 'I suppose I'll have to take Carphew—he's new to the game, but it's really my job to show him the ropes.'

Carphew, Rubin's subaltern, a tall fair young man seconded from a cavalry regiment, and extremely pleased with himself, had just arrived in the station.

'Carphew!' said Rackham. 'He played for his regiment in India.'

'No—did he?' said Rubin, appearing greatly surprised. 'Then you'd better have Honeywood.'

Honeywood was a pretty man in the saddle. He talked much of hunting, and he had read all the books. He kept two good ponies at Rimi, and played in every game. But for some reason, which he described as the run of the game, he very seldom came near the ball. His attitude was graceful, his seat was beautiful, his boots shone like a chef's copper, but by the time he had carried out the movements of a finished horseman, in checking, turning, and putting his mount to a gallop, some other player, miserably inferior in grace, had carried the ball out of sight.

'Thanks,' said Rackham. 'That's a kindly thought.'

'It does make you a bit heavy for us,' Rubin agreed, 'so we'll take what's-his-name, and you can have Rooty.'

What's-his-name was Fisk, who had never been in the saddle except in the Banbury road. But he had been commanded to play polo, and he had played already twice. He had fallen off three times in the first game and once in the second. On the other hand he had hit several long shots, for he practised every spare moment on the wooden horse in the polo pit. His aim was erratic. He had put one ball through Mrs. Pratt's front window, and split Rackham's hat with his stick. But he was often in the way when the enemy attacked, and what more could be asked of a beginner?

Colour-Sergeant Root was a long-bodied, short-legged cockney with a singularly long, wrinkled face and a very short nose. The moustache which covered his upper lip and fringed his small open mouth was as high as it was wide. It resembled one of those straw mats placed above basins.

As an officer he was extremely efficient, sensible, devoted to his regiment and adopted regiment. His opinions on any subject were old-fashioned, but strong and clear. He was greatly respected in Rimi. But as a polo player he wanted presence of mind. As soon as the ball was rolled in, Root would begin to utter loud shouts of advice and encouragement to his side, and set his pony galloping, stick whirling. Nobody worked harder or performed braver feats then he. But he never hit the ball. Sometimes he hit the ground, sometimes he hit his pony, very often he hit some other player; once he had given himself, by some extraordinary shot, two black eyes; wherever he went on the field he was surrounded by dust and frightful curses.

Root himself never uttered a damn. It was against his principles. Besides, as he said to himself, 'The thing about this gyme of polo is to keep your 'ed. Fine gyme for soldiers. That's why they myke the young orfcers ply it in Ninja. It's part of their tryning—to go 'ard and keep their 'eds.'

He enjoyed polo very much.

'Did you say Root for me?' said Rackham.

'And I'll take the other one—the child. I suppose we'll have the usual ten bob on it?—Though it's giving it to you.'

'God bless you, Rubin. I'll say this for you: you were always a fair man—before your hair fell out in horror of your life.'

Rubin answered in the good-natured tones of an old English gentleman: 'After all, the game's the main thing.'

'Whose game?'

'You'll walk over us, I'm afraid. But if I took Root, it would be soldiers against the rest, and that's so bad for feeling in the station.'

Rackham answered that he would be the last man to deny that, and summoned his side with these words: 'We're Whites—put on your shrouds.'

The polo ground at Rimi is the parade ground of hard earth. But a thick covering of dust is supposed to act as a break-fall. It is the orderly sergeant's duty to go over the ground on the morning of a play day, and remove any ants' nests that may have arisen since the last. But he rarely does so. On this evening, Carphew found an ants' nest in the first two minutes—when his pony fell over it—and called loudly for the game to be stopped.

But it did not stop. Nothing could stop Root or Rackham or Rubin until the end of the chukker, and Fisk did not always stop even then. He was lucky if he could stop; or if he held one rein after the first minute.

Carphew therefore remounted, but during the rest of the chukker it was noticed by the spectators that he never went out of a canter, and that he watched the ground very closely. He did not pay much attention to the ball. There was no score in the chukker.

In the interval, Dick Honeywood explained that he had been deprived by the run of the game, of two goals; Rubin apologized to Carphew for the ant-heap, and assured him that in Nigeria ants will make a new heap actually in the course of a game, and Root, covered with dirt and sweat, explained to the ladies, for the special benefit of Dryas Honeywood, who had not seen African polo before, that 'this gyme 'as more tactics than you'd think,' and that was, in fact, why it had such military value.

In the second chukker, Carphew back-handed a drive from Rackham to Rubin, who carried it down the field until Honeywood, still seeking the ball in the direction of the north-west where it had been two minutes before, and in the act of performing a movement similar to the curvet, of the Vienna riding-school, crossed him at about half a length's distance. Rubin pulled to the left, Honeywood to the right, and, while Rubin was telling Honeywood to take his bloody rocking-horse home and burn himself, Carphew picked up the ball again and shot a long, straight goal.

Root, who was number three, made a gallant attempt to stop the shot, with a back-hander, but unluckily caught his stick between his boot and the saddle, while the ball passed under his pony's belly. In the last second of this chukker Rackham shot a goal, with the help of Fisk, who made his finest shot yet, but, unluckily, in the wrong direction.

Thus ended the chukker except for Honeywood, who wheeled his horse, found the ball, and carefully shot a goal, after everyone else had turned off the field, and Fisk, whose pony was cantering towards the river with the boy's whip under its tail. Fisk had not lost the reins, but he held them only by the buckle. They flapped in the air, useless for control.

Rackham caught the pony, and received the boy's polite thanks— 'It's most awfully good of you.'

'You ride too long. That's why you can't get him by the head. Take up your leathers.'

Fisk obediently took up his stirrups a hole. They were still too long, but it did not seem so to him. He felt safer when he could curl his legs as far as possible round his pony.

The interval was passed in listening to a story from Carphew of how he with several lords had defeated a crack regimental team, before several princes and dozens of maharajahs, at Boojah, or some such name, in India.

Rubin, with a worried brow, enquired of everybody where Honeywood had gone to—'because I'm afraid he may have misunderstood something I said to him just now.'

Honeywood, who had gone to change his pony, and see the last one dried, sulked; and Root explained to Judy that the art of polo was to keep your eye on the ball—'because the 'and follows the eye—like in shooting.'

In the third, and last, chukker, Carphew shot another goal for Red, in the first minute. Carphew was visibly inspired by his own story. He meant to show these provincials how polo should be played. But, unluckily, in the next minute Root walked his pony over the ball, treading it deeply into the dust.

In a moment, he was surrounded by the whole field; five ponies faced inwards. Even Honeywood's horse, seeing this gathering, rushed off, in spite of the horse-master, to join in, neighing defiance.

The six horses then rose on their hindlegs, with loud screams of rage, and boxed with their forefeet. Nigerian horses are all entires. They are always looking for a fight. As soon as they stop galloping, and come face to face, they get up on their hindlegs and strike out at each other and at the riders. This adds an interest to Nigerian polo.

Rubin, in the attitude of Marlborough at Blenheim teaching the battle where to rage, was bellowing, 'Get off the ball, damn you! The ball, blast you! Get off the ball—the ball—God damn and blast you!'

Sergeant Root looking fiercely round, and, working his arms and legs with exactly the motions of a wooden monkey on a string, shouted, or rather sprayed, 'Now then, Whites.' His face was entirely composed of concentric folds, with his pale blue eyes starting from two whirlpools in the middle, like two fish noses in a muddy mill dam.

Fisk, with a polite expression, was holding his pony's mane and saddle with both hands, and saying politely, 'I'm awfully sorry, sir.' He was quite sure that he had broken some rule or other. Dick Honeywood was slipping over his pony's croup. He considered it beneath the dignity of a subscriber to the Blankshires to hold on to the pommel of his saddle. Just as he fell off, and Carphew shouted, 'Man down,' Rackham, who had his left fingers locked into his pommel, stooped forward, while his horse still reared, and hooked the ball from its nest directly under the sergeant. And while Carphew was still shouting, 'Man down. Stop the game,' he galloped off with it and shot a goal.

Carphew protested. He also complained that Rackham's black pony had bitten him in the leg. But nobody even listened to him. The game, having been rather dull, was now beginning to have some excitement. Rubin, as he rode in for the hit-off from his own end, exclaimed proudly to the subaltern, 'Warming up at last, what?'

The game was now equal. Two all.

From the hit-off by Carphew, Rubin picked up the ball and took it to within ten yards of what was now the White goal. A mêlée followed. Root hit the ground so often, and so hard, that dust rose ten feet in the air, no one could tell friend from enemy, and the ball sank out of sight.

Rubin was now quite mad. His face was the colour of a ripe strawberry; his polo hat, a very small high-crowned helmet which was held upon the extreme top of his bald head by a native-made chin-strap of red morocco, vibrated with the agitation of his nose, moustache, cheeks, jaws, and both his chins, while he bellowed curses and moaned appeals: 'Damn you, sir! Damn—damn you, Root—for God's sake get off it! God damn it! Where is it, then? Where is the god-damn ball? For Christ's sake, gentlemen! Damn and blast you, Honeywood!'

Rackham, leaning far down from the saddle, perceived the ball and hooked it out, back-handed it, with a short swing, to Honeywood, who hit it forty yards. His pony at once galloped after the ball. Carphew pursued on his light bay; Rackham followed Carphew. As the soldier leant forward and hooked Honeywood's stick, Rackham's black pony, making a long rein, stretched over the bay's croup and bit the rider in the bottom. Carphew uttered a yell, twisted in the saddle, and his pony, mistaking the signal, wheeled off at a sharp angle. But Honeywood, finding his stick unexpectedly freed, struck at the ball too late for a swing, and knocked it two yards sideways out of the line. Rackham, galloping all out, overrode it. Root following up, with a shout of, 'Come on, Whites,' missed it by a foot and struck Honeywood's pony such a blow on the left hindquarter that it kicked him out of his stirrups.

Rubin and Fisk, in headlong chase of Rackham, had already wheeled, and now, with triumph, rushed at the ball. Nothing, and nobody, was between them and the White goal.

Rackham, turning his black, felt that he could have lifted the pony into the air and made him fly. His whole life was bent on winning this game. He would willingly have made a bargain with the Devil, to die and go to hell in five minutes, if only he could get that ball.

Rubin hit a long shot towards the goal. Rackham, galloping after him, reached for his stick. Fisk whirled his stick to hit the winning goal, but suddenly disappeared beneath his pony's belly. Rubin, with locked stick, overrode the ball; Rackham circled, picked it up.

When Rubin wheeled, he found himself without a side. Fisk was running after his pony, which was frisking towards home; Carphew was limping towards the doctor's house, with his hand on the seat of his breeches. Rackham, therefore, dribbled the ball the full length of the field and shot the winning goal. Root, cantering after him, very upright in the saddle, prepared to support him to the death, shouted several times, in an encouraging voice, 'That's it, sir. Take it on yourself, sir.'

Honeywood was seen near the goal in the exact attitude of Mr. Schumann at the Bertram Mills Circus, when he makes his pony dance the one-step. But no one was surprised by this; and his sister was heard to say to Judy, 'Dick always was wonderful with horses.'

The game was over. For though it was agreed in Rimi that the third chukker is always the best, and that the game, to be really good, should go at least two more, Root, Honeywood, and Fisk had only one pony each, and Rubin had been warned that his blood pressure would not stand more than three chukkers at most.

'You ought to have done better than that, Jock,' said Rubin, still glowing like red-hot metal. He took off his puff-ball hat, and wiped his large shining head with a red silk handkerchief. 'With all the old hands on your side.'

'What's happened to Honeywood?'

'Yes, yes. Where is he? D'you think he's upset about anything?'

'Why should he be?'

'No reason at all. But he *looked* upset.'

'What was it you said? Get to hell off this field? Most delicately put.'

'H'm, I'll just see if he's behind the house. He's a nice chap, Honeywood. Don't want him to feel that he's been badly treated.'

Rubin walked off, with his chin in the air and his stomach well forward, straddling his legs in his most imperial manner. He could always be seen thus, after polo days, approaching someone or other with an apology.

Carphew now returned in great indignation. He demanded that Rackham's pony should be barred from the field. But he heard that it was the best pony in the station, and most of the others had a worse bite. 'Satan has never taken a piece out,' said Rackham, 'but that hyena which Rubin was riding would bite your leg off, and he's got pyorrhœa too.'

Rackham was in excellent form. Excitement made him more Irish, reckless, and voluble. He now, within a yard of Carphew, began to make some jokes about polo as played by the Rajah of Bong, which had so pointed an application that Judy put her hand in his arm and guided him towards the Scotch club. But she chose a roundabout way in order to let her excitable friend cool.

VIII

ALADAI HAD TWO ROOMS to Makurdi's behind the store, facing west towards the town. They looked across a dirty alley upon the native compounds outside the town wall—an overflow of beerhouses and hovels full of broken roofs and rotten mats and occupied chiefly by riff-raff.

Aladai did not like the view, but he knew that the rooms were Makurdi's own—the best he had, with the only tin roofs in his compound, except the stores.

This place was already his council chamber and court. When he returned from his visit to the Resident, he found the alley in front of his door blocked with deputations come to offer their homage and support. On the next day the people from the villages began to arrive, many from great distances; they had heard only that a man had come, a Rimi, the son of Rimi kings, who promised to give them freedom, to obtain justice for Rimi, to help Rimi people, and that he had a white man's *ju-ju* in his coat stronger than any other, a *ju-ju* that defied death.

They did not know what he meant by freedom; and as for justice to Rimi, they supposed that someone had misunderstood and repeated nonsense. Rimi didn't commit murders, or eat, or have children, or marry, or catch the fever.

All that was nonsense, it did not concern them. But food, wives and children, illness, concerned them very much; and they wanted the biggest *ju-jus*, as well as the best advice, to defeat bad crops, disease, and the spite of enemies.

All the morning from six o'clock Aladai sat at his door, receiving his people. He wore the grey coat at their special request.

Already he was treated as a chief, the source of help and advice. Old farmers complained of pains, bad crops, and enemies; young men had been deserted by their wives; village chiefs wanted advice about the tax assessment.

Aladai felt pulses, looked at tongues, and gave out his own pills, or letters to the town dresser. He said often, 'I am not a doctor, and there is no *ju-ju* will do you any good. Go to the hospital, or the dresser.'

He explained to the old farmers that old land needs manure; and he spent hours with pencil and paper doing sums for anxious chiefs required by Government to divide a total tax of thirty-two pounds seven shillings and fourpence equitably between nine families, all differing in size and wealth: two butchers with farms; one dyer with a horse but no farm; the village idiot; a widow with two grown-up sons, one a prosperous thief; and a fisherman suspected of being, at will, a hyena, possessing unknown sources of income.

One early morning when Miss Coote, who complained that there was nothing to read in the station, called on him to borrow a book, she found him already at duty, and said, 'But you work harder than the Resident. I saw you sitting here at four o'clock yesterday. Don't you keep any hours?'

'I tried, but there are so many coming all the time.'

'Let them come. You can't see all Rimi.' She was looking curiously round the little sitting-room, furnished with a drawing-room suite in pink plush, a cottage piano with pink silk front, a carpet striped like a rainbow, a brass standard lamp with pink silk shade, two brass spit-toons. On a shelf, where, had there been a fireplace, the mantelshelf should have been, there stood a skeleton brass clock under a glass globe, and three pairs of green and gold vases. The clock was Makurdi's chief treasure. The curtains were of white lace tied back with pink ribbon; the tablecloth was pink plush. The pictures, in large gilt frames, represented the King and Queen, King Edward, Queen Victoria, the Kaiser, the battle of Magersfontein, and the young Queen—apparently Queen Victoria—at Buckingham Palace.

When she had seen his room, she felt a new and slightly different kindness for Aladai—more protective; more maternal; deeper.

'It's not much to do, to talk to them,' the boy said.

'They'll wear you out if you let them, and I think that would be a pity, even from their point of view.'

She sat down at the piano and played the first few bars of Handel's Fantasia in C—her test piece for pianos. It was a bad piano, but in tune.

'They make me feel small.'

This sentiment, which might have come from the mouth of any young English missionary or colonial official, made Judy look round and up at the man with a chaffing smile. But at that moment he did not like to be chaffed.

'It's true,' he exclaimed. 'They are so simple, so brave. They expect so little. Talk of the poor in England, and then meet some of these people and see how patiently they suffer.'

Judy peered at his music.

'I talked of loving Rimi, but it is only now I begin to know what it means.'

Judy strolled to the bookshelf and looked at the titles. She mur-mured, 'Rimi—or did you say the Rimi?'

'It's all the same, isn't it? At least, to me.'

Judy took out a book and opened it. She said carelessly, 'Are Rimi and Rimi people the same thing? I mean, the people have feelings and wants, but I suppose Rimi, strictly speaking, is chiefly silicates mixed with H$_2$O.'

'You have no patriotism, Miss Coote.'

'Oh, but I have.' She slapped the book to and cocked up her nose. 'I am a regular romantic about England—but then I mean by England, the English people and all the things they've done, all they stand for and what they have *made* of England.'

'And Rimi doesn't stand for much?'

She took out another book. 'Well, Louis, I didn't say that.'

He laughed and answered, 'It is no good arguing with you. But you will allow me to say that I admire and love the Rimi people—the individuals that come here.'

'I'm sure they're very nice, and, if you make them a Rimi that will be worth living in, you will do them very well. I see you like Russian novels, Louis?'

'Yes. Do please borrow any you want.'

'May I take this?'

'What is it?'

'*Notable Sex Crimes of the Nineteenth Century.*'

The young man looked surprised and embarrassed. 'I didn't know I had that.'

'I am very interested in crime,' said Judy gravely, 'and I see this is supposed to throw a new light on Crippen. I always felt so sorry for that man. And it's so hot in Rimi; too stuffy for Dostoievsky.'

But Aladai was much embarrassed. He thought plainly that this was not the kind of book which gave credit to his taste; and that Judy, in her grave approval, was perhaps pulling his leg. He was sophisticated; but there were odd holes in the polish of his surface.

He was still a little embarrassed when Judy took it home. She thought, as she picked her way through the crowd of clients in the alley, 'He's losing his sense of humour already. Is that princedom, or Africa?'

But when she looked back from the end of the alley she saw that he was already at work, and thought, 'What time has a man thrown into a position like this for trivial little jokes? They are really beneath his interest; he literally hasn't time for them.'

In fact, Aladai, listening to the story of a man who had been robbed by one of Waziri's servants, and flogged when he complained of it, had already forgotten his trifling discomfiture. He could not even hear the other women, his aunts and cousins, thumping corn in the yard, or his uncle Makurdi, round the corner, cursing and screaming at his staff.

Makurdi was always busy in the morning, and did not trouble to dress. He still wore the singlet in which he had slept, a banty, and a dirty rag, or kilt, wound about his stomach and tucked in at one side.

Makurdi spent all his working day in quarrels and abuse. He abused his clerks, porters, family; and he was always engaged in furious quarrels with clients. Two or three dissatisfied clients were always hanging about Makurdi's; they squatted on the quay, or planted themselves beside the door of the store. They all had the same air of melancholy and obstinate disgust. The Rimi hates to be swindled. It depresses him; he cannot reconcile himself to loss.

Makurdi was fighting with three pagans and a boatful of traders at the same time. The boat was being unloaded of what seemed to be mats; but it was probably smuggled gin. Makurdi was waddling to and fro on the quay, shrieking abuse at the traders for their late arrival. They were bawling that the current had been too strong for them; how could they reckon with the Niger?

The pagans did not say very much, but they followed Makurdi with their eyes as he rolled up and down, and now and then one of them— the middle one—would raise a cheap clock and say in an angry, obstinate tone: 'But look at it. It's dead.'

Makurdi would then rush at the pagans as if to throw himself on them and smash them. His voice screeched like a machine saw; his language was terrifying even to Rimi pagans. But they did not shrink. They only remained silent; turned up their frightened eyes; and the man with the clock slightly moved it upward with an involuntary motion, as if, though he himself were crushed, his arm would still protest against this swindle. And Makurdi never did fall on them or even strike them. After abusing them to the fourth generation, backwards and forwards, he would turn again upon the boatmen.

Even Makurdi's figure seemed different at this time—in the working hours of the morning. His great rolls of fat now had a dangerous aspect, like cumulus cloud with the sun on the other side of them. His grotesque figure was quite dissociated from ideas of good nature and a summer day of easy living; it appeared inhuman and horrible, so that the man's savage threats and spiteful screeches were inadequate to express what might be expected from his carcass. Nobody can appear so malignant as a fat man.

A young girl, one of the nieces, at the door of the private quarters, was weeping loudly; and another, with her round shining face thrust through the door, suddenly withdrew it as the tyrant turned away from the pagans.

The only happy person in sight was Akande Tom, dressed in a new white linen suit two sizes too small for him, a check cloth cap, cup-tie pattern, black sun-goggles, and red morocco slippers. He was walking to and fro by himself on the town road, apparently careless of the fact that nobody was looking at him. The delight of his new clothes, put on for the first time, about half an hour before, was so intense that he had forgotten the world. He was completely removed by his joy—like a mystic in contemplation.

He walked with dignity, moderating his porter's swagger to the discreet pace of a clerk; and at every few steps, taking off his goggles, he carefully wiped them on the inside of his coat and then, raising his nose and eyebrows, pursing up his lips, and contriving even, by blinking and screwing up his eyes, to seem shortsighted, he put them on again with both hands, and carefully adjusted them.

At one o'clock Makurdi's clerk, Jamesu, came out of the store and shouted, 'Hi, you, Tom.'

Tom jumped.

'You bring dem clo'es back now.'

Tom began to walk away slowly, with his head twisted over his shoulders, like a dog going off with his master's cutlet from a picnic party. The clerk ran out; he was perspiring and furious; he seemed to have a fire burning in him as hot as the sun overhead; no doubt he was burning with the same rage and hatred which tortured all Makurdi's family on a week-day morning.

'Hi, you, Tom,' he bawled, 'you want I call po-leeceman, den?'

Tom suddenly broke into a run, and vanished round the corner of the Marine building towards the station.

The clerk uttered about ten frightful curses, each louder and worse than the last, and then two more mild and feeble ones, in a weak tearful voice. He threw up his hands and, as it were, sank into the dark doorway of the store, like a suicide.

It was very hot. Aladai was exhausted in his tight, smart suit, soaked with sweat. But there were still at least forty people waiting to see him. He did not say for the last time, 'But it is no trouble; I come only to help you,' until past three.

He took off coat and waistcoat, collar, tie, and shoes, and lay down on his bed. But he had much to think of. What did Fisk mean by his hints that he should go to the mission and stay there till the situation in Rimi was clarified? Fisk came from the Resident. And what was Coker doing in the town? And what did Elizabeth mean by suggesting that she should make a woman's war? What was a woman's war?

He could not sleep because of the yelling of the women. He heard Makurdi, too, screaming at some wretch, 'You pagan swine! Another word and I'll have you put in prison.'

Suddenly there was a knock at the door. He started up and reached for his coat. His heart almost stopped; he thought, 'Miss Coote—Mr. Fisk.' He shouted, 'Just a moment, please.'

But the door opened and Akande Tom tiptoed into the room, in his white suit, spectacles, and the cup-tie cap still on his head. Aladai felt annoyed. He had already had two visits from Akande Tom, who was studying English. But when Tom went up to him and held out his hand, Aladai shook it warmly and at once liked the boy because he was friendly.

'Good afternoon, Tom. Isn't that cap rather hot?'

Tom shook his hand up and down so vigorously that his goggles began to fall off. He secured them with his left forefinger while he completed his handshake.

'Loo-iss—you quite well, Loo-iss? I come see you.'

'It's very good of you. Have some tea.'

'I gree for you, Loo-iss. Dem *ju-ju* people wild too much—too much savages for Rimi. I tink I come live for store.'

'I don't think my sister will like that.'

Tom laughed, raised one shoulder, and wagged his hand in the air; the exact gesture of a French actor who says, 'Ah! the ladies, how they pester me!'

'I don't think she'll like your suit either.'

Tom suddenly became angry and contemptuous. 'I no small boy to Lisbet—I no savage man. If Lisbet make palaver for me, I go way. I catch plenty money. How she like it den if I go way?'

'Perhaps she'll send to bring you back again.'

Tom laughed. 'You tink she make *ju-ju* catch me back? Dem *ju-ju* fool *ju-ju*—I Cristin man—*ju-ju* no fit catch Cristin. I laugh for dem *ju-ju*.'

Akande Tom had already assured Aladai several times that he was a Christian man. The truth was that he had attended one of Coker's meetings, and had added to the *ju-jus* tied to his right forearm a cross sewn up in leather.

'Yaas, I Cristin man now, Loo-iss. I no savage man. I come talk to you.'

'Sit down, then.'

Akande Tom glanced anxiously out of the window and said, 'I no catch time'; then, still more hastily, 'Loo-iss, you fit teach me book?'

'You want to learn to read?'

'Yaas, learn book. I want dem big *ju-ju*—white man *ju-ju*—to beat dem fool Lisbet *ju-ju*.'

'But it isn't a *ju-ju* at all.' Aladai sighed and stared at the boy. How could he explain to Tom what he meant by education? It was impossible.

'You say you give me book *ju-ju*,' Tom cried, opening his eyes widely, wrinkling his nose, and expanding his mouth—a negro expression meaning, 'What are we getting at—are you mad or am I?'

'I said I'd teach you.'

'You say you give me book.'

The clerk, Jamesu, bounced through the door and seized Akande Tom by the collar. 'Oh, you Tom, I catch you,' he screamed. 'Take off dem clo'es, you fool swine! You want I call po-leeceman, damn you?'

Tom cringed to the floor and shouted upwards, 'I pay for dem.'

'You pay tree shilling for one morning, you damn tief. Hi, po-leeceman, you come here with yo stick.'

There was no policeman outside, but Tom at once unbuttoned his coat; the clerk, Jamesu, looked it over and pointed at the dirt inside the collar. You damn swine, you pay nudder shilling for mark dis coat.'

'I no pay nudder shilling. I no got shilling.'

'Hi, you po-leeceman!'

'I no got shilling,' Tom shrieked.

'Makurdi, dis damn tief Tom make palaver.'

'Leave him alone, Jamesu,' said Aladai.

Jamesu, driven to the limit of nervous exasperation, turned upon him and shouted, 'I do ma job. If I no do ma job, you no fit go home to Oxford.'

'I'll pay you a shilling.'

'You no pay me,' screamed Jamesu. 'Makurdi pay. Why you no do yo' job. Your money Makurdi's money. You tief it, den?'

Jamesu was suffering from envy. He too was a nephew of Makurdi's; but he worked for Makurdi at ten shillings a week, of which the larger proportion, when it was paid at all, was in goods; and Aladai had been given a thousand pounds in three years. It was true that Aladai's mother had been a princess; but Jamesu was descended from an elephant, and he was far cleverer, far more deserving, than Aladai.

'You job make fool talk to fool bush people,' he shouted, 'My job make money pay you chop. Now you, Tom, I done finish with you. Hi, po-leeceman!'

Tom, half stripped, yielded, and was dragged away, protesting, towards the store.

Aladai had not condescended to answer Jamesu. He sat with a dignified smile, regretting only that he was unbuttoned and barefooted. But as soon as Jamesu had gone, and Tom's puppy-like cries of despair and protest had been shut off by the crash of Makurdi's back door, he felt sudden depression and fear. It did not seem to fall upon him from outside; but it expanded within him with overwhelming force and speed, as if he had carried in some lower part of his brain a genie or devil imprisoned in a hidden oubliette, to which Jamesu's stupid hatred was the key; so that, at the touch of it, the lock smoothly opened and the genie spread out of it.

This genie, risen out of Aladai's self, seemed to say, like Jamesu, 'You fool'; and it added the question, 'What's happening to you? Do you know? No, you don't know.'

Aladai not only felt like a fòol, but as if he were helpless in ignorance and weakness; as helplessly driven and used by circumstances as Akande Tom himself.

What had Fisk meant yesterday? What was the Resident up to? The Emir, Elizabeth, Coker, Makurdi, those farmers with their flattery? Why did that spear not kill him? Why had he been sent to England, out of a million Rimi?

He felt as if fate had hold of him, but this time in the shape of a devil. But the devil only commanded him for a moment. Then he jumped off the bed and began to dress. He said to himself, 'Poor Jamesu, he's no better than I am'; and the thought occurred to him again, 'One in a million.'

The devil suggested the thought, but it seemed to be a two-edged weapon. It instantly struck at its own producer. It acted on Aladai's demon, to use the English phrase, like a charm. The devil sank down before its bright, flashing power, and shrank away like a pantomime demon when Mr. Maskelyne waves his wand. It disappeared altogether, as if through the floor of his brain. There was nothing left of it at all except its memory, and a few drops of sweat on Aladai's forehead.

He was now fully dressed. He looked about his rooms as if assuring himself that the devil's visitation had not altered their appearance for him, walked to his books and ran his hand along their backs, tidied the music on the piano.

Aladai had detested his rooms, furnished by Makurdi with all his treasures; he had submitted to them only because Makurdi had absolute power over him, and because he was too grateful to him to wound his feelings. But now, after a week, he delighted in them. They were all English.

He went to the corner, where, on the bookshelf, he kept his tobacco-jar with the college arms, his straight-grained pipes, and his photographs of college friends. The captain of the boats had written, 'Prince Aladai, from yours sincerely'; the senior scholar, 'Louis, with love': his tutor had signed himself, 'Yours affectionately'; the president of the Shakespeare Club, 'Yours to a frazzle.' Lesser men were his affectionate, his very sincere, his ever.

He filled his favourite pipe with a tobacco bought in Oxford High

Street and looked smilingly at the captain of the boats. He had not been very clever; he read tripe and listened to trash; but he had been a good fellow, a good friend. To look at his photograph was still like a communication from England itself.

A girl brought tea. She was one of Elizabeth's girls, sent apparently in the hope that he would be caught by her. She was a pretty, impudent young Rimi, pure bred and much fairer than himself, by name Obishala. She was certainly a spy.

Aladai paid no attention to her. He despised Elizabeth's tricks, her cunning of a savage.

He sat down at his writing-table and pulled out a sheet of paper; began, 'Dear Mr. Burwash.'

How did one address the Resident: 'Dear sir,' 'Dear Resident'?

He wrote: 'I would want, if elected, to co-operate in every possible way with your side of the government. I believe you would not object to my education policy except perhaps on financial grounds, which could be discussed later'; and then he read it again. What would the Resident think of that? Of the phrase about education?

Was the Resident really his friend, or a secret and cunning enemy? A letter to an enemy would be dangerous, whatever it contained. It would be better to see the man informally. Burwash himself had suggested it.

The girl said in a disdainful voice, 'Your tea, Galadima Aladai,' and went out with her nose in the air, banging the door behind her.

At a quarter to six the sun touched the edge of Rimi hill, so that the shadows of the station bungalows striped its whole surface like a woman's cloth; and Makurdi came out of his house in his white suit, smiling and rubbing his hands. He had swallowed by now about half a bottle of gin rather cruder than sulphuric acid, and he was feeling kind. The women who had quarrelled and worked all day were chattering and laughing among themselves in the yard. The time had come for play: food, dancing, drumming, singing.

Only Akande Tom looked sad. He was now naked, but he could not go away from the place that held his suit. He dawdled in the road and gazed at the store. His face was that of the one-eyed porter of the Arabian tale who wakes from his millionaire dream to find himself in the ditch. Even his shoulders mourned; his feet were dejected as he slowly rubbed one over the other.

At this moment Aladai walked out of his house, dressed in tussore silk, with a blue shirt and white shoes. He stood and looked about him; his smile of confidence and enjoyment made Akande Tom retreat among the shadows of the native compounds behind. He did not feel equal to meeting Aladai now.

Aladai was turning his head this way and that; he looked at the sky, the shining river; turned right round to admire the station. The change from his narrow, hot room to the fantastic and marvellous scene made him laugh like a child who gets out of a cab and goes into a pantomime. The sun had just fallen below the edge of Rimi hill; but all that side of the sky was like still champagne; on the other it was a deep peacock blue, like oil blue on water; and in the two curving arms of the river the two reflected colours ran down like inverted blue and yellow flames, as if the oily water was on fire.

The sky overhead, freshly opened to the stars, had suddenly become enormous, so that the station, with all its houses, looked at the moment, to an eye that had last measured it by the sky of the afternoon, like a set of nursery bricks, left on the floor after the children have gone to bed, in the light of a fire almost out, and a cold side-ray from an uncurtained window.

'Beautiful! How lovely it is, this Rimi,' said Aladai, standing on his toes as he looked at the sky. Then he went into the house and changed his white canvas shoes for a pair of white buckskin strapped with blue, to match his shirt.

He had not dared to wear these shoes before, even in England, but now it seemed to him that he could do anything.

The women in the compound suddenly broke into the strains of a song; a drum was heard to beat in the town a steady invitation, 'come-come-come-come.'

Only Akande Tom was dejected. He wanted to cry; he could not hold up his head as he slouched down the road. He was not going anywhere; but away, far away from the suit and from Aladai. His legs felt weak; his arms were too heavy for his shoulders.

Aladai shouted loudly for his boys. He had a cook and three boys.

The boys wore dark-blue jumpers with the initials L. A. embroidered in white letters six inches long on the breasts. He had once seen a Resident's servants in this uniform.

He said to the boys, 'Get my lantern, chair, and whisky. I am going to see the Resident at the club.'

This simple order made great excitement. Aladai was going to the white man's club. All except the women, who knew nothing of clubs or men's politics, and cared little more, ran out to watch the procession: Aladai and his three boys, carrying lantern, chair, whisky bottle, sparklet, and box table.

A dozen or more followed it the whole way in the dark, to see with their own eyes Aladai take his seat among the whites.

Aladai did not turn round; but he knew that the procession was there. He was excited by this discovery. He had not fully under-stood that he was making history, but he was also alarmed. The fear and the delight were, as usual, there together, maintaining each other.

When the Scotch club has no invitation, it meets on Oxford Circus, where the town road and river roads cross. Often the chairs extend over the circus, but this is no disadvantage to travellers, because the ground on each side of the road is made of the same material—hard earth. By arrangement with the police, a fire is lit at a spot near the circus on the town side, as soon as the members' chairs are in position. A fire used to be lit for one member. But Rackham, always a stickler for detail, and a defender of the police and the convicts from being put upon, had ordered that the fire quorum be a minimum of three.

On this night there were twelve chairs round the fire, which was proportionately large. Aladai could see them and their occupants from twenty yards away. Miss Judy was sitting between Captain Rackham and Honeywood, and opposite them Sangster and Carphew were talking together. Two Hides Store clerks, Prince and MacNeil, with a Marine man in for the day, sat beyond Carphew. Four chairs, including the Resident's well-known *rhoorkee*, taller than the rest, were empty.

When Aladai saw that the Resident was not at the club, he felt panic. He had counted on the Resident. He had heard that the Scotch club met at six, and it was now a quarter past. Like other people, Aladai imputed more regularity to arrangements which he did not know by experience, than they were meant to possess.

He had not realized till now how much he had dared by this expedition, how much his longing for the company of white people had influenced him to risk it, and how much he had depended on the Resident.

He was for the moment blind with panic. The chairs at the fire wavered in front of him. But he did not stop walking calmly forward, because he found it impossible to do so. He was the prince among his people. He was with his own servants, and under the eyes of townspeople. He could not turn back and acknowledge to them, 'I am a conceited fool, and not even a brave one.' He could not have made his muscles and his nerves accept such a humiliation; for they were prouder than his mind.

He walked up to the circle, said, 'Good evening, gentlemen,' pointed to a place—one removed from Honeywood—where there was room for his chair, sat down, and lit a pipe.

No one seemed to have heard his salutation. Carphew and Sangster, the clerks opposite him, stared. The members beside him had not noticed him. Honeywood, who was grumbling to Miss Coote about Rubin's bad manners at polo, continued to do so; and Rackham, beyond her, wearing a huge British warm over his polo kit, had sunk so far into its turned-up collar that nothing could be seen of him except the tip of his nose and cigarette.

111

'Captain Rubin is a little hasty at polo,' Miss Coote said, in her most sympathetic voice.

'He's lost his nerve, that's the truth of it,' grumbled the other. 'Why, I wasn't within six lengths of him. It's his own business if he has to pull up because he's in a blue funk, and it was the same on Monday. I'm getting sick of it.'

'I'm sure he'll apologize.'

'I don't want his apologies.' The man finished his drink—a powerful one—and looked at the glass, as if the whisky had also ill-treated him. 'Who does he think he is, I'd like tò know?'

Suddenly Carphew and Sangster got up, and Carphew said, 'Come over to my place.'

Miss Coote exclaimed in surprise, 'Where are you off to?' and in the same moment, glancing in the direction of Carphew's parting glance, saw Aladai. She turned red, and stared at him in plain dismay. Aladai, with an uncertain smile, said, 'Good evening, Miss Judy. The Resident's not here yet.'

'No, not yet.' There was a slight pause. She looked round her with rather a wild expression, and then exclaimed, 'What a sky? I never saw it so black.'

'It is a black sky,' Aladai agreed. 'The air must be unusually clear.'

There was a short pause. Dick Honeywood was looking from side to side with an expression of bewilderment and consternation.

Rackham suddenly leant forward and said to Aladai in a good-natured tone, 'Is that why it's blacker some nights?'

Aladai answered at once: 'So I believe. When the upper air is quite clear of vapour, or more than usually clear.'

His voice shook a little. He sat forward in his chair, leaning towards Rackham with an eager politeness. His voice was eloquent of his grateful feelings.

Rackham's hand holding his glass was quite steady. He also sat forward in his chair, with his booted feet on the ground; peeping sideways over his huge turned-up collar at the negro.

'You interested in astronomy?'

'I haven't studied it. But I've read something about it. It's a fascinating subject.'

'Yes, I should think it was.'

'Just look at the—the—what is it?' said Judy. Her remark was really an explosion of relief and joy. Her pride in Rackham, and in something deeper and wider than any personal feeling—in her people—had taken her by the throat. She gulped, 'The—the—bright one—the frightfully bright one—just next——'

'But that's Venus,' said Aladai, smiling.

'It's absolutely marvellous,' said Judy, 'to think we sit under a show like that and don't notice it. Talk of fireworks——'

Aladai quoted in his finest voice:

> *'There was a time when meadow, grove, and stream,*
> *The earth, and every common sight,*
> > *To me did seem*
> > *Apparelled in celestial light,*
> *The glory and the freshness of a dream.'*

Rackham suddenly muttered, 'Oh, Gawd,' got up, and disappeared. His movement was so quick that he seemed to have shot into space. There was a short silence.

But the movement had broken the tension in which all the others had sat, suspended between the action of Carphew and Sangster on one side and Rackham's and Judy's on the other.

Prince, on the other side of the fire, said, 'Come on, boys, this is no place for the likes of us,' and walked off. He was followed by the stranger and MacNeil. The Marine, left by himself, looked hastily over his shoulder, half rose, and then with a red and embarrassed face, sat down again.

Dick Honeywood, who had sat like a man under a spell, now said loudly, 'Well, I'm damned!'

'Shut up, Dick,' Judy whispered. Aladai heard her clearly.

'What do you mean, shut up?' Dick Honeywood was a big man; his build and colouring were like Fisk's, square and blond; but he was six foot to Fisk's five foot eight, and he weighed fifteen stone. Now he seemed to swell. His polished pink cheeks became red, as if swollen with blood. He twisted slowly round to glare at Aladai.

'Be careful, Mr. Burwash asked him,' Judy murmured, inventing the lie most likely to have influence with Honeywood.

'I don't care who asked him,' shouted Honeywood. 'It's not Burwash's club—it's the station club.'

'Then go quietly,' Judy murmured in agony. 'That's the best thing.'

'I am going,' said Dick solemnly. It was obvious, however, that this action had only now occurred to him, and that he was pleased with it; as a suitable and appropriate gesture, commensurate with his dignity as District Superintendent. He rose slowly, staring at Aladai all the time, and called his boy.

The boy, a Hausa horse-boy, clad in a few fluttering rags not much dirtier than his body, was folding up the chair when Dick caught him by the tuft on the top of his head and twisted his face towards Aladai.

'You see dem black man, boy?'

'Yaas, *zaki.*'

'You fit to sit for club now, boy.'

'Yaas, *zaki.*' Honeywood released the tuft and marched off, plainly delighted with his last shot. The boy, grinning so that all his gums could be seen, trotted after him.

The Marine man, turning scarlet, murmured something that sounded like an apology, and hurried away.

Judy and Aladai were now left alone with the fire and eleven empty chairs. There were four chairs between them.

Judy said to Aladai, 'You'd better come nearer.'

Aladai replied, 'That's not my chair next you.'

'Then bring your own,' said Judy. She spoke shortly to the boy, for she thought he had behaved foolishly.

'Do you want me to?' said Aladai.

'Don't be silly, Louis. Of course.'

Aladai got up and called his servant, and had his chair placed in the opening left vacant by Honeywood.

Judy sought for subjects of conversation, but she was angry with Aladai, and her anger jumped out. 'Do you think it was wise to do this without warning anybody?'

'I came to see the Resident. He said he wanted to see me.'

'But you know this is a kind of club.'

'I went to clubs in England. I went to much *better* clubs than bounders like Prince and provincials like Sangster. And I only wanted to be friendly. If the Resident had been here, he would have made it all right.'

Aladai spoke excitedly, and she could see that if he too had not been conscious of the eyes upon him he would have waved his hands, nodded, worked his eyes, teeth, shoulders, in the expressive Rimi manner. But now he was holding himself rigid; only his voice gesticulated.

Judy was sorry for him. 'Never mind, he'll be here soon now. He must be coming, because his chair's here. And I'm sure he'll understand the situation. I think you've made an impression there—quite definitely.'

'The Resident is my worst enemy,' Aladai answered in a bitter tone. 'He wants to drive me out of Rimi. He sent Fisk to say so.'

'You must be wrong about that, Louis. Why should he?'

'Oh, Fisk didn't put it like that. But that was what was meant. He wants me to go to the mission. And that would ruin me—to go to the mission. There are two thousand Christians in this whole country, and a hundred thousand Mohammedans, and four hundred thousand pagans; and so my enemies will say, "He is a Christian. He will destroy your *ju-jus.*" That's what the Resident would like.'

'He doesn't realize——'

114

'What, you think he is stupid, Mr. Burwash? Oh, no, he is very far from stupid, and he is my enemy—now I'm sure of it.'

The boy was gesticulating now; sweat stood on his forehead, the whites of his eyes rolled in the firelight. Judy heard a laugh and looked up. It came from the nearest bungalow—Carphew's—fifteen yards away. But behind that, over the sharp line of the fort wall where it cut the dark-blue sky, she could see a row of heads. The soldiers of the guard were looking on from the gallery.

She tried to soothe the boy. 'But, Louis, you have plenty of friends to see that nothing like that happens to you.'

'I'm not afraid. Do you think I'm afraid? But what could you do? You're not an official.'

IX

RACKHAM had meant to be polite to Aladai on general principles. His exclamation had exploded out of him without any premeditation. He did not know what he had said until he had said it, and, as he darted up the road as if shot there by the same explosion, he still did not know where he was going or what he was going to say.

Meeting Mrs. Pratt and Rubin on their way to the Residency, he said, 'Why not the club? You'll have the pleasure of meeting Mr. Aladai there.'

'What!' cried Mrs. Pratt.

'He's just arrived. He's been giving us a lecture on the stars, with quotations from the poets. It was a touching scene.'

'But can't we do *anything?*' Mrs. Pratt screamed.

'I'm afraid not. You see, Mr. Aladai happens to be black, and so he can do what he likes.'

'Yes, with a Resident like Mr. You-know-who. But really—this is too much!'

Mrs. Pratt began to exclaim and cry out for help in her usual manner, but Rackham was already disgusted and bored with her. How silly she was in her violence and fear. She depressed him; or, rather, she increased his anger and depression by adding to it material of exactly the same sympathetic quality from her own silliness and violence. She made him savage. He would have been rude had not Rubin, seeing that there was something wrong with his temper, reminded the lady that they wanted to catch the Resident about the next chapel service before he came to the club.

Rackham, left alone again, went to his house. He stared from there at the club, right below him. Judy and her friend were talking with great animation.

He walked round the floor and back; looked again; then sat down, tore off half a sheet of paper, and wrote, 'Come at once. Urgent. To J. R.'s.' He did not sign the note, and he wrote in a hand unusual to him, large and slow. But he was barely conscious of stratagem. His brain suggested it. He sent this to Judy at the club and watched her read it, jump up, excuse herself to Aladai, and come, almost running, towards his bungalow.

As she panted up the steps she saw him, and exclaimed, 'What is it?'

'Come up and I'll tell you.'

'I thought you'd broken your neck, at least, doing some of those horrible stunts. I suppose it's only a button.'

Judy already had taken charge of Rackham's buttons; and he was already, like any husband, aggrieved when one was missing.

'No, I only thought that the demonstration had continued long enough.'

Judy, now at a level with him, stared at him and said, 'Don't let's use that kind of words.'

'What good are you doing that ape by giving him a swelled head?'

'That ape, as you call him, is more of a gentleman, and a better man, too, than most of the white men in the station. Infinitely more, and you know it as well as I do.'

Judy knew that this was not quite true, but when she was angry she exaggerated. So, however, did Rackham. After another violent exchange, she cried, 'And now I'm going straight back.'

'No, you're not.' He caught her by the wrist.

'But you really can't do that, Jerry.'

'Why not? If I love you. It's just what I ought to do.'

The words 'If I love you' were so unexpected that they shook her resolution. She said in a doubtful voice, 'But, Jerry, my darling, it seems such a small point. I can't understand. If you can give me any good reason——'

'Oh, for God's sake, don't come the don.'

But even this could not make Judy angry again. She apologized for coming the don. She did not want to quarrel. There was relief in her voice when she said, 'Here's Dryas at last. Would you mind very much if I took her with me as a chaperon?'

'Don't be silly.' But he turned round.

Dryas Honeywood had just come in sight, strolling up the river path behind her lantern-boy. She was in her white tennis-frock.

'It's like a circus,' Judy said. 'I wish the Resident would come.'

The ring of chairs was in fact very like a circus. The bungalows were the boxes. In one Carphew and Sangster were seated on upright chairs beside a table; in another Colour-Sergeant Root and Prince were leaning on the rail, gazing at the ring; in the third nothing could be seen but the projecting legs of three occupants; in a fourth Honeywood stood, a distinguished figure with a glass in his hand, talking to the Marine man, who had his back towards the ring.

Beside every bungalow, in the shadows of bushes, beside the road, the grinning teeth of servants, horse-boys, small boys, soldiers and soldiers' women, carriers, filled the pit.

The top of the fort wall was lined with a row of soldiers, and even from this distance it could be seen by their stillness that they were intent on the spectacle.

'I must go back,' said Judy. 'It really is a shame. Look at the poor boy. His pipe's gone out, and he's too nervous to light it again. 'No'—as Rackham caught her waist—'you mustn't—please, Jerry.'

At this moment they both saw, out of the corners of their eyes, Dryas's white dress turn towards the club chairs. They looked round. The girl was walking with her usual self-contained air, full of awareness; the proper carriage of a school prefect and débutante; but probably she was not so wide awake as she looked. She passed a good deal of her time in an absentminded state; not dreaming, because she did not think of anything; not sleepily, because she was acutely conscious of being herself and alive; but enjoying existence like a bather escaped from the office, who floats on bright waves, sharply felt.

Probably she was in this mood when, obeying the routine of a week, she turned towards the club chairs and walked into the middle of the circle—the circus—before she noticed Aladai, on her left hand.

Then obviously she received a shock. The watchers saw a perceptible jump, and a deep blush rising slowly from her chin to her forehead. She half turned as if to run. Just then, Aladai, equally embarrassed, began to get up from his chair. He might have been rising to greet the girl, whom he had never met; or simply to be polite in a lady's presence. Then he saw her turn away.

For a moment Aladai was hovering in the air, with one hand on his chair, half up and half down, while the girl stood on one foot, like a stork.

Then she turned towards Aladai and, now apparently quite collected —the young lady of the finishing school—walked up to him and shook hands with him. Aladai, in his sudden leap of anxious politeness, nearly butted her in the face.

She sat down beside the man on a footrest, accepted a cigarette from him, and, after a little thought, made some remark. He answered with his most Continental gestures. He looked at one moment as if he was going to fall on his knees beside her and put his head in her lap.

Dryas looked at him with her prefectorial manner, and made what was a long speech for her.

Meanwhile Judy and Rackham were having a serious quarrel. For, to Judy's surprise, the unexpected support of Dryas had made Rackham even more unreasonable. He said that what a silly little girl like Dryas did was no criterion for Judy, who had got to live in West Africa.

'And I'm not going to let you mess up your whole life out here before you've started it.'

Luckily, before Judy had said anything difficult to forgive, the Resident, with Fisk quick-marching beside him, was seen approaching the club.

Aladai rose to receive him. Burwash gazed round with surprise at the empty chairs, and then for an instant at Aladai, nodded, and sat down. Fisk called a boy to make up the fire, looked about with the eyes of a sporting dog who, after a day's work, visibly asks himself, 'Anything else for master?' turned himself round once, and dropped his stern. He sat alert, ready at any moment, to take Aladai off master's hands. But Burwash, discussing Rimi antiquities with the visitor, had never seemed better amused, more friendly and attentive.

However, in ten minutes Aladai rose, bowed, excused himself, called his boy, and walked away towards the waterside; and in another five minutes the Scotch club, except for Rackham and Judy, was assembled at full strength.

Captain Rubin, finding the party slightly embarrassed, made a favourite opening, 'When I have a drink, it makes another man of me, and then the other man wants a drink.'

As nobody laughed, he repeated it and remarked to himself, 'Damn good, old chap, though nobody gives you a hand. The more chaste, in fact, the less heed.'

The reason why nobody gave him a hand was the visible embarrassment of Miss Honeywood, who sat stiffly in her chair, with a face like marble, and could not be persuaded to speak. Even the Resident's good-nature rebounded from that catalepsy.

Judy, asking her afterwards why she was so preoccupied, received this answer: 'How exactly did we get hold of Rimi?'

Judy gave a long historical explanation. The girl's only comment was: 'I don't really like negroes, all the same—though I suppose one ought to'—which had nothing to do with the explanation.

118

X

Rackham had fitted up a horizontal bar, rings, trapeze, and punching-ball in the empty education bungalow next his own. Here he taught his men gymnastics, boxing, singlestick, and amused himself by the hour.

He had already persuaded Dryas to show him what she could do on the bar. On the day after the famous Scotch club, Dryas was in the gymnasium from three o'clock. The rest of the station were still sleeping, or, at least, resting. The heat was little past its maximum. But Rackham never took a siesta, and Dryas was unusually restless this day—restless and lively.

Rackham was also in an unusual mood. He was full of praise and encouragement. He smiled in the most charming manner, and, when Dryas missed her swing and fell on the mattress, instead of saying, as he would have done the day before, 'Serve you right,' or, 'Clumsy,' he cried, 'Oh, good try,' and ran to pick her up with a most solicitous face.

But in fact, as they both acknowledged by coming together, as if by spontaneous attraction, at this hour when everyone else in the station was resting or asleep, they were now in a special relation—something closer than their former friendship—admiring on the girl's part, appreciative and brotherly on his. They were in secret sympathy, and, although neither mentioned Judy, she was in their thoughts when Dryas said, 'It was funny last night—me having to do the polite.'

This was also a defence against the suspicion of priggishness. The girl had been taught that priggishness was a crime. She therefore spoke and acted in a careless, agnostic, unpatriotic, modest kind of way.

If anyone waved a Union Jack in her presence, she would say, 'Oh, why the flag?'; and when anyone spoke of religion, she would remark, 'Oh, dear, we had enough of that at school.'

She described politics as a bore, and the Government, whatever it was, as those cretins. If anyone mentioned Chinese labour, or Abyssinian slaves, she would add modestly, 'But, of course, we can't talk! Look at London!'

Rackham at once came to her rescue. 'Just bad luck, turning up then.'

'I nearly ran away. I simply can't get used to black men—socially, I mean. I suppose I'm an ass.'

Rackham knew that she was an ass, but he said warmly, 'Not a bit of it. I know how you feel, because I feel that way myself.'

She frowned. 'I don't feel that way about them when they're really native—dressed or undressed.'

'Better undressed.'

He was impatient with the subject. He wanted to forget it and enjoy himself with this charming and simple girl, so easy to amuse, so ready to agree with him in his prejudices as well as his pleasures.

She laughed, and said, 'They've got such good figures, it seems a pity to hide them.'

'A good figure is the gift of God'—with an intonation which left her in doubt whether he was paying a compliment or not.

'Come now, up you go.' He caught her by the waist, and tossed her to the bar. 'You don't want to waste any time on philosophy, or whatever you call it. Put your legs through your arms—carefully—don't turn over.'

Dryas, upside down, with her short hair falling downwards in a cascade, smiled broadly at him, and said, 'I'll never do it.'

'Yes, you will'—patting her behind. 'You could do anything with that build. You were born to be an acrobat.'

She toiled to please him; and he to please her with his compliments, to teach her his art, which was the best of him. They encouraged each other to extraordinary efforts, Rackham performed a back somersault off the bar. Dryas attempted a back lift. But her arms were not strong enough. In the middle of her pull, while she was hanging head downwards from the bar, her legs swung outwards and she fell, landing so badly that she dived forwards between the uprights. As there was no mattress on this side of the bar, Rackham jumped in her way. Her head struck him in the chest, he threw his arms round her and tumbled backwards with the girl on top of him.

When Dryas, giggling helplessly like a girl of fourteen, had got up, and Rackham, who was also laughing, had sat up, they saw Judy standing in the room with a letter in her hand.

Her cheeks were flushed, and she looked the most embarrassed of the three. Rackham, indeed, was not embarrassed at all, because he did not choose to be so needlessly troubled.

'It's for you,' said Judy, handing the note to Dryas, who was putting her hair out of her eyes. 'It came from Makurdi's.'

Dryas did not know who Makurdi was. Still smiling, though in a shamefaced manner, with damp pink cheeks, a smear of dirt on her nose, dirty hands, and the seat of her white flannel trousers black with dust where she had fallen, she was at a disadvantage. She kept her eyes down, while she again wiped her forehead with the back of her hand, and opened the letter.

She read in silence, looked up with an expression of wonderment, and exclaimed, 'But it's that man!'

Judy and Rackham watched her while she read the note again. This time she breathed as if awestruck. 'But how queer!'

'What's queer?' said Judy.

'Well, his letter.' She began to laugh and then checked herself. She handed the paper to Judy. 'Look at it yourself.'

Judy read:

Makurdi's
Friday

Dear Miss Honeywood—I could not express to you this evening my gratitude for an action of kindness, to use a very inadequate word, which was so spontaneous and magnanimous that it surpassed my belief in human nature; I almost put here my belief in white human nature, but now your pure and disinterested goodness forbids me to write that libel.

It is for that character from which it sprung that I treasure and shall always act upon the advice which you gave me, equally wise and honourable spirit of the noblest and most magnificent not only of your own race but of all humanity; of P. Sidney, E. Burke, F. Nightingale (etc.). Not merely a body, but a soul lay dying on that chair, in an agony beyond what body can suffer, and you gave up for it not merely a cup of water, but the precious draught of your worldly position. If I could be honoured to die for you, I should not yet be satisfied. It is easy to die—a mere gesture—it is not easy to defy the scorn and hatred of one's friends, and for what, to succour an impudent negro,

Who remains, in the strictest sense
Your humble and devoted servant
Louis Aladai

Dryas and Rackham stood on each side of Judy, reading with her in silence. When Judy had raised her head, Dryas uttered a sudden giggle, but at once turned very red, and looked gravely at her friend.

'It's good enough for *Punch*,' said Rackham.

'He means it,' said Judy, to Dryas.

'But I didn't do all that.'

'From his point of view, you did a lot. What did you tell him?'

'Tell him? Oh, I don't know! I just buttered him a little. He was so upset.'

'He mentions advice.'

'Well, I said that he oughtn't to mind too much about things that didn't really matter—the usual stuff.'

'It seems to have had a strong effect.'

'But, Judy, all that stuff—about Philip Sidney and his soul. Isn't it rather wash——?' The girl, still flushed, drew her thick brows together in a puzzled look.

'Well, is it? What do you feel about it?'

Dryas looked down; and then turned her eyes out of the door, as if to hide them. Rackham, who found himself ignored by both women—not rudely, but simply dropped and overlooked in a fashion that irritated him far more than a snub—jerked the letter out of Judy's fingers and began to read it aloud, in a mock heroic style.

They neither applauded nor protested. Dryas glanced at him with an air of surprise, and, when he had finished, took the sheet from him with the remark, 'Thank you, Captain Rackham, but it's my letter.'

'Tie it up in blue ribbon, and put it among your other love-letters.'

'But you've done more than me. Why didn't he write to you?' said Dryas to Judy.

Judy reflected—'You're much younger and prettier,' but she perceived also that Dryas, for this reason as well, had really done more for Aladai than she. She answered: 'I left him in the lurch.'

'He knows you didn't.'

'If you want to fight for him, I can lend you some gloves,' said Rackham.

'What had I better do?' said Dryas to Judy.

'There's nothing to do.'

'The incident is closed,' said Rackham.

'Except that you might tell the messenger that you've had the note. He was rather worried when I took it from him.'

'He knew you were the wrong girl,' said Rackham.

'Where is he?' said Dryas.

'At the bungalow. I told him to wait there.'

Dryas went out. Rackham called to her angrily to put on her topee. Judy took it to her, and dusted the back of her trousers. The girl herself, thus reminded of her clothes, looked at the knees of her trousers, and said, 'Oh, well, they don't *really* matter.'

She walked off, swinging her legs in a hockey stride. Rackham turned to Judy, and said, 'You've no business to encourage her. She's only a kid.'

'She's older than either of us, in some ways. I don't know anyone so responsible.'

'Exactly. Half a giggle and half a revival meeting—and she doesn't know which, herself.'

Judy, who had resolved to be polite to Rackham, and to say nothing about the gymnastics of the afternoon, who had, besides, seen the

122

whole episode of the back lift and knew the innocence of its climax, said, 'Which was the one you were embracing on the floor?'

'You're not jealous, are you?'

'No; but if you want the engagement broken, I'd rather you told me.'

'Thanks, I will.'

'Why not now?'

'Because I don't want to break it. I want to marry you. Strange as it may seem to you, I prefer you to any other woman—even a silly little schoolgirl who happens to play tennis well. But, of course, if you go on hammering at the thing you'll damage its constitution in the end. And it will break itself.'

'Please, Jerry.'

Rackham walked up and down the room on his toes. He was white, or rather, blue, with rage. 'The idea of marriage is, I suppose, to be happy together,' he said. 'That's the general object. So we must hope that our marriage will turn out better than the engagement.'

'Jerry, don't rub it in, for God's sake! I know I was being stupid.'

XI

THERE WAS A CLERK'S CHAPEL in Rimi station, and Coker's in the town. Most of the whites did not know that they existed. But for some time past a certain Doctor Schlemm had given occasional services in Rackham's gymnasium, usually on a Tuesday evening, and these had been attended by all the official staff, except Burwash, and most of the traders.

Burwash explained that he would like to attend, but was prevented by the amount of work on Tuesday, which was a mail day. But, in fact, as he had confessed to Fisk, he thought it improper, or, at least, injudicious, in a Resident to show religious prejudice. On the other hand, he had the highest regard for Doctor Schlemm.

So had everybody in Rimi and several neighbouring provinces. It was the accepted thing to say of Schlemm, 'The man isn't a mish at all. He's a real good chap,' or, 'If they were all like Schlemm I'd be a Christian myself.'

He was a very short, thickset man, stooping slightly, with a fair beard and a bald head. His nose was long and crooked, justifying the nicknames sometimes applied to him of Fagin, and the Wandering Jew. But he was not a Jew. He was a German-American. He wore extremely thick spectacles on his shortsighted pale blue eyes, and his favourite costume was a Norfolk jacket and breeches, in the style of 1880, made of grey cotton.

This dress, with the stoop, the nose, the beard, an enormous German topee, at least six inches wide all round the brim, and a peculiar walk, at once very rapid and shuffling, made a figure which could be recognized at great distances. He belonged to some Danish branch of the Protestant Church. His English services were a mixture of the Anglican prayer-book and his own, composed by himself, or perhaps translated from the Danish.

He was not a good reader, and his sermons were extremely dull. They resembled university theological lectures, and they were delivered in a thick guttural voice which, with their original obscurity, rendered them extremely difficult to follow. To Dr. Schlemm, however, they were perfectly clear, and he would smile for an hour after one of them, gazing absentmindedly about him like a man who has just enjoyed a remarkable and unexpected triumph.

Captain Rubin, who had suggested the Tuesday services in the first place, and who, as he expressed it, whipped-in for the congregation, used to invite a newcomer in these terms: 'The old bird is a real fountain of eloquence, so bring your umbrella.'

Why was Schlemm so popular? He was not a back-slapper. He did not drink or smoke, or attempt to be one of the boys. He would sit in the Scotch club, but he did not tell funny stories, and his presence stopped others from telling them.

Rackham's theory was that he was a character—'that Norfolk suit and beard have put him over.' Burwash, who was greatly interested in the question, declared that Schlemm had 'the right touch.' Rubin, when the question was put to him, was greatly surprised at finding that there was a question, and then declared promptly, 'Nobody could help liking the old beak. He's a Christian.'

But Rubin also described his head horse-boy, a Rimi pagan with three or four wives, as a real Christian. 'See him handle The Kraken!'

Colour-Sergeant Root said he was a real gentleman, and not so foreign as you'd think to hear him or look at.

Probably all these judgments were right. Schlemm owed something to the Norfolk jacket and beard, something to his tact and excellent manners, something to his horse mastery, or, rather, man mastery, and a good deal to the quality recognized and admired by Sergeant Root.

It was worth noticing the adjective 'real.' For Sergeant Root, a real gentleman was not simply a person of good class and accent and polite education. For instance, he utterly despised Dick Honeywood, first cousin to a peer; and did not consider the Resident, a man of charming manners and some wealth, and Fisk, whose father was a general, as anything better than gents. He had been heard to say of Fisk: 'He's one of those young Oxford gents, 'opping about.' Root did not allow the title to his own officers. Rubin, he considered too free and easy altogether, and Carphew, ' 'E's swallowed the ramrod.' His ideal was a former Captain Jones, who had been invalided out with delirium tremens in the last year of the war. Jones was the reallest gentleman he had ever known—'drunk or sober'—and everybody who had known Jones—that is to say, everybody who had the necessary critical apparatus—agreed with Root.

What Schlemm and the late Jones had in common were fine manners, a complete lack of chicane, moral repose (in Jones's case only after his first whisky of the day) based upon a sure faith (Jones believed in the British Empire), and reserve or moral dignity. As Root put it. 'You knew where you were with 'im—'e didn't come it over you, and you couldn't come it over 'im.'

Schlemm's mission was at Kifi, thirty miles from Rimi. The main road in that direction reaches only half-way to Kifi, so that the doctor usually came up on foot and bicycle, and went down by dug-out. He usually came up on Tuesday morning and left on Wednesday morning.

Rubin was therefore surprised to see his guest's loads arriving on a Monday morning. But he was always glad to see any guest, much more the doctor. He ordered a special breakfast—that is to say, sausages as well as eggs and bacon.

The doctor would not wait for breakfast. He was very hot, obviously very tired, but he explained that he had urgent business in the town.

'But, doctor, the more haste, you know—you'll be going to hospital unless you eat your breakfast.'

'It is a matter of life and death.'

'Who is ill?'

'No, no. It is a poor girl they have taken for a witch. She may be dead already. I must go on——'

'Now, I tell you what, doctor: if you sit down and eat your breakfast like a sensible man, I'll make them saddle a pony for you—that will get you into the town in five minutes.'

'Yes, a pony. Thank you. But now, at once.'

'Sit down at least while they saddle it.'

The doctor consented to sit down while the pony was saddling. The saddling took some time. Meanwhile Rubin had persuaded him to drink a cup of coffee and eat the eggs and bacon.

'A witch trial,' said Rubin, stroking his moustache with some natural satisfaction, as he watched his guest taking a second sausage. 'You ought to tell Burwash about that.'

'Oh, what is the goot! I cannot trace anything. The people disappear

—that's all. And I do tell him. I wrote about this case, and look at this.' He handed Rubin a letter from his pocket. Rubin read:

Dear Doctor,—Thank you very much for your information. Immediate enquiries were made in the town, and, though they have been fruitless, they will be continued. But I think that your fears have probably been exaggerated. Witch trials, though they may possibly occur still among the more primitive tribes, have not been known in Rimi for many years. The last reported was in 1912, when the victim was fortunately saved from her terrible position by a court messenger. But the situation has greatly changed since that time.

I must thank you again for your letter. Your magnificent work at Kifi has placed us all in your debt and I shall always be glad of your co-operation in Rimi.

Very sincerely yours,
J. O. Burwash

'What is the goot?' Schlemm said again, when Rubin handed him this letter. 'They tell him lies. He is the last to hear anything.'

Rubin, who was perfectly sure that Burwash knew more about his own business than Schlemm (dear old Schlemm), answered, 'Do they still hunt witches?'

'Still! It is the curse of Africa. The *ju-ju* and the witch-doctor. Oh, if one could say truly that there were no more witch hunts. For think, captain, what that means.' The doctor stared earnestly at Rubin. 'To be accused and tortured—when you are innocent. It is the cruellest suffering of all, and every day in Africa it happens to thousands and thousands—every day.'

'Try another sausage, doctor. They're rather a special brand.'

'Thousands and thousands. And then you say: the missions do harm; they upset the people; they do not consider native institutions. Native institutions!—that is, *ju-ju*, witchcraft, witch trials.'

Rubin shook his head and looked sympathetic. Then he said cheerfully, 'Well, what do you think of them?'

'Think of them?'

'The sausages?'

Schlemm gazed thoughtfully at his friend for a moment and then he said, with great emphasis, 'You are quite right. They are remarkable. Most splendid sausages. You must tell me where you got them. But now I fear I must really go—pony or no pony.'

'But, doctor, what's the good of hurrying away now? The pony will take you in a couple of minutes.'

'But he is not ready. Forgive me, Captain—I am so impatient. Suppose the poor girl is in torture at this very moment—how should I feel?'

126

Rubin shouted, 'Hurry up with that pony, Maidoki, you *wofi*'; then, beaming on Schlemm with the smile of a wise old nurse who says to a nervous child, 'There now,' he remarked, 'You'll be off in one minute. What about a touch more of bacon with the other egg?'

'No, no, no, Rubin. You are too goot. But I have eaten well, and I must truly go. Where is the pony? May I see him?'

Rubin saw that the game was up. He went himself therefore to see the pony saddled, moving with as much speed as his figure and natural majesty of action allowed; for he did not want the doctor to find that nothing had been done about the pony.

Schlemm, however, with perfect tact, satisfied himself by going out in the sun in front of the bungalow and standing there. This secured the utmost speed in saddling without exposing Rubin to the feeling that he had been too clever.

The pony was brought round in three minutes, and the doctor, who in spite of his heavy figure rode very well, cantered away towards the town.

It was a little past eight. The roads and markets were filling, but when Schlemm asked the farmers, 'Where is the *ju-ju* house?' no one seemed to know. Several told him that there was no such thing in Rimi.

At last he remembered Coker. He had met Coker once, after a mission meeting at Kifi, and he detested him. To men like Schlemm—scholars and, at the same time, Churchmen—the species represented by Coker is especially disgusting, because it is at once the worst enemy of Christianity and the most difficult to tackle.

Schlemm was not permitted to hate Coker, but it was difficult not to hate a man who was capable of so much harm and did it all in Christ's name, who was completely self-satisfied in his ignorance.

But now he remembered Coker and asked for him. He was directed at once to a compound in the second ward on the upper side of the main city gate. But Coker was not at home.

Coker was at Aladai's. As soon as he had heard of the incident at the Scotch club, of which all the town was talking, he had hurried to his friend with what he believed to be Christian consolation.

'It is a chastisement,' he declared joyfully. 'It is de Lord's work. To cut you off from de wicked men—from de proud stiff neck and dem dat hate him. What you got to do with dem white people, Aladai?—Aren't you black like me? Aren't you African like me? Dey no gree for you—dey no good for African men.'

Aladai was sitting on the side of his bed, smoking, with a reflective air. Outside the sitting-room fifty or sixty visitors had already gathered in the street. Many had been sitting there for two hours, waiting patiently for their hero. Aladai did not notice them any more than he heard Coker. He looked thoughtful, and he supposed himself to be thinking about his plans. He had promised the Resident to go away for at least a fortnight—until the Emir could be pacified. Burwash, on his side, had promised that the Emir would get rid of Saïé for an even longer period. The bargain had seemed a good one. Aladai was now supposed to be deciding when he would go, but, in fact, he was still running over his letter to Dryas Honeywood.

Had he made a fool of himself in writing such a letter? His feelings answered at once, 'No, not even if those white cowards think so. She said, "Don't mind them," and I don't mind them.' His nerves thrilled to the phrases that he had written to her. He had meant them, and he stood by them. If that white trash did not know the quality and power of their own spirit, he, a black man, could know it—in their great men, in a woman like this girl who had said, 'Don't mind them, you have much more important things to do.'

He felt power and excitement, as if he had been repeating a poem or singing; his languid stillness, as he drooped from the bed, which seemed to Coker dejected or bored, was in his own feeling, the rest of a wound-up spring whose power is at the full and waits only to be used.

'Resident go speak you,' said Coker. 'He drive you way now—he spoil you—I say, no good ting come from devil—dey spoil you now—for a chastisement—to bring you back to de Lord.'

Aladai continued smoking. He felt, 'I'll show them, black and white.'

'No man can be saved, save by de blood of de lamb,' said Coker, letting his voice boom and his eyes close, 'for in dat blood all men washed clean of sin—all men de same—poor man and rich man, white man and black man.'

Just then Doctor Schlemm knocked on the outer door of the sitting-room, and the boy put in his head and said to Aladai, 'It's the doctor from Kifi.'

Aladai jumped up. Schlemm was not a man he wanted to see, for he knew the danger of a visit to Kifi. That would prove him, in the pagans' eyes, a Christian, and lose him the support of half Rimi.

Schlemm walked in and held out his hand; Aladai shook it, but without warmth, and said, 'Excuse me, doctor, I'm not quite dressed.'

'I beg your pardon, Galadima, but this is important—urgent.'

Schlemm had felt himself unwanted. He therefore addressed Louis as Galadima.

'Can I do anything?'

Schlemm explained the position. News had reached him from a

128

Christian in a certain village that a girl, Osi, was accused of witchcraft, and that she was in the house of the cannon *ju-ju*.

'Do you mean, at my sister's?' Aladai stared at him with wide-open eyes.

'I hear of dis girl,' said Coker. 'She kill many people.'

Schlemm made a quick nod of irritation—a bow cut short, as if he had acknowledged a position but was ready to demolish it. 'Your sister is in charge of this *ju-ju* house—that is goot—because you can help me.'

Aladai saw the extreme danger to him of enraging the Emir, Elizabeth, and the Resident at one stroke. He answered, hesitating between the phrases, 'But, doctor, I'm not allowed into town—and you see—it's rather critical with me.' He made a quick gesture with both hands, but he was frowning. 'I can't really believe that Elizabeth—she wouldn't dare——'

'It is true. I do not say it is your sister. Where is this cannon *ju-ju*? But I was sure that you would not agree that Rimi girls should be tortured, and perhaps murdered, for crimes that do not exist.'

'Excuse me,' said Coker, getting up. 'Dis woman is a witch.'

'She is accused of it.'

'She kill many people—she is a witch.'

'How can she be? There's no such thing.'

Coker's face became animated; he was angry. 'You say dere is no such ting.' he said. 'You, white man, say witches no live. But how you say so, when Bible say plenty witches, plenty evil spirits, yea, in beast and man, for a chastisement?'

'Never mind about the Bible, Mr. Coker.'

Coker's lips worked and expanded as they did when he was about to be inspired. Coker hated the whites, but, above all, he hated the white missionaries of every sect, because even if they claimed no superiority over him, he felt it.

He did not acknowledge it even to himself. He did not see it. He thought of all of them as backsliders, far behind him in loyalty and devotion. But his nature felt it, and responded like that of an animal which feels a rival or enemy even in the dark, and bares its teeth.

The man's profound spite, double-edged in austerity against himself and hatred against everybody else, rose in him like the inspiration of a spirit, the only one he knew.

He exclaimed suddenly, in a loud sonorous voice, 'What you say, never mind de Bible, Doctor Schlemm, you say you no hear de Bible? But as de minister of Gawd in Rimi——'

'Please, Mr. Coker, let us discuss this question some other time. I have no time now.'

'Doctor Schlemm, you have no time for de word of Gawd. And here in Africa we tink de proud man what set himself against de word of Gawd not fit to call himself minister of Gawd.'

Doctor Schlemm, perspiring with rage, glared at Coker as if his spectacles were weapons capable of throwing flames at the man and burning him up. But Coker was enjoying himself. He opened his mouth for another broadside.

Aladai said, in Rimi, 'Hold your tongue, Coker. You don't understand what we're talking about.'

Coker, astounded, revolved slowly till his face was turned towards his friend. He opened his mouth again to flout him, but Aladai glanced at him, and said again, in a savage voice, 'I told you to hold your tongue.'

Coker fell back a step, and his expression changed to that ludicrous dismay of the self-confident negro who has suffered an unexpected repulse. He muttered 'Pardon; excuse me; I didn't mean——'

Aladai had already turned towards Schlemm, and said again, 'I'm sorry, doctor. But it's impossible. It would be too mad for me.'

Schlemm looked at him, blinking, and then exclaimed, 'But even now she may be suffering! No, no. I can't believe you are indifferent, Louis. You were not so when I knew you at Kifi—four, five, three years ago. And then you were going to do great things for Rimi. You were the man of our destiny.' He smiled to show that he was not angry in his reproach.

Schlemm held out his hand. 'At least you will not quarrel with me, Louis. Why? I don't want to. I see that you are in a difficult position. Yes, very difficult—more difficult than anyone can understand.'

Aladai shook hands politely. 'I am sorry, doctor, but you see how I am placed. The position is good enough, but it does not allow me to be stupid—not if I want to do anything in Rimi.'

Schlemm made suitable noises in reply, and produced another smile. He could not speak in his bitter disappointment. He left the room suddenly, as if in flight, and had gone some twenty yards in the sun before he remembered to put his hat on.

Schlemm was a man devoted to one cause—the alleviation of human misery. There was very little of the ecclesiastic about him. He did not despise the professional Churchman, for he knew the need of organization and its power to drive back the enormous forces of ignorance and fear—the Devil's powers renewed in every generation to drag it into hell—and to keep them back. He knew that a Church staffed by a continuous succession of routineers may accomplish more permanent good than one saint. In fact, one of his favourite sermons began, 'As my friendt, that truly great man, Doctor Schweitzer, has said, isolated effort in the mission field is too apt to be wasted. For the impression that it makes, however great at the time, is not permanent—it is not fixed—it is not institutional. This question of the sphere of the institution or Church and the individual worker is one of great importance and much interest,' and then he would begin to talk about the Gnostics and Aquinas, and, sooner or later, Hegel appeared; and the congregation meditated upon polo ponies, cocktails, and sweethearts, or simply nothing at all. Rubin snored gently, with his chin on his vast chest, and Rackham fidgeted.

But though Schlemm in his sermons was much too theological and philosophical, in his work he was practical and individualist. He had come to Africa to make people happier, and he dealt directly with persons.

Louis Aladai had been one of his favourite pupils, and he had built great hopes on the boy. What could not be done in Rimi with a Christian chief as intelligent and courageous as Louis? Already he had been disappointed in Aladai; first by his ceasing to write from England, and then, on his return, by his failure to visit Kifi.

'But that will be easily explained,' he told himself. 'He has so much to do in Rimi.'

Schlemm was an optimist. If he had not had faith in human nature, he could not have set out to be a missionary. It was his strength and his weakness that he could not believe in the treachery or wickedness of his beloved pupils.

Why had he not come to Aladai's house in the first place, when he was seeking help? He did not know. Perhaps he feared a snub. Now he was so wretched that he scarcely knew where he was going. 'He does not understand,' he muttered. 'He does not think—he is only a boy. I should not have gone. But what could I do? This poor girl!'

Schlemm had once seen an old woman with her legs burnt off to the knees. She was still alive and conscious. She would not say why she had been treated so; she was too frightened. Schlemm had not forgotten her agony and terror. 'This poor girl!' he said, standing in the sun; and then, unconsciously repeating Coker, 'Poor Africa.'

Aladai sat down on the bed, but he felt a loss of power—as if the refusal of action had by itself taken strength from the spring.

'You see now?' said Coker.

'He thinks I'm afraid of Elizabeth,' Aladai reflected, 'or even the *ju-ju*, but I'm not—I'm not afraid of anybody.'

He sat still. But now the phrase came into his head, from his own letter, 'spirit of the noblest of your race.'

'He came here to catch you again,' said Coker, 'for de white man's god.'

Aladai jumped up and ran out of the house, in his bare feet, through the patient crowd, who, with the early shoppers, outside Makurdi's store, saw the great Galadima, in purple and green pyjamas, shaking hands with the old doctor, whom they knew as nosy, and heard him shout, in Rimi, for a boat.

The pair then returned to Aladai's house, whence, in ten minutes, they came out again, with Aladai dressed in his grey suit, and at once stepped into the dug-out. The polers drove it rapidly, in the shallow water near the shore, towards the town.

'But if you are not allowed to come into the town——' Schlemm said to his friend.

Aladai laughed, and cried, 'They won't expect me by river, and, if they did, they could not catch me!'

'You seem to have confidence in yourself—that is goot.'

Aladai replied that he had reason for some confidence: the people in the town were rallying to him. He added gravely, 'They are also inclined to rally round the *ju-ju*. But I think I am stronger than the *ju-ju*. We shall see.'

Schlemm, now that he had Aladai's help, was growing uneasy.

He said, 'But, Louis, you don't think that your sister would turn against you?'

'We shall see,' said Aladai, smiling. As usual, he could not resist the temptation to dramatize a little. He waved his hand: 'We shall see. But what does it matter? It is no good talking about consequences in a case like this. One knows what has to be done.' He made a gesture expressing, 'And that's all to be said about it.'

He reflected a moment, and said then, 'I was angry when I saw you this morning. I knew you were going to ask me to do something like this.'

'I'm afraid I have often asked you to do things that did not suit your convenience.'

'They were always good.'

'But I do not like to ask you to come to Kifi.'

'Why, doctor?'

'Because it would be, perhaps, to our advantage. When the people saw that you were our friend, it might help us very much.'

Aladai hesitated a moment, then exclaimed, 'Of course I will come—I must come!'

'I am quite proud of you, Louis'; and then again he was anxious, 'But will it do you harm?'

He answered himself at once by faith—'No, it can't do you harm.'

Aladai smiled. He said, 'I suppose that it is a toss-up!'

'No, no, Louis,' said Schlemm severely. 'You don't believe that.'

'No, perhaps not.' Aladai saw that he must not talk of toss-ups. But he thought, 'There is luck, all the same; look at me—one out of a million.'

Aladai landed at the compound of a friend, and so passed quickly, without being seen, through a piece of waste ground to another compound and the back of the *ju-ju* house.

To his great relief, Elizabeth was away. Elizabeth had three or four mysterious *ju-ju* holes and swamps in the bush, to which she paid visits at their appropriate seasons.

Aladai was known to the assistants, and had entry to all parts of the *ju-ju* house except the inner compound of the women. He therefore, with Schlemm, was able to go right up to the door of it before the old woman porter, dozing in the porch, saw him and opened her mouth to protest. He laughed, said in Rimi, 'I am the Galadima Aladai; it is all right—tell my sister Lisbet I said so,' and strolled past her.

He looked quickly round the compound within, and noticed that out of a score of huts only two had closed doors. They were in the furthest corner, where the mud wall of the *ju-ju* house almost touched the mat wall of the outer yard and the street.

He went directly to the first, pulled up the enormous bar of palm-wood which held the door, and walked in. It contained only the ashes of a fire, and a few sticks and whips hanging from a wooden bar.

As he came out of this hut he heard the porter shrieking the alarum. She had awakened more quickly than he had expected.

Schlemm was running from hut to hut. He had not noticed that some had doors, and some nothing but doorholes open and unprotected. He could not diagnose a native compound.

Aladai pulled up the bar of the remaining hut and went in. The hut contained the fœtid corpse of a boy, and a girl, thin, filthy, who seemed unable to walk. She shrank away from Aladai to the furthest wall, staring like a lunatic, and working her lips. She did not utter a sound.

Aladai did not want the doctor to see the corpse. He quickly snatched up the girl in his arms, holding her like a baby, and rushed out, almost knocking the doctor over as he ran. 'Come on, doctor,' he shouted. 'Don't stop now.'

But he saw already, through the porch, five or six women running from the outer huts. He turned aside, therefore, and made for the wall behind the corner huts. He had noticed already that one of them had no roof.

'Quick, doctor,' he said. 'Behind here. Now hold on for a moment.' He put the girl in his arms, and said to her in Rimi, 'Don't make a noise.'

133

The wall was ten feet high, but the roofless hut, as he had expected, was four feet lower, and within a yard of the wall.

He put his foot in a window-hole and scrambled on the hut wall, stooped and dragged up the girl, until, leaning his shoulder against the yard wall, he had her once more in his arms. Then he heaved her to the top of the wall, and said in Rimi, 'Hold there.'

The girl, though her legs appeared to be useless, at once began to haul herself over the wall with her arms, wriggling her body. Aladai, meanwhile, stooped and gave the doctor a hand. The doctor was breathless. But, also, he did not see the reason of this indignity.

'But they will not stop one,' he panted.

'I don't trust these ladies,' said Aladai, as the women, armed with pestles, broke into the compound behind, shrieking, 'I see him—go away—catch him!'

The doctor had made a strong effort and reached the window-hole; Aladai heaved again, and brought him to the wall-top. Meanwhile the girl had disappeared—she had wriggled herself over the wall and fallen, on her head, beyond.

Aladai and the doctor then put their legs over the wall. This brought them into view from the *ju-ju* compound, and the women made a rush. But the fugitives were in the alley before the first pestle came cracking against the top of the wall, aimed at the doctor's fingers.

The girl was lying crumpled in the ditch. Aladai picked her up, and sprinted along the lane, encouraging Schlemm with, 'Come on, doctor—the last lap.'

Schlemm ran well. But the pursuit was not energetic.

Elizabeth had few women in the *ju-ju* centre at any one time—perhaps six, at most, of which three were servants. They were not a garrison. She knew that no man would dare to break the taboo on the inner court.

Two or three of the women did appear in the lane, and one of them, an old one, probably a cook, ran some way along it, uttering violent threats; but, as soon as Aladai and Schlemm had disappeared round the corner, they gave up the chase and returned, chattering furiously together, to their fortress.

Aladai and Schlemm, meanwhile, travelling fast downstream, had brought the girl already to Makurdi's, where she was carried into Aladai's room.

She was not apparently hurt by her fall from the wall. But her legs below the knee were raw flesh, through which the bone appeared in several places—but not white bone; it was brown.

'Burns,' said Schlemm. 'She must go to the hospital at once. And I go to the Resident.'

But the girl would not go to the hospital. She found her tongue soon, and screamed that she would not leave this place. It was long before Aladai could persuade her, by this promise—that he or Doctor Schlemm would not leave her there.

The question of reporting to the Resident was a more delicate one. When the girl was finally in Pratt's hands, and Aladai had agreed to take the first watch, until her legs were dressed, he said to the doctor, 'You said you were going to the Resident.'

'Most certainly; now I go. It will be some other poor wretch to-morrow.'

'It's my sister who will be held responsible.'

Schlemm had not thought of that. He answered, 'But, Louis, what do you want? Can we let it go on?'

'Let me speak to her. I won't let her off.'

'I must go the Resident. I must! But I could wait to-day.'

This was agreed. But during the day their trouble was saved. Burwash's political agent, Audu, hearing that a white man had taken a witch from the *ju-ju* house, and knowing, therefore, that the case would be reported to his master, hastened to report it first. Audu was a good and experienced agent. He had never told the Resident anything about anyone in Rimi unless he was obliged to; and so he lived there in health and peace. Yet he had never been anticipated by a scandal. He was always first by at least five minutes.

Burwash at once demanded a report from Waziri, and sent Fisk to the hospital to examine the victim.

Waziri, who was in strong hopes of obtaining Elizabeth's support, declared that the story of the witch trial was a lie invented by her enemies, and that the *ju-ju* house was only for 'good medicine.' The pagans would never agree for anyone to injure the *ju-ju* house.

Fisk's report, obtained after much patient questioning, was this:

'"My name is Osi. I came to see the woman doctor in Rimi for a cough, and also because I wanted a baby. I fell in the fire and burnt my legs. She gave me a cure, but the white man made me go to hospital."

Question: "Were you shut up in this woman doctor's house?"
Answer: "No."
Question: "What is the woman's name?"
Answer: "I don't know."
Question: "What kind of a fire burnt your legs?"
Answer: "A fire; I fell into the fire."
Question: "Did you hear of a witch being tried in Rimi?"
Answer: "No, no, no. There are no witches in Rimi!"

'*Note.* She refused to answer further questions and became distressed. The fire mentioned was possibly the fire in the third ward which consumed two compounds during the late troubles in that ward.'

The Resident then sent for the priestess; but it appeared that she had been out of town for a month, and would not return for another month.

At the same time that Burwash was receiving this news in the office, Elizabeth was standing in front of Aladai, on the town road outside the hospital, about forty yards from the provincial office. She was in full view of Audu, as he squatted in front of Burwash's table and reported her absence.

Elizabeth had come to find her brother. Aladai, released from his attendance on the girl, who had just been drugged to sleep by Pratt, was on his way home.

As soon as Elizabeth saw him, she shouted, from twenty yards, 'What have you done? What have you done? Are you mad, then? You fool boy.'

But Aladai was in the most European and nonchalant mood. He answered coolly, 'You are the mad fool.'

'The *ju-ju* will kill you for this.'

'It's I who will kill your *ju-ju*.'

Elizabeth stood speechless with horror and rage. She raised her huge arms like a black Bernhardt, and stood like stone in the pouring sunlight. She, too, had dramatic powers. The spectators—shoppers, boatmen, riff-raff from the tumbledown compounds on the edge of the town ditch—stood silent and joyful with suspense.

Elizabeth dropped her arms, and crossed them over the slope of her breasts. 'You're a Christian, then,' she shouted at last.

Aladai at once lost his nonchalance, and threw up his arms.

'No, I am not a Christian, and you know it.'

'How do I know it? You go with white men and Christians—you break down the *ju-ju*.'

'You do know it, and I didn't break your vile *ju-ju*—but I will!' And he shouted at her, 'You are the fool—to deceive me.'

'Fool, you—fool that thinks he's a white man.'

'I saved you from the judge, you lunatic.'

'The *ju-ju* will blast you, fool. You're finished.'

'That for your *ju-jus!* All of them.' Aladai's gesture, made with both hands, chin, lips, and eyebrows at once, was expressive of the last degree of contempt. 'And if you dare to try another witch—just one— I'll go to the judge, and you'll be hanged—hanged. Do you hear that? It's my oath.'

Elizabeth untucked her black cloth, retucked it, and walked away to the town. This was meant to say, 'I cannot notice this scum any longer,' but, in fact, it was perceived to be a defeat. Aladai's reputation was increased. They looked at him with awe, while, still frowning and breathless, he walked up and down the road in front of them.

He knew it, and took another turn or two, with a slightly increased frown.

Some of them pointed at his coat. He heard the word 'coat' in Rimi. He thrust out his chest a little as he strode towards his house for an evening drink with Makurdi and Coker. He had no other companions.

XII

JUDY FELT SLIGHTLY FEVERISH. She had never had fever; never been salted; and so the doctor gave her ten grains and sent her to bed, as a precaution.

Her temperature was only 99. The doctor said that this was no proof that she had not more malaria in her blood than was good for her, but she herself knew that malaria was not her trouble.

She wondered if it were true, after all, that unhappy heroines could die of brain fever. Was jealously amenable to quinine? It ought to be, she thought. It was a disease of the body—a disorder of the blood.

As soon as she was in bed she suspected that she had got herself there, with the doctor's involuntary help, to avoid seeing Rackham's eyes when he looked at Dryas in the Scotch club.

But the girl would be in the gymnasium all the afternoon.

Was Pratt's help really innocent? These people in Nigeria seemed to know all about each other by telepathy—as if the wall of surrounding barbarity acted as a whispering gallery to their thoughts. They were watching her already—with pity or curiosity.

She got out of bed and dressed. She felt still more feverish, weak in the legs. Perhaps, after all, she had fever. Never mind. The station should not suppose that she was using it as a funk-hole.

Pratt had talked about the danger of a chill. He had pulled a medical face and spoken of pneumonia. That proved that the danger was slight. Or perhaps he was treating her as an intelligent person and telling her the truth. She might die, in fact. And a damn good thing too.

She put her dress over her head, and fought with it. 'And a damn good thing too,' she felt. She was surprised by her feeling. She had never before suffered from these morbid ideas. It appeared, on careful examination, that she was afraid of the future—or, at least, her nerves were afraid. They were trying to push her into another funk-hole.

'I'm getting jumpy,' she thought. 'They say it's quinine. I must really pull up my stockings.'

It was Rackham who had suggested to her this feminine form,

saying, when she failed to catch one of his mixed allusions, 'Now then, Ju, pull up your stockings—if you have any.'

So that the phrase made her nerves say again. 'And a damn good thing too.'

She couldn't live without Rackham now, any more than the famous fish, taught to live on dry land, could go back to the water. She would be suffocated for lack of the sun and the wind.

She pulled on her frock, crumpled and crooked, snatched her hat, and ran downstairs. It was still not past eight o'clock. She did not know where she would go, but at least she would escape from thinking.

Half-way downstairs, she stopped. She had caught sight of a figure, in the distance, which she recognized as Doctor Schlemm. She had never met the man, but nobody else could be anything like the object now approaching with Mrs. Vowls.

Judy had wanted to meet Doctor Schlemm, out of pure curiosity, but now, the moment she saw him, he suggested peace, escape, a respite. She would go to Kifi. She rushed back to her room to change her frock. take off her spectacles. Bless Doctor Schlemm, whatever he was like How wise of her to think of Kifi.

She looked in the glass, powdered her nose. Already she felt the zest of a campaign. She might be snubbed by Mrs. Vowls, but the man would not snub her. She could manage most men, except Rackham— and he was half woman.

Meanwhile, Dryas had been sitting on the verandah below, with a book—Burnaby's *Ride to Khiva*. She had borrowed it from Rackham, for she saw that he had a high opinion of it, and she considered that it was a book which she ought to have read. But she found it extremely dull. She could not concentrate on it.

While her eyes read Samarkand had been annexed, her mind was planning a secret visit to the gymnasium, in Rackham's absence, in order to practise the back lift. She was sure that it was a knack. She was strong enough.

A shadow fell on the steps. She looked up, and saw Mrs. Vowls with a very odd-looking old man in a preposterous hat. She was seized with laughter, but hastily jumping up, and turning round to put her book down, she was able, by strong effort, to make her face rigid.

She turned round again, and, greeting Mrs. Vowls, said, 'Dick is in the office.'

Dick Honeywood and Mrs. Vowls were old friends. Dick had subscribed to Mrs. Vowls's local charities, and often said of the lady, 'She may be a bit off, but her religion's all right. You can't get round that.'

Dryas therefore supposed that Mrs. Vowls had come to visit Dick. But the lady answered, with a most gracious smile, 'I was coming to see

138

you, Miss Honeywood. Let me introduce Doctor Schlemm, who is very anxious to make your acquaintance.'

The old gentleman took off his absurd hat with a tremendous sweep, and bowed over Dryas's hand until she was afraid he was going to kiss it. 'Yess,' he said, 'I was fery anxious. I am fery pleased to know you, Miss Honeywood.'

Dryas knew that she had heard of Doctor Schlemm, that he was famous for something—she could not remember for what. But she was greatly interested. Celebrities excited her curiosity and attention.

Doctor Schlemm, retaining her hand, threw back his head, so as to direct towards her a bayonet charge of beard and said, 'I have just been speaking with a friend of yours—Mr. Louis Aladai.'

'But I hardly know him.'

'He is very grateful to you'—bowing his head, and looking over his spectacles.

'But I didn't do anything.'

'He thinks it's a great deal. It *was* a great deal. It was a *Christian* thing to do.' He threw up his head again and bristled at her.

Doctor Schlemm spoke this with force and also with power—that is to say, he caused Dryas to feel this word as if it meant a good deal; perhaps because it meant a great deal for him, and she was unresisting and receptive.

'Oh, no,' she murmured, blushing.

'You are a Christian'—again aiming his beard at her in defiant manner.

'Not properly. I mean, I've no right to call myself one.'

'That is a very *goot* answer. You mean that no one can *be* a Christian —they can only approximate to it. That is true, and it is easy to forget.'

'Oh, no. I only meant that I myself wasn't. Not anything like.'

'That makes me think that perhaps you are nearer than a good many of us who are more pleased with ourselves.'

'No, really. In fact'—straining to repudiate this terrible charge of virtue—'I'm not a bit like that. I don't even believe the right things. Though of course I know that I don't really understand anything about it.'

'So. But that is not so important. What you believe is not so important—it is what you do. And you have done very well—very very well.

'Oh, no, Doctor Schlemm.'

'That is why I haf come to ask you to do more.'

'But what do you want me to do?'

The doctor now began to speak volubly, and rather thickly, so that it was not easy for Dryas to follow all his complications. But his meaning was plain. Aladai, he said, was a Christian, and the Christians at Kifi had long arranged to give him a welcome as their chief and comrade. In fact, he, Doctor Schlemm, had come to fetch Aladai. It had been understood that they would go next day. The boats were ordered.

'And we hoped,' said Mrs. Vowls, 'that you, too, might like to see Kifi. Most visitors are glad of any opportunity to see Doctor Schlemm's work at Kifi.'

Dryas said, oh yes, of course she had heard of it. But Doctor Schlemm, whose politeness barely obliged him to pause during the interruption, rushed on at once: The boats had been ordered—all prepared. But now it seemed that Aladai was wavering. He wished to put off the visit—and he had been talking in the most foolish way about Christianity being the white man's religion and not for Rimi people. And that kind of thing. 'Now I ask you, Miss Honeywood, could you not aid us with this unhappy young man? I think you could—very much.'

'You want me to ask him to the mission?'

Doctor Schlemm bowed. 'As a Christian—I do not hesitate to repeat that name—I ask you. But not only for Christ's sake—for the sake of that poor young man, and poor Kifi. Poor Rimi,' he ended with an exhalation like a deep sudden sigh.

The girl was too astonished to hide her feelings. It was obvious that she felt inclined to laugh. Her eyebrows were raised; her smooth cheeks, shining in the reflected light of the river, were slightly dimpled; her eyes turned from Doctor Schlemm to Mrs. Vowls with an expression which said, 'Really, these people are too cool.'

'Of course there is no need to invite him as from yourself,' said Mrs. Vowls hastily. 'But if you could mention that you were going, and suggest that it would be nice——'

She was interrupted by Judy's breathless voice, 'Good morning, Mrs. Vowls. How lucky I came down. I would have hated to miss you. Doctor Schlemm, I have been longing to meet you for weeks.'

'Yess, yess. I am. And you, excuse me. How do you do?'

'Coote is my name. C-o-o-t-e. In English it's a kind of bird.'

'Coote—so. A bird——' Schlemm was puzzled.

'I suppose you hate visitors at Kifi? You have so many.'

'No, no. We have not many. Not enough. You would like to see Kifi?'

'I'm longing to see it.'

'But there is nothing—a few mud houses—a great many people with stomach-aches.'

Doctor Schlemm gave a loud laugh. The ladies therefore laughed, and Judy said, 'Why didn't I think of that?'

'You thought—Miss Coote?'

140

'Of having a stomach-ache.'

'So.' Doctor Schlemm was alarmed. His eyes and mouth opened.

Dryas said quickly, 'Miss Coote means that then she could have gone to——'

But Judy flew on: 'I was thinking—how do you go? By Duchi is the nearest road.'

Doctor Schlemm's face was already sagacious and benevolent. 'But, Miss Coote, you come as my guest—and we——' He stopped, staring at Mrs. Vowls. Dryas turned towards her also. But Judy, knowing that the woman had made a face at the doctor, did not. Instead she said quickly:

'That is very kind of you, doctor. But are you sure I won't be a nuisance? Will you let me know soon? Perhaps next week?'

'Oh, yess, yess. Next week. Why of course. Next Tuesday I shall be home again.'

'I think that's Captain Rubin,' said Mrs. Vowls. 'So we'll have to be thinking of breakfast.'

Captain Rubin was not to be seen. But the doctor at once agreed that they would have to be thinking of breakfast; and, after a gallant farewell to the two girls, he went stiffly up the hill beside the prancing Mrs. Vowls.

'Now why on earth mustn't I go to Kifi?' said Judy, turning and climbing the stairs. 'What has the old cat got against me? Who could be more respectable than I? But I mustn't call her a cat—she's only a lunatic.'

'They've asked me to go to-morrow,' said Dryas, behind.

Judy stopped and looked down at her.

'You! How extraordinary! Really, how very queer!'

'No, but what is queer is that they want me to ask that man. Did you ever hear of such cheek?'

'Louis. To Kifi? No! That's the limit!'

'Well, I think the limit is to ask me to ask him.'

'Don't you do it,' said Judy, going up to her room. She didn't want to talk to Dryas at that moment.

'I didn't propose to. Why should I? It's none of my business whether he goes *ju-ju* or not.'

'Goes *ju-ju?* Is that it?'

'They didn't say so exactly. They only complained that he's not being a good boy to the mission.'

'I should think not. Why, it would ruin him. But he knows that quite well, so you needn't worry. If he wants this job in Rimi, he can't afford to get mixed up with the Christians. And don't you let him, Dryas. It will finish him if he goes to the mission. The pagans will write him off. But he knows that well enough himself.'

141

Dryas was just mounting through the trap; her head was level with the floor. She looked up at Judy, and said, 'Doctor Schlemm accused me of being a Christian.'

'He's an old scoundrel.'

'And I suppose I am, an't I? though I'm a pretty rotten one—I'm nothing else, anyhow.'

Judy fell into a chair, and carefully arranged her skirt over her legs. She looked at Dryas, and said, 'Nothing else, certainly.'

'And I suppose a Christian ought to be one,' said Dryas lounging in a window. She lit a cigarette and reflected.

'To be what?' said Judy abruptly.

'Well, to help it on. I don't mean to ask the man. I couldn't. I was only wondering——'

'It's not worth wondering—the thing's impossible.'

'I was wondering if——'

Judy's gaze stopped her. Judy was thinking: 'She's in love with him already, and she doesn't know it. She thinks of nothing else. And if he drops her, she'll go to bits and not know what's wrong with her.'

Dryas, seeing that the gaze did not preface a remark, repeated, 'I was wondering if you would——'

'Would what?'

'Rescue Mr. Aladai for them.'

Judy was at first too astonished to reply. What was the girl's object? It was suggested to her that it might be a bad one. But instantly she knew that it couldn't be deliberately so. Dryas was incapable of meanness. Besides, it was a reasonable suggestion; she knew that Judy was Aladai's friend.

She said, 'But why should I ruin Louis? That's the last thing I want to do.'

Dryas did not seem to hear this. She was still reflecting on the moral problem which had suddenly been put to her. 'It's really not my job—though I suppose it would be a good thing for the mission to have one of their people bossing Rimi.'

'How pretty she is,' Judy thought. 'Young, pretty, and decent. Decenter than I. Much better temper.'

'But perhaps Doctor Schlemm will try some other way,' said Dryas, carefully putting her ash in a tray.

'I should think after this specimen of his powers, that he'll have several good tricks.'

'Is he a schamer?'

This was one of Rackham's Irish words. Judy gazed at Dryas for a moment, and the words jumped out of her mouth, 'How English you are, Dryas.'

The girl slightly coloured, and asked, 'Isn't he straight?'

Judy was also flushed. She said vigorously:

'Schlemm? Good Lord, yes! He's a saint. Oh, yes, he's a saint all right.' She picked up her book and looked for her place.

'You said tricks.'

Judy gazed at her vaguely. 'A real saint. There are real saints. People who really do love goodness and give up everything to help it along. But, of course, that's obvious—only one keeps forgetting it.'

Dryas was walking about the room. She was always restless in the house. She passed from one window to another, watching the company on parade—toy soldiers glittering on the toy mountains of painted brown and metallic green; the Union Jack flapping slowly on the Resident's flagpole, like a naïf old soldier; a row of carriers trotting along the town road like a centipede with a yellow back and black legs.

'If he's a saint, he can't be tricky,' she said at last.

'Good gracious, Dryas, all saints are tricky. You can't trust 'em a yard—not an inch—at least in religious things.'

'Well, I suppose I'll have to go to Kifi.'

She spent all the afternoon at the gymnasium, but did not go to the Scotch club. Her object was to avoid hurting Judy. In her mind, the gymnasium was neutral athletic ground; the Scotch club social. But Rackham also stayed away from the club. He called on the Honeywoods at the Hides bungalow.

Judy rose at six the next morning and went to find Doctor Schlemm. The old man was still in bed, but when he rose he was delighted to hear that she, too, would visit the mission. When Judy returned on one of Rubin's polo ponies, she was surprised to see Aladai standing at the edge of the Hides stoop, in eager conversation with Dryas. But he went away as soon as he caught sight of her.

'So you asked him?' said Judy.

Dryas was not at all put out. She answered readily, and without defiance, 'I just said that Doctor Schlemm seemed to expect him.'

'You've probably done him a very bad turn, but I don't suppose you mind.'

'I think Doctor Schlemm is a very good man—really good.'

'So do I. But not good for Aladai—not till he's elected. And so, perhaps, not very good for himself, either. But I suppose you can't expect saints to have any respect for politics.'

'Salé has been sent away to Makker.'

'What? Where? Mecca, I suppose. How do you know?'

'Mr. Aladai told me just now. The Emir sent for him and ordered him to go to Mecca—he said, "Makker." He's going like a lamb, and

143

he won't be back for a year, and Mr. Aladai seemed very pleased about it.'

'You're getting quite an expert on the political situation.'

Dryas's eyelids flickered. But her temper was perfect. This was the quality that had made her loved as well as disliked.

Besides, she acknowledged that she had been wrong to use the word schamer twenty-four hours before. That had been tactless; and so Judy had a right to be tactless now—even rude.

She answered gently, 'Of course, I don't really know anything about it. It's only what I heard. Perhaps I've got it wrong.'

There was a short silence. The two women looked at each other. Then Judy, flushing, exclaimed, 'Do you know how pretty you are, Dryas?'

'I was just longing to be as slim and distinguished as you.'

They spent the rest of the morning together; and Rackham himself, when he came to ask Dryas to see his new parallel bars, could not separate them. They preferred, for the moment, each other's company, because nobody else could understand so well each other's complicated and female feelings.

XIII

It was true that Salé had promised to go to Mecca. The news raised great hopes in the Aladai party and put Elizabeth into so good a temper that she gave Akande Tom five shillings.

Akande Tom added this five shillings to four others in his purse, levied sixpence from the queue of clients in the street, and went to Makurdi's, where he paid the last instalment on his suit—all but sixpence. Makurdi, on account of his family connection, forgave him the sixpence. The suit, having been worn many times by Tom in his visits to the station, was crumpled and dirty; but had it been rags, so long as they were European rags, it would have given Tom an indescribable happiness.

No one can feel that happiness who has not been in Tom's position: a naked savage. The successful grocer who puts on a coronet for the first time, the suburban climber who first hears herself called 'My lady,' cannot come near it. For the difference, even in a snob's imagination, between a peer and a tramp is nothing to that in a savage's between himself and a white man. It is so great that the bush negro does not concern himself with it. His indifference to the white man and his ideas

144

is founded on a feeling of difference so profound that his mind will not attempt to pass over the gap. Only the most enterprising, like Tom—men of ambition and ideals—attempt it.

When Akande Tom had put on over a naked skin linen coat, trousers, cloth cap, and black goggles, he felt as near a white man as it was possible for him to be, and enjoyed an exaltation which might possibly be compared with that of a risen soul on his first morning in paradise. Because, for Akande Tom, the change was not only one of appearance, but of being and power. Akande's reasoning was not logical or definitive. It was part of his feelings. The whole process was one of thought-feeling carried on by every part of his nervous system, from the ends of his crinkled hair to the tips of his long, thick-jointed toes; and now, when he took his usual turn on the town road, walking by himself and for himself, he felt to the end of his toes and hair the quality not merely of a white man, but all that belongs to him—the power of his engines and guns, the magic of his telegraphs, gramophones, radios, motors, ships, and his mysterious being. By wearing white man's clothes, it seemed to Tom's bodily and natural logic, that he became one with the white *ju-ju*. For ten minutes he walked to and fro, stopping now and then to look downwards at his lapels, his buttons, and the trousers below. He did not even notice the huge bare chest, with the thick muscle-pads of a negro, under the bulging lapels. Then he turned towards the town. The suit was his; and he was free to enjoy a public triumph.

This triumph, even in Tom's consciousness, was quite different from the joy of possessing a white man's suit. It was an inferior thing; like the pleasure of a great man in being cheered by ragamuffins in the street. The real joy and achievement was in possession, in the power. He disdained the loungers in the main street, of whom some looked at him and one or two recognized him. They were savages. He did not deign to notice, though he knew, that ten or a dozen idle carriers and small boys had presently formed behind him; and when one of them, Musa, a well-known pest of the markets, began to imitate him, walking in front of him with a peculiar toe-and-heel movement, like a white man in boots, peering, with thumbs and fingers for goggles, to right and left, and shouting, 'I am the big judge Akande Tom, brother of the Sultan of England, not very distantly related to the cannon *ju-ju*, and closely connected with the backside of a camel,' he did not hear him.

Yet two days before he had chased Musa half a mile, in such rage that he could hardly speak, for a much inferior insult. The white suit gave him such power that insults to him were no more than the chattering of monkeys; or, to a white man, the things muttered after him by riff-raff in a ditch.

He was proud, however, of his train, especially when, augmented to

145

twenty or more, it followed him right to the *ju-ju* house and took up places there—in the porch, or clinging to the street bank, and pushing its noses through the mats, to see his apotheosis.

Akande Tom had not formed any scheme in returning to the *ju-ju* as a white man. He had simply followed a course of action laid down by forces which he did not examine. But he was confident now—that is to say, every part of his body was confident—that he had established himself as master of the *ju-ju* and Elizabeth.

'Lisbet,' he called in a white man's voice, high and flat. 'Whar are you, ma dear?'

The impudent girl Obishala came out of her hut and gazed at him. She made a very rude remark about the inconvenience of trousers to an animal when he wanted to scratch himself.

Akande Tom, who had raged against this girl for weeks, smiled at her now, and said in English, 'I tink you ni-ce girl, Obishala. I gree for you too much.' Then, seeing from the corner of his eye, in the doorway of the *ju-ju* yard, Elizabeth slowly approaching, he coughed—exactly the Resident's cough—poked his head forward, took off his spectacles, breathed on them, wiped them, put them on again with both hands, and, only then noticing, cried, 'Lis-a-bet—ma deah girl—how do-do?'

Elizabeth took his hand in her left hand, hooked her right hand into the top of his coat. Then, with a strong downward stroke like that of a leopard's forepaw, she ripped it open, making one button fly and tearing out a buttonhole.

Akande Tom gave a scream of surprise and anguish and jumped back; but Elizabeth was still gripping the coat and hand; he swung sideways, and his weight against hers tore half the coat-front from the collar downwards through the seam of the sleeve.

'Lisbet,' he shrieked; and then in Rimi, 'Let go—you spoil my coat.'

Elizabeth, who had in sudden action the momentum of heavy bush animals like the elephant and the rhinoceros, had made another plunge. Her hand was in the waistband of his trousers; one heave of her shoulders, as large as a York ham, opened them like a paper bag and split one leg to the knee.

Akande Tom was falling all the time. He fell now on his back with his legs in the air; but, rolling and doubling himself like a hare knocked over by a greyhound, bounded to his feet.

Elizabeth, nearly as quick as a greyhound, had him by the tail of his coat, and as it began to tear, he stopped and cried imploring, 'Lisbet, they're so nice.' He spoke like a child, he was tearful. 'Don't spoil them, Lisbet.'

With a quick, deft movement, as if her fingers were pecking birds, she took the spectacles off his nose, threw them on the ground, and trampled on them. He gave a scream of rage, and flew at her with his fists. But he only struck her once, in the breast. The next instant there were twenty men and women sitting on him, clawing at him. Five minutes later they threw him into the street. He was stark naked and much scratched.

The crowd was still laughing at him. Elizabeth, standing outside the porch, since it was too low for her, with one leg of the trousers still in her hand, now spoke to him for the first time. She said in Rimi, 'Come in now and put on a banty, like a Rimi woman's husband.'

But Tom bounced up and walked off.

'I tell you, you can come in now,' Elizabeth shouted.

Tom still walked away.

'I shall fetch you,' Elizabeth said, 'and then you will catch trouble.'

Tom turned round and shouted, 'I'm not afraid of your fool *ju-ju*. That's for savage men. I don't care for you or your *ju-jus*. I'm a Christin man. Good-bye, you damn witch Lisbet.'

Elizabeth was surprised. She returned thoughtfully to her yard. Afterwards she went to the *ju-ju* house and made medicine for Tom's return.

This medicine, sold to many women in Rimi, obliges a husband's return within so many days, on pain of death. The death is by wind. The man, wherever he is, swells up and dies in great pain.

The news that medicine has been made for a certain man's return is always broadcast. Elizabeth and her assistants take care of that, for it usually brings the man back at once, unless he has succeeded in getting an antidote at some other *ju-ju*.

Tom, meanwhile, having dodged about the alleys of the third ward for half an hour, to shake off the jeering boys, was making for Makurdi's. He covered himself as well as he could with his hands. He had no friends to lend him a rag or a penny in Rimi town. The favourite of a *ju-ju* queen is even more unpopular than a prince-consort.

But just as he slipped past the town wall where it touches the river-bank, a slim young man, who had been sitting in front of Makurdi's, jumped up and approached him. He carried a rolled bundle under his arm.

'Greetings, Akande Tom,' he said politely. 'The Master of the Horse has sent me to greet you with this present. He thinks you badly treated.' He unrolled the bundle and showed a fine blue gown, embroidered in white—a chief's gown.

'Thank you,' said Tom; but, when he reached out his hands for it, the polite youth drew it back. 'Pardon,' he said; 'perhaps you had better not put it on now, for if people saw you in it they might wonder where you had got it.'

'Why shouldn't they know?'

'I'll explain. It would be better if you could see the Master himself.'

'What for?'

'He would like to be your friend.'

Ten minutes later, after a long détour, Tom and the polite youth, still carrying the gown, entered the palace by a back door and made their way, by a more than usually obscure route, to the Master's compound, immediately behind the main building.

The Master was one of Aliu's favourites, an old soldier picked out of the ranks for his valour. He was about forty years old—a big man, like a gorilla, with a body large enough for two men, and short, twisted, thick legs. His head, much narrower than his huge neck, was sunk into it like the ball of a ginger-beer bottle into its patent groove. His ears were so small and flat that they could not be seen at all from a front view; they lay behind the spread of his wide cheeks, which seemed to be expanded for the purpose of providing a base for his nose. This was in shape like half a purple fig cut off short at the thick end and scooped out into two craters below.

The master had the rough, frank manners of the warrior; his manner seemed to say, 'You can trust a man like me. I've got no use for any kind of finesse.'

He condoled with Tom like a fellow tough. 'That Lisbet, I know her. I've been there myself. She's a hard one.'

'A fool,' said Tom with dignity. 'But I shall not go back to her.'

'You're right—she's a fool. Look at the way she goes on with that brother of hers. He will smash up her *ju-ju* if he is elected, and, if he is not, Salé will break it.'

'I don't care for the *ju-ju*. It is only pagan wild men believe in her *ju-ju*.'

'Quite right, my lad. Though it pays money, a lot of money, I should think. And there's no harm in money.'

'I'm not going back again. I'm not a small boy.'

'But look here, Tom, if Salé was emir, you would not be a small boy. You would be a big man, bigger than any of us—anything you wished.'

'Oh, yes, I know how you palace people talk. But you can't take me in. I'm not a savage man.'

The master laughed loudly at the notion of taking in Akande Tom. 'Ah! you're not to be had, I know that. But neither are we. That's what I want to say. You help us and we help you.'

'What do you want me to do?'

'You can make Lisbet a bit more sensible—show her where all her real friends are—then, if we make Salé chief, you shall have pay on the paper' (i.e., a salaried position in the Treasurer's official account).

Tom already looked as if he was a Minister of State. His chest stood out like a duck's; his eyelids drooped like an emir's; he said, 'I shall want four pounds a month.'

'Four! Five is what I was going to suggest.'

'A horse and a sword.'

'A horse and a sword, of course. Also uniform money.'

Tom, suddenly remembering his side of the compact, lost something of his majesty. 'But Lisbet is hard to manage—she is a big fool. She won't listen to sense.'

'That's all right. That's easy. We'll tell you what to do. We only want a little news now and then, and you can say something for us to Lisbet at a good time—you know when.'

'I know. Ah! you can trust me there.'

'Ha-ha! I believe that.'

'The fool woman, who thinks herself clever—but I play with her.'

'Ha-ha! I'm sure. And now perhaps you'd better be getting back. It's late, and they say she's making *ju-ju* to catch you.'

'I don't care for the *ju-ju*.'

'Neither do I. That's woman's talk. But still, since you are going, this is a good time—before she gets angry. She's got a temper, that bitch, as you know.'

'I don't care for her or her temper.'

Tom got up and reached for the gown, which lay, rolled up, beside the master. His eye had been on it for a long time. The master put his hand on it and pressed it down. 'You'd better leave the gown, perhaps.'

'Leave it? You gave it to me.'

'It's yours, my boy. And it's worth six pounds, that gown.' The Master spread the gown out across his knees. 'Just look at that work.'

The Master gazed at the embroidery with the eyes of a connoisseur. It was, in fact, the best in his collection.

'I wouldn't have changed it for the Emir's black horse. But now it's yours, Tom, my friend. And that's why I say, leave it here. For if Lisbet were to see you in such a gown as this, a gown she couldn't get the like of in all Rimi country, what would happen to your gown?'

'I'll take the risk of it,' said Tom, reaching for the gown. 'It's my gown, so it's my risk.'

'But, my dear boy, if Lisbet sees you in a Mohammedan gown she may think you've been at the palace. You know what women are. And then, if she suspected that, she wouldn't talk to you.'

'I'll risk it,' said Tom. 'You leave it to me.'

Nevertheless, when he returned to the *ju-ju* house at sundown he was wearing a banty. He possessed in revenge, not one, but two gowns, at the palace.

Elizabeth received him in a very affectionate manner. She had never been so tender, so kind. But Tom was sulky, and when, gazing at him with a caressing smile, she said to him, 'You see, it is no good to run away from me; my *ju-ju* is everywhere,' he answered, 'I didn't come back because of you. Your *ju-ju* can't touch me. I Cristin man.'

Elizabeth was silent for a moment; and her expression became threatening. It would have terrified any one of a million Rimi people into a fit. But Tom did not see it. He was feeling still some of the power of that white suit, and even a little from the gown.

The power of a white suit is so great that it sinks through a whole body in a few minutes, and something of it remains for ever afterwards, either as pride, aspiration, envy, or bitter regret.

Elizabeth, however, almost at once ceased to be dangerous, and became still more affectionate.

'You came back for love of me,' she said.

'No,' said Tom.

'Why, then?'

'Because I wanted to. I'm not a small boy.'

The impudent girl's voice from the doorway said, 'Perhaps somebody sent you back,' but Elizabeth at once snubbed her in a severe manner. She talked of whips.

Elizabeth, like other autocrats, did not like unsuitable interruptions, even from her best friends. But she soon forgot her anger in looking at Tom. The boy was still sulky. He lounged across the bed, propped on one elbow, with one shoulder up to his ear. The full roll of his narrow hips, the bend of his neck, his half-closed eyes, and the huge sulky mouth, expressed with the utmost dramatic force, with their curves, bends, and their whole systems of weights and balances, the languid and insolent sufferance of an adored beauty. His whole body was expressive of one complex but connected idea: it had the force of old and elaborate art.

Elizabeth could understand, or rather appreciate, with her own African senses, its African beauty and rococo exuberance. She gazed, silent and motionless, on the boy, with a fixed smile curling her upper lip; not doting upon him, for there was no softness in her, but rejoicing and triumphing in him.

In the night, all Rimi, town and station, was kept awake by the drumming at the *ju-ju* house, where Lisbet was making a dance.

150

XIV

KIFI IS DOWNRIVER from Rimi about thirty miles. Doctor Schlemm travelled downstream in one dug-out, with a kind of dog-kennel, made of dirty straw, amidships. This was his cabin. Mrs. Vowls was to share the dog-kennel, by her own request. But for this picnic, recollecting that young girls (to him Judy was also a young girl) expect luxuries, and determined to do them well, he had provided another larger dug-out and another bigger dog-kennel, big enough to shelter both of them, sitting back to back, as far as the waist, and allow them to take off their hats. His own was nearly sun-proof, he told them proudly; but not sufficiently so for young ladies. He seemed to think that young ladies' brains were more likely to heat than his own and Mrs. Vowls's.

Neither Judy nor Dryas liked the dog-kennel, even back to back; and they were delighted when, about two o'clock, after a very bad lunch of sandwiches, they saw Aladai, on the deck of a big southern trader, charging down on them. The trader had a sail, unique in Rimi, and a large crew of polers, who, now and then, used their poles as oars.

He was towing two more dug-outs, carrying an escort of spearmen, servants, the servants of his escort, and the servants' small boys.

All this, of course, was paid for by Makurdi; Aladai had nothing of his own. But he did not explain this; to his friends and servants he was the lord. He insisted now that the girls' dug-out should turn in to shore, so that they might come on board the trader. It was not safe to tranship in mid-Niger from a dug-out with, at the highest, six inches, and, at the lowest, three, of freeboard.

The boat was a Kakanda; built of broad planks sewn together with iron wire and caulked, apparently, with silk-cotton. It was steered by a long oar, and, after tea, Dryas, feeling the need of exercise, demanded to be taught to handle this oar. She spent the rest of the evening on the poop with the helmsman.

She felt in her muscles and nerves the delight of riding and managing the power of the immense river, pouring towards the sea its thousand miles of flood. As its lift and pressure twisted the pliable craft under her, she balanced with springing knees, waiting to pull against the next gust or freshet which would send them yawing out of their course.

151

Judy and Aladai were chatting on the forecastle head in the shadow of the sail. She could hear them clearly except in the gusts. Their talk amused her, like the chatter of passengers overheard by an officer during a difficult crossing.

They spent an hour discussing native education; and with what excitement!

Education! On a day like this!

A gust caught the sail; the helmsman gave a shout; Dryas, her hair blowing in her eyes, threw herself back, tugging with all her might at the loom; the ship swung wildly, rising at the bow, then, caught by the oar blade, checked, heeled till the water was within a foot of the gunwale, and slowly was brought back to her course, wriggling underfoot like a snake in a forked stick.

The helmsman shouted at her in Hausa one of the two African words she knew, 'Good,' and she laughed in triumph.

It was good to escape from Rimi, from the wretchedness of being in love with a man whom you could not have; whom you were obliged to snub when he made love to you. Why did Judy insist on keeping him? Had the woman no pride? She rested, breathless, against the black polished wood; her arm, lying along it, touched the thin, filthy arm of the helmsman—a typical river-rat in middle age; his muscles gone to string, his face into holes, a gap-toothed, foul-tongued blackguard whose skin had the very texture of dirt, granulated, cracked mud-crust.

She looked down at Judy across the waist, where the crew lay inanimate, like a heap of shining black fish in a small basket. The little woman was waving her thin hands and speaking very fast. Aladai was looking down at a girl with bandaged legs who had sat crouched against the half-deck all noon; Dryas had noticed her because she moved her place when Aladai changed his, following the shadow. She thought, 'One of his wives, I suppose. I expect he has plenty. They all do.'

The girl had fine eyes, which she was now turning up towards Aladai with an imploring and terrified look. She looked very ill. 'I expect he beats her,' Dryas thought.

'Out of hospital,' said Judy, in a surprised voice.

'She ran away,' said Aladai.

'I'm sure she ought to go back.'

'She was afraid to stay because——'

A current from some cave or bank, or perhaps from some unseen tributary out of sight in the forest half a mile away, made the boat swing; Dryas briskly returned to her duty.

It appeared that the sick girl was a witch; no, accused of it. She gazed about her like a guilty dog, hanging her head, while Judy discussed her.

'Why must Judy discuss her?' Dryas thought, angrily tugging at the oar. 'Can't she see how she feels? But Judy can't leave anything alone.'

Aladai was taking the girl to the mission, but she did not want to go. 'Then why make her?'

'Jealousy, I expect,' said Judy, in a sharp, loud tone. 'That's at the bottom of most witch trials.'

Her sharp voice made Dryas smile. She thought with pity and a little contempt: 'I suppose she doesn't realize how mean it is—and how stupid. I believe Jerry is beginning to hate her. I wouldn't blame him.'

Judy and Aladai were talking about jealousy. Judy said that it was the first and worst of all vices.

'So it is,' said Dryas to herself.

It was at the root of all that was bad in everything you could think of—human relations, nationalism, religion. 'Scotch clubs,' said Aladai; but Judy hurried on in her fury against jealousy. It was the voice of the devil himself—the angel that would not stay in heaven because he could not be king of it; and it was as cunning as the Devil——

'The Rimi say that blood is jealous.'

'So it is. Creeping everywhere—into your brain and into your nerves—that's absolutely true. All the jealous gods love blood. Because jealousy is a cannibal, feeding on itself. It would rather destroy itself than help another.'

Wind and current together swept away the ship. It was growing dark, and the wind was rising. Dryas and the helmsman threw themselves on the oar with a common shout. He pushed, she pulled; it seemed that the boat would break in half. But she was as flexible as a snake. Her sewn, leaky planks were like the scales of a snake, opening, sliding; and her keel had the sinewy whip of a snake's backbone. She straightened, wriggling. The helmsman roared 'Good,' breathing his crocodile breath into the girl's face, not a foot from his tettered nose. But she was complimented. She smiled at him broadly, like a fond daughter and pupil congratulated on her progress.

'Human nature,' Aladai was saying in his rather sententious manner.

Judy jumped on him. '*That* was no excuse,' and she exclaimed, with some warmth, 'Nature—I hate nature. Most of it ought to be abolished. Don't laugh, Louis. I do mean it.'

It was growing dark; the dug-outs behind were brought alongside, and Dryas, at last giving up her oar, came to fetch her jumper from the bow. She was standing in the waist with one foot touching Osi's thigh, balancing herself with her legs apart while she put the jumper over her head. When her head came through, with closed eyes and the disgusted

153

expression of a child whose face has just been washed, she said, 'Oh! Judy, you don't really think that.'

'Think what?'

'You know you love nature—hills and trees.'

'No, I don't. I love what poets have made of them for me.'

Dryas smiled, and, putting her hands on the half-deck, vaulted neatly upon it, with a round turn so that she was sitting with her legs dangling in the waist. She tossed back her hair, looked about her, and said, 'You can't say this isn't lovely.'

Judy answered, 'I didn't,' and then, looking at Dryas in what the girl called her donnish manner, she said, 'It's a stupid point—not worth bothering about.'

She had been extremely kind to the girl ever since that unfortunate exclamation about her Englishness, which Dryas had easily forgiven, for she was profoundly convinced that the English were the best people in the world. It was not a thing you talked about. But it was obvious.

But Dryas could not be offended by anything that Judy said or did; because she was sorry for her; with the unconscious pity of a younger, finer body. There was no arrogance in it. And she refused to hate Judy or to take advantage of her.

If Jerry tries to flirt with me, she thought, I'll go away.

To steal the man would spoil her happiness. She did not reason this out. She knew it only as her nerves knew that dirty sheets would spoil her sleep. She was used to clean ones.

When dark fell, Aladai called for music. The band, who had been the crew all day, now put down their poles and took up their lutes, flutes, and drums. There were five or six lutes of different sizes, three wind tubes—sounding like oboes, but rather harsher than the European oboes—and four drums. But only the smallest, not bigger than a child's, were played with the strings. The artists sorted themselves in the waist and began to shout at the dug-outs; laughter, exclamations, and loud spittings presaged a Rimi concert.

Dryas settled herself on her perch, her foot swinging against Osi's shoulder, which to her seemed some projection of the luggage. She was going to make and use, her holiday, her day or two's escape from what seemed to her inexperience, the last tragedy of fate.

She looked about her. How absurd of poor Judy to say that nature was not lovely in itself; lovely and exciting! Could anything be more obvious? Sky and water were the same colour and brightness; sheets of blue light as dark as a new gun-barrel, but hollow and transparent. The mission boat trailing far behind seemed to float on air; carried on a dark bird with outstretched wings. It carried no light, steering by the lights of the trader. Its bow waves were the wings of the bird, gliding in the blue night air a foot above its own reflection.

The spearmen in the dug-outs over-side began to sing; and the band at once threw in the accompaniment—a wailing tune, lightly syncopated by the drums.

The voices rising from the dug-outs, unseen beneath the overhanging sides of the trader, seemed to come up from the river itself; as if the Niger, the Gwarra, were singing.

'But is it a sad song?' Judy asked.

'I don't know,' said Aladai, in the tone of one interrupted by a guest in the middle of music.

'What does it matter what they're singing?' Dryas reflected. She did not think that the music was worth listening to. It was merely a savage noise. But she enjoyed it because it suited her mood of calm unhappiness.

'He'd rather have me. But he'll marry her. She loves him so much and he hates a mess.'

It seemed to her a long time since she had been in love with Jerry Rackham. She had, she supposed, begun to love him when she saw him fighting with The Kraken; not that she had liked him then, but that he had given her a certain kind of excitement, the kind that might turn into love.

'How do you mean, you don't know?' said Judy. Her curiosity was not to be put off.

Aladai said something to the singers, and they paused; he translated a line, in a kind of recitative, accompanied by one lute:

> *'In the dark water, under the dark trees.'*

The spearmen shouted another line; their voices crashed through the air like a wind blowing down a tree; Aladai's tenor, and the single lute, floating out of their noise, were like birds rising from the branches after the tree has fallen.

> *'The father of all things.*
> *O father, father of rivers.'*

Dryas was annoyed to be distracted by words from her sadness. The song, in English, made her feel more unhappy. It excited her unhappiness out of its calm.

Aladai sung in his light tenor:

> *'Young children weep in the dark,*
> *They die in the dark.'*

Then, with the spearmen, sang the refrain:

> *'Father, father of men.'*

155

The voices of the spearmen burst out always with unexpected power, musical and harsh at the same time—like brass, and thrilling like brass; and when they were cut off abruptly, as if by an unseen conductor, Aladai repeated in English, liquid and sibilant:

> *Because of his anger*
> *His eye is red like an ember,*
> *Father, father of men.*
> *Evil spirits wait in the dark.*
> *They eat your children.*
> *Father, our father,*
> *We starve, we are afraid,*
> *Because of your anger.'*

There was a silence. Dryas, looking calmly about her, admiring the view, kept her face turned away from the lantern on the half-deck. Her heart was swelling. How absurd! But she would never get her man.

Judy said, 'Osi wants you, Louis.'

Aladai said something in Rimi to the girl beneath Dryas's feet in the waist, and went to the edge of the deck. The girl crouched again. He said to Judy, 'I was too far away,' and then at once he began to sing to himself in Rimi, with a quick throbbing note, full of a new elation.

The spearmen broke in like a crash of trumpets; the strings shrilled like a chorus of women:

> *'Father, I am old, an old woman,*
> *My womb is barren, my breasts are dry,*
> *I cannot bear sons, I cannot feed your sons,*
> *They starve in the dark. The children weep for food,*
> *Father, accept me, take the old woman to soothe your anger,*
> *Take me to feed them.'*

The tune changed again, became slower, louder, and, as it seemed to Judy, more triumphant.

She said to Louis: 'I believe you like this song better than Schubert.'

He answered with a little impatience: 'But this is real—it is a family song. She was a real old woman—of my own blood. We are proud of her; and I think you would be proud of her'; and then, as the spearmen broke off, he sang with the same triumphant, proud voice:

> *'She threw herself into the black water.*
> *The river accepted the old woman.'*

Then, quickening again to a dance rhythm:

> *'The black water is joyful with her blood.*
> *It runs and leaps. It is dark and thick.*
> *The great fish moves its tail and swims in the thick water.*
> *He is not angry. His people remember him.*
> *Father, my father, your children are fed.*
> *See to the fish feast all the village crowd.*
> *The sandbanks are full of laughter and dancing.*
> *O father fish, many are your children.*
> *You give amply and in abundance.*
> *Once I was in the water and swam twisting my tail:*
> *Now I dance with my brothers on the sandbank.'*

There was a few minutes' silence after the song. Then Judy said: 'But it is worse than sad; it is terrible. And why does the father want a sacrifice?'

'I suppose he is a jealous god,' said Aladai. His voice was uncertain. He could not yet control his excited nerves.

Judy changed the subject. 'But they're not usually so sad in your Rimi.'

'They're sad now because they're poor.'

'But all people feel so now—all over the world.'

'No; white people are full of hope, because they say, "This bad time will come to an end"; or they say, "We may not beat the bad times, but our children will, and now we will fight." But these poor people do not know how to fight anything. They do not know how to fight sickness and pain and grief. They do not even know how to fight themselves.'

'And that's why you want schools?'

'Yes, to teach them to be free.'

Dryas said suddenly, 'I hope you will be King of Rimi, Mister Aladai.'

'I shall be king, but hope for me that I shall be a good king. Pray for me, then, Miss Dryas.'

'That isn't much to do.'

'A great deal—perhaps everything.'

'I think it's time for dinner,' said Judy briskly, putting off her blanket. 'I like the singing, Louis. I wouldn't have missed it for anything in the world, but I was glad when it stopped. It was spoiling the best appetite I've had for a week.'

It had been agreed to camp for the night and dine in the bush camp. Aladai had already ordered huts to be built and fires to be lit. But Judy ate very little at dinner. Dryas, on the other hand, and Doctor Schlemm, made an excellent meal.

The camp was only half-way to Kifi, and an early start was arranged for the next day. But Aladai, pointing out that the big trader could reach the mission in three hours, invited the party to spend the morning on a visit to what he called his iron-field—a village of smelters about five miles inland from the camp.

Aladai was proud of his iron-field. It was strange to see, even in this sophisticated young man, a naïve desire to show off Rimi to visitors.

Judy foresaw that the iron-smelting as practised in Rimi could not be impressive, and that the visit would disappoint Aladai even more than his party. She hinted to him that Mrs. Vowls and Doctor Schlemm were not interested in manufactures.

'Miss Honeywood and I will come with you. I love to see any kind of works.'

'These aren't exactly works, you know; the furnaces are in the open air.'

'But so they are in England.'

'I'm going to put up some works as soon as the iron trade revives,' said the young man. 'In fact, I am getting out estimates.'

Judy, seeing how much he would be gratified by a tin shed, said that this was an excellent plan.

'Of course, it will be a State factory.'

'Excellent. But I hardly think Mrs. Vowls understands much about ores and blasts.'

'I've got a hammock for her specially.'

But Mrs. Vowls herself was determined not to be left out of the party; and in the upshot only Doctor Schlemm was left behind. His excuse was that he had to be back at the mission that morning. He left, therefore, in his own dug-out; the ladies would follow in the big trader.

Aladai had gone forward an hour before these arrangements were made, in order to see that the lunch was prepared at his smelters' village. The three women and the hammock travelled at their leisure. Mrs. Vowls refused the hammock. She preferred to walk; and she walked bareheaded. Judy ventured at last to point out that it was eight o'clock; but Mrs. Vowls answered, 'I never put on anything till half-past eight.' Her tone was defiant; as if she had been threatened.

At twenty-past eight Judy asked her, 'Have you the time, Mrs. Vowls?'

Mrs. Vowls answered, 'Don't mind about me. I've been in Africa before.'

Judy, snubbed, reflected, 'Yes, and, according to report, you've had two sunstrokes already.'

At twenty minutes to nine she put on a light felt hat—the lower half of a terai.

At half-past ten, when Mrs. Vowls and the two girls were still half a

158

mile from the ironmen's village, Judy noticed that the woman was breathing hard, and that her face was flushed to a dark red. She asked her, 'Wouldn't you like the hammock, Mrs. Vowls?'

Aladai's hammock chair had been brought in case Mrs. Vowls got tired.

She answered shortly that she preferred to walk.

A minute later, Judy, alarmed by the heavy breathing and mahogany-coloured cheeks, said, 'Are you all right, Mrs. Vowls? I'm sorry to fuss, but it's so hot.'

'Quite,' said the other sharply.

'I'd rather like to cool off myself. Shall we sit down in the shade for a little? There's plenty of time.'

'You can if you like. I don't find it too hot.'

Two minutes after, she fell down unconscious. Judy and Dryas carried her into the shade. The boys ran to find water. The excited headman waved his arms and exclaimed, 'Cut—cut—cut—for blood,' and pointed at the woman's arm. He wanted to bleed her. But Judy thought that bleeding was out of date. 'We must get her back to Rimi— it's only twelve miles overland. But somebody must go and bring the loads back.'

'I'll do that,' said Dryas. 'I'm no good here. I can't even talk to the carriers.'

'You may have to bring them overland,' said Judy, who was stooping over Mrs. Vowls, squeezing the water over her head.

'I'll manage somehow.'

Judy felt a great relief. She was delighted. She thanked Dryas in a manner which obviously pleased the girl, and said at last, 'And, if you get stuck, you can always rely on'—she was going to say Aladai, but changed it, without enquiring why, to 'the headman. Just shout Rimi at him and point at the mountains.'

The girl strolled off with her easy gait; Judy called after her: 'Don't lose your way. The river is due south.' On second thoughts, she sent the hammock headman after her, as a guide and assistant.

She felt still a deep obligation to Dryas.

She was very tired when she limped over Rimi hill at four o'clock and descended upon the station.

It was just waking up for tea; Rubin was to be seen walking thoughtfully on his verandah in very short white pants and a shorter vest, which did not meet the pants, and red slippers. He was scratching his neck with a fly-whisk; but, seeing Judy and the hammock, he started and suddenly disappeared.

Rackham came out, fully and neatly dressed. He said, 'Hullo, Ju. What's happened? Sunstroke. Probably heat apoplexy. Where's Dryas?'

159

'She's coming with the loads.'

Judy hurried on to the hospital, and, when Doctor Pratt had put the patient to bed, escaped out of the back door to go home by the town road. She wanted to avoid Rackham. She was not fit to be seen.

But he was waiting for her. He saw her, and came quickly.

'Did you say Dryas was bringing the loads?'

'Yes.'

'But your boy tells me they were in the big boat.'

'Yes, that was the trouble.'

'Did you realize that you'd left her alone with that nigger?'

'She's perfectly all right. She can come overland if she likes.'

'What was the idea? Didn't you think, or had you a reason? You're taking a pretty large responsibility.'

Judy, hot, dirty, with wisps of hair glued to her forehead, and patches of sweat on her thin dress, had no will or courage to fight him. What was more, she felt that she had no right. She said only, in an imploring voice, 'Not now, Jerry. Wait till I've had my tea.'

He walked off, and for the next two day, though they met at the polo ground and the club, and spoke politely, they were enemies of the most intimate kind; as much beyond hatred as an old married couple are beyond romance, but with more power to hurt each other, and less means of reconciliation.

Judy asked herself why she had left Dryas alone in the bush. Was it because she had not wanted her to be alone with Rackham in Rimi? She could not decide. She knew only that she was dealing with motives below reason; and when one entered into such motives, or surrendered to them, one was lost and contemptible.

What surprised Judy was that every event now turned to her disadvantage; and she thought, 'When one is happy, everything is lucky; and when one is not, everything is unlucky. It is as though luck were the flower of happiness.'

XV

ALADAI, as soon as he heard of Mrs. Vowls's illness, mounted a pony and galloped back to the river. He found no one there but Dryas Honeywood and the headman. They had sent for carriers, and proposed to take the loads back to Rimi overland.

'But why?' said Aladai. 'Here's my boat.'

'I thought you were going to Kifi?'

'I'd be quite glad of an excuse to get out of it, and now I have a good one.'

'Won't it take longer by water?'

'You'll have to wait three or four hours for carriers.'

The girl hesitated. She did not know that half a day's journey down the Niger is equivalent to a day or two days against the stream. But she was influenced, above all, by her desire not to offend Aladai.

It was not only because she felt a nervous disgust of his black skin that she was particularly careful to be polite to him—she sympathized with him for being black. She thought already that she could see disappointment and suspicion in his face.

'But perhaps you'd rather not,' he said.

'But it's awfully good of you. I was only afraid of being a nuisance.'

'A nuisance!' He threw up his head, eyes, and one hand. 'But you know how delighted I am to be able to do anything for you.'

'It would be doing quite a lot if you really could lend your boat.'

She wished to be kind to the man, to put him at his ease and make him happy, but she did not flirt with him.

During the long afternoon, while the rowers tugged painfully up five miles of the Niger, they talked about the most serious things—the war, the Irish rebellion, Gandhi, sovereign and subject races.

Neither chose these latter subjects. Dryas did not want them, and tried to escape from them; Aladai, seeing that they embarrassed her, willingly let her diverge from them.

From Gandhi she abruptly turned to Rimi weaving; she had bought some specimens.

'They are not much good, I'm afraid,' said Aladai.

'But they're lovely.'

'Do you think so? The strips are too narrow for a dress, and not good for anything else.'

'But they're the real thing. I mean, they're what the people make themselves.'

'They make many things very badly. If they had better tools, they would be better off.'

'Ah, but it would be a frightful pity to spoil their native dress!' And then, seeing her mistake, she blushed, and said, 'I mean, as a rule.'

'You agree with the officials—you like to keep the Rimi picturesque.'

But the girl stuck to her opinion. She would not change her mind or belief even for politeness. She said, 'Why should they dress like us? We don't dress like them. I mean, I should feel all wrong if I dressed like somebody else. I wouldn't mind about the stuff being cheaper, or even more comfortable.'

161

'You put national feeling before national efficiency.'

'Is it that? Yes, I suppose it is. I know I thought Gandhi absolutely right to dress in his own native clothes. It's obvious.'

'To your feelings.' He smiled at her.

'I suppose so; but it's obvious, anyhow.'

'I feel like that too—but I might be at a disadvantage with Mr. Burwash if I visited him in a banty.'

'Oh, of course! You have to be careful with officials.'

'I hope not.'

'I only mean that they're foreigners, to you in Rimi. Your interests are different.'

Aladai did not answer this. It amused him to perceive that this white girl was simpler than himself; that her ideas were little deeper than any Rimi woman's, who concludes, by force of nature, that all strangers must be enemies to each other; that there is one way to do everything—to dress, to cook—and all others are bad. Miss Honeywood's only extension of this creed of instinct was by sympathy; she could project herself into a stranger's place. But she gave that stranger her own naïve ideas. Naïve and exciting. Aladai felt a sudden elation. He said slowly, 'But I think you're right.'

'About officials?'

'No.' He smiled. 'I was thinking about trousers: they don't quite suit Rimi, do they?'

'It's obvious,' she said bluntly.

Both laughed. But Aladai looked at the girl for a long time, delighting in the sensation of their sympathy, while she coloured and glanced at him—carefully without reproach.

'Our feelings are rather alike; and that's nice,' he said.

The girl did not see this. She did not agree with him, but she saw that she was making him happy—making him forget his inferiority; and so she smiled, and said that everybody must feel like that—every fair person, at least—because it was obvious.

She did not flirt, but every time her eyes turned towards the man's face they paid a compliment, and, though Aladai had the subtlety of Hamitic blood in him, he was not subtle enough to know that the compliment was not so much for him as for his disabilities.

They camped at Duchi, just before sunset. It was not yet too dark to see the snags, but the crew were tired and wanted a meal, which they could not get except at Duchi.

The rest-house at Duchi is on a bluff which stands twenty or thirty yards back from the river. It overlooks a broad space of both banks, covered with shrubs, which were now black and leafless after the forest fires of the last winter.

While Aladai was shouting at his boys in the rest-house—who ran to and fro, falling over each other in a confusion of loads, village girls bringing water and fuel, chickens and half-packed boxes—Dryas walked on the bluff, to stretch her legs and to enjoy a night in the African bush. She meant to enjoy it. She thought, with contentment, 'Now I am a real African traveller.' She looked at the view.

The boatmen had already lit a fire down below; its flames made a little dome of light in which they sat, like a private congregation of devils over the mouth of hell; the blackened tufts of last year's grass, a few trees, trees twisted and dwarfed by fire, caught the flickering light which made them seem like the burnt skeletons of the damned thrown out on the rubbish heap of the earth's surface.

The sun had just gone down; it, too, threw up a dome of yellow light, steadier and paler than the boatmen's fire, but of the same shape, fading quickly, like the fire, into a greenish halo, and then into the blue-black of a sky more luminous than the burnt earth, but strangely like it in colour.

The small broken clouds which dotted it represented the burnt-out grass tufts. Its faint stars were like drops of water stuck upon the oily surface of charcoal, or the blue-grey ash of fallen trunks. It was as though two camp-fires burnt in the same African desolation, above and below—not a grand, but a mean, desolation: raw, senseless nature.

The Niger glistened like a new-split coal.

Dryas stood staring for some minutes, smiling in the proper enjoyment of a view. But her smile disappeared. She was a sincere young woman. She did not know why she felt troubled and inadequate, as if, after all, she did not know what to think of this view. She did not pretend that she was liking it. But she continued to look at it. It was, after all, a view—sunset in Africa. She must not slight it.

Aladai was so happy that he could not help making a noise. He shouted at his servants to express the elation of his spirits and feeling.

He was a prince among his people—a fairy prince, a national deliverer; he was at home again; he was in love, and he thought that he had made an impression.

He did not suppose that this girl loved him, any more than he would have expected love from an angel.

This feeling of the loved one's angelic separateness may belong to any Englishman, but not in the same degree, for, though angels may exist for them as ideas, potent and real as Britannia or La France in action, they aren't to be met with in flesh and blood—creatures visible of a different colour and beauty from one's own mortal race.

Aladai therefore hurried his servants and his cook to make a special feast. Coloured lights, at least a dozen, were hung on the two dead thorn-bushes in the waste before the tumbledown rest-house; artificial flowers stood on the table; the cook opened all his most treasured tins containing halved partridges and Christmas puddings; and a dozen labourers staggered from the town, half a mile away, with a roof on their heads, to build a new house, for the guest's private accommodation, on clean ground.

Aladai was glad that the girl had walked away by herself. He had wanted her to be surprised. He was so delighted by her surprise when at last she came into the circle of his fire, the fairy lights, the table candles, and the lamps, that he could only grin.

The girl shivered, and said, 'It's really lovely to see a clean tablecloth.'

Aladai flew at a passing boy, and shouted in Rimi, 'What are you doing with that can, idiot? Where's the hot water?'

Dryas's house was already set up. The builders, having placed the round roof on six-foot stakes, unrolled mats, and tied them round with a rope. The house was ready for occupation in five minutes. Within another five it was furnished with bed, table, chairs, and a bath full of hot water.

Dryas congratulated Aladai on the smartness of his boys, but he made no answer. His silence, now unsmiling, a little disconcerted her, but she forgot it instantly when she saw the warm water. That was what she needed.

'He really couldn't be better at this kind of thing,' she thought. 'But I suppose he ought to be.'

The dinner was excellent. She smiled at its richness, but she ate well. She was hungry. She did not want to talk now; she was enjoying herself too much. Aladai said little, and looked preoccupied.

After dinner, he asked her if she would like to see a Rimi dance.

'Oh, please; I should love it.' She lay in her long chair, smoking a very good cigarette, drinking coffee—which was, at least, better than she had feared—replete with Christmas pudding, and as happy as she could be. Her enthusiasm for the dance was not affected; it was simply a way of saying 'Thank you' to her host. For the dance bored her. She would have rather enjoyed her peace than sat up to watch forty pagan girls, in couples, dancing a monotonous kind of czardas.

Apparently one of each couple took a man's part, but each seemed to perform the same wriggles, hops, and jerks—all equally boring, or, if not boring, slightly disgusting.

She could not understand Aladai's keen watchfulness and sudden cries of appreciation and encouragement. Sometimes he clapped his hands in a complicated rhythm which seemed to have no connection, to her ear, either with the rapid irregular beat of the drums or the wriggling of the girls. It was not even syncopation—as she knew it, in an English ballroom.

She became rather sleepy—lay back; she was glad when Aladai dismissed the girls and set the gramophone going. Suddenly she heard him say, 'Do you dance?'

She looked up, and saw him waiting; understood that he was giving an invitation.

She felt a shock of fright or repugnance—she did not know which— and at once mastered it. She smiled and jumped up, raising her arms.

She was a good dancer, like any other long-legged athletic girl, and she found Aladai the best partner she had known. In spite of the rough floor of mud, the poor rhythm of the gramophone, she thought, 'This is real dancing—how I should love it if it wasn't for——'

What she disliked was his hand touching her back, but again she suppressed her distaste; and when he said, 'How beautifully you dance —we must try another,' she smiled again, and raised her arms to be taken.

For real dancers, like Rimi people, dancing like poetry is a communication as well as an expression. They speak in the movements of the body not only of passion, but tenderness, sympathy—such as an Englishman may feel and think he expresses while he treads on his partner's toes.

Aladai had never danced so well, so expressively. He was a poet expressing passion in rhythm, but, unlike a poet, he had immediate power of expression. It was not remembered feeling carefully and elaborately suggested by an artful construction, but feeling in its real presence, directly carried into action. In revenge, it was a simpler feeling.

But Dryas felt nothing but its unusual quality, and she began to dislike that. It did not frighten her, but it made her feel, as she might have said, silly.

She suggested a rest. Aladai stopped dancing, and said to her unexpectedly, still holding her, 'I need not tell you what happiness you have given me—what great happiness—and—and confidence. I think I owe very much to you—I must not say what I feel.'

Dryas coloured deeply in her surprise, and, for a moment, seemed about to pull away her arm. But at once her breeding controlled her. She said cheerfully, but warmly, 'You have given me a perfectly lovely day, Mr. Aladai. I'll never forget it. Really—never!'

Aladai stepped back. But he still looked at her. There was still a tension. Therefore she waited to play her part.

But she was glad when a trader with a huge load of kola-nuts, the fifth that evening, came panting and groaning into the rest-house clearing.

Aladai and the boys rushed at him, shouting. The poor man, exhausted, raised his downcast eyes and stared at them, muttered, 'I'm staying here.'

By the time that the boys had explained to him that he could not sleep in the rest-house that night—that, in fact, he had no right to sleep in rest-houses any night—Dryas had been able to say 'Thank you' again, and to escape to bed.

She had meant to sleep under a tree, but now she chose rather to stay in her house—partly to let Aladai believe that she appreciated it, partly because she liked to feel the walls round her. She had seen wild Africa, and she could now write home about it.

Aladai stood on the bluff for a long time, staring at the same view which had disquieted his guest. The boatmen were growing more animated. Duchi had provided beer for the prince's escort. The sky was black and dead, as if smoked out. The river was only a faint rustling noise, like a creeping animal in the black waste. But to Aladai the scene was beautiful, because he felt its savage desolation, which was at the same time a challenge and a delight. Its wildness entered into the exhilaration which made him feel that he too, like the boatmen, would like to drink, sing, and dance all night, to perform astonishing feats of rejoicing; and it was also a challenge. It challenged the Englishman in him, who wanted to build, to enrich.

A touch on his trouser-leg made him look down. Osi was kneeling at his feet. He was startled, and said, 'But what are you doing? I told you to go to the mission.'

The girl turned up her face to him, and said, 'Pardon, lord.'

She was shivering with cold or fear. Aladai was touched with pity. He squatted down in front of the girl, and said, 'But what are you afraid of, Osi? No one can touch you now.'

She looked ashamed; bending down her head.

'You will be happy at the mission—they will make you well and strong.'

She whispered something. Aladai could not hear, and said:

'Good girl; now you'd better go to bed.'

'I'm afraid,' she whispered.

'To go to bed?'

'I'm afraid—don't send me away.'

'But, Osi, you can't stay with me.'

'I could work—my arms are good.'

Aladai sent her to an empty hut. But, when he got up in the early morning, he found her lying on the mat beside his bed. She was awake. She looked at him in such breathless terror, with such imploring eyes, that he could not send her away. Was it not good to have her with him, to show how he had beaten the *ju-ju?*

XVI

WHEN ALADAI'S BOAT turned upstream, a watcher on the bank, a thin pagan in a loincloth, popped a kola-nut into his cheek and ran off at full speed towards Rimi. His full speed was a little over six miles an hour. He left the river-bank at half-past three and reached the station at twenty minutes to six. Here he was delayed for five minutes. Two policemen caught him, put a machete in his hand, and sent him into the bush to cut wood for the white man's fire. He walked to the police lines, took a bundle of wood from the back of a cookhouse, and carried it to the policeman, who rewarded him with a single cigarette.

It was growing dark when he reached the palace, but giving the word 'News,' he was at once admitted to the guard-chamber.

He was told to wait. After ten minutes he protested. He was a Rimi pagan, half Yoruba, half Munshi; brave, bumptious, full of rustic cunning and persistence. His name was Guinea-fowl, on account of his habit of jerking his head as he ran, or simply Fowl.

'What have I run here for—to sit and smell your breath? I tell you I've got news.'

'Shut up, guttersnipe.'

'Very well, I shut up and you get your bottoms skinned.'

The guards, sitting in undress of singlets and drawers, ignored him. There were three: a tall thin Fulani, a tall thick Yoruba, and a little thick Munshi. All had a look of imbecility and experienced depravity combined, common to all pretorian guards. They were smoking a huge brass pipe, shaped like an elephant and holding possibly a quarter of a pound of green tobacco in its hollow back. It was the guardroom pipe, passed from hand to hand day and night, and filled by subscription or levy upon the Emir's suppliants.

They were talking about love and money, the staple of all guardsmen. The room was tall and narrow, with one window high up on the inside. A lantern stood in a blind embrasure next the door. The big outer door was faced by a smaller door, in the other wall. A fire burned in one side of the room, where the guardsmen were sitting; its smoke filled the air with blue haze. In the other half of the room two horses were tied up. Their dung had not been cleared for several days, and covered the whole of the floor at that side.

Fowl, though he assumed an easy air and spoke cheekily, was much impressed by his first glimpse of a palace. The height of the room, the red painting of the ceiling, the idle guards with their pipe, the extravagant fire, the horses, the rich and plentiful dung left lying—all these spoke of luxury, power, and grandeur. Even the conversation of the guards excited his awe. He listened closely to the details of fashionable life. The tall Fulani, who now held the pipe in his hands, deep crimson with henna, was describing a conversation with his lady friend, ' "But look here, my girl," I said to her, "what about me? You don't think a man in the police guard can keep up his position on his pay?" So then she began to cry, and she said it was the bad trade. She'd never seen trade so bad. There was a curse on Riimi, she said. "I was out all day yesterday and didn't have a customer, and all the other women the same." And she says it's because the *ju-ju* didn't get a sacrifice—not a proper one.'

The little Munshi at the other side, who had been watching the pipe calmly, reached out his hand for it and, to cover the hint, remarked, 'She's right there—can't expect a *ju-ju* to work for nothing.'

The first man affected not to see the hint. He puffed a great cloud of yellowish smoke and continued, 'That may be. But what I say is, if a girl wants a man of position——'

'Here, mate, I think you've had enough.'

The tall man started, and seemed to notice the hand for the first time. He at once apologized and handed over the pipe. He was still apologizing when the orderly officer, in full red dress, strolled in. But the sullen Munshi, smoking like a steam-engine, made no answer. The orderly carried a spear as well as a lantern. The reason appeared at once when he led Fowl from the guard chamber into an ante-room with four doors, and, turning left, dived at once into a maze of passages, small low chambers, compounds full of surprised women and terrified goats, stables. At every minute he was prodding at man or beast with the butt of his spear and shouting 'Pardon,' or 'Rascal.'

When Fowl had passed a hundred times from the stinking darkness of narrow rooms full of breathing, tranquil beasts, screaming children, staring, frightened women, to the thin, bright dark of a yard covered with stars, he suddenly found himself in a small room brightly lighted by an oil lamp with a glass shade.

The *dogarai* salaamed and went out. Fowl, blinking in the strong light, could see, beyond the lamp, two men sitting on a raised dais.

He recognized the Waziri. The other was a pale-coloured man, who

168

looked like a Fulani. His face was the colour of sun-dried wall; his nose was long and hooked; he had a small black moustache and beard.

He was dressed like a Mohammedan chief, in a tall turban and many robes.

'What is the news?' asked the Waziri.

Fowl had not saluted. He had rustic manners, and now made a crooked jerk towards the left and pulled off his cap.

'Quickly,' said the Waziri.

Fowl was confused, but he did not lose his air of impudence. It is the last thing that fails a Rimi farmer. He said, 'You see, I came to see somebody else.'

'You said you had news. What is it?'

'You see, it wasn't you that——'

Waziri called out; two servants came in, laid hold of Fowl, and put him down on his face.

'Give him six,' said the Waziri.

But Fowl, even before the first lash cut him, was shouting, 'I only said it was someone else—that's not a crime.'

'Wait a minute,' said the Waziri. 'Now will you tell me?'

'You see—it was the other one.'

Down came the whip, and Fowl let out another yell of, 'I haven't said anything—I only said——'

'Tell me the truth, or you'll get fifty,' said the Waziri; and, suddenly squealing at the man, 'I'll kill you, you fool.'

Fowl stood up again, and at once assumed the most impudent and disgusted air. 'But, you see, I didn't come to you. I came'—and, just as the two men were throwing him down, he finished with a yell, 'the Master of the Horse. That's not a crime.'

'Why didn't you say, you fool? You can tell me anything for the master. Now.'

'But you see——'

The two men leapt upon him; the Waziri raised his hand, checking them, and said in a weary, exhausted voice, 'No, no, this fool is beyond hope. Go and fetch the Master.'

In a few minutes a deep voice was heard mumbling pardon, and the Master of the Horse entered, stooping below the doorway. He smelt strongly at this hour of stale beer. He was dressed in the rags of an old blue gown, and carried on his shaved head a small piece of dirty red felt that had once been a fez. A four foot two-handed sword was slung from his shoulders by two yards of red curtain-rope.

He greeted the Fulani by the name of Salé, with a careless salute; he ignored the Waziri.

Salé slightly bent his head, then threw back his sleeve with the gesture of a fine lady arranging her tea-gown, and held out a long, slender hand. His splendid melting eyes, painted with antimony, looked up at the soldier with affectionate enquiry.

The Master touched the hand, made another jerk of the elbow, and then, turning to the farmer, said, 'Hullo, Fowl. Let's have it.'

'They're coming back, sir.'

'Who is?'

'You know, sir. The one you wanted to know about.'

'Why did you say they, you fool?'

Fowl, who knew the Master well in the village, promptly shouted at him, 'Because you didn't want anyone to know about Aladai except yourself.'

'Get out.'

'Where's my money?'

The Master gave a shout, but, before it was answered, the Waziri with an impatient jerk threw a penny at the man and said furiously, 'Go.'

'But I wasn't working for you, and the Master said sixpence.'

The Master pushed him out of the room; whereupon he began to shout at the top of his voice, 'A penny, a penny, for news like that!'

The Waziri uttered a kind of scream. Steps came running.

There was a scuffle; yells; thumps; silence.

The Master called out, 'Don't kill him. He's my man,' and the Waziri added, 'Keep him quiet till to-morrow. You understand. Till to-morrow—quiet.'

Fowl was now perfectly quiet.

The Waziri turned to the Master and said, 'That means we'll have to move at once.'

'That wants talking about,' said the other.

The Waziri's eyelids never ceased blinking; under the eyelids, his yellow eyeballs jerked towards the Master's face, and suddenly he gave a little squeal. 'What's the good of talking? D'you want to be thrown out—all of us?'

'That may happen anyhow,' said the other, not looking at Salé.

The graceful prince opened his lips, smiled, and declared that, by Allah, were he Emir, he would know how to reward their services at a better rate than they were valued now—much better.

The Master, not looking at him, but speaking into the air, repeated a Rimi proverb which means that promises fill nobody's pot.

Salé replied, 'This woman Lisbet is said to have much power.'

The Master answered, 'She has.'

'She is a friend of yours, Master?'

'I know her.'

170

'She will support her brother, of course.'

'I don't know about that.'

'But she won't support a Mohammedan.'

The Waziri interrupted. 'She doesn't like the Christians. Aladai was a Christian, and now it seems he is going with Christians again. If anyone could manage the witch properly, she would desert him.'

'It would cost much money,' said Salé.

'My friend the Master knows her mate, Akande Tom. Akande is his friend. Perhaps through Akande something might be done. With women, influence goes further than money.'

'That is very true, Waziri. You understand men and women to a marvel. No chief of Rimi could do without your help; and you, Master, I have always known your soldier's loyalty and influence with the pagans. Tell your friend that, if I were Emir, a woman like his wife, with her great power in Rimi, would not be left out of the State council. And, of course, in Rimi her *ju-ju* must always have the first place. It is the greatest *ju-ju* in all the Sudan.'

'I could talk to him,' said the Master. The Waziri paid even less attention to flattery. He sat blinking; it was like the pressure of the whole man revealed in the jerking of two valves. Suddenly he gave a faint scream, and just as Salé, with the same ingratiating smile, was about to speak, caught his wrist. There was a sound outside like the wheezing of an old bicycle pump; the scraping, tapping noise of a house-tortoise. A lantern-boy slowly crossed the door, walking sideways; then a tall spearman, with half-closed eyes, yawning; then the Emir.

He approached the door, and the spearman called, 'The Lord of the Earth comes to Waziri.'

That was the worst of the Emir. Like other old men, although he fell asleep twenty times a day—in court, at council—he could never sleep when he wanted to; and he had a taste for wandering at night.

It was obvious to the enraged Waziri that this visit, too, was a whim of the moment. The Emir was dressed only in a skull-cap and a dirty singlet, so that, as he hopped and struggled towards the Waziri's door, he was like a performing cat. His little twisted legs hobbled and staggered over the ground, stopping and falling all the time, like those of a cat when it balances on its hind pads. His body was arched like a cat's when it walks on its hindlegs. His gold-ringed pupils glittered in their socket-holes like a cat's in the dark; his teeth had long fallen out, so that his long, flat nose came down to the shallow, far-projecting chin. His beard was a few white hairs, stiff as wire, scattered here and there on cheeks and chin. He had, even in old age and sickness, a tom cat's tiger-look of coiled force, dangerous life.

The Emir's appearance was so sudden and close that none of the three men had time to move. But, just as the old man stood in the door, smiling, swaying to and fro, and saying, 'Waziri, are you there?' the Master struck at the lantern with the point of his sword, broke the glass, and knocked it over. It flared up, throwing out a thick black flame; and then went suddenly out.

The Waziri came bowing out of the door, full of apologies for his stinking lamp. 'You could not bear the smell in here, lord.'

'What are you doing, knocking over lamps?' said the old chief. 'What have you got to hide?'

'Lord, you know my heart, the heart of Waziri, the faithful one.'

'Yes, yes. Tell me, Waziri. . . .' The old man wanted to know why a certain wall had not been repaired. He took the Waziri to see the wall.

This was another of his troublesome ways. At all times he was prowling. At any time of night he would come to wake some officer of State to know why a horse had not been cleaned, or a roof repaired. He would be heard in the darkest hour of the night, shouting somewhere: 'Oh, the rascals! See the rotten work. Where are they?' and they would find him prodding at some piece of brickwork, perhaps fifty years old, with his stick. Then the builders had to be found; or some rascals willing to pretend to be builders in order to be told that there were no builders any more; no honest craftsmen anywhere.

But the Waziri got rid of him at last by reminding him that he had a new wife. He staggered away to the women's court; the Waziri hurried back to his political affairs.

'He didn't hear anything,' he told Salé. He seemed angry with his chief also for that. 'He saw nothing either. There is no need for fear, and now he is with the women. He will be safe for two hours, at least.'

'You said that you had a suggestion,' said Salé.

The Waziri answered in a mild tone: 'I have a suggestion—a plan'; then, after a pause, he added: 'The Master said something about an arrangement.'

'What is your plan?' said Salé.

'Let us consider the arrangement.'

Then began the negotiations, at once tortuous and circular, always hopeless, by which, since the beginning of time, the dependants of an autocrat have attempted to secure themselves in a change of masters by binding the new in some dependable manner before the old is done with. The problem is always the same: to buy trust with treachery; and the bargainers, seeing very well that there is some fundamental weakness in the offer, are the more obliged to aim at security; at the highest

172

degree of security—very strong oaths; immense assurances of truth—but never can be satisfied. It stands to reason that self-made men are not such fools as not to know what kind of faith can be bought with lies.

On the other hand, the Waziri had three wives and seven children. He loved his children. He was surrounded by a thousand deadly enemies made in the course of his duty. Unless he could make sure of the new Emir's favour, he would certainly be a beggar, and probably a convict or a corpse within a few days of the old man's death.

'Where is my old friend Waziri Suli?' the Resident would ask; and the new Waziri would answer, 'Lord, he is sick,' or 'He has gone to his farm.'

Salé, of course, as everyone knew, had already promised every post at Court to at least a dozen of his own party. Only the Chief Justice and perhaps the Treasurer were safe in their posts.

For Residents demand that Chief Justices should know some law and have some experience of judging; and that Treasurers should be able to count up to ten. The only way to get rid of these officials is to poison them; and even that method has caused more trouble than the posts are worth. Blackmailers take too much of the emoluments.

Nevertheless, as the Waziri and the Master were obliged to be assured, and Salé to give assurance, both sides at last declared themselves satisfied.

They were, however, not so, because that was impossible.

The Emir had been reminded of a new young girl, a pretty and young one called Shaker, lately found for him. It had also been suggested that she would make him a good wife. But he had not seen her yet, because she was never to be found when he came to the women's yard. The Emir felt that it was time he did something about her. But he had so much to do. There were half a dozen court cases that he had to think over; and the market dues; and a dozen appointments; and a sick horse, and two or three new huts. There was this trouble with the fool of a judge about the succession; and the butcher had charged seven shillings for the last sheep, which, so the guard said, had no fat on it anywhere. He had too much to do to think of little girls; but he supposed he must attend to her now. It was a good moment when other duties had to wait.

The Emir of Rimi, in spite of his name, and although, like others nowadays, he kept a Mohammedan state, was a pagan chief. His attitude to his people, his duties, was entirely pagan. He was the father of his people, irascible, unreasonable, often brutish, but he called them his children and he felt like a father to them. Like an old pagan in his

173

own compound, patriarch of three or four generations and fifteen or twenty families, he valued above everything the title of father.

Because he was a pagan and not a Mohemmedan, he had still, as a very old man, purposeful activity of mind and body. Mohammedans may live old and remain active; but not in purpose. They contemplate, and enjoy, waiting for paradise. But the religion of the waiting-room, of resignation and renunciation, had never soaked into Aliu. For him there was only one world. One lived among men, trees, and beasts. One reckoned with them, handled them, fought them, loved them; and, when one died, one was born again a man, a tree, or a beast, to begin again with loving, fighting, and striving for the glory and the honour of creatures.

A pagan is alive to the last jump of his pulse. If he is bad, he dies bad; if he is good, he dies good. But the Mohammedan saint lives only to the glory of God. Nevertheless, a patriarch can be a trouble to his tribe. Aliu was a troublesome father. He wanted to see everything done before his own eyes; for he could not trust anyone else to know how it should be done.

He would, if he could, have done the whole government of Rimi by himself: seen every house built; tried the hanging of every door; advised every young husband and wife; heard every case.

He spent long hours at the judgment-seat—a little gilt drawing-room chair, given him by a former governor, which stood in the great hall behind the ante-room. He did not sit in it except to receive the Resident, but sat below on a leopard-skin, among a crowd of Rimi litigants who treated him with little ceremony. This was because they were Rimi. For none knew when he would take fire at a piece of insolence, and shriek for his guards to throw the visitor into gaol, to flog him, or, if a woman, to shave her head or put her in the town stocks.

He would take three days over a single case about the ownership of a tree, or the theft of a yam, talking and listening to the family history of Rimi, with shrieks of laughter, furious denunciations, and every kind of stratagem to extract the truth or a new story out of the witnesses.

Rackham declared that his favourite gambit was precisely that of the Old Bailey; 'When did you leave off beating your wife?'

He was supposed to try only pagan cases; but he used every possible device, by hook or crook, to take Mohammedan cases too from the Chief Justice. He was jealous of the other and more formal court. He was sure the Chief Justice did not know his job.

He was a father to his people. He felt so; he behaved so; and so they called him. He loved them. No doubt they loved him. For they told him so—at least, whenever he pointed out to them that their country manners were not suitable to Court.

The women's yard was waked up by hearing the Emir shouting at the doorkeeper. It seemed that the fellow had not had the door mended since his last visit. Fanta came waddling to him. It was not her turn for a visit. It is wrong for a wife to leave her own hut when her husband may intend to come to her; neither must she go to meet him; otherwise he would be exposed to all kinds of embarrassment by the importunities of women.

But the women's yard at Rimi had long given up any kind of rules; and Aliu scarcely distinguished between his wives and their children.

He had no children of his own except grandchildren, girls already married in the far south. Fanta had borne him two sons, but both were dead, one in battle, the other of small-pox.

She came waddling now, in a crowd of scared women, and kneeled on one knee to greet him.

'Ai, ai,' he said. 'There you are, children. Quick enough to salute the old man, but none of you to see anything done for him. Off with you, you lot of lazy wenches; d'you think I've nothing more to do than stay and play with silly children? And how many cigarettes are you selling, I'd like to know! Ai, cigarettes—cigarettes. Do you eat them as well as drink them?'

'You are so good to us, father,' said Fanta. 'No one in the world is so good as you are.'

'So there you are, Fanta. Now what do you want? But I tell you I can't stay long. I've got other things to do.'

'Father, but you'll kill yourself with walking about all night and day.'

'Who is there to do the work if I don't do it? Tell me that.'

'You must sleep.'

'Sleep, sleep. No time for sleep. It's you that sleep—all you lazy wenches. Nothing but sleep and eat and drink tobacco, and nothing done all day.'

'Oh, father, but we know the King of the World has much work.'

'He has, he has.' The old man followed her into her hut and sat down on the bed. He nodded, and in a moment he was asleep, drooping forward till his nose almost touched his knees. Fanta spread a cloth over his shoulders and sat down beside him to prop him up. But she dared not put an arm round him. She was still afraid of the man who, as a warrior king, forty years before, had carried her off from a raid on Bida; who had chopped fifty heads off with his own sword before her eyes, in order to discourage slackness and disloyalty in a conquered town.

She scarcely breathed for fear of waking him. But after a quarter of an hour he opened his eyes, and said in a loud, brisk voice: 'Those rascals the Chief Justice and the Treasurer are up to something. They've

175

been talking to the judge about the market dues. Let them take care, or I'll put them down and give them fifty each.'

Fanta agreed that the rascals should be put down; and she said that she did not like the Waziri's looks either. He too was up to something.

'He, the old rascal—he wouldn't dare anything. He owes everything to me. That's why I chose a guttersnipe for Waziri. He depends on me and so I can depend on him. Why, if I was to be lost'—using the polite word for death—'the Waziri would be ruined. He knows that well enough.'

'But they say that Salé——'

'Salé—that woman-man! Ah! he's nothing. And Aladai, that clerk—he's less than nothing. Eff!'

'Are you going to put them in prison, then?'

Aliu laughed and slapped her big leg. He didn't tell women his secrets. He said only, 'We've settled 'em, Waziri and I. Ah! he's a tortoise for guile, that boy.'

'Yes, lion, but the Master. I don't like that Master, and they've been saying—you know how he's been playing with Akande Tom, who belongs to that nasty bitch Lisbet, the witch.'

'Ha—ha! So I heard. But why not? It shows his sense. Ah! what a lad that Tom is. What shoulders! What a beautiful man! It's good to look at him. A real pagan. And what a soldier he would make! What a chest he has! What strength! That's the kind of man I like. And, do you know, when I was his age I could bite a spear-shaft through. But those were the days of the Bida war—the first one.'

'Everybody knows that you were the greatest war chief in all the Sudan.'

'True, Fanta, I was. I was a good warrior. Those were sweet days. War is a sweet thing. There is nothing so sweet as war. Men of good heart, how they love war! It is good for the blood to fight, to do brave things to make the enemy fly, to triumph over the rascals that would not own your lordship.'

'You are the greatest king that ever ruled in Rimi, and that's the greatest in the world.'

'It's not true, Fanta. No, I am fallen away. The Emir of Kano has five thousand pounds a year, and I have only eight hundred. Those damned Mohammedans have stolen all my greatness.'

'Lion, you are the most famous of kings.'

'Yes, I suppose that is true. My fame is very great. It is known to everybody in the world. But I am fallen away, Fanta, from my greatness. Where are my armies? I had two hundred gunmen when I went to Bida—two hundred of the best gunmen in the Sudan—and now, I have not twenty. Twenty scum not fit to shoot chickens. Many years ago I could have beaten the whites themselves. But could I beat them now?'

'Lord, you could wipe them off the earth if you gave the word. All the people would fight for you.'

'Yes, they would fight for me. We should make a good fight. But would we win the victory. Fanta? No, I doubt it. No, the whites are stronger now. And yet I could have beaten them when they first came to this land. It was only because of the famine that I did not destroy them all. For I had a good army then.' He began to describe his army. He described all the chief captains, and some of the horses, by name; even some of the camels. Soon he was fighting Bida. He related deeds of bravery half a century old, and said, 'Poor man, he was killed. What a pity. Such a big fine young man, like that Tom.' And he mourned over his dead captains as if they had died yesterday. At last Fanta, stroking him, massaging his limbs, had him asleep again. He dozed; she sat with his head on her thigh, soft as a pillow, and felt the triumph of an artist. But suddenly he jumped up and cried, 'What was that?'

'Nothing, my lord. Some horse eating.'

'What time is it? But I've no time to waste here. Where's that boy?'

He called the lantern-boy, staggered away. At the yard gate the spearman was asleep on the ground. He left him to sleep. He was always considerate with anyone that could be called a soldier. Besides, the spearman dawdled and he was in a hurry. He had wasted quite enough time with that old chatterbox Fanta. There was that spout to look at; and the hinges of the great gate; and he had to go over the court cases with the court scribe. This was a good time for court cases, when nobody could interrupt them.

'Where does the court scribe sleep?' he screamed at the boy.

The boy, reeling, half asleep, through a dark hole that he had never seen before, stopped and raised his lantern as if the scribe might be found on the floor. Moans, grunts were heard. Dark, contorted figures about their feet untwisted, stared with eyes like lantern flames, and suddenly started up, disappeared. They fled in all directions, like beetles startled by a flash of light. A sheep dashed itself wildly against mats.

But the Emir had already tottered past. The boy trotted after him with anxious eyes, open mouth. Where did the scribe sleep? But luckily the old man had already forgotten about the scribe. At half-past five o'clock in the morning he was staggering across the flat roof of the highest tower. He had come to look for the defective spout. But now on the roof he was staring at different aspects of the town and pointing them out to the boy. 'That's where old so-and-so had his compound. He was the best bowman in Rimi.'

177

The boy looked on in terror, expecting every moment to see his master tumble into the market-place. But instead he sat down against the low coping and fell asleep. He slept for an hour as the dawn rose; any early riser in the market would have seen his head, like a sleeping bird, in one of the deep embrasures of the tower.

At half-past six he jumped up and waked the boy. 'Go to the Waziri at once and call the council.'

He was impatient. He came tumbling down the enormous steps, each a foot high, with shrill cries. 'Hurry, hurry up! What are you waiting for?'

It seemed to the Emir Aliu that every day he had more to do, and less time to do it in. And who could do it for him? Who had his experience? Who could do anything properly? Nobody. All depended upon him.

The council was assembled ten minutes before the Emir's coming, at six. This was not the stale artifice of a parvenu lord, but accident. The old man had gone out to see a new kid, born that night, and stayed to make sure that the proper *ju-jus* had been summoned and placated to ensure its health and fruitfulness.

Meanwhile the six great officers of State, with nine secretaries and pupils, sat motionless in the great hall, forming a half-moon before the dais and the leopard-skin; wide in the middle, narrow at the ends, where it terminated in the Chief Justice's youngest clerk and the Waziri's kettle-boy. Nobody spoke or moved because the Waziri did not speak or move.

There was a quick, bird-like tapping on the floor, and the Emir appeared from the back of the room with a hop, a stand, and a totter. He was alone; by day he usually ran about alone. He was too impatient for ceremony.

He was dressed still in his singlet and drawers. A few years ago he would never have appeared before his council except in full dress—robes and turban and chin-cloth. But as he grew older he became more impatient of forms; he had other things to do besides dress himself. In the last ten years he had gradually thrown away all the dignities of a chief. This was thought to be a sign of dotage.

The assembly bowed to the earth. Aliu smiled at them and cried 'Children!' This was his usual salutation. He was thirty years older than the oldest of them.

He collapsed on the leopard-skin and said again 'Children!' He beamed upon them, blinking his eyes.

They bowed again and cleared their throats. This was a ceremonial act. It sounded like the scraping of six or seven old dustbins.

'I hear Aladai is coming back,' piped the Emir. 'That will make more trouble. Fool people will make trouble. They know how to talk lies.

178

Now, I have thought how to stop this trouble. I shall say to Salé, 'If you go to Mecca now, and if you stay out of Rimi till the time comes when you are wanted here" '—Akiu never spoke of his death—' "I shall make you Galadima." What do you say to that, my children?'

His voice was full of triumphant satisfaction. The assembly bowed; Waziri, who had been urging this plan for six days, again cleared his throat, and, rolling slowly from side to side on his hams, said, 'That seems to me a very excellent plan. A very wise and clever thing.'

'Unless that rascal didn't keep his word,' said the Emir. 'I know these yellow men.'

'But if all of us know your will.'

The Emir shook his head. 'It's the Bridegroom who's got to do it.'

The Bridegroom was Burwash's politer nickname. It referred to his smiles, to his charming manner, and also to something of fatuity in the man. In Hausaland the word 'bridegroom' has much derision in it.

The Emir should not have used a nickname in council. It caused pain to the Chief Justice, who was a gentleman of the old school.

'You mean, he shall keep Salé out?'

'We shall tell him of the bargain. Salé shall put his word to it. Then, if he comes, the Bridegroom will know he is a rascal. Is that good, judge?'

The Chief Justice answered in a gentle and sad voice, 'The white judges are strict that faith should be kept. But they change often. I am told this great judge Burwash desires a greater position. He will go from Rimi. The new judge will not know us or our difficulties.'

The Waziri said sharply and contemptuously, 'We can tell him.'

'We can,' said the Emir. 'Besides, there's nothing else to do. For, thanks to these two bastards and liars who have bewitched our people, we'll have a war if we do not choose one or other.'

After this, the matter was quickly settled. The Waziri was sent to find Salé and bring him to the council. To do this the Waziri left the palace, for Salé was strictly forbidden the town and palace, and he had slipped away, hours before, to his farm.

The Emir went to rest before his State visit to the Residency. Four men, shouting and wincing, brought out the black stallion from his private stable. His screams of rage could be heard in the market-place. He was full of corn, and his exercise was chiefly calabash-biting, groom-kicking, fence-eating. This was at half-past six.

XVII

Burwash liked to spend the three hours between six and nine in quiet, working at his letters and reports, which cost him much thought and trouble. He was a slow composer in English, and, moreover, a very cautious one. Like a bad chess player, he spent a long time in anxious meditation over the simplest moves. The reason was that he had been greatly impressed by the disastrous consequences arising from a single bad move—such as a word too much, or an unguarded admission. He never forgot that the most promising and heartfelt ambition of his early years in the Service—to realign his divisional boundary, and restore to several thousand starving farmers their ancestral village lands, cut off by the mistake of a map—had been frustrated by the phrase, 'to all intents and purposes,' which he had thrown in simply to make weight. He had written, 'To all intents and purposes the man Gani's evidence is the same as the witnesses on the other side'—meaning that Gani could be depended on. But the redoubtable Cock Jarvis, his opponent across the river, fighting on the behalf of *his* farmers, had answered to the adjudicating Resident: 'The intents and purposes of the man Gani, mentioned by my esteemed colleague Mr. Burwash, are no doubt the same with those of his other witnesses—to collar someone else's property for the purpose of increasing his annual drunk from six months to twelve.'

Experience, therefore, had convinced the Resident that, in a world where it is impossible for the rulers to have personal contact with the ruled, and government must willy-nilly depend chiefly for its data on reports and discussions by letter, the wording of reports and letters is an important matter. Real things—the lives, happiness, destinies of living people—depended quite as much on the literary skill as on the political ability of an officer. For what was the good of a sound case if you could not present it?

He had hoped that a scholar like Fisk would give him useful help, but up to the present he had been disappointed. His efforts to instruct the young man without hurting his feelings (for he did not like to hurt anyone's feelings) added greatly to his difficulties.

At this time in the morning there was no sound or movement to be detected anywhere. The two daroa-trees in front of the office were as stiff as toys, the gowns of the two messengers squatting against the wall in the verandah had not changed a fold for half an hour. The police orderly was asleep on his back. His fez stood upright on the floor, behind his shaved skull, like a dark-blue flower-pot. But, though his mouth was open, he did not snore, and the fly which was hovering over the crater of the fez danced on the still air without a sound.

Burwash, at his table, was smoking his first pipe over the mail, stacked in its file baskets on either hand. The low beam of the sun, coming in at the window, fell on his left cheek, and put a halo round his head. He looked his handsomest in the side-light, as Fisk, now and then, glancing up from his work in the corner, never failed to notice. But he was also looking worried. He laid down the paper he was reading, and studied it with the most anxious attention.

'This draft of yours about the town planning,' he said, at last. 'You write: "I can't find the old letters about Joseph Makurdi's claim to this site, as the files have been eaten by ants." ' He shook his head, 'I'm afraid they won't like that.'

'But I showed you the state of the files, sir.'

'Oh, quite. It's not that. It's just the way it's put. I'm afraid it will upset them at Kaduna. They'll probably answer that in that case Makurdi had better be left where he is, and give us a rap over the knuckles about the state of the provincial files. We don't want to throw away the position at this stage.'

'Perhaps I'd better leave out the ants, and say "disappeared." '

'No, no. "Disappeared" would be suicidal. What about this?— H'm—"Referring to Joseph Makurdi's claim—there is—appears to be—a breach in the correspondence—or gap—that's it. Gap in the correspondence. This has produced an impasse which may prove difficult to surmount." '

Fisk opened his mouth to say that impasses were not surmounted, but, seeing his master's look of quiet satisfaction, closed it again. Situation, impasse, he noticed, were highly official words, and favourites of Burwash.

For instance, Burwash had corrected a letter of his: 'The trade situation is bad, and is getting worse,' to, 'The trade situation is un-favourable, and shows signs of further deterioration, due to the new railway.'

'I think that does it,' said the Resident, smiling with the pleasure of an artist. ' "Gap in the correspondence" is much better than "ants." We must get rid of the idea that we've actually lost anything—that's what the Secretary won't stand at any price—no, no, "disappeared" would be suicidal. What about this?—H'm—"The present situation in regard to Joseph Makurdi's claim is complicated by a gap in the correspondence relating to the original application"—or hiatus—yes, "hiatus in the correspondence. This has produced an impasse which may prove difficult to surmount." '

He put it in the basket marked 'Clerk,' and took up another paper. 'Ah, yes, Mister Aladai again. More of his friends complaining against the Waziri. You'd better enquire about that, Fisk. I'm sorry, I know you've had a lot of trouble with Aladai's friends, but we must take notice of complaints. In fact'—glancing at Fisk over his spectacles, which meant that he was conveying instruction—'the only safe rule is, *all* complaints must be noticed—even the obviously factious. People who make factious complaints are just the ones to make the worst trouble if they are disregarded. It's the type. So be careful of that one.'

He took another paper from his file, and he was once more deeply concerned, frowning, puffing clouds of smoke: 'You say here—"The old mosque is already in ruins, and the Limam states that he would be glad to accept twenty pounds compensation in addition to the new site." That's the most tricky part of the whole business—they hate anything like a religious question, and I don't like "old mosque" either. It will bring Lepper down on us to know if we are proposing to destroy a local antiquity.'

'Well, sir, you know it's only a heap of mud.'

'It's a pretty old heap, though.' Burwash did not like to hear anything old and honourable, even if it was only a tumbledown house of rain-washed clay, described as a heap of mud. His chivalrous instinct to defend the weak, his British leaning for giving every creature, of any kind of clay, even pure clay, its freedom to exist and go about its own affairs, stirred at once. 'I shouldn't be surprised if the mosque was really two hundred years old, as they say it is—that takes you back a long way.'

'I thought, by what you said yesterday——'

'Oh, yes, I'm afraid it's got to be shifted, but we mustn't rouse old Lepper. What old Wood did, I remember, in a similar case——'

It was at this moment that the Waziri, Salé, and his forty horsemen arrived in the compound. The messengers, the orderly, sprang to their feet, the clerks took their noses out of the file-boxes in which they were dozing, and Burwash hastily put on a neck-tie and struggled into his coat.

The Waziri entered. He had brought news. The Emir had appointed Salé dan Seriki, Galadima Rimi. Burwash had met Salé before. He greeted him politely, congratulated him on his appointment, and made a little speech explaining that it did not, however, fix the succession until the governor and the King of England had approved it. But he had no doubt that Salé, if appointed, would be an excellent chief. Then he made another little speech on the duties of a just and progressive ruler, and sent his greetings to his friend the Emir. At the last minute he recollected something he had heard from Sangster, and said, 'I hear you are going to Mecca—that is a great journey.'

Salé smiled, but said nothing. The Waziri answered for him. No, it was spoken of. But now the Galadima must stay in Rimi, to learn his work.

Burwash warmly approved this plan, and dismissed the party, which at once galloped away down the hill. As he took off his coat and neck-tie again, he said to Fisk, 'I wish they could learn to give me this hour free for real work. But I suppose they're rather relieved about this appointment. I must say it's a good thing. It doesn't commit us, and it will stop all this agitation in the town.

'I think we managed rather well, don't you? It seems that the Emir can sometimes take advice.'

Fisk, much impressed by the Resident's success in this menacing problem, answered, 'You certainly know how to manage them, sir.'

'I won't say that,' said Burwash, who was not a conceited man. 'But sometimes I am lucky in the way a situation develops.'

The Waziri's plan was going well. He had not been alarmed by Burwash's reminder that the Emir's choice needed confirmation. He had expected it. But he knew that governors did not set aside a Galadima who had nothing definite against him, and who was supported by a strong party in the State.

He now returned to the town, with Salé, in order to gather that party, and to raise a popular cry for the Emir's removal.

He did not trust Aliu so long as he was Emir and and alive. He knew the force and evil of the old warrior, who had turned so many defeats into victories. The Emir was a pagan. Although three-quarters of the whole Rimi population were pagans, and less than a third were Mohammedans, he knew that he could raise a cry that would seem irresistible. A mob of one per cent. was more than was required to speak the voice of the people.

It was true that Aladai had a much bigger following. The Waziri had made overtures to the boy a week before. But Aladai had refused to see him, and he had said since, in public, that the palace gang ought to be hanged.

That was why the Waziri had joined Salé.

Salé's followers in the countryside had been gathering for the last three days—the streets were crowded with them when he came in at the main gate with the Master of the Horse and most of the palace guard riding behind him. His reception was even noisier than Aladai's. It had been better managed.

The dual government of Nigeria is leaky at both ends. The Waziri had stopped up the palace end, but he could not stop up the office. Three of Burwash's clerks were members of Mr. Coker's chapel. Two of his messengers were ardent supporters of Aladai, and the wife of the police orderly was Elizabeth Aladai's club organizer in the barracks. Five minutes before Burwash had finished his complimentary and instructive speech to Salé, on the ideal of the just and progressive government, two different messengers had reached Makurdi's. Elizabeth was in her *ju-ju* house, and Coker in his chapel, before Salé had mounted his horse outside the provincial office.

Meanwhile the Emir was sitting in his private room, or cell, opening from the back of the hall, where his State robes were kept in tin boxes and servants' trunks. There was a bed here, a bare frame without clothes; a few *ju-ju* images, whips, a Koran; spears and guns, odd objects used in court cases or impounded from convicts. The room had a very strong and complex smell, but one that always pleased and soothed the old man with the sensation of activity. The room was his office.

He sat down on his bed, and reflected upon his cleverness in solving the problem of the succession. He thought: 'Aha, my children! You didn't think of that. It took Aliu to think of that.'

Opening his toothless mouth, still smiling with pride, he uttered a scream, which meant, 'I'm here when that blackguard the Waziri comes back from the bush.'

Burwash had barely sat down again when a messenger came panting from Sangster.

'D.O. Rimi pagans to Resident.

'1. Duchi pagans report that the man Aladai is returning to Rimi and will land at the Hides Wharf about ten o'clock.

'2. Large crowds are assembling to meet him and I understand there is grave danger of a clash with Salé's people.

'3. Suggest landing should be prevented, and wharf cleared. Police action will be required in any case to prevent a breach of the peace.

'B. C. SANGSTER,
'D.O. Rimi Pagan Div.'

Scrawled at the bottom in pencil was this note: 'Large party pagans just arrived but waiting river bank. Im'te action nec'ry.'

'H'm, h'm,' said the Resident, a trifle startled, and even piqued, by this postscript. He did not like to be hurried by anybody.

He looked at the messenger over his office spectacles, and said, 'Well, I suppose if Sangster wants the police——' He wrote across Sangster's neat ladylike script his own bold words, 'I can see no objection. This will do for Rackham,' read it over twice, and added, before the first sentence, 'On the information available'; once more read over the amended letter, improved the capital I, and slowly, as with reluctance, handed the paper to the messenger, who, with joyful cries of relief and gratitude, shot from the office, scrambled into his saddle, and galloped recklessly away down the hill.

'There seems to be a little excitement down below,' the Resident said then, smiling at Fisk. 'Where were we?—Yes, about the mosque. Now, how about this? "The other buildings near the market-place, including those formerly in use by the Limam, could be removed for a total compensation of twenty pounds"; or, better still'—making an alteration with his pencil—' "The remainder of the buildings in the neighbourhood of the market-place——" '

'There aren't any others there, sir. The mosque stands by itself since the fire.'

'Yes, but we don't want to rub it in, and the secretariat *may* know what a Limam is. Besides, you have to consider style in these things. It's a funny thing that I should be the one to consider style. But, of course, you were a classical man, weren't you? Nevertheless style matters a lot in this job—I found that out pretty soon when I first—— Hullo! What do you want?'

One of the messengers was bobbing up and down at the door, with the expression of a frightened watchdog.

'Zaki—the people from the town—many people.'

Burwash stood to look out of the window. He continued to stare for a moment, then, with a peculiar expression at once bland and innocent, walked out to the stoop. The whole brown hillside below the town was peppered with black specks slowly moving downwards, and on the road ascending the station hill there was a long crowd, like a thick black caterpillar. Hundreds of black feet could be seen in rapid motion, but the thing itself seemed to advance with labour, slowly coiling itself past each twist of the road. Faint shouts could be heard, and in the town a drum began to beat a fierce lively air.

The Resident recovered quickly from the first shock of surprise. He did not waste time. He turned to Fisk: 'This looks serious—I'd no idea the whole town was coming out—those police must be stopped. Go at once to Sangster, as fast as you can—take my pony—or, better'—he remembered that Fisk was not horseman enough to ride without stirrups, and that his leathers would need adjustment—'you go to Rackham and I'll go to Sangster.' By this time the big man had his foot in the stirrup, and the horse-boy was gripping the bridle in one hand and the off-side leather in the other. 'You know what I mean.' He was speaking over his shoulders, while Fisk, with his hat on, stood, in the very act of going, on one leg, facing downhill. 'Mustn't do anything— keep still, you brute—inflame passions.' Burwash, boy, and the restless game little chestnut, wild to be off, were now skipping about together in a kind of dance. Burwash's last instructions were punctuated by

185

gigantic hops. 'But mind—let him—understand—no wish dictate—not time—formalities—trust you—consider situation—needs—— Damn you; all right—leggo.' He swung up his leg, and was off at a gallop before his foot had crossed the brute's croup. His last shout, flung over his shoulder, was something about apologies to Sangster.

The D.O. pagans Rimi office, once the rest-house, a long narrow mud house with a very high-peaked thatch, of Sangster's own design, was surrounded by a huge crowd, standing fifty deep in a great semi-circle. Their eyes and open mouths were directed towards Sangster himself, who stood in the centre, with his hands in his pockets and his battered old Cawnpore over one ear. This pose showed the man's hollow face and huge Voltairean nose to great advantage. He was speaking, his small pursed mouth moved, but Burwash, on the other side of the crowd, could not hear a word. Sangster never troubled to shout, and rarely even to speak loudly.

Burwash had to push his way through the thick silent crowd, which did not oppose him except by its weight and immobility. The people stood like tree-trunks, all their faculties were concentrated in their ears and eyes—their very jaw muscles, for lack of nervous reinforcement, could not hold up their burdens.

Some were turning their heads this way and that, as if to find out if one ear could hear any better than the other; one impatient angry voice, as the Resident pushed forward, snapped in Rimi, 'Be quiet, there.'

'Just as you like, friends.' Sangster's mild tones reached him now. 'If you hold up the town-planning scheme that you don't like, I shall have to drop the boundary division which you want so much. And it's no good, you know, making all this palaver. The town-planning scheme is to be carried out, every bit of it. And it surprises me very much that you oppose it, because it is a very good scheme, devised by the great judge, Burwash, entirely for your own profit and advantage. I think, myself, that only fools or blackguards could oppose this excellent plan. That's all. Except that if you waste any more of my time with rotten appeals I'll pull down the whole town. Good morning, sir. Come and have breakfast.'

He smiled, but his blue eyes had a certain expression reserved for the Resident and his staff, even for his orderly. It meant, as Burwash knew very well, 'What wangling business is he about now?'

Burwash explained that he had countermanded the police, as, owing to the unexpected development of the situation, he considered that any sudden provocation might be dangerous. Meanwhile he hoped Sangster would watch developments, and he thought that the crowds did not intend to be troublesome or they wouldn't have brought out the women.

186

Sangster did not answer, but, fixing his little blue eyes on the Resident, he nodded twice, and then suddenly said to the crowd, 'Make way, there, for the great judge—you bandy-legged baboons.'

They gave way hastily. Burwash walked to his pony and rode off. Sangster's rudeness, the rudeness of a bush officer, a poor devil who would certainly stick in the outer provinces for all his service, did not wound him in the least. He was mildly sorry for the man.

XVIII

RACKHAM was one of those men who seem to have a spring in them, always wound up, and ready to go off at the lightest touch. His wit was like that, and his work. Within five minutes of getting the Resident's note he was walking up and down the police lines, in full uniform, waiting for the men. The sight of him, though he did not look at them, and though it was the sergeant who bawled, 'Quick! Quick!' made them quick. In another five minutes they were on the river road, fully equipped, though not in parade neatness. They were on the Hides Wharf, and Rackham was explaining the situation to Honeywood when the messenger came rushing through the crowd with Fisk's note.

The crowd was not yet thick in this part of the station, half a mile from the town. It was in groups, each apparently homogeneous and not closely attached to the others. One or two parties were obviously down-river boys. They wore shirts and trousers, cloth caps. Another seemed to be Christians, listening to a preacher. A group of young Rimi women were squatting together on the roadside, screaming and moving their bright heads, in blue, green, and red handkerchiefs.

They did not look dangerous to a stranger; but to Rackham, who saw their eyes roll sidelong at the police, who knew that none of them had any business there, and who saw the town gate in the distance pouring out its black stream like soldier ants from an alarmed nest, they meant a first-class row.

He looked at the note, crumpled it, threw it on the ground, said to the messenger, 'Thank you. Tell your master, all right'; and to the sergeant, 'Sergy, we are going back. The judge says he doesn't need the police.' He turned to Honeywood—'I'm sorry about this, but I don't think the stores are in any danger.'

Honeywood, who was pink and damp, looked round at the crowd, and exclaimed, 'Damn it, they'd better not be. I suppose Burwash thinks he needn't worry about a few bloody traders? My clerks swear there's going to be a war.'

187

Rackham was silent. The sergeant and the detachment were ready to march. The sergeant looked at Rackham for orders. Honeywood, taking a few restless steps each way, exclaimed, 'Look here, what do you think, yourself? Those chaps over there in the caps are a well-known longshore gang—every one has a knife.'

'I'm sorry, Dick, but——'

'The fact is, of course, that Burwash would see any of us cut up rather than get in the wrong with black brother. Can you understand it, Jerry?' Honeywood stopped and gazed at him in amazement. 'A white man—I suppose he is a white man?—just selling us to a performing ape like—it's not even a decent ape—a bloody swollen-headed monkeyfied——'

The sergeant marched up to Rackham, stamped his foot to attention, slapped his carbine-butt, and stood saluting, with his chest at its major dimension. He wanted to get back to breakfast and the safe and comfortable barracks. Rackham said, 'All right, Sergy—you take 'em back. And keep every man and woman in barracks until further orders.'

The detachment marched off. Rackham said to Honeywood, 'I'll come in, if you don't mind.'

Honeywood was delighted. He caught Rackham's arm. 'Come to breakfast. That's splendid.'

'I suppose it is nearly breakfast-time.'

'Go upstairs, Judy's up, I think. I'm just popping into the store for a minute.'

Rackham, however, followed him into the store. He did not know why he had stayed with Honeywood, or why he now stuck to him. The Hides Wharf suddenly had a strong attraction for him, and though he knew quite well, by his jumping nerves, that it was a dangerous attraction, he gave way to it. He had been indulging in the same manner for the last four days—ever since his little row with Judy about the Scotch club. For instance, he had spent all these evenings with Honeywood and his chaps, as he called them, at the store, discussing Aladai. When Honeywood called Aladai a performing ape, or a monkeyfied Bolshie, he was using Rackham's own words. But Rackham knew perfectly well that Aladai was worth six Honeywoods, both as a man and an intelligence; he was worth an infinity of Honeywoods, because Honeywood was a robot, a set of reactions, a creature ruled entirely by prejudice and a mass of contradictory impulses and inhibitions, which he called his opinions, and thought of as his character. He was a wooden man danced on strings; and anyone could make him kick. The word Bolshie, for instance, caused one reaction—not a mental, but a nervous, reaction —and the word nigger caused another.

His brain did not seek to judge and know; it existed to scheme defence and satisfaction for the beasts and parasites lodged in the zoo of his character. His will was the servant of nature, the crocodile in the swamp. He had no freedom. He was not a living soul, but a tumour—something pushed up by the blind force of life; as innocent as an imbecile, as a fungus that eats the face of a corpse.

To Rackham, people like Honeywood were more disgusting than to a tolerant and patient Englishman, for he loathed his stupidity. He was a dull fungus. He had not even colour or interest as a curiosity. Millions like him spawned every day in the national mushroom-beds of the world.

But for four days he had spent almost all his spare time with Honeywood, living his kind of life, drinking too much, and listening to a stream of senseless remarks on every possible subject.

The station had noticed this change in him. A station notices a change of mood—a liver attack of three hours' duration will cause tactfulness at two days' clubs. Rubin had said to him: 'He's a good chap, Honeywood—I—like him.'

This was very severe from Rubin, for whom the world was divided into damn nice fellows, first-class lads, real Christians, and real gentlemen (these two titles entirely reserved for blacks or the lower order), people you could trust anywhere (black and white, of a slightly inferior range; murderers, ex-thieves, grooms, bookies, etc.), and lastly, at the very bottom of the bucket, good chaps, whom, after a very slight pause, he liked.

But, in case he had injured Rackham's affection, he added at once, 'What a first-class girl the sister is—a real peach too. Of course, I'm not comparing her with Miss Coote.' This meant, 'Of course, I know why you're going with the man—it's because you're smitten by the young sister—and I can understand it in a young ass like you; but don't forget the fact that Miss Coote is a pretty good proposition, especially for a young ass like you.'

Rackham had answered that he didn't agree; Miss Honeywood had many serious faults. She was not only sticky in talk, but a bit of a prig too—much too girls'-public-school for his taste. Then he went away to drink gin and It. with Dick and Prince, and discuss for three hours the criminal policy of the mission in encouraging niggers to be impudent, and so on. Honeywood and Prince always attacked the Resident and the Government, but Rackham did not join in to this part of the entertainment. He only signified, by silence, that he agreed with it.

Now, again, he was in the store, perched on a box behind the counter, with a gin beside him, and Honeywood saying, 'I'm going to send Dryas home. I told her I would if she insisted on this trip.'

'It wasn't her fault that that ape joined in.'

'She asked him.'

'That lunatic Mrs. Vowls made her do it.'

'Don't tell me. You can't make Dryas do things. I've tried. She's as obstinate as a blind mule. She just took it into her head, because she'd made a fool of herself at the club; she was jolly well going to carry it through and justify herself.'

Rackham refrained from saying, 'What nonsense!' It was not worth contradicting a man who believed what suited his temper.

'But *dancing* with him!' said Honeywood, in a kind of explosion. 'That's a bloody lie! It's the kind of bloody lie these apes would invent about a white woman!'

Rackham did not believe that casual traders, gossiping up and down the river, would invent such a lie. It was too small. But he wanted to believe it. He had been adrift now for some days; carried about by various currents; and his nature did not like muddle.

He sipped his gin, and thought of the girl's serene and joyful face, in which the joy, the enjoyment of everything about her, seemed to be just restrained from breaking into smiles, exclamations, by an acquired dignity; and her strong round body, full of the power of joy; her strong arms and legs, adept in the joy of their play. And then he thought of her in Aladai's arms.

Rackham himself did not enquire why he wanted to feel hatred, but as he sat idle, with the gin in his hand, he allowed it to mount in him. It was strong and lively, full of purpose, regenerative, making a new man of him—a new kind of man.

The store was an oblong building of tin, forty feet long, fifteen high, with a hard earth floor. It was dark and dirty, and stuffy with the metallic smell of cheap clay-filled cotton, cheap soap, the hot stench of raw hides. The counter ran the full length of the floor. Behind it, in pigeon-holes and piled boxes, the stack of goods walled it almost to the roof. In front, two upriver traders were arguing with Prince over a roll of skins from Borgu.

The skins were still on the scales. The weight was agreed. But Prince was objecting to their quality. He kicked them scornfully with his slippered foot. They were from the Borgu cattle road, he said—from beasts that had died at the roadside. They were poor stuff.

The traders, two old Hausas in gowns, waved their hands, called on Allah; the beasts had been slaughtered for meat—the finest beasts in the herd.

An old pagan came in with a single goat-skin over his arm. He stopped at the door, looked suspiciously about him, scratching his left buttock. He wore only a banty and two *ju-jus* tied to his right arm. His head was old, wrinkled, and dry, but his body was strong and fresh.

A black clerk called him to the counter. He started, strutted forward with an air, saying in Rimi, 'I was just passing, that's all. I don't want to do business. But, say, do you buy skins here?'

The clerk, used to this preamble from the Rimi, pulled the skin out of his hands, and threw it on the counter. His heavy-lidded eyes, his flared nostrils and protruding lips expressed a degree of contempt impossible to European features. He drawled, 'What's this?'

The pagan gave a loud whinny of laughter, then suddenly became serious and indignant. He snatched at the skin: 'That's enough. I'm off. Makurdi will give me two shillings for a skin like that.'

But, though he snatched at the skin, he did not snatch it away. He had expected the clerk to keep hold of the skin. The clerk did not do so, and, while he turned listlessly away, the skin moved very slowly towards its owner.

'Good-bye,' said the pagan.

'Good-bye,' said the clerk.

The pagan burst out: 'Swindler, thief—I know you ones in the white man's store. I'm going to Makurdi.'

Unfortunately Makurdi paid the lowest prices, and gave the worst goods, on the waterfront. He dealt only in the worst. But the skin was a good one—unusually thick, and free from holes and thin places.

The clerk had taken down a box of handkerchiefs, which he now began to fold and sort. The pagan's eyes could not leave the box. Probably he was dealing for some lady-love. Probably the clerk knew it—he knew a great deal about his customers.

'What rubbish is that?' said the pagan. 'That's for the market women. They'll take any rubbish in the town.'

The clerk continued to fold and sort. Prince struck a bargain with his Hausas, who were taking their price in cloth. A clerk was measuring out the cotton, the cheapest cloth, half filling, while they lamented their bargain. It was probably a good one. Prince was no match for the Hausas.

A whole family party—husband, two wives, or wife and sister, three children—had come in with sheepskins. Prince wearily leant against the upright iron post of his scales and lit a cigarette. He was a long-necked pale youth, who wore for morning dress a dirty grey shirt and dirtier flannel trousers. He had become dirty as soon as he reached the store, straight from some Midland town, with a grant for a dinner-jacket.

MacNeil was not dirty, and Honeywood was a dandy. But for Prince the correct dress for a tropical adventurer was rags, or at least dirt. Even his hat was a ruin, though it could not have been more than three months old.

He looked with hollow-eyed disgust at the black family, with the weariness of the exile. In fact, he was thrilled to be an exile instead of a shop assistant in Manchester, and his eyes had always been hollow. The romantic pallor of his cheeks was, however, new. Partly dirt, partly lack of soap and exercise, partly too much exile's compulsory gin, had produced it in the last six weeks. He was delighted with the black family, and felt like Stanley at the Congo while he stood before them. But it was the proper thing for an exile to be sick of niggers, and to hate the country.

'This bloody country,' Dick was saying, 'is going rotten with sentimentalism. I'm just about sick of it. When an ape like Aladai——'

A crash against the side of the store took him to the verandah. The store verandah was not raised. It was simply a part of the hard earth in front of the store, railed off and covered by a roof. Honeywood was heard shouting angrily, and came back more flushed, damp, flustered. 'Some b——r's head,' he said. 'I wish he'd cracked it.' He came up to the counter, hitched himself upon it, sipped his gin, and gave a heavy sigh. Then he said fiercely, 'If they do any damage here, I'll make you people pay! It's up to you, by God it is!'

'Up to Mr. Aladai now,' said Rackham.

Dick Honeywood's blue eyes popped again in angry amazement. 'By Christ, yes! That's it! Think of it—that monkeyfied——' And he added, wondering, 'D'you think Burwash wants him to get the job?'

'God knows!'

'It will finish this place if he does—finish Nigeria—finish the bloody Empire. Once you get that type——'

Prince turned his head from the scales, and put in, 'Look at Inja'; but added, with weary disgust, 'But they haven't the sense—— Now then, mammy, hurry up with your stuff. Though what you expect to get for it——'

Judy came in, and said that breakfast was ready. She had red swollen eyes, and Rackham did not look at her. But, seeing him, she said, in a voice of delight, 'Hullo, Jerry!' Surprise had caused her to forget that she was wretched about Jerry.

'They never have the sense,' Honeywood said, in his tone of astonished indignation. 'All your blasted politicals are the same. Selling out to Gandhi in India and your Aladai here—what I can't see is, how they think it's going to pay them.'

'They don't think, they get pushed,' said Rackham.

'What pushes them?'

'Chiefly funk.'

Judy was standing away with tightly-closed lips. She had sworn that she would not fight again with Jerry about this ridiculous question. What did it matter? What good could she do? And perhaps she had feared, sometimes, that another quarrel with Jerry would make it impossible for them to be happy together at any time. Their memories of each other would be spoilt.

'Funk of that baboon!' said Honeywood savagely.

'It seems funny,' Rackham agreed.

Judy had turned very white, so that her eyes looked still more red. She said suddenly, in a mild thoughtful voice, 'Oh, but do you think he's like Gandhi, Jerry?'

'I haven't gone into it.'

'I should have said that Gandhi was a regular mystic. He goes by the inner light, and the inner light tells him that the holy life is like the life he first saw in his village as a little baby—the life of an Indian village. He wants to go back to that and knock out everything that stands in the way, including motor cars and machinery. But Aladai's quite a modern young man—I mean, a sensible one. He's not a bit mystical—not even a mystical Communist or Socialist. In fact, I'm sure all that kind of mystical people would rather despise him, because he wants so little—and such reasonable things.'

'I know what he wants.'

'Do you, Jerry, how?'

'We've got four of his speeches in the office.'

'I'd like to see them.'

'They're the ordinary Socialist type. Give me the job of boss, and I'll make everybody happy ever after. Slogans for the sheep-market.'

'He's not a sloganeer. Not a bit of one.'

'You know he's been dancing with her,' said Rackham suddenly.

Judy looked at him with cool surprise, which made him colour. She said, 'Mrs. Pratt had some story.'

'They were seen at Duchi—before the whole village.'

'What's it matter?'

'What's it matter?' said Honeywood. 'Do you realize——?'

'You danced with one of the Blackbird girls, you told me so.'

'Well, that was—well—in London—after all.' Honeywood was taken aback.

'What's the difference?'

'All the difference,' said Rackham briefly, coming to the rescue.

Judy, who knew that there was a difference, shifted her ground. 'I don't believe it, anyhow. And I'm sure he's treated Dryas like a princess. I know him pretty well, and he's always been most respectful. Rather too much so. He thinks she's a kind of angel. That's the terrible mistake you're making about Aladai. He's most frightfully anxious to do the right thing and to be appreciated. He's just pathetically ready to take advice, and he really does know something about the position too. He's been thinking about it ever since he was a boy. I know he's got rather romantic ideas—about the duty of a king and about freedom and education—but he doesn't use slogans.'

'You wouldn't call "Free Trade for Rimi" a slogan?'

'It's only about market dues—and you know the dues are too high.'

'How do you know?'

'You make me tired, Judy,' said Honeywood. 'You women treat politics as a game, but it's not a game to us. It's our lives.'

'What Mr. Aladai wanted was a kick up behind,' said Prince, from the scales. 'About a week ago.

'He'll get it before he lives much longer,' said Honeywood.

'Is that politics?' Judy asked.

Dick flushed. He hated this woman, whom he blamed for Dryas's adventure with Aladai. He knew that she was not responsible, but he blamed her all the more vehemently on that account. He hated her also for being more intelligent than himself—more unselfish. He ignored her now because he did not know how to retreat, but he said, 'There's only one thing a dirty swine like that understands—and it would be worth five pounds to let him have it. It would be a public service.'

'Meanwhile breakfast's ready,' said Judy. 'Your breakfast. I want to do some shopping.' She went to the counter, and placed herself beside the pagan, who was examining handkerchiefs with a disgusted face, muttering, 'Makurdi's, that's the place.'

Honeywood and Prince, waiting for Rackham at the door, saw that Judy was speaking to him and went out.

Judy said, 'You don't really believe that kind of thing, Jerry?'

'What's it matter if I do?' said Rackham, hopping over the counter with his usual neatness.

'I think it does matter.'

'I'm a Tory.'

'But Dick isn't. He doesn't believe in anything at all—even traditions. I'm a Tory myself, with people like Mrs. Vowls and Mr. Coker.'

'Who's he—the yellow friend?'

Judy turned white and came up to Rackham. Disregarding clerks and pagan with the unconscious arrogance of a white, an aristocrat among slaves, she took him by the lapels, and said, 'My darling Jerry, what's wrong—what's wrong with you? If it's the girl, I don't mind so much——' She choked, and tears could be seen in her lower lids.

Rackham's face assumed an odd expression. He said, 'That's all right—it's not the girl, and it's not that man, either. I'm going up the hill. I'd better not see him, I suppose.'

'I'm sorry, but I can't bear—you to be like Dick—and you aren't— you aren't—not the slightest bit——'

He kissed her, and patted her shoulder. 'I'm not going to be. All over. Go and put your eyes in cold water.'

His kiss did not help her to control herself. He took her by the arm, and led her out of the side door, which opened direct, by three steps, upon the back verandah of the bungalow.

He was glad to get her upstairs and leave her there, so that he could return to the store and be alone. He walked up and down impatiently.

A boy came to say that his breakfast was going cold, and he followed him like a saviour.

XIX

An hour later, when the town drums were beating a war song, and the Hides bungalow, all the stores and houses on the waterside, were completely surrounded by Aladai's followers, carrying clubs, Sangster returned from breakfast to his office. It was empty. Messengers, clients, even the clerk, had disappeared.

Sangster was putting his head into the clerk's office and reflecting, 'This looks like a real war,' when he heard a quick step behind him, and turned. Fisk, in full uniform, fire-new, was stepping smartly down the river road.

'Good morning, sir.' He saluted Sangster.

'Don't call me "sir." I'm not the Resident. And where are you off to?'

'I was going down to intercept that chap Aladai.'

'A nice scheme. Intercept.'

Sangster looked sharply at the boy to see if he was using the word with any sarcastic overtone. But he answered with the same cool, brisk air, 'The idea is to turn him back to the mission.'

'You can try. Don't get killed.'

'No, sir'—with a smile; and then, quickly, 'I beg your pardon.' He took off his hat and marched on.

'These new lot are very polite,' Sangster grumbled. He tried not to like Fisk; for it was, he felt, a religious duty to hate everything that belonged to the Resident.

Fisk was in the highest spirits. It was the first time that he had been sent out on an independent commission, and he knew that it was an important one. Burwash had said, 'You'll have to keep all your wits about you.'

At this time the mob had not reached the top of the station hill or the doctor's compound, which at Rimi is opposite the station landing; the only part of it yet in sight from the south slope was a thick column advancing along the riverside to Fisk's left, and the crowd round the stores.

The river under the nine o'clock sun had shadows behind its ripples, shading it with green strokes which relieved the sight; but close in to the shore, where the slack water reflected a broad sheet of light, it made the eyes blink, and ate into the outline of the stores and bungalows, so that their black edges seemed to be corroded by a fiery acid. In this dazzling sheet of flame three native boats were moving slowly towards the bank; but Fisk, though he screwed up his eyes, could not distinguish their particulars; only that one was a big trader with a mast; the others, dug-outs.

In two minutes he was involved with the crowd: bush pagans with spears, gazing towards the boats and chattering among themselves like starlings. It was plain that they feared to penetrate further into the station. But now he was among townsmen, also with spears, fishermen with clubs, and everywhere groups of women, standing about with their heads, or at least their shoulders, turned inwards; pressed together in excited clusters.

This part of the crowd was noisy and excited. There was an incessant shouting as men here and there—but so often that there were always three or four at any moment—threw out their arms and uttered yells. Some of these yells were directed against himself. One man seemed to threaten him with a spear. But he paid no attention. He did not suppose himself to be in any danger. He had the immense courage of inexperience and a limited imagination.

He was now caught in the stream pouring between the store buildings. The people crushed in upon him without ceremony. He could hear his orderly crying out, and felt himself lifted off his feet. A woman in front, being carried backwards, pointed at him and made some joke which she herself laughed at. No one else heard it.

The stream opened suddenly, and he fell, landing on his sun-hat. The orderly, with a terrified face, puckered with fright, picked up the hat and dusted his master's knees. He said, 'We go, sah. Dey fit to kill us—no fit speak to Galadima Aladai. Dey kill us, Master. Dey——'

He answered, 'If you are frightened, Ali, you'd better go home.'

Somebody charged into his back and nearly threw him down. The topee fell over his eyes. He said mildly, 'Damn these people,' meaning the London firm which had provided him with his hat—a hat too small, and boots too tight.

When he had put his hat straight, he was looking at Mrs. Vowls's face, crimson, sweating, which was not more than a foot from his own. She gasped, 'They'll kill us—they'll kill us!'—and then, suddenly, 'We deserve it.' She was idiotic with fear.

'There's no danger,' he assured her, but she did not hear him. She had already turned away and was caught in another eddy. He could see

196

her lips moving; her eyes were staring, and he thought, 'What's she doing out of hospital?'

He was now wedged in another side-rush of the mass; but, working himself about, found himself above the level of the heads in front of him. He was jammed up against the wall of the Hides bungalow. The congestion which held him there was due to a gang of fishermen on the wharf, who were pushing back the mob with the flat of their poles, clearing the wharf.

On his left hand was the wooden rail of the Hides stoop, about a foot above his head. Through the baluster he could see Dick Honeywood and prince sitting in long chairs. A boy was clearing the breakfast-table.

Prince had a glass beside him on the table; Honeywood a coffee-cup.

He heard his name, and looked up. Miss Coote and Rackham were leaning out of the window. They seemed amused by his situation, and Miss Coote offered him a banana. He made comic gestures displaying his helplessness; Rackham answered by turning up his hands and shaking them quickly, in the attitude of the Jew who says, 'It's not in my power. All is in the hands of God.' It was obvious, in fact, that no one could move a yard out of the Hides bungalow.

Fisk tried to push his way forward. The wharf in front was clear except for Makurdi, Elizabeth, and four younger women.

Makurdi was in a complete suit of white linen, in which he resembled numerous bladders of lard well pressed down into a bag too small for them. It was bursting in the back seam. He was crowned by a helmet of French make, like a straight banana cut in half. It was yellow in colour; extremely tall and high, and segmented into broad seams. Its brim was an inconsiderate fringe round the lower edge, like the frill of a lawn sleeve.

Elizabeth was wearing black velvet, many yards in length, and on her head a cloth of gold. She carried a long, thin, white staff in her hand, with which she now and then pointed at the crowd, as if giving directions.

Makurdi rolled to and fro, clasping his short arms, first upon his large behind, then across his stomach. Sometimes he was all dignity; and the next moment the picture of doubt, confusion.

The big trader was now close to the wharf. Aladai could be seen standing on the half-deck. He was wearing the grey suit; the slit in the right breast could be seen. It appeared larger.

Miss Honeywood was sitting in a deck-chair just behind him, with a book open on her knees. She seemed nervous, by her frequent picking up and laying down of the book.

The boat touched the wharf; Aladai said something to Miss Honeywood, now below the level of the wharf, and then stepped ashore. Yells went up from the crowd. They continued for a long time, because those behind the stores, hundreds in number, who could see nothing at all, continued yelling long after Aladai had raised his hand, Elizabeth her staff, Makurdi both his hands, his chin, his stomach, and his heels, in the effort to silence them.

At last the fishermen began to strike with their poles, women shrieked, and silence grew quickly. In half a minute it was complete.

Aladai stepped forward and made a little speech in Rimi. Fisk had already learnt a little Rimi. He carried two little books in his pocket— one for Rimi phrases, one for Hausa—and he wrote down in each ten new words a day.

He heard Aladai say that he had come back to his people and would never leave them again; that he knew their poverty and (something that Fisk had not learnt), and he would cure their sufferings, or (another unknown word). Although the wicked Salé had (unknown) the white judge, he would not succeed, because the people were against him. He, Aladai, would promise them that. They must win. The palace robbers who had (unknown) them would be driven; and no Rimi man or woman would any longer suffer the (unknown) and bad taxes of the (unknown) and thieves who had deceived the Emir Aliu and robbed the people. Let them only be careful to (unknown) and make no trouble, and he would lead them to victory.

Ten minutes' cheering followed before the crowd in front of Fisk, breaking through the guard, weakened by their own enthusiasm, gave him the opportunity to push forward.

The fishermen, seeing him and knowing him, hesitated to thrust him back. The crowd, still yelling in a frenzy of loyal excitement, suddenly saw the little judge, in full uniform, with a police orderly, walk out upon the wharf. He stopped there for a moment to put his hat straight, adjust his tie, pull down his coat, and then made for Aladai.

A woman's voice shrieked, 'He's catching the Galadima.'

This was a fair suspicion. A judge does not put on uniform and take a policeman except to meet a great man or catch a bad one. The woman, living in the back parts of Rimi, had only seen judges performing the latter duty.

Instantly another wilder yell went up, and the fishermen were blown away like grass in front of guns. Fisk felt himself seized as if by an engine of a thousand horse-power, which lifted him like a straw.

Then he was once more on his feet; Makurdi pulling down his coat, gasping apologies. Aladai was driving back the crowd. His attitude was not that of a lion-tamer, but an angry young fish-wife. He shook his fists at them; jumped off the ground with both feet.

The fishermen were pounding heads like corn. The crowd was broken; retreating, all rolling eyes and open slavering mouths, without a word in them.

Aladai turned round, became an English gentleman, and advanced with a solicitous air. Elizabeth, picking up Fisk's hat, made three majestic strides and planted it on his head, back before. At once Aladai whipped it off again, brushed it with his sleeve, replaced it the right way round.

'I'm most frightfully sorry, sir.' He began to bow, but recollected himself and squared his shoulders, thrust his hands into his coat pockets. 'I do hope you're all right.'

'Yes, thanks. Look here, you can't go on with this, you know.'

'I beg your pardon.'

'You don't want to start a riot in the station.'

'No, there won't be a riot in the station. As for the town'—Aladai, though he was speaking to an Englishman, could not help a slight shrug—'It's not my fault if the people object to a stranger being put over them.'

'Salé is not Emir yet. Look here, Mr. Aladai, my orders are to stop your landing.'

Aladai smiled. 'I have landed, you see.'

Fisk was a little put out by the accident to his hat and Elizabeth's contemptuous handling of it. He answered brusquely, 'You *can't* land here, you know. This is a private wharf.'

'I'm awfully sorry. But Miss Honeywood is staying here, and the idea was that I should put her ashore.'

'She can come, of course, but I'm afraid you can't. I'm sorry, but I think you'll agree that it might be in your interests to——'

The crowd was silent, staring with concentration at the scene. Prince's voice, from the bungalow six yards behind, said clearly and loudly, meaning to be overheard, 'D'jever see Consul, the chimp, Mr. Honeywood? He wore trousers too.'

Fisk was startled; he half glanced back at Prince and then continued, still brusque in voice but not so assured in manner: 'We can't allow a political demonstration in the station.'

'But, Mr. Fisk, I didn't arrange this reception. I did not know that Salé had been made Galadima till ten minutes ago, when I arrived. It was my friends in the town who decided to——'

'The Resident understood you were visiting the mission.'

'He wants me to go back to the mission?'

'You will be held responsible for——'

'But, Mr. Fisk, if I go away now, a riot is certain—a dangerous riot, because it may be directed against the officials—British officials. That is the real danger, and that is why I must stay. While I am here, there will be no attack on the station. You can be sure of that.'

Makurdi, revolving slowly round the couple, now on this side, now on that; now grinning as he looked from Fisk's stolid, calm face to

Aladai's animated and confident air, and then suddenly grave, immensely grave, like a statesman at a War Cabinet. Sometimes he moved his lips, bent his head forward, waved his little short arms, so that through a telescope he would have seemed to be giving most eloquent opinions, but in fact he never said anything. He had nothing to say. His dumb show was like the gestures of a child who runs about at a party because the others run; or of a lamb that skips when the others skip and pretends to eat grass when the ewes put down their heads.

'If you have so much influence,' said Fisk, 'why not send the crowd away now?'

'And then you'd let me stay?'

'I'm afraid that's impossible.'

Aladai smiled. 'A general who dismisses his army is not in a good position for a peace conference.'

Fisk could not be bothered with this kind of talk. He thought the reference to generals and armies silly and inflated; typically negro. He answered, 'No, I'm afraid that we couldn't let you stop—not at present. Of course, in a week or two, even a few days, when things have settled down——'

'And Salé is well established as Emir.'

Fisk did not trouble to repeat that Salé was not yet Emir.

'Then we are at loggerheads,' said Aladai, 'for I cannot go. "There is a tide in the affairs of man," you know. But it is for your own sake as well as my own.'

'Consul had a better figure,' said Prince's voice. 'Not so much like a ring-tailed baboon, he wasn't.'

Aladai glanced towards the bungalow and drew himself up. His chin projected as his head was thrown back. The sidelong turn of his eyes under the half-dropped lids gave him for an instant a menacing expression. Makurdi, who had jumped at the words as if prodded from behind, twisted himself round, and then round again in an agony of confusion and anxiety to please. His flippers were clasped before his chest, as if to say, 'This way, gentlemen—peace and goodwill department'; his whole body bent forward in a continuous deferential, imploring bow, directed first at the white men in the bungalow, especially Prince; then at Fisk; and then again at the bungalow. His lips moved silently; his eyes besought. He was much alarmed.

Fisk had turned red. He did not look towards the bungalow, but after a moment he said to Aladai in a severe voice, 'Don't pay any attention to what that fellow says.'

'Good heavens, no,' said Aladai.

'He doesn't represent—ah——'

'No, no. At Belton we used to call them snaggers.'

This remark had an extraordinary effect on Fisk. He knew, of course, that Aladai had been at an English public school. But for Fisk, with his slight powers of imagination, the fact had been registered like description of nature to a blind man.

Aladai's remark instantly made him see the man at school: among other boys, white boys like himself. Why, there had been a West Indian at his own private school—a very small, very black boy, blacker even than Aladai—who had been the spoilt favourite of the whole place.

Fisk's sympathies were visual. But they were effective. In a moment his whole feeling towards Aladai was changed, and, though he did not know it, his voice also changed. He said, 'Yes, I knew you were at Belton. Look here, it seems we're in a bit of a fix.'

Aladai's voice was also changed, and his manner. He no longer stood stiffly and behaved with a nonchalance which was slightly mocking. His neck bent; his hands went up; his back stooped; his eyes were full of sympathy and affection. There is no other word for their eager response to Fisk's change of tone. He exclaimed, 'Fisk, will you believe I am not an enemy? I am very loyal; perhaps I am more loyal than you yourself. I am a prince—a very little prince, I know, but still a prince—and to me the King of England gives feelings of great tenderness and honour. We in Rimi are only too willing to be his people.'

As Aladai gave rein to his feelings, he was carried into Rimi thought and his English suffered.

'Yes, but what are you going to do? You won't go. Very well. That's clear. But what will you do?'

'Mr. Fisk, may I make a suggestion?'

'I wish you would.'

'Suppose the people were all sent away, and I went to the Resident? You shall come too—with me you are safe.'

Fisk looked doubtful; Aladai poured out explanations, arguments. He repeated several times his favourite gesture: an outbend with both knees; an inclination of the head downwards and sidelong to the left; an upward roll of the eyes and a throwing out of the hands.

Makurdi was still wringing his flippers, one over the other, but his legs were now bent outwards; his head rolled down, his eyes up; it was a caricature of Aladai's appeal—Teddy Brown performing the part of Othello.

'I shall say, "The Resident wishes to see me. We are going to talk about your wrongs. But you must go peacefully." '

'Will they go?' Fisk asked.

'See here.' Aladai turned to the crowd and began to speak. At once Elizabeth intervened. She too became animated. The large woman, dignified as a mountain, screamed like a parrot and raised her immense arms like a black Ahmed Madrali about to seize Hackenschmidt by the

201

neck. She shook her fingers and her wand waved in the air; she seemed about to throw herself flat on Aladai, who shouted even louder, so that one wondered he did not burst every seam of his suit. But even its wrinkles, in their violent agitation, were expressive of his urgency, his excitement and resolution.

Makurdi joined in. Makurdi could talk to Elizabeth because she was, after all, a woman. He tossed up his chin and shouted at her; he was extremely indignant with the wench, who paid no attention to him. Suddenly she became calm, contemptuous. The arms fell; she hitched up her cloth under her armpit and walked towards the crowd. It fell back before her; all the women in it began to scream, struggling to join their leader.

It turned out that a high proportion of the crowd was women; as they poured towards the town after Elizabeth, they left big gaps in the mob. It was no longer solid black, but dots and rings of black; drifting, moreover; uncertain of their right to be there.

The drift was away from the waterside, where Aladai was shouting; and the fishermen, no longer obliged to use their poles as bars, used them as batons and blind spears. The drift became a current; the triumphant fishermen were heard shouting, 'Now, then, you bastards!'

This meant that the mob was in retreat. The word bastard is never applied to a threatening mob by its opposers.

Aladai and Fisk were now alone on the wharf. Makurdi was shooing the crowd; the younger women had followed Elizabeth.

They were waiting till the station roads were clear. Aladai did not want to take any risks.

Suddenly Rackham, followed closely by Honeywood and Prince, came out of the bungalow, walked to the quayside, and called down to Miss Honeywood, 'Are you coming up?' She jumped up at once and held up her hand.

Aladai had meanwhile turned round. He said now, 'I'm sorry you had to wait all this time.' He reached down for the girl's hand; Rackham, as if by accident, jostled him to one side, but. Aladai, skilfully recovering himself, jumped down on the half-deck and said something to Dryas, smiling in a friendly manner.

The girl, startled and obviously frightened by the sudden crisis, turned red; and Rackham, instantly jumping down beside her, gave Aladai a strong push in the chest which caused him to stagger back. His heel caught in Dryas's chair, and he fell flat on his back. His legs went up in the air.

But at once, in the same roll, he was on his feet again, and flew at Rackham with both fists. Rackham was a good lightweight. He would probably have taken a Cambridge Blue in 1917, if the war had not carried him straight from school to a training camp. He sidestepped

Aladai, and, as the man turned again, gave him a flush hit on the nose, which visibly jerked his head back.

Fisk had rushed to the quayside; but, before he could jump, Honeywood had him by the coat. Honeywood seemed likely to have a fit. He was yelling something about an insult to his sister. Prince, with a fine gesture, swung his long arm across the A.D.O.'s chest, and said, 'Keep the ring, gentlemen.'

Honeywood threw himself down into the boat, caught hold of Dryas, and lifted her bodily towards the quay. She protested furiously, and it was impossible for Honeywood to lift her to the quay-deck, five feet above. But he continued to try. It was quite like the films. Luckily Dryas' fingers hooked a plank. She pulled herself up. The hero brother pursued her, on guard. Meanwhile Aladai was still rushing at Rackham, whirling his fists, screaming curses and threats in English and Rimi; and still being sidestepped, and punched in the face, which was now covered with blood. Rackham's blows excited in Prince the highest degree of admiration.

'Look at that jab,' he said to Fisk. 'Beautiful—right in the kisser.'

Fisk, who had been shouting 'Captain Rackham' with great indignation, ducked under the arm at the second attempt and vaulted down. But, just as he established his balance on the narrow deck, Rackham, probably by design, managed in the same adroit movement to side-step a rush of Aladai's and jolt Fisk off the half-deck into the hold, where he floundered among paddles, ropes, calabashes, and Dryas's loads.

But Rackham had now decided to finish Aladai off. The next time the boy turned, therefore, after being dodged, and made a rush, he was received, not with one punch in the nose, mouth, or eyes, but half a dozen smashing blows in face and body, which knocked him across the deck, and finally heels over head into the river.

Prince clapped, and began to count 'One—two—three——'

Fisk, who had found his feet, balanced himself on Dryas's tin bath and said with dignity, 'I shall report this, Captain Rackham.'

'Certainly,' said Rackham, in his most charming tone. 'Don't forget that last cross to the ear.'

Aladai had already come up. He was swimming with the current and rapidly leaving the shore. Fisk began to wave his arms at the fishermen, now fifty yards away, and shout. But a boat had already put out from Makurdi's—one of the dug-outs which had accompanied Aladai on the expedition. It was full of excited paddlers.

Rackham made a leap at the quay, and was up. He held down a hand to Fisk, who did not take it. This made him laugh. He turned away.

Honeywood and Dryas had already disappeared into the bungalow. He walked off towards the station with a distinct swagger of the shoulders.

Fisk, having with some difficulty scrambled back to the quay, looked anxiously round. But the stragglers of the mob had seen nothing. The whole episode had been hidden from them by the quay.

Aladai himself was now a speck, far downriver; the dug-out less than fifty yards away. Fisk waited to see him picked up, then set off at full speed towards the provincial office. On the way he met Rubin and Carphew. They both wore serious and important faces. They greeted him gravely, and Rubin said, 'I say, old boy, have you a clerk called Paterson in the office? Treasury I think he is.'

'I believe we have.'

'I was wondering—could I see him now? Just for a moment. I don't want to bother you on a busy day, but the fact is, this lad Paterson's got a pony.'

'Oh!'

'Are you in a hurry?'

'I am, rather.'

'I'm sorry, old boy. I thought you people finished about now. But I'll just come along with you, if I may. It's rather urgent.' He strolled along beside Fisk. 'The fact is, that pony is not getting a fair deal. I've just seen it on the road, and the thing's becoming a scandal. I'm sure it's not the lad's fault. I believe he's quite a nice chap, but he doesn't seem to understand how a pony like that ought to be cared for.'

Fisk left him in the Residency compound, talking in a fatherly way to the clerk Paterson about grooming, feeding, and exercising an Azben pony.

Burwash was in consternation about the fight. He said several times, 'I shall have to take very serious notice of this. It's outrageous.'

XX

THE NEWS OF THE FIGHT passed round the station, and reached the town within twenty minutes. The first report in the town was that Aladai had been murdered. The effect was a popular frenzy, rare even in Rimi, and surprising to the townspeople themselves. It frightened Salé's party out of their plans. But a good half of the third ward wanted to attack the station. These were Coker's people. He himself was there, having arrived, unluckily, that morning; and he was screaming in the streets, 'It is the sign of blood—it is for a chastisement—for the Lord's people—and a destruction for the wicked man, the rich man, the proud man who did not keep the word of God.' That was to say, the white man in all his varieties—trader, official, and all missionaries except perhaps the fundamentalists from whom Coker himself had had his teaching.

Coker's power in Rimi, which astonished everybody in the next weeks, was due to much more careful preparation than anyone then supposed. He had been touring the country for a long time, especially in the neighbourhood of the mission, with his propaganda.

Nobody knew exactly what this was, because all the missions deny that Coker was ever seen in their places. Of course he was not seen, he did not work in the open. It is certainly wrong, however, to say, with Burwash and a good many more, that he was a Communist emissary. If Communist money has ever been spent on the coast, it did not go to Coker, who was not their man at all. Neither was he a lunatic. He was a preacher of natural or primitive religion—herd communism, herd fear and herd love, blood ties and race hatreds.

Such a religion is pre-human, even in its ritual of blood. Beasts fear blood, and drink blood. It has a special significance for them.

Coker's slogan was, 'Africa for Christ,' but his conception, if you can describe his mental processes as such, was a kind of bloody sacrifice. Africa would offer herself up to Christ, in blood—not only the blood of the whites, but her own.

It seemed odd to suggest that Coker's real motive in murdering several white people was to provoke reprisals, and so bring the necessary suffering upon Africa. This theory could not be proved, of course, because Coker's motives were unknown to himself; but it was suggested by a man who knew something about morbid psychology and primitive religion—which are nearly the same thing.

On this morning at Rimi, while Coker was screaming for the blood of the whites, Elizabeth, who remained cool and seemed to be amused by the turmoil, was telling everybody, 'Don't listen to that yellow fool; he is half a white man himself. This is a women's war. Leave it to me. If you go with that lunatic Coker, the soldiers will shoot you. That's all you'll get. But if the women go, you will get all you want. Aladai shall be Emir, and no more taxes. Besides, the white men are too stupid to shoot women.'

However, Coker's mob was actually moving towards the station, which had not the faintest idea of what was going on in the town, when the news went through it that Aladai had arrived at the waterside. Almost the whole fighting force of the river wards at once rushed to the shore.

Aladai had been picked up by a dug-out a hundred yards below the station, and taken slowly upstream towards Makurdi's. But he did not land there; he ordered the men to go to the town.

When he landed, he was in his wet European clothes, which clung to his legs. The front of his shirt and coat was spattered with blood, and blood was still trickling from his nose and swollen lips. The people arrived at the shore before the dug-out touched it. Some of them at once went down on their knees to salute, others shrieked for war.

Aladai, when he stepped ashore, paid no attention to them. He carried his swollen face high, and marched through the yelling mob as if it did not exist. His arrogance offended many of his supporters, and filled old Makurdi with despair—who had run after the dug-out, along the shore, and now stood flapping his hands and moaning, 'Oh! dis very bad day—very unlucky day—he woan speak to me—he too mad now.'

But Aladai had no motive in his bearing. It was as instinctive as the reactions of one proud wild animal suddenly attacked and rolled over by another.

He was conscious of rage and hatred, but his thoughts were confused. He scarcely knew what he was doing. When he entered the compound of his town house, he said to the people gathered there—the old uncles and cousins, the crippled dependants and parasites who had used its shelter for the last three years, in his absence—'I have come home to Rimi.'

This was, of course, an act of defiance, at least to the Emir, and caused enthusiasm among the young men who were shouting for war.

'Look at them,' they screamed. 'There are ten of them and thousands of us—we do not need spears. We shall walk them into the ground with our feet.'

The word war caught Aladai's ear, and he said, 'Yes, it is war now.'

The house was filled with the leaders of the party. Some of them were looking frightened; their anxious faces, their mouths, set in the form of an appeal, filled him with contempt. He said, 'War has come to us. It can't be avoided, except by cowards.'

Elizabeth came to him and examined his wounds. She made him sit down where he was, in the middle of the compound, and took off his wet clothes. Then she said, in a sarcastic voice, 'Perhaps you want a white doctor!'

Aladai answered coldly, 'I am a Rimi man. Take these clothes away and burn them.'

Elizabeth smiled, and began to wash his face and body with medicine water. The crowd of men, women, and children stood round, watching the process. The young men were talking of how they would destroy the whites. Elizabeth told them that they were a pack of young fools. The whites would destroy them. It was the women who must manage this war.

'Why?' said Aladai.

'Because white men do not shoot women.'

'But is it a war if no blood is shed?'

Elizabeth pushed his head sideways, till it almost touched his naked shoulder, in order to wash the blood off one ear. But this posture did not remove the gloomy dignity of the chief—it rather added to it, as a grotesque circumstance adds to the weight of tragedy—neither did it interrupt the council.

'What fool talk is this?' said Elizabeth, carefully handling the calabash that none of the water, containing Aladai's blood, should be spilt. It would not do to let it fall into an enemy's hand, even mixed with dirt.

'The white governor pays no attention unless there is blood shed.'

'Then shed somebody else's.'

'Are you too selfish to give something to Rimi? Is not Rimi worth a sacrifice?'

'For Rimi? What's that? I want you to be chief.'

'And yet your own aunt threw herself into the river for Rimi, for the people's sake.'

'That was for good fishing, and the fish came. But it won't make you chief if I get shot by some rotten Hausa with a white man's gun.'

There was a commotion, and Coker broke in. He seemed mad, or drunk. 'It is the sign of blood,' he shouted. 'It is a chastisement for you—and for us—for us and for you—to bring this land to the Lord—and to drive out the wicked.'

The whole yard burst into yells; Elizabeth stormed at Coker, who flourished a cook's knife at Elizabeth. Outside in the market-place, crowded with the supporters of each party, the knife was taken for the war signal. Coker's hooligans shouted, 'To the *barriki*'—that was, to the station.

Aladai got up and strolled thoughtfully into the inner yard. He did not yet know what he would do, but it seemed to him that the decision was already prepared within him, and that he was prepared for it. He would do what he had to do for Rimi, for Rimi people.

Which was the cry? There was, somebody had said, a difference.

XXI

THE RESIDENT's anxiety about the station had dwindled and gone with the crowd. But he was the more agitated about Rackham. He sent for him. Rackham came up half an hour later, in his own time and at his ease. He offered no excuse, but said, 'If you want to run me in, do so.'

'That depends on Mr. Aladai. I think you would be well advised, though, to make some kind of apology—before the situation gets any worse.'

'I don't owe him an apology.'

'A serious position may arise—I mean for you—if he brings an action. In your position, as a police officer——'

'You think H.E. would take Mister Aladai's side? Yes, I suppose he would!'

'If you approached Mr. Aladai, now, at once——'

Rackham shook his head. 'I don't propose to crawl to your friend—but I might throw in my hand. I suppose that would meet the bill?'

'Do you mean—resign?'

'That's the idea.'

'Of course, if you persist in this attitude, you will find yourself at an impasse from which there might be no way out.'

'Except home—and not such a bad way, either. I'll think it over. Good morning, sir.'

As Burwash said to Fisk, this suggestion of Rackham's, though Irish in its hastiness, was really a good solution of their difficulties.

He was still discussing its implications, about ten o'clock, when Doctor Schlemm called on him. Doctor Schlemm had heard a rumour that Aladai was in Rimi town, and the town were arming. Burwash was able to tell him that there was no cause for alarm.

Officially, cause for alarm is the best reason why an official should say to a layman, a member of the general public, that there is none. But Burwash really knew of none. The station wore its usual morning appearance. The station gardener, with the aid of the chain gang, was watering the Residency flower-beds, and Sergeant Root, on the distant parade ground, could be heard talking to some recruits in a voice that brought Aldershot directly to his desk.

Schlemm had a proposal, with apologies—might he go and see Aladai, if possible, in the town? Burwash smiled benevolently at the good doctor's disquietude, so natural in a private person, but also so pitiable. He picked up a file, as if to get on with real work, and said, 'Very kind of you, doctor, but not really necessary. And it might cause misunderstanding.'

'But why cannot I see him in the town? That is just the place I must see him. It is the worst place for him. Do you mean the town is not safe?'

'No, no, no—not at all. That is, I believe there is, or was, so Pratt tells me, a slight disturbance on the waterside, but the town itself is quite calm—in fact, unusually quiet. It is only that Aladai himself, and his immediate followers, might be in resentful mood, after this very unfortunate incident——'

'Yess, that's why I want to see him. I think, Mr. Burwash, it would be goot for me to see him—if you do not absolutely forbid.'

Burwash would have liked to do so, but he had already declared the town unusually quiet, and he knew that Doctor Schlemm was not one to miss a debating point. He therefore consented; saying only, 'At your own risk, doctor.'

The doctor replied, 'Of course—of course. That goes without saying. We are all at our own risk.' He then thanked the Resident as if for a boon, bowed twice, and shuffled away towards the town, looking like an animated toadstool.

Obishala, when Aladai asked for native dress, brought him a blue kilt, white singlet, and a white cap. He examined each attentively, but his mind was still idly reflecting, 'Rimi—Rimi people—what is the difference?' Miss Coote had said there was a difference, but what was it? Who had said, 'France is the living soul of Frenchmen'? Then why not Rimi the living soul of Rimi people? Miss Coote said that Rimi had not enough—what was it?—history, literature. But perhaps these only came to a nation when it had a soul first.

He threw the singlet aside, and said in his grandest manner, which he always used involuntarily before Obishala, who seemed to despise everybody except Elizabeth, 'That is for servants.'

But he put on the kilt and white cap.

'How does a nation get a soul?' he asked himself; but he knew that this was a foolish question. Miss Coote would smile at such stuff.

Obishala brought him the grey coat, dried. It had a large white patch sewn on the right breast, round the spear-hole, which was outlined in black thread.

Aladai looked at it, and said, 'But who did this?'

'Lisbet told us to do it.'

Aladai smiled and put on the coat. He was not afraid of *ju-jus*. He was not afraid to make them useful if they served him.

Obishala, after admiring Aladai in his native dress, and the white *ju-ju* on the *ju-ju* coat, but with a slightly scornful air, said, 'The white doctor.'

'What do you mean?'

'Nosy, from Kifi—in the outer yard. He's been there for some time. But perhaps they will kill him.'

Aladai went through the hut, and saw, in the outer yard, Schlemm pressed against the left-hand wall. The yard itself, like the square outside, was crowded with a mob, chiefly of young people, now in the highest or last stages of nervous hysteria. They did not even know what they meant while they yelled, 'To the *barriki!*'—or, 'Kill the whites!' They were simply nerve centres, intoxicated by noise, and the stimulation of various glands by hatred, fear, rage, and excitement, to make more noise and to produce more hatred and blood lust, not consciously directed at any special object. They would have murdered anybody at the slightest direction from outside. They only wanted cruelty, blood, more stimulation—the only way to release.

Schlemm was staring at them, through his thick glasses, with a look of mild curiosity—like a zoologist who has seen this species of animal conduct before, but not in such perfection.

The moment Aladai saw Schlemm he knew what he had to do. It was as if in Schlemm, both his enemy and his power came to him—white civilization. He shouted at the top of his voice, 'Silence!'

He was not heard; no sound less than gunfire or thunder could have been heard six feet away in that yard, at that time. But the nearest lunatics saw their chief dressed like themselves, standing among them and apparently speaking to them. They stopped screaming, therefore, by a mere reaction, like insects that roll themselves up when the ground shakes.

In this manner, when Aladai had walked, shouting, right through the yard, he had brought half of it to silence, and his voice could be heard.

'See, I am a Rimi man like you.'

After a moment, some of the people raised a thin cheer, but these, though feeble and scattered, had quite a different sound from the shrieks of a moment before. They had a motive—attention.

Aladai put up his hand. 'Now I am with you—I shall not leave you again. I live for Rimi, I die for Rimi—if Rimi wants my life.'

The cheers were now louder, deeper, and distinctly coloured with human intelligence.

'Therefore you must trust me—you must do what I tell you.'

There was silence in the yard, which made the all-devilish shrieks from the back parts of the square more noticeable. Coker's voice could be heard somewhere near by explaining, in Rimi, why the white devils must die because Africa belonged to Jesus.

Aladai now turned towards Schlemm, who at once, as the people

210

divided to let their chief pass, stood forward from the wall, made his involuntary Continental bow, without which he could no more begin a conversation than a Catholic priest could eat without crossing himself, and said, 'I am fery sorry about this attack, Galadima. It is a disgraceful thing.'

Aladai, throwing back his swelled face with a proud and, indeed, arrogant gesture, answered, 'It is very good of you to say so, but it is nothing.' He made a slight gesture brushing away the incident. 'What happened between Captain Rackham and myself is, you understand, quite a private matter.'

The man spoke with the dignity of a grand duke who has been spattered by a street boy—and no doubt with the same motive.

Schlemm made a little bow. 'I understand your feelings, perfectly, Mr. Aladai. It is fery sensible of you to overlook such a schtupid thing like that. But I fear your people are not so wise. I hear some of them call out, "We want war"—or something like that. I tell them it is not only wicked, but it is schtupid'; and he repeated again, with emphasis, 'Most schtupid! What is the good of war? You will kill some of Salé's people and he will kill some of yours, and then the police will come and shoot a great many on both sides, and you will have to answer for them all.'

'I don't agree, Doctor Schlemm,' said Aladai; and now, in spite of his dress, he was easy and nonchalant, already the European. 'When there was a rising in Kaiama, against Moshi, plenty of people were murdered, but the Government did not punish the leaders of the anti-Moshi party—they put them in power. And we shall beat Salé.'

'Salé is very strong.'

'If he were as strong as the British Government, it would still be my duty to fight him, because the people have chosen me. You don't ask me to desert Rimi?'

'But, Louis, think what you are doing!'

'We shall win.'

'How can you know?' Schlemm's eyes fell on the coat with its white pocket—'Not by *ju-ju*.'

Aladai was angry. He said sharply, 'I am a Rimi, Doctor Schlemm, but not a savage.'

The doctor, much disturbed, begged his pardon effusively, but Aladai walked off into his room. The doctor, distressed by his failure in tact, walked out into the square, and looked with surprise at a number of rioters who appeared to be beating each other, and now turned and ran towards him.

'But how could I put it?' he asked himself. 'Luck—destiny—perhaps he would not have minded that so much! But then I wanted him to mind—to know—to see.'

Burwash sat down to compose his report on the Rackham affair. It was a difficult report, because he wished it to combine the minimum of information with the appearance of complete openness. He was anxious to avoid an enquiry about what might bring out his own dealings with Aladai, and especially Fisk's various missions. Then, just when he was trying to find another phrase for 'delicate situation' which would convey a reason for the gravity of the assault, without betraying the existence of a crisis which he ought possibly to have avoided, a messenger brought in this letter.

From *Louis Aladai, Galadima Rimi*
　　to *Mr. J. O. Burwash, Resident.*

Sir,—I understand that a certain Salé, foreigner to this country, has been made Galadima of it.

This man has no title to any rank in Rimi, because his father was bastard and his mother was a foreign slave.

I Louis Aladai am the only rightful heir to the ancient title and honour of Galadima Aladai, attached by Rimi law to the presumptive successor of the Rimi emirate. My right is acknowledged by the people's acclamation.

In case this interloper Salé should be allowed to remain in Rimi, the people will move against him. The Rimi people are too proud to bear the rule of a foreign upstart. Within twenty-four hours the Rimi people will make war upon this man and his accomplices, and if he remains in Rimi, I forgo all responsibility for the consequences, be what they may.

Louis, Galadima

Headquarters,
　Rimi City

Burwash showed it to Fisk, and said, 'I was afraid it was going to be about Rackham.'

'He seems to be letting that go.'

'I hope so. Though it's more than Rackham deserves.'

'But do you think there'll be trouble, sir? There was a big crowd out this morning.'

'Personally, I believe we're over the worst. You heard that the hospital is full up with the riff-raff of the third ward—all from the same ward.'

'I did hear Pratt was busy.'

'All third ward—one of Aladai's holds. Now what does that convey to you?'

Fisk didn't know. Besides, he saw that Burwash wanted to tell him. 'Putting that fact and this together'—Burwash tapped the ultimatum;

he then leant back in his chair and smiled at Fisk for ten seconds with a knowing benevolence—'what would you say?'

'That his people are a bit out of hand.'

'No, no.' Burwash rolled forward like the wave of doom. 'No, I don't think that. I think he's on his last legs. This'—and he tapped the ultimatum again—'was produced by that'—pointing at the window, which gave, approximately, in the direction of the hospital, near enough for rhetorical purposes.

'I see, sir. You think he's taken the knock already?'

'There's a split. You hear what Audu said—that Aladai's crowd were—decidedly—undisciplined. He was right. I don't think we'll have much more trouble with Aladai.' He got up and reached out for his coat. 'I'm sorry for the chap. I don't agree with Sangster. I liked him. I think there were great possibilities in him. It's a real tragedy, this business. What about lunch? You'll stay? Yes, of course.'

It was not till the middle of lunch-time that Doctor Schlemm re-appeared. He was very hot and dusty, and he was wearing a piece of lint and a cross-over of sticking-plaster, about three inches square, across the bridge of his nose. No lesser nose could have carried such a dressing. No lesser man could have carried himself with dignity under such a handicap. But the doctor did not even refer to it. Having mounted the stairs, he was breathless; he therefore only bowed, and made apologetic gestures with his hat for the first half-minute, while Burwash caused the boy to bring a chair and coffee-cup. Doctor Schlemm shook his head. 'It is fery kind of you,' he said, 'but there is no time. The situation is fery serious. I was surprised—most unpleasantly surprised—at——'

'I hope you aren't hurt, doctor?'

'Wot? Oh! that is nutting. I hat an accident. Mr. Burwash, would you'—he looked anxiously and thoughtfully at Burwash—'would you tink it impertinent off me to suggest something?'

'I should be most grateful, doctor.'

Doctor Schlemm then committed the impertinence. He drew out a paper, sketched the position of Aladai's and Salé's forces, pointed out that they were divided roughly by the main street running east and west through the market, and proposed that this should be patrolled by the police, or even the troops, 'because the situation is so fery dangerous.'

The Resident was polite. But he was a little surprised that Doctor Schlemm, a minister of religion, should advocate the use of armed police, and soldiers.

'I do not like force,' said the doctor, 'but sometimes it is necessary to avoid worse things. Firmness at the proper moment is of great falue with negroes. My friend, Doctor Schweitzer, says——'

213

'Excuse me, doctor. I have to go back to the office. But I'm afraid I would hesitate very much before carrying out your suggestions. In these cases, it is of the first importance to avoid any great provocation.'

Doctor Schlemm therefore returned to the hospital rest-house, where he was staying with the Pratts. Even Pratt.could not discover the mystery of the nose which had been dressed by the town dresser. Doctor Schlemm declared that it was an accident. The fact was that the doctor had received a shock to his ideals, and he did not like to admit it. Schlemm, in spite of his shrewd criticism of the negro character and his devotion to 'my friend, Dr. Schweitzer, with his sensible views,' was an idealist. If he had not been so, why should he have come to a West African mission, or remained there? So that he had been painfully surprised, in every way, when, being attacked in the town by a mob of young hooligans armed with canoe paddles and sticks, he had recognized among them several pupils of his own from Kifi.

He had reproached them by name, whereupon one of them, a youth of fifteen at most, had struck him in the face with his stick, skinning his nose and injuring his precious hat. Schlemm had been rescued at once by Makurdi. His nose had lost much skin, but it was not broken. He thanked heaven that his spectacles had not been cracked. But he could not admit to anybody that it was one of his own pupils who had struck him, and, rather than tell a lie, he said, 'It was an accident?'

The argument was—'Young Frederick is a goot boy, a very goot boy. He could not have meant any harm. But he was excited by the trouble; he had a stick in his hand; he had been fighting, and he thought that I was going to catch him and punish him. He struck to protect himself, and hit me. It was an accident.'

But he did not quite believe this, and the effort to do so depressed him. By nature he was an honest man.

What happened in Rimi the rest of that morning is not exactly known. All the station knew was that Pratt had a queue of out-patients with broken heads and stabs, and all his native beds full of fractures, including three skulls. But it was heard through the political agent Audu and the Resident that the man Coker had quarrelled with Aladai and attacked his party; that Aladai's people had defeated him, and chased him out of Rimi. He had been last seen about four o'clock, heading for bush at high speed, with half a dozen battered elders or deacons in front of him, and fifty enthusiastic pagans, armed with spears, knives, hatchets, hoes, and dane guns, close behind.

XXII

THE EMIR waked up with a start, hopped off the bed, and uttered another scream which meant, 'Where's that damn rascal the Waziri?'

He was startled to see how far the sunray had walked across the floor. It must be ten o'clock; past ten. He had expected the Waziri back from the bush in an hour at the longest. What had happened to the man?

Outside, in the town, he could hear an unusual volume of noise, shouts. It sounded far off through the thick, high walls of the palace keep; but he recognized its volume.

He stood in anger and surprise, saying, 'It's a fight'; then he thought, 'It's Salé, and those Mohammedan rascals are cheering him.'

This notion increased his anger. He shouted for his servants.

Nobody answered. He shouted for several minutes, and then, in an undignified rage, hopped out into the yard. But there was no one in the boys' huts.

He thought: 'The rascals! They've run out to join the other rascals and make a noise.'

He sat down in a hut to await their return.

They did not come, and he went out to look for them in the stables. There was no one there; the big stallion had gone. He thought, 'Ah, they've had trouble with that villain of a horse—took all of them to get him out. All the same, the Waziri will be here soon. I must be dressed.'

He went back to the room where his state clothes were kept, the office. He had resolved to dress himself.

To his great delight, he found that he could dress himself. He put the heavy gown over his head; and then, after a rest, the big turban and the chin-cloth. He put his baldric over his shoulder. He did not need to put on his boots. He was accustomed to wear moccasins, with feet of soft leather. Upon these he wore loose slippers—walking-slippers or riding-slippers. They stood in a row on one of the tin boxes. He shuffled his toes into riding-slippers and tottered into the main hall, trailing his sword.

'Curses on that Waziri,' he said, 'the lazy rascal. I'll teach him.' He sat down on the leopard-skin, and at once his head drooped. He fell into a doze. He was tired from his exertions during the last night.

When he waked up he was much surprised to find himself alone. He was also thirsty. He began to shout, and soon lost his temper. Furious, he tottered and reeled from room to room and yard to yard. But they were all empty. Gradually this emptiness surprised him. He thought, 'There must be a big market to-day'; and then, 'Somebody's got the smallpox. Oh, dear! my poor children.'

In one remote yard that he had not visited for years he found a collection of broken crockery, including a blue-and-white teapot given him by Lugard, that he had valued and lost. This angered him. He said, 'Look at that. Ah! the rascals!' and, picking up the teapot, he began to shout furiously. Nobody answered. The walls echoed. Still holding the broken pot, trailing his sword, his feet, he slowly made his way towards the women's quarter. He was sure of an audience there. Moreover, the women would understand his feelings about the teapot.

It was a long way to the women's compound; back to the main hall and then by a separate and private route to the other side of the palace. Twice by the way he sat down for a rest; and dozed. Once he left the teapot behind. But he went back for it.

When he saw the great hall, he reflected that the Waziri was a long time finding Salé. 'But he's a lazy fellow, Salé—all these Fulani are lazy, useless good-for-nothings. They're the worst kind of white man. It will take him an hour to get shaved and dressed and painted; and then he has to say his prayers.'

There were more than thirty huts in the women's quarter, but only seventeen were in use. Of the others, some were used as storehouses, some as quarters for the women's friends and visitors, aunts and cousins; many were unroofed. Aliu wanted his favourite. He began to talk to her at the door of the hut.

'See here, Fanta, the thing that gamna Gular gave me. The pretty blue things for tea. Didn't I tell you the rascals had broken it?'

The hut was full of smoke and smell from the embers of the fire on which a pot of porridge stood. The porridge was burnt to a thick bluish coke, shiny and full of large, smooth-edged holes.

'Oh! the slut! That's Fanta all over,' said the old man; and he shouted, 'Fanta, you slut, look here—wasting the good porridge.

He waited. Nobody answered. He thought, 'They've all gone out to see the fun. Ah! these women, they never get any sense.'

But the sight of the pot and the smell of smoke made him hungry. He continued to shout for Fanta; not with much hope of bringing her back from the palace market—or the nearest point of vantage on the wall—but because it relieved his indignation, and because it pleased him to use a name which meant food and the comfort that women impart. Women were silly things, but they were faithful, and at peace. They gave repose.

How often had he lain against Fanta's warm, thick shoulder, in the

216

corner of the wall, while she gently stroked his cheeks and forehead and he described to her his old battles, his feats of skill and bravery?

'Fanta!' he called. 'Ah, you rascal, you wait!' He climbed on the bed and curled himself in the corner against the wall. The large turban drooped; the toothless mouth fell open. The Emir was dozing once more with his favourite wife.

The palace had been expecting war for the last month; and a great many of the parasite families had taken away all their movables a long time before the Waziri and the Master of the Horse resolved that the time had come to secure a new job.

Nevertheless, there was a panic when they rode away with the guards. A great many people, especially young people and women, had not really grasped the fact that a change was coming—a change that affected them personally. They discussed it, of course. It was the topic of every hut. When would the Waziri desert? Was he with Salé or Aladai? When would the Emir die? Would they poison him or shoot him? Would there be a war? Where was the best place to go—to some relative in town, or to the country?

They discussed it, but they did not realize it, so that when the guards rode off, and the forethoughtful ones promptly took up their remaining loads and disappeared out of the back gates, they were panic-stricken. They packed in confusion, and rushed away without knowing where to go to.

The return of Aladai and the fighting on the waterside increased the panic; also some of the roughs and blackguards who formed a large part of the population in the palace, which they used as a refuge, now feeling confident that the old man was finished, began to loot.

In the harem, Fanta was running round like a hen in a grass fire. 'They're mad! Wait till my lord catches them!'

A dozen times she had sent messengers to the Emir, but the messengers had, of course, left the palace by the nearest door. Meanwhile the women continued to pack and gather their children for flight. They were in such a hurry to go that they left their pots on the fire.

Fanta called them all the names that she could think of; but they did not even answer her. They were too frightened, and she shrieked at them, 'What you want is the whip. You wait till my lord hears about this.'

She could not understand what was happening. She had never heard of the fall of princes. She knew plenty of stories but no history. When she screamed that everybody was mad except herself, she believed it. But she was greatly disturbed. To be the only sane person in a lunatic asylum is not a pleasant situation for a lazy, self-indulgent old woman.

Fanta, having thrown the most violent curses she could think of after the last of the women, was walking with great dignity to her hut, when she noticed a child's foot projecting from behind the large water-pot. It was shaking. She dived behind the pot and saw Ibu. She was delighted 'Ah! you're not going to run away for nothing, like a fool, and get the whip for your trouble. You have sense, at least, my dear, and good manners. Come with me, and we'll see if we can find you a cigarette and a sip of gin. Don't be afraid. You're a good little girl.' She took Ibu by the body and set her on her feet. 'Though you are such a little trembler, you've been well brought up. Anyone can see that. I'll tell my lord that when all his people went mad you had sense. And you know he's going to make you his wife.' Breathless, she drew the child towards her hut. 'He is a good man, the best in the world. He gives you all you ask. Life is good here. It is the best life for a woman. Yes, you shall be his wife, my dear, and I shall teach you how to rub his legs and his body. That's what he likes. It sends him to sleep. For he is old, you know, my poor lord. He can't fight or make love any more, or enjoy his food, or even sleep. Ai, ai.'

She sat down on the bed and uttered a deep, tremulous sigh. 'Life is hard for him. It is terrible to be old. But you will like him; he is so kind, so wise. He tells such good tales. And he is a great lord. It is a great honour to be his wife. He will give you all you want—cigarettes, gin, beer, and no work at all. And when you are old enough, he will say, "Shaker, it's time I had some children by my pretty dear. You must find yourself a nice young man. For, you know, he loves children very much, and when he likes a girl, then he wants very much to see her with a child. Ah, he has plenty children. You see how many. This yard is full of them. But of course they're gone. Ah! how angry he will be with those mad fools if they lose any of his children! He will beat them when he catches them. You can be sure of that. I remember once, when there was talk of an evil spirit and they all ran out into the town, it was two days before the Waziri had finished beating them. He doesn't let them go into the town. Anywhere in the palace, but not the town. If they go out there, the fools are sure to get robbed or stolen. Get me the bottle, my dear. I'm tired with all this silliness.'

Ibu fetched the gin-bottle from the water-pot where it stood cooling, and a tin cup. Fanta drank about half a pint and said mournfully, 'My lord won't take gin nowadays. It makes him drunk. Ai, ai, the poor old man. I weep for the old. It is terrible to be old. But he is strong still. He will live many years. He has a big heart, a lion's heart. And you shall be his wife, my dear. I'll show you how to rub his legs, and you shall do it this very night. Then he will say, "Who is the pretty shaker? I like her; and you must say, "Your slave, lord," and he will say, "If Fanta chooses, you shall be my wife. Ask her to-morrow, and say I wish it." But of course I agree, my dear. You're not like that girl. . . .'

And she began to tell a long story about a girl who had been introduced to the Emir and who had seized the opportunity to tell stories about Fanta herself and her dealings in gin.

Fanta, by arrangement with Makurdi, had the monopoly of gin sales in the women's yard. She received a commission, which she spent, no doubt, on her numerous dependants and young men.

The story diverged into another, an amusing one, about another girl who had, while drunk, been carried off by the horse-boys; and Fanta roared with laughter while she described the girl's surprise on awaking in a stable. She acted it. 'Am I a mare, then? Some witch has turned me into a mare. Hin-hin-hin (an attempt to imitate a whinny). No, I'm not a mare. But perhaps I'm a goat.' Feeling her head. 'No, I'm not a goat. Then I must be a horse. No, it seems not.'

This was an old story of Fanta's, elaborated by many years' relation. The old woman told and performed it with extraordinary zest and the louche mimicry for which she was renowned. Ibu did not laugh. She was frightened of Fanta in this noisy mood; and she disapproved of her language and gestures, though she barely understood them. She edged towards the door. But Fanta did not need an audience yet. She was in the full course of art; at once delighted spectator and performer.

Suddenly Ibu saw Musa. He had run out of the opposite hut. Ibu called him, and Fanta at once turned round. She too perhaps was glad to see a familiar in the empty yard.

Musa was carrying a roll of new mats under his arm, a tin pot on his head, and a box of cigarettes in his hand. When he saw Fanta, he shouted at once, 'They're mine—presents.'

Fanta rushed at him. She was furious. 'You rascal!—You, too—dirty thief! Put them down. You'll be whipped for this. Yes, I mean it.'

Musa retreated, screaming, 'They're mine. What are you talking about? You'd better be careful. They're a special present from the old man himself.'

'Liar, you son of a hole!'

'I swear by Allah. It's a fact. He came to me just now and said, "Musa, I like you. I gree for you. Take them mats, this new pot, and go to the judge for me." It's a message,' Musa yelled, thinking of a new stratagem. 'I'm taking a message to the judge. Don't you dare to stop me.'

'And the cigarettes, you villain?'

'They're mine. What are you talking about, you old trot. Who takes the gin money—and half of it water?'

'Old trot, you bastard! What language to a lady. I'll call the guard.'

Fanta, breathless with anger and exertion, waddled after him, while he dodged her. But, though the way was open to him, he did not try to escape out of the yard. He was too angry with the woman's foolishness.

'You old fool, there isn't any guard,' he yelled. 'They've all run, and you'd better run too. What are you staying here for? D'you want to get your belly opened? Take what you can, and clear out.'

'Ah, you villain, you talk like that, and I'll whip you myself!'

'But they've all gone, I tell you. Here, Shaker, you've got sense. Tell the old fool.'

'What if they've gone? They'll only get the whip.'

'It's you—you'll get it, and a knife in the belly too. I swear by Allah, Mother Fanta, you can't stay'; and he appealed to Ibu: 'Tell her that she can't stay here.'

Ibu did not trust Musa, but she owed him gratitude and admiration. She said, 'The others have gone away.'

But nothing could have moved Fanta. She had not been out of the palace for twenty years. Ten minutes later she was still disputing, when the looters broke in, knocked her down, and stripped her in a moment of cloth, necklaces, rings, anklets. The rings were tight, and one of them proposed to cut her fingers off. But another said, 'Rip her up first. That's what she deserves, the old whore.'

These men were all known to Fanta—favourites of the women, to whom Fanta herself had given cigarettes and money. She kept screaming their names in pitiful astonishment at their cruelty, while they dragged her about the ground, trampled her, kicked her, and clawed her as if she had been a corpse.

Musa was her only defender. He, with his usual truculence, had flown at them as soon as they appeared. 'Get out,' he shrieked. 'How dare you come in here! Do you know who I am? The son of the Emir of Rimi, the friend of the great judge of Rimi. Leave go of the woman. I'll tell the judge, by Allah!'

One of them turned round from tearing the coral stud out of Fanta's nose and with one blow knocked the flimsy Musa right across the yard. He lay bleeding against the wall, and for a moment he seemed to be dead. Then, just as they were debating whether to kill Fanta or not, he got up and screamed at them: 'You murderers, you wait!—The judge is my intimate friend, you dare to touch me.—Let her alone. I tell you, do you want to be skinned?'

One of them gave a curse, took out a pestle, and knocked him senseless. He then gave him another couple of blows to finish him off; and the party ran out with their booty.

They had, however, forgotten to kill Fanta. A second party, five minutes later, in their disappointment at finding her stripped, had resolved to do so, out of pure irritation, when one of them had a better suggestion, and they dragged her off to ransom her. if possible, to her friend Makurdi, for gin.

Ibu had crouched behind the water-pots during the whole attack of the robbers; but as soon as the second gang had passed she rushed across the yard and made after them. She did not want to be separated from Fanta, whose screams and curses were her guide. The looters dragged Fanta through a gap in the wall abutting on the compound of the palace butcher. The gap had been made by the weight of terrified women and old people trying to force their way, all at once, through a narrow doorway. All the palace posterns stood open. The gang dragged Fanta, not towards Makurdi's, but northwards into the rabbit-warren of the first ward. They did not mean to take her directly through the town. And, catching sight of Ibu as she followed, one of them ran at her with a stick, and drove her, flying like a burnt dog, back towards the palace. But she dodged aside into the alley or drain which led to the market-place.

She intended—or, rather, she was instructed by her feelings—to make for the waste land in the third ward. This was the only other part of Rimi, except the *ju-ju* house, that she had known before. It therefore seemed to her the nearest thing to home. She did not know the exact way to the waste, but she knew it was directly across the central market square.

This was occupied, when she reached it, by fifteen or twenty horsemen, prancing round Salé and the Waziri; and a large crowd saluting the new Galadima. Ibu, giving both the horses and the crowd a wide space, bolted along the side-walls of the market until she had passed them both, and then made direct for the river, which now appeared below, glittering over the tops of the houses, which appeared like a wall keeping it out of the hollow market-place, still shaded grey-green below the flat rays of the half-risen sun. Ibu, with the glitter in her eyes, was running at full speed towards the nearest alley, going down to the river, when a woman, labouring uphill towards her, with an immense netful of calabashes balanced on her head, suddenly came face to face with her.

They stared at each other. Ibu recognized a calabash maker of her own village. She stood like stone. She did not know whether to run or speak. Then the woman gave a shriek, dropped her load with a crash, and ran away as fast as she could run, uttering still louder shrieks.

Ibu stood in wonder. Then a hand fell on her shoulder and a voice said, 'You're Ibu.'

She looked up, and recognized one of the two girls who had received her at the *ju-ju* house and put her into prison. She leapt like a caught fish, and tried to run. But the girl held her firmly. In three minutes Ibu was back again in the *ju-ju* house, in the same cell from which she had escaped. But now the ceiling was mended and the dying boy had gone.

But Ibu knew where he had lain. She even thought that she could see a mark on the floor where his head had rubbed it for many days. She went as far from that place as she could, and crouched behind the old stocks. Her legs began to shake so violently that she wanted to cry with weariness. But she was afraid to cry.

The butcher's family, in terror, were already fetching mats to repair the break in the palace wall. Within a few minutes of the flight of the last gang of looters, and the ceasing of the tumult from within the palace, all its doors were closed and blocked from the outside.

For, though the Emir was deserted, the people feared him. He was still the father king, the old man, the invulnerable. None in Rimi could remember the time when the Emir Aliu had not dominated its life. He was seldom in their minds, but he was present in their lives like the weather; like the sky and the earth. If market dues went up, and the people were ruined, it was the king, complain if you like, but it made no difference. It was waste of time. When the stores were built and the river trade came to Rimi, making it rich, so that even the poorest could buy gowns and every man had employment for money, carrying, building, trading, it was because the Emir had made a treaty with the white men, and put a guard on the waterside to protect the traders' goods. He did it because it pleased him. Thank him if you like; but it made no difference. It was, besides, a great waste of time.

He was a great king. He knew things that ordinary people did not know. He had power in him. He was to be feared.

The way to treat this wise and powerful man was to go down on your face before him and throw dust on your head. You could cry out to him for help, but whether he gave it or not was his own mysterious affair. His gifts were like the rain; his anger like a draught. If you give thanks for rain, it is not from gratitude but to keep the god in a good temper; if you complain of draught, it is in this form: 'We are sinful people.'

Although by the afternoon it was suspected that the Emir might be alone in the palace, nobody dared to go in, or even to approach the walls. The back doors were all blocked; the great front door had been barred inside, as usual, on the departure of the Waziri. The quarter guard of the palace, called the gate guard, had retired to join their captain by one of the posterns.

The matter was, however, quickly forgotten, because there were more important things to think of. What would Salé do? And Aladai? Which to join? Three-quarters of the family heads in a town like Rimi did not care who ruled so long as they were on his side. Their motives were not purely selfish. A mistake might bring misery on their wives and children. They were in an agony of perplexity and anxiety. The mobs who rioted in the third ward during the morning were all young people and visitors, or country people. Five thousand is a large mob, capable of devastating a town. There were at least thirty thousand people in Rimi, but they trembled at the shouts of Coker's three or four hundred, Aladai's fifteen hundred or so, Salé's thousand.

In the afternoon it became known that Aladai had threatened war: some people said war against the whites. The town fell into silence. This is a time of silence in Africa. The whole continent of men and beasts is resting then. But the Rimi people did not sleep during the afternoon. They argued, packed their goods, buried their money, sharpened their knives, or sat and trembled.

At night, when all Africa is awake, the town was still silent. Every soul was on watch. A single tap upon a drum would have made thirty thousand pulses flutter. The moon was three-quarters full. At ten it was high above the town. Soon after ten the watchers in the compounds surrounding the market-place were terrified to see the big door of the palace jerking and shaking. This continued for a long time—perhaps half an hour. Then the door disappeared; it had fallen backwards into the dark room behind. It made a heavy, dull crash, which was followed by a long, high, screeching noise. Some women near the market-place had hysterics.

After this nothing happened for so long a time that many people, saying that a ghost had pushed down the enormous door, began to beat their heads on the ground and repent.

But about eleven or twelve, when the moon was near the zenith, a small white object appeared under the arch, on the top of the fallen door. Here it remained for a few minutes, giving an occasional peculiar jerk, and then suddenly advanced into the square. It was the Emir in his white robes, wearing his largest turban—almost as big as himself—and trailing his biggest sword.

He nearly fell in stepping off the edge of the door; but recovered himself, after five or six staggering steps, by a violent jerk. Then he moved slowly across the huge square; three steps totter, two stagger, a stop, another totter; dragging his shoes like a chief. His sword, trailing on the ground, clinked against the humps like a cracked penny.

Either because his vast turban was falling over his eyes or because he was weak and giddy, the man did not hold a line, but, after each stagger and stop, set off again in a new direction. Once he started in the opposite direction. But there was purpose in his determined progress. He meant to reach the houses.

In twenty minutes he was near the compounds on the east side of the square. A last stagger brought him to a door; he drew himself up, threw back his sleeve, and tapped upon the wood.

Naturally the people of the house did not answer. If they had not feared the old man, if they had not been paralysed by terror of his mysterious power, they would still not have dared to offend Salé,

Aladai, or Coker. The Emir tapped again, listened, fell back, and gazed at the door. He was heard to say something in a tone of mild surprise. He then went painfully to the next door. It is said that the old man continued through the streets, knocking at different doors for three or four hours. Once he was seen to sit down in the middle of the street and go to sleep for twenty minutes. About four in the morning the moon set. After that the trembling people could only hear the staggering shoes, the clink of the sword, the tap, and the surprised voice saying, 'Nobody there.'

At the first light of dawn the Emir had returned to the market-place, on the west side.

He knocked at a door near the middle of that side. At the same time another door, further down, was opened, and a girl came out with a calabash. The door shut quickly behind her. She was dressed like a bride, but she appeared in the last stages of terror. She walked a few steps, then she fell on her knees.

The Emir came up to her, took the calabash, and said, 'Thank you, my child. I was hungry.'

He asked her what had happened to all the people. Had they run away? She answered, 'No, King.' But he didn't attend to her. He took the calabash, collapsed on his hams, and ate without ceremony. The girl crept away, and knocked on a door. But the door did not open. She went on creeping away, crouching almost to the ground, till she came to the main road and disappeared into it.

The Emir suddenly dropped the calabash and gave a scream; jumped to his feet and ran about twenty yards, screaming; then he fell down, rolled over on his back, kicked up his little legs, and lay dead in that position, like a beetle.

Nobody approached the body until, after dawn, in full light, the native administration dresser, coming to work, saw it lying there and shouted indignantly for it to be removed. The dresser was a Christian from Kifi. He had no respect for the Emir.

His cries brought out more of the bolder people. But they stood at a distance, arguing with the man. It was not till some of Coker's people came up from the third ward that the body was carried into the palace.

The girl who had poisoned the Emir came out of a compound belonging to a dyer of Salé's party, but no one in the house admitted any knowledge of her. She herself was found the same evening, on the riverside, with her throat cut.

The Resident was informed that morning, by Salé and the whole Court, of the Emir's death by a fit; and Salé then took up his residence in the palace.

He brought with him seventeen women of his family, three pretty boys, two young brothers with their families, and seven grandmothers and great-aunts, thirty odd servants, small boys and hangers-on, with their families; an old *mallam*, who had done two years in Kaduna gaol for fraud and who was Salé's chief adviser; and horses, goats, chickens, and sheep in proportion.

Salé's personal servants at once began to build up the walls and to repair the great gate. Old Aliu, unable to open the gate or lift the bars from it, had picked away the mud holding the upper hinges and the bar sockets with a spear. This feat must have taken him many hours.

The rest of Salé's following went through every cranny of the palace for loot, but they found nothing except broken pots, one small boy with a broken leg, and a scared little girl who was giving him water and keeping the flies off his wounds.

No one had time for these children at the moment. It was a crisis for all these people, and they knew it. The huts, compounds, alliances, positions, secured in these first hours would probably fix the rest of their lives. There were six fights within the first hour; and one obscure rascal, whom no one had seen before, was stabbed to death by another equally unknown, who was afterwards found established as the doorkeeper of the women's yard, a position which soon made him rich.

But on the third day, when the women complained of the boy's cries and the girl's importunities, Salé sent for the town dresser who set the leg. Meanwhile the little girl, having been pinched and tormented enough by the new children of the women's yard, was received into friendship and allowed a reasonable share of cigarettes.

In the evening, Ibu was taken out of her cell. The girl led her into the *ju-ju* yard and through the main door of the *ju-ju* house.

Ibu found herself in the outer room, full of *ju-ju* sticks and bags of medicine. But the girl brought her to the door of another room, where the priestess whom Ibu knew as Lisbet was waiting for her. Lisbet took her by the hand and said, 'Don't be afraid.'

Ibu was very much afraid. Her teeth were chattering; she could hardly stand. Lisbet had almost to carry her past the cannon *ju-ju*. Here another door, hidden by a mat, was opened, showing a dark cell beyond, with some huge object in the middle of it, like a door. It seemed to be made of cracked mud.

Lisbet herself did not enter the room. She pushed Ibu into it and shut the door behind her.

Ibu knew that she was in the presence of a terrible *ju-ju* of which even Lisbet was afraid. She would certainly be killed now; but she was used to fear. She could not be more afraid than she had been. She pressed back against the door, whose heavy planks shook with her body. But she did not scream. She was afraid to offend the thing, the power. She could not see anything now, not even the big door, in the thick darkness; but the darkness itself seemed to be the life of that power. It did not breathe or move. But it was alive; waiting. She, too, waited until she slipped down to the floor, exhausted with her fear.

Light was falling on her face. It was moving. The girl Obishala was looking down on her with a strange, sharp look. The girl jumped. The expression changed, and she said, 'You're not dead.'

Ibu said nothing. She got up and slipped out of the *ju-ju* house. The girl caught her and took her into a hut, gave her a basin of warm gruel, very good, and a new cloth. Then she led her to Lisbet's hut and said, 'Here is Ibu. She was quite well this morning.'

Lisbet was lying on a bed. She smiled at Ibu in a manner that the child knew instantly for friendship. She did not smile in return, only because she was still afraid, and cautious.

Lisbet took her by the hand, pulled her close to her, and asked again, 'How did you fly out of the prison?'

'I don't know.'

'You have a very strong spirit, Ibu. Would you like to be a priestess?'

'Oh, no.' The child tried to retreat.

'But the *ju-ju* has accepted you. If the *ju-ju* had not agreed for you, you would be dead now.'

Ibu gazed at her with wonder.

'Ibu, anyone can see that you must be a priestess. You are different from other people.'

Ibu gazed at her. She was still full of confusion and perplexity. Although she was now called Ibu again, she did not feel like Ibu; or, indeed, like anybody. But the word 'different' remained distinct in her head in the middle of her confusion. Among all the words flying about there, and changing their shapes every minute, like bats in a dark hut—words like shaker, emir, witch, *ju-ju*, judge, wicked—this word stood still and bright.

'I'm different too,' said Lisbet. 'I can make people live and I can make them die too, if they are bad. I have a strong *ju-ju*. You shall stay with me, and I shall teach you how to make medicine. You will be my daughter in the *ju-ju* house.'

'Oh, no. Oh, no, I don't want it. I want to go home.'

'But how can you go home? They would kill you for a witch. This is the only place where you will be safe.'

Ibu began to weep. It was the first time that she had done so since before her first accusation. Since then she had always felt too much anxiety. But now, the whole events of the last week—her imprisonment, her angry parents, the flying, terrified woman this morning, the stare of the girl looking down at her in the *ju-ju* house, and Lisbet's kind, appealing voice—seemed to join, for her feelings, at one point. She was different. She belonged to this place, where the different people lived. She would never get away.

Lisbet made her sit down on the bed and began to pet her, smiling at her tears. 'But this is a good thing for you, Ibu. You will have great power. The *ju-ju* is your friend, and you need not fear anybody. You will be able to cure the cough and pains in the chest. You will make women bear children. And perhaps you will be able to find witches. I shall try you. I shall teach you plenty of things.'

Ibu was calm again. But now already she felt like a person; she was a different person.

XXIII

AFTER HIS DEFEAT OF COKER, Aladai was in authority over three-quarters of Rimi town. But he withdrew from his own central house on the market-place to a compound behind Elizabeth's—a fortress surrounded by other compounds full of his own supporters and by the whole of the third ward.

His books, bed, and clothes were brought here. Makurdi brought the clothes, but Aladai refused to wear them. His dress was still the blue kilt and white cap. Usually he went naked to the waist, but on official occasions he wore the *ju-ju* coat. The people demanded it. He put it on when he sat as judge in their cases every morning. But he would tell them—'Don't believe in *ju-jus*. This coat is nothing but cloth and silk. This spear did not go through it, because it hit a book in the pocket. Rimi people must put away *ju-jus*, and then they will become great and wise and strong—as they are meant to be.'

When Aladai said Rimi now in any connection, the word affected his nerves, pulse; he felt it through his whole body; it made his blood tingle. He understood that the people did not love Rimi as he did, but he said to himself, 'They are too poor and ignorant to feel any ideal. They must be taught.'

Two days after the Emir's death, when it was seen that the Resident made no attempt to turn Salé out of the palace, Aladai decided to fight. He was no longer so confident of victory. But it was obvious that, come what may, he must resist the betrayal of Rimi to an alien and Mohammedan like Salé.

Rimi could have no future, no development, under Salé. It would probably sink further in real quality of life—especially if the Mohammedans increased, and the Rimi women lost their traditional freedom.

He went to Elizabeth. She was sitting, as usual in the morning, in her private yard, on a steamer chair which looked incongruous and vulgar under the barbaric exuberance of her figure. A small naked girl squatted beside her on the ground, gazing at her with eyes rounded by the necessity of looking upwards.

Aladai said, 'The judge has not answered my letter.'

'I know—I am ready. The women are ready.'

'But no killing—unless they begin.'

'I tell them.' Pointing at the child, she said proudly, 'This is my daughter, Ibu.'

Aladai answered shortly, 'It's not play, Elizabeth; this is war. And no *ju-ju* tricks. Because if you try them, I'll smash your *ju-ju* house to pieces.'

'No; no *ju-ju* tricks,' said Elizabeth easily. 'Ibu, go over to the wall. We shall play as we did yesterday. The Galadima will like to see in.'

'I smashed Coker, and I could smash your *ju-ju* house just as easily.'

Ibu had gone to the other side of the compound, six yards away, and stood with her face to the wall.

'You must forgive me, Lisbet, if I am hard, but I am thinking of Rimi. I belong to Rimi now.'

'Don't look, Ibu.'

'Why do you play like that? It's stupid,' said Aladai, annoyed.

Elizabeth liked to play with her brother. It was part of the dramatic relation in which she lived with Aladai that she should sometimes curse him and sometimes be capricious. With Akande Tom, on the other hand, she was always the queen—even in their most intimate relations she did not relax her dignity.

'We had better talk of plans,' said Aladai. 'What will these women of yours do, Elizabeth?'

'What I choose. You say war—we make the war. But we make it by ourselves.' She said then, in English, 'I go call her—when I move my han' so.' She slightly moved her hand on the far side from Ibu, out of the child's sight.

But Aladai took care never to be impressed by Elizabeth. He said, 'You'll have to tell me what you mean to do. You will need my men's help.'

'We need no man's help. You will spoil everything if you are stupid.'

'You will spoil Rimi if you are stupid. If you don't tell me, I shall make the war myself.'

'If you start, I do nothing.'

'What a pity you don't understand anything. Stupid people are so obstinate.'

Elizabeth sat silent, looking at Ibu. Then she moved her hand. The child slightly moved her head, as if listening; then slowly turned round and stared at her with an anxious face, open mouth.

228

Elizabeth clapped her hands, and cried, 'Good—good—you are really my daughter! Now go in there behind the cookhouse.'

Ibu went in behind the cookhouse, where its round wall made an angle with the wall of the *ju-ju* compound behind it. She stood in this corner, with her face to it. She became at once tense, as if listening for something far off—not with her ears, but with her mind. Ibu had played this game many times already. The first time, Elizabeth had said to her only, 'Go over there; turn your back. Wait till I want you. I won't speak, but you will know. Then turn round.'

How was Ibu to know when she was wanted if Lisbet did not speak? But it was not for her to ask. Probably it was a simple thing that any grown-up could do. Yet, as she stood against the wall, she was anxious, and her anxiety inside her was like an ear listening intently.

Now, for the first time out of sight of Elizabeth, she felt still more anxious. She held her breath in her anxiety, her concentration. She was eager to please Lisbet.

The Galadima was still talking, in a loud angry voice. She wished he would not do so. Lisbet was not angry; she was laughing at him. Lisbet laughed at all the men, because she had such a strong *ju-ju*.

She could not hear Elizabeth while the Galadima talked, because his talk got into her mind and it could not listen.

Elizabeth said angrily, 'Wait, Louis—this is not play—this is important'; and then again she spoke in English.

Ibu listened with all her body, tense as an ear-drum.

She felt an impulse—was it Lisbet calling her, or a thought of her own?

She felt confused, tired. The Galadima began to talk again, still more angrily. Lisbet called to her, 'You can come out now; you didn't hear me that time.'

Ibu came to her. She felt dejected and angry. She thought, 'Yes, I heard you. But I didn't know because of the Galadima's talking. He spoilt it.'

But she said nothing. Even when, in this serious compound, she found herself at home among people she understood and respected; who ground corn and cooked, and marketed, and were busy every morning; who had not used bad language, and were particular about other people's language and conduct—she had not yet learnt to chatter.

She looked reproachfully at the Galadima while he walked up and down the compound, waving his hands, and shouting that he knew all about Lisbet's tricks and he wasn't going to give way to the *ju-ju*.

'No more witch tricks, Lisbet—whether I'm Emir or not.'

Lisbet smoked her cigarette, and smiled at him. Ibu highly approved of her mistress, of her calmness, which defeated the angry powerful man.

The Galadima soon went away, in a very bad temper, but Elizabeth lit another cigarette, and gave one to Ibu. This was her reward for being a good girl.

Afterwards they both went into the *ju-ju* house. In one corner of the compound, Ibu had already noticed a bushy tree somewhat like a dunia, but with a longer, narrower leaf.

This tree was carefully tended and watered; it belonged to the *ju-ju*, and was inhabited by the mother of the cannon *ju-ju*.

Elizabeth and Ibu cut twigs from the tree, and reduced the number of leaves on each to three without blemish. On each leaf she cut, with scissors, certain nicks.

They worked all day, and at dawn handed the twigs to three young girls, chosen for their speed, who carefully wrapped them up in a cloth, put the cloth in a bag, and the bag on their heads.

The messengers then ran off to the nearest villages, where twigs were handed to the chief club members in the village.

Only those were given twigs who could be approached without suspicion, alone in the bush or close to the wall of a compound. But each was given several to pass to others, during the day, with similar precautions.

The girls ran to the next village at once; but each, after visiting two villages, handed over the whole bundle to the local club chief, who then gave it to a fresh runner, already chosen and tested for the honour.

In this way the twigs reached every village of Rimi, which is ninety miles across and seventy long, within twelve hours.

The women's war began the next morning, so peaceably that nobody noticed it. The Waziri, who, in the interregnum, continued to bring daily reports to the Resident, assured him that there was no danger in that quarter.

On the same afternoon the Resident drove out to a place on the great south road, about six miles from Rimi, to inspect Sangster's new bridge.

He was met at the bridge by the native Minister of Transport and two of his assistants. These men and their assistants cut their salutes very short. Burwash was surprised at their haste. In the last days he had been accustomed to extreme and troublesome civilities from the native officials, who wanted their posts confirmed in the new administration.

They conducted him, at high speed, across the bridge and as far as the village. In the village no women were seen, but this did not strike him as unusual. Women do not appear in village streets on ceremonial occasions.

The village chief was also hurried and short in his answers. Burwash left early, and was surprised to find the bridge crowded with women.

They blocked it completely, as close as third-class passengers on a coast boat. Those on the outside plainly had difficulty in holding on; and at every movement of the mass loud yells were heard from them—like the shrieks of monkeys elbowed off their perch. A row of legs dangled over both sides of the bridge, like a fringe, but some of the women were being thrust out backwards, so that it was their behinds, in tightly-stretched butcher-blue or purple, which stuck out, over-hanging the river, ten feet below, in a very dangerous manner. Many more for whom there was no room on the bridge sat on the road and the river-bank. Three or four were squatted, knees to chin, on a big flat rock at the bridgehead, not four yards from the car bonnet.

All were chattering, twisting their heads and eyes about. Their faces, turned sometimes towards the car, did not express anything but the usual indifference of women in a mass towards an unfeared stranger, a neutrality mixed a little contempt. The women on the shore were talking the loudest, especially the one nearest the Resident. She was a young and handsome Rimi girl, chocolate brown, dressed in black plush. She wore a red handkerchief, and silver bracelets as large as wooden curtain-rings. Her big liquid eyes, and huge mouth, hands, neck, and body were in ceaseless movement while she uttered a succession of cries sometimes harsh like a parrot's, sometimes like a 'cello's, sometimes like an oboe's. She had every quality from the most rich to the harshest, and every sound had a gesture. She clawed the air, wriggling her toes; twisted her head almost to her shoulder and threw out her arms as if repelling a seducer; yelled and bounced up and down like a frog; or, nodding her head, ear-rings, neck, and eyebrows together, sadly fluted, and rocked her body in unison; at once mourning and declaring that destiny could not be turned aside.

When Burwash jumped up and shouted his ultimatum, the women on the bridge paid no attention. It was only when the chauffeur, Ojo, spoke in Rimi that a majority of them stopped their tongues. But the woman on the stone talked louder than ever. She uttered a succession of screeches mixed with laughter, that irritated the white man's nerves as directly as a road-drill or slate-pencil.

He turned round, fell back in his seat, and said to Ojo, 'Drive on.'

Ojo twisted his eyes back and opened his sausage lips. Burwash shouted at him, 'Drive on—I tell you.'

Ojo let in the clutch, and the car gave a leap and then stopped again.

'Not like that, you fool!' Burwash grabbed the sides. 'D'you want to kill somebody?'

'No, no, sah—no, I no want. Das what I *no* want.'

The woman on the shore continued to screech.

'Damn you, Ojo, go on. Push 'em out of the way. Wait a minute. Let me.' Burwash scrambled over the back of the front seat, took the

231

wheel, and suddenly pressed the horn. It screamed, and the nearest women on the road, taken by surprise, scrambled into the bank. Burwash let in the clutch. The car jumped, struck something, and the engine stopped. A shriek was heard under the wheels.

The women rose in a wave and threw themselves towards the car. Burwash, white as his shirt, was already in the road. A young girl of about fifteen was lying under the running-board. She was screaming like an engine whistle. The women uttered yells of rage, and now it was seen that most of them carried clubs. Some of these clubs were corn pestles, of iron-wood, four inches thick and fifty pounds in weight.

But before any could reach Burwash the girl in plush was on her feet screeching at them. Her large mouth opened as if from ear to ear, and her big teeth glittered pink in the sunset while she spoke, nodding now to Burwash and now to the women, admonishing the women with a finger, and bending her neck towards Burwash with a grin. Indeed, she seemed to be smiling during the whole speech.

Burwash had dragged the girl from under the car. Her leg was broken. He knelt down to devise a splint out of his walking-stick and a stake cut from a tree by Ojo.

The women stood in a circle, watching him, chattering. No one offered help. He completed his work with a bandage made of the girl's own cloth, and he and Ojo lifted the girl into the car. Then he returned to the driving-seat. But at once the women lay down in the road, touching each other. The whole visible surface was flesh.

Burwash jumped up, and shouted in Rimi, 'But it is for this poor girl—she must go to the hospital.'

The woman on the stone screeched in answer, smiling so that her gums were visible to the root. She bowed towards him from the waist, and at each bow, taking her cloth, by its two top corners, in her two hands, she opened it wide, so that her milk-chocolate body was seen naked within.

These bows, smiles, and the gestures with the cloth expressed a coquettish triumph.

'What's she say?' said Burwash, who could not follow the high, rapid scream.

'She say she woman.'

'What do you mean? She's just said something about the bridge.'

'She say she woman. Dis women's war now. So she no fear you.'

'But this girl must go to hospital.'

He pointed at the hurt girl, and said in Rimi, 'I take—hospital—with motor.'

The woman on the bridge repeated her pantomime, speaking quickly, and ended with peals of laughter.

232

'What's she say now?'

'I no fit tell you, sah.'

'What is it? Tell me at once.'

'She say, you come from woman—all mans come from woman—you drink life from woman's blood—she fit take her blood back—make other men. You make palaver, she cut you. She say old time, women chiefs for all dis land. Now dey chief again, make Elizabeth Aladai queen this land, Aladai king, no more pay more money for tax.'

Burwash was compelled to go back to the village, where he found the men in a panic. They were, however, not so much afraid of the women as of the Resident's anger. The chief said that the women's war was not their fault. That it was no good for them to argue with the women, because if anyone offended them they would kill him in a very painful manner. 'But so long as you do not annoy them too much, they will only talk and laugh.'

When this was interpreted to Burwash, he pointed out that he had been prevented from crossing the bridge.

The chief answered carelessly, 'Oh, yes; that was the women's war.'

Burwash had to leave the car and the girl, ford the river a mile below the bridge, and walk seven miles back to Rimi. On the way he passed many groups of women camped on the road, who laughed at him, but did not prevent him making a detour to pass them.

They laughed, but they did not jeer. They seemed like good-natured girls on a bank holiday.

When he reached Rimi, very exhausted, he was told that all the wires were cut and the motor bridge on the main road to the railway had been carried off. This was put down to the hill pagans, whose women were fond of telegraph-wire bangles, and who had once before carried away the road bridge to make spear-heads.

Sangster was highly amused by these feats of his darling pagans. He seemed to think that they had done something meritorious in breaking up communications.

Sangster was a good pagans' man, but, unlike Bewsher of Gwanki or Bradgate in Yanrin, he had never done anything to make them richer or to develop their government. He liked the pagans, as he said, primitive.

But he made them keep the peace. He went off now, in the highest spirits, with ten policemen, and chased some of his oldest friends round the mountains. He took care, of course, not to shoot them. He only burnt their houses. But he enjoyed himself quite as much as the pagans, on the other side, and he would have spent the rest of the dry season on patrol if he had not been recalled after a week by the later, and more dangerous, explosion in the Rimi district.

Meanwhile Rimi station and town were isolated. But, though the women deserted the market-places, they were behaving very well. The small parties who now began to stroll about in the station behaved like sightseers, staring at people and things. A dozen or more amused themselves watching Rubin at his evening bath. They came up to the verandah to see him in it.

The boys made no attempt to drive them away. Rubin, who knew the curiosity of the negro women, and who had, in the bush, often looked round to find grinning women's faces and round eyes at the window-holes, was highly amused, and exchanged sallies with them so much to their taste that their shrieks of laughter could be heard at the Residency.

As Mr. Burwash afterwards wrote, 'There was only one incident in the early days of the strike'—Burwash always called it a strike;—and that was an attack on Mrs. Pratt by a party of girls whom she met on the road. They were too slow to make way for her, and she screamed at them. Suddenly they flew at her. But luckily she was able to escape into the fort. The sentry closed the gate in time to save her from them. He, too, was behind the gate, and he seemed glad to be there.

Burwash at once took steps to catch Mrs. Pratt's attackers, but he found himself in a difficulty. No one could give him any information. The women's leaders did not appear. they only sent letters making absurd demands—the abolition of all market dues and taxes, the expulsion of unmarried girls from the markets, the cessation of retail trade in the stores, including Makurdi's, and the election of Aladai as chief. They refused to negotiate until these things were granted.

The Waziri, from whom he usually got information, had suddenly retired from his post. He was said to be ill with fever, and the Master of the Horse, who had taken his place, was only interested in enlarging the bodyguard and getting himself a rise of pay.

Salé had no information of any kind. He was, he said, too new in the position to know what was going on in the town. He was, however, so polite, so ready to help, if he could, that both the Resident and Fisk had greatly taken to him. He was, compared with the Waziri, the Master, or any of the old Emir's pagan rascals, so much of a gentleman.

Burwash enquired once or twice if Aladai's sister, the woman Elizabath, had not been associated with the women's clubs, but Salé, it seemed, had never heard of Elizabeth.

The political agent, Audu, like all the native men about the office, was reticent about the women's war. They did not show fear or amusement, but simply a kind of wary neutrality, as if to say, 'This is not our business.'

When information did arrive, from various sources, in the next few days, it was contradictory. Salé assured him that the women were making play, and it only required a few policemen with sticks to give them sense. His political agent told him that the women wanted to make someone called Lizbet Queen of Rimi, and Aladai her Waziri; to abolish all market taxes, and prevent the town-planning of the third ward.

Two trustworthy spies brought news that a *ju-ju* man called Coker was preaching war against the whites, and that the women were his tools. Another, from the bush, said that it was all due to the big fish. The big fish was angry because he had no sacrifice. He wanted blood. But fish were plentiful at Rimi.

This conflict of evidence had one advantage—it gave the Resident a free hand in the composition of his report, which was therefore very satisfactory to him. It explained that the slight disturbance caused by the sudden death of the Emir and the disputed succession had died down, 'but the market women have, in some places, taken advantage of the situation to advance certain local grievances. The interruption of the wires is believed due to irresponsible elements among the hill pagans. Mr. Sangster is enquiring into this matter. The situation is well in hand.'

He sent this off by a runner at four o'clock in the afternoon. At six, on reflection, he composed another—longer—one, on the succession, in which he pointed out that, 'Although the claims of Salé dan Seriki are very strong, it should not be overlooked that there are several other claimants from this branch of the family; while, on the other, Aladai is in some respects unusually well fitted for the position of Emir. The political situation——' and so on for three pages. A first-class report, leaving open at least three paths of escape from too hasty judgment.

But the man was tired and harassed. It was not surprising that, for once, he allowed a little irony to appear in his face, when at the reduced Scotch club, consisting, with a highly embarrassed marine and Colour-Sergeant Root, of five members only, Rubin asked him to sit on the committee of a new bagatelle competition, took half a crown from him as entrance fee, and said gaily, 'What Rimi wants is stirring up. We're all getting sleepy. I believe that half the station rows in Africa are due to boredom and nothing else.'

'Bagatelle,' said Burwash, now clearly ironical. 'Very good idea. But I'm afraid I'm rather busy at the moment.'

Rubin, an acute man, noticed his tone at once, and answered, 'Yes, I noticed the lady friends. I suppose the Probate and Admiralty Division is working overtime. Some of the co-respondents were calling on me this afternoon—made me feel like Moses in the bulrushes.'

XXIV

As soon as she had declared war, Elizabeth disappeared
into one of the *ju-ju* places in the high bush, about five miles from
Rimi. Nobody except the staff there, an old cook and Ibu, Akande
Tom, whom she took with her, and Obishala, knew where she was. It
was given out that she was in the bush making *ju-ju* for the war. Her
object was not only to escape from the police and Salé, but from Coker
and Aladai—especially Aladai. She was a little afraid of Aladai, but
she knew that if he could not find her, he could not threaten her, or use
any of his white man's *ju-ju* upon her.

On the second day of the war, when the women in Rimi, astonished
by the ease of their first triumphs, were singing—

> *'The big judge is become a little boy.*
> *He said to the women, let me by,*
> *They said to him, making play,*
> *Out of a woman and into a woman.*
> *The women make play with the big judge.*
> *Be careful, judge, of women, they are strong.*
> *Out of a woman and into a woman:*
> *The world is a woman, big judge,*
> *Bringing forth all things, all men,*
> *Out of a woman and into a woman'—*

not only Burwash and Fisk, but the Salé party, alarmed by the same
triumphs, were trying to find Elizabeth. But no one in Rimi, not even
the women, had any notion where to look for her.

Aladai was especially disturbed by the outrage on Mrs. Pratt. He
could not apologize for it, because to do so would be to acknowledge
responsibility for the women. But he wanted to make Elizabeth understand that she could not afford to allow such outrages.

But when he went to the *ju-ju* house to ask for her, he found there
only the two assistants, impudent and bored.

'Go away, you white man,' screamed the hag at the inner door.

'She is making strong *ju-ju*,' said two young women.

'Do you know where she is?'

They were chattering again. They did not trouble to answer. They
had their orders, and they obeyed them exactly. But underneath that

obedience was a belief in Elizabeth and her *ju-ju* that nothing could shake. It defeated Aladai.

Meanwhile Elizabeth was at breakfast. She sat in a room, at a low table, while Akande Tom, having served her, squatted down behind her, in his usual place, and gossiped. He was still wearing a banty, and during the last week or two he had been kept very short of cash.

'It's a pity,' he said, 'that Galadima Loo-iss is a friend of Coker's.'

Tom, though he was not permitted to see his mistress eating, gossiped freely to her at all hours. She liked his chatter.

Elizabeth assured him that her brother was not a friend of Coker's.

'I hope not, then,' said Tom, 'for Coker hates you and the cannon *ju-ju*. All the Christians hate the *ju-ju*. They want to spoil it.'

'I thought that you were a Christian, Tom?'

Tom paused, seeking an answer. Elizabeth smiled, and picked up a chicken drumstick, which she placed entirely in her mouth. Then, taking it by the knuckle, she drew it out between her teeth, stripping off the meat like the flesh from a date-stone.

'I'm a good Christian,' said Tom. 'Coker is a very bad Christian.'

'But my brother isn't a Christian at all.'

'He is friends with Coker, and Coker is getting stronger than all, except Salé.'

Elizabeth said, indignantly, that this was market talk—all nonsense. Tom knew by her annoyance that his arguments were having effect.

'It's a great pity that Salé isn't your brother. He would do everything for you,' he murmured.

'Ah! He talks.'

'All the people say, "Give us Salé. He will stop all the dues, all the taxes, and pay the *ju-ju* a hundred pounds first-fruits in new silver." '

'Ah! That rascal!' Elizabeth jerked her whole huge body in contempt and disgust.

'But he likes you so much, Lisbet. What a pity you can't see him! He wants to have you on the council.'

Elizabeth, who had been approached before, both by the Waziri and the Master, with all these suggestions and offers, answered, 'We'll see what happens.'

But, when Tom began to press her, she grew impatient with the boy. She was like an old statesman with a butterfly of a wife, who attempts to interfere with State affairs. At first she had put him off with jokes, smiles, caresses. But now he was becoming a nuisance, and she began to lose patience. She was especially irritated because he had managed to find exactly those points of anxiety which were disturbing her. She said sharply, 'You don't understand these things, my friend. You'd better let them alone.'

'But, Lisbet, if you would only see Salé—he will come to you himself.'

'I tell you, that's enough. Where are the cigarettes? They're never here when I want them.'

Tom, grumbling, went for the cigarettes. But he sulked all the morning, and renewed his attack at eleven, at the morning meal. Elizabeth turned him out of the room, and threatened him with a whipping. She had never whipped him, but she said, in her rage, 'That's what he wants, the big head. He's been spoilt.'

During this day it became known to Salé that Burwash had written to the Governor advising him that Aladai's claim should be considered. The report came from the provincial office, through Salé's agent, the head clerk's house-boy, who was on good terms with the clerk's wife. The Salé party then held a council, and agreed that the judge was principally influenced by the women's war. They sent for Akande Tom.

The same evening Akande Tom came to Elizabeth with a message that Aladai wanted her. Elizabeth said, 'Then let him come to me.'

'He's sick,' said Tom.

'Why didn't he write?'

'He's too sick—I think perhaps he has been given some poison.'

Elizabeth was frightened. She asked no more suspicious questions, but called her lantern-boy and set out for the town, following the bush path known only to herself, Tom, and her servants.

Within half a mile she was set upon by three men lying in an ambush, trussed up, gagged, and carried off into high jungle near the river, where they put her in a grass hut, newly built with strong stakes. Elizabeth fought them like a leopard, kicking, scratching, doubling her body, and pushing the men to and fro with her powerful arms. The men were terrified of her; and, when they had placed her in the hut and untied her, they at once retreated into the bush, as far as they dared, to keep their watch from a distance.

Elizabeth did not attempt to break out of the hut; finding herself untied, she at once became dignified and calm.

In an hour Salé, the little old *mallam* who was already acting as his Waziri, and the Master, came to her.

Elizabeth cursed them, but Salé had no fear of her. He was wearing all his talismans from the Koran.

The little old *mallam* said to her, in Rimi, 'My master has arrested you for murdering many people in your *ju-ju* house, and to-morrow we are going to take you to the judge.'

'You will die,' said Elizabeth. 'All of you will die in two hours.'

Salé smiled politely, and said, 'It is you who will die, if we take you to the judge.'

He then swaggered away, making his big sleeves flutter.

The *mallam* said, 'My Master is sad because you will not be friends with him. He wishes to be your friend.'

238

'Go away, you old ——'

'He wonders that you support the Christian Aladai who will destroy the *ju-ju*. My master is a friend of the *ju-ju*.'

Elizabeth lost her temper, and rushed at the old man; she would probably have murdered him if the Master, even stronger than herself, had not jumped between them and pushed her back. He told her, 'Don't be a fool, woman—we are trying to do you good.'

The *mallam*, gathering up his old ragged gown, slipped out.

Elizabeth screamed at the Master—'I kill you! You will die! Your blood will turn black!'

'Now, Lisbet, it's no good making fool talk.'

'Your feet are cold now.'

The master shrugged his big shoulders and threw up his chin. 'What's the good of doing anything with women? They have no sense.' He went out.

Water and food was brought, but Elizabeth refused to take them. She demanded live chickens, a goat, and a new pot. These were brought, and she killed a chicken, boiled it in the pot. Then she milked the goat and drank the milk.

The next day Salé and the Master returned. They offered a hundred pounds in new silver for her co-operation. She would not even speak to them; but, as they were going away, she said to the Master, 'This is your plan.'

'Ah, what fool talk! Did I know where you had gone to?'

'Akande Tom is a silly boy. It is you who caught me. Now you will die—your feet are cold.'

The Master burst out laughing, spat on the floor, and walked out. But outside he kicked up his left foot and felt it with his right hand. It was warm and strong. He laughed again.

On the third day Salé offered Elizabeth two hundred pounds in silver. But again she would not speak to him. The Master did not come on this occasion; he said he had better things to do. But afterwards he attended a council of the three conspirators, when they discussed their next move.

They had never intended, of course, to take Elizabeth to the Resident. There was no advantage to them in denouncing her, and a possibility of making enemies of all the pagans in Rimi as well as the women. They had only wanted to obtain her support; or, alternatively, by depriving the women of their leader, to make the women's war fail.

But the women had been leaderless for four days, and so far from going home and abandoning the war, they were growing bolder and more turbulent. The Resident was said to be in a panic.

No one had realized that the women were organized by villages, and that every branch was self-operating, nor that women do not need leaders as much as men. If they are given a simple object, they pursue it with great resolution, and often will continue to do so in spite of leaders. Their regard for leaders is as feeble as their discipline is bad.

The Rimi branch chiefs had not realized that Elizabeth was absent from headquarters; and her own assistants at the cannon *ju-ju*, who knew that she had disappeared from her hiding-place, supposed that she had gone elsewhere on her own *ju-ju* business. Akande Tom was also absent, and this supported their belief.

Elizabeth was beyond *ju-ju*. No priest in Rimi would undertake to put a spell upon her. The plan was, therefore, to poison her, and then to throw her carcass into the bush. Salé would then report that he had arrested a *ju-ju* woman for murder, but that she had escaped, by her magic, and disappeared, or possibly been killed by some beast.

Once a person is dead, there is no difficulty in getting rid of the body. Throw it in the bush, and the leopards, hyenas, and ants will pick it to pieces in a night.

The old *mallam* went into his own room, which was the late Emir Aliu's office, and sent for some chickens. He took a small thin knife, made a cut in the leg of each chicken, under the feathers, and with a thin split stick, hinged at one end, pinched some darkish powder out of an old scent bottle. He pushed this powder deep into the cuts.

The chickens squawked, but, when they had been released, they ran off in a lively manner. Half an hour later, two were dead, four others seemed to be dying, three were pecking corn. These three were sent to Elizabeth in the forest; and the same evening, when the old *mallam* and the Master were summoned to the hut, they found her rolling on the floor, foaming at the mouth. All the muscles in her body seemed to be twisting and knotting themselves separately.

When she saw them, she tried to raise herself up, screamed some curse. Then she fell back and lay motionless. They called the men, took her into the bush, and threw her into a hole. To make sure of her, they pegged her feet and neck to the ground with crooked branches—they did not use cord, in case of frightening away the beasts.

Just as the Master, whose strict orders were to see the end of Elizabeth with his own eyes, stooped to test the pinning of her neck, she turned her head, and, with a contortion of her whole body, spat on his hand.

'I eat you now,' she croaked.

The Master sprang away from her with a cry of rage and surprise. Then he kicked her furiously, three or four times, driving his heels into her spongy body. She screamed at him again, 'I'm eating you now.' He lifted his sword as if to hack at her, but, meeting her bloodshot eyes glaring at him, he let it fall again, and said, 'It is you die now. Yes, you die now. The hyenas will eat you to-night.'

He marched away, jerking his head in his contempt and indignation.

The whole party then mounted their horses and rode off towards the town. Salé was in good spirits. As soon as he arrived, he sent for his new favourite, Musa, to amuse him with his mimicry. For two hours, the boy, whose leg was still tied up in splints, shouted and pranced among the new Court, imitating the judge, the captain, the old Waziri, and Fanta in the hands of the robbers.

This was the most popular performance in the women's yard, and what gave it a special zest was the presence of Fanta herself, who had, some days after Salé's entry into the palace, been found, naked and starving, in the back ditch. She had got as near home as she could. A *dogarai* found her there, and took her in as cook. But she did nothing but weep and moan for her dead Aliu until, having beaten her till he was tired, he sold her for a cigarette-case to the women's doorkeeper. She was now, having learnt resignation, cook to the doorkeeper, who kept her in very strict order.

But Salé always insisted that she should attend Musa's performance, and he would say, when she failed to laugh at it, 'The queen Fanta is displeased with you, Musa. You don't please her. Do it again and make her laugh.'

Then Musa, to whom Fanta, as a cook and a butt, was worth no more consideration than he expected for himself, would waddle slowly into the middle of the yard—waddling only with one leg, but contriving to make it give all the effect, thrusting out his skeleton chest like the woman's deep bosom—and scratch his buttocks, and yell, 'Now, then, you lazy sluts—hurry up, there.'

He would strike a haughty pose, and say, 'My lord is the greatest king in the world'—then belch loudly.

He would then turn laboriously round; sit down, and begin to gossip—talking about his great lord, and also telling dirty stories, with screams of laughter, rocking himself from side to side.

He could even do Fanta half drunk, smoking a cigarette and getting the smoke up his nose. But his best turn was the old woman screeching in the hands of the robbers, rolling on the ground, and shouting at them, 'You dare to touch me—you'll catch it.' This was the part that made Salé laugh aloud—as much to see Fanta's face as she tried to grin at it, as Musa's gambols. Salé had a strong sense of humour, and liked every kind of amusement. He always attended a flogging by the native Court, and regretted very much that the white judges prevented the giving of the full number of lashes, as laid down in the Koran. Salé was also generous. He was already spending more money in the palace

241

than Aliu. He gave presents even to Musa, and he had promised several times to make him Waziri as soon as he was grown up.

He also gave presents to the girl Oya, whom Musa called his wife, and who, at Musa's special request, attended all his performances. Salé was willing that she should. He had noticed the child's firm limbs, well-shaped body, and neat head, and had already promised her to himself, in a couple of years.

The Master, who had introduced Musa's gifts to Salé, was the chief appreciator of his mimicry. But to-night he was sitting in his hut, staring at his hands. Now and then he rubbed his right with his left palm. Was it swollen or not? He could feel nothing. But it looked different. Had it always been different? No man's two hands were the same size. Or were they?

He called the *dogarai* guard. 'Look here, bastard'—holding up his hands, backs outwards. 'Look at these.'

The *dogarai* stared at him with an open mouth.

'My hands, you fool, not my face,' shouted Master. 'Are they the same size, or are they not?'

The *dogarai* began to splutter. He took a step backwards, and bumped his head on the doorway.

'At my hands—my hands!' the Master yelled.

'Hands, hands,' said the *dogarai*.

'Are they the same size?'

'Yes, Master—no. The right one is.'

'Is what? You cursed son of a bitch! Is what? This is the left, you fool.'

'It's the same. But not that one.'

'Get out! Damn and curse you to extinction!'

The *dogarai* ran away. The Master got up and walked round the room. He slapped his hands together. Then he sat down again, and stared for a long time at his right hand. It was aching now—there was no doubt about it. Or was it aching? Had it perhaps been aching all day?

Since the Waziri had been sent away, it was the Master's duty to attend the Resident every morning. Salé intended to make his old *mallam* Waziri, but he was not yet Emir, and meanwhile he knew that the Resident was accustomed to the Master.

When the Master arrived at the provincial office, the next morning, he was carrying his right hand in a sling and a large bandage. He had not news of anything—none at all; but he wanted a letter to the doctor to cure his hand.

Burwash was sympathetic. He liked this bluff old soldier. He asked him what was wrong with his hand.

The Master groaned, rolled his eyes, and muttered. Audu said, 'He says that it's a witch has done it.'

Burwash, who took every opportunity of attacking this absurd superstition, and who had an excellent little speech for use on just such an occasion as this, explained to him that it was impossible for witchcraft to affect the human body at a distance. It had no means of doing so. And, reaching out his hand, he said, 'I can strike a man with my hand —but I cannot hurt him with my mind, because my mind has no hands.'

Audu said to the Master, in a flat voice which disowned all responsibility for the white man's nonsense, 'He says there are no witches, because witches haven't got hands on their heads.'

The Master made his salute, as he sat, and said, in a loud voice, 'I thank you, judge. Your wisdom is my salvation. Give me a letter to the doctor.'

He had his letter, and went direct to the hospital, where Pratt gave him a purge and entered his disease as 'rheumatism.'

But he was back that night, in a hammock. His right arm was as big as his leg, and he was in high fever.

Pratt opened the hand, but there was nothing in it. The patient's fever did not abate.

XXV

Rimi station was split by the Rackham affair. Mrs. Pratt proposed a petition to the Governor, declaring that his brave and unselfish action had saved a catastrophe. She was supported by all the traders and all the officials except Rubin, Burwash, and Fisk.

For Mrs. Pratt this petition was a crusade. She visited every house in the station during the heat of the next morning, with her draft, asking for signatures. She had been at Rimi for thirteen months. She was as thin as a consumptive in the last stages; a little skeleton, white as paper. But her energy—at least her nervous, feverish energy—seemed to increase every week.

She darted along the fiery paths with her chin in the air, her eyes blazing, while the sweat dripped from her eyebrows and cheekbones; and, pausing by Carphew as he came from parade, she screamed, 'Have you heard? They're going to turn Captain Rackham out of the service. The only man who's done *anything*—the only *man* who's done anything. But it's going to be stopped. I'm writing to my cousin at the War Office and we're sending a round robin to the Governor at once, and I'm going to write to all the white men in the country to get up a petition—we'll send it to the King. My cousin will get it to him.'

The little woman was shaking with excitement and ardour. In her own mind she was defending civilization and a hero. Carphew had taken the draft from her hand, and was signing it in pencil on his knee, when Judy and Dryas came out of Rackham's house. They had been breakfasting with him.

Mrs. Pratt flew at them and made her appeal, but with more vigour, more fierceness. No doubt she expected opposition. Judy and Dryas, however, were quite ready to sign anything.

For the moment all the women were agreed in supporting Rackham: Mrs. Pratt because he was a hero; Dryas because Aladai, she said, had hit him first; Judy because it was abominable, she said, that a man's career should be ruined by so stupid an accident. 'Besides,' she said, 'It was my fault.' But the others did not ask why it was her fault. They were too excited.

Doctor Schlemm and Rubin, coming out of the company office, found themselves in the midst of their shrill babble. Mrs. Pratt turned upon them. 'I suppose it's no good asking *you*, Doctor Schlemm, to do anything for *white* people. Though I don't believe the Germans were nearly so considerate to their *own* natives. But I know Captain Rubin understands the real nature of this country.'

Schlemm took off his hat and stood inclined, but he looked confused. He was easily thrown off his balance by an attack of this kind. He did not know how to answer it. Rubin took the draft, and, holding it at arm's length, read it through. Once or twice he stopped to glance uneasily at Judy.

She saw it, and said sharply, 'Why are you looking at me, Captain Rubin?'

Rubin was as disconcerted as Schlemm. He begged Judy's pardon and held out the paper to Mrs. Pratt.

'I want you to initial it now,' said Mrs. Pratt, 'to give a lead. I haven't much hope of Mr. Fisk, because, of course, he's hopelessly under Mr. Burwash's thumb, but he might come in if he sees that everyone else has.'

'I haven't got my spectacles here,' said Rubin.

'But you don't need spectacles to sign your name.'

'I shouldn't like to sign anything like that without spectacles.'

'In fact, you're afraid, Captain Rubin. You don't care if Captain Rackham is sacrificed.'

'But Rackham has sent in his papers.'

'He had to—he was forced to. Without any chance of being heard.'

Rubin answered with a joke about the fear of the pen being the beginning of wisdom, which made Mrs. Pratt so angry that she was incoherent. She said that Rubin was typical, and that of course no one expected him to take a serious view of anything. He was in good

244

company, however, with Doctor Schlemm, who was of course quite *disinterested* in his views about a question affecting *British* officials.

Doctor Schlemm could only open his mouth and bow. But he and Rubin were greatly disconcerted, and retired looking foolish. It is the fate of most men in controversy with a woman like Mrs. Pratt.

Rubin was hurt and surprised. He said to Doctor Schlemm, who was breakfasting with him, 'I can understand the little Honeywood girl'—Dryas was as tall as himself—'but I was surprised at Miss Coote.'

'Miss Coote is in lof,' Doctor Schlemm sighed.

'It won't go on much longer if Jerry goes on playing with the flapper.'

'Perhaps it will be worse then—I tink it is fery bad now.'

'Jealous, what? Poor little girl. Jerry is a first-class chap, but Miss Coote strikes me as one of the best.'

'She is fery clefer—perhaps too clefer.'

'Rackham likes 'em clever. He's clever himself, you know. Regular scholar—hell of a chap for the books.'

'I meant perhaps Miss Coote intellectualizes too much her view of life. I do not mean that she is not a goot-hearted woman—no; but that from a religious point of view . . .' And he began upon one of those long and elaborate analyses of conduct, full of fine distinctions and dissolved philosophies, which in his Rimi sermons caused Rubin so much delight, though he did not understand a word of them, and everyone else such acute boredom; and which, in this case, amounted simply to the statement that Judy, though an intelligent, well-educated, and affectionate woman, did not see eye to eye with Doctor Schlemm about several doctrines of his sect. Doctor Schlemm was unusually long-winded and boring during these days because he was anxious about the mission. There was a rumour of trouble at the mission. The Resident had sent him a note to say that 'the man Coker is reported to be in the Kifi neighbourhood. Have you any reason to fear his influence in your mission village?'

Doctor Schlemm answered that no Coker or anyone like him had influence in the mission village. But he could not forget that mission pupil in Rimi rushing at him with a stick, and shrieking, 'Death to the whites.' He would have liked to forget his face, but he could see the lint and plaster on his nose every time he turned his eyes anywhere out of a direct line.

He was angry with Burwash for suggesting that anybody could have influence in the mission village except himself or the members of his staff.

Mrs. Pratt attacked Rubin again several times. She was enraged by the attitude of Burwash and Fisk, and said, 'But it will do them no good at the enquiry.'

245

In the evening there were only three chairs at the Scotch club. Everybody except Burwash, Fisk, and Rubin went to Mrs. Pratt's, by invitation.

Rubin was in great distress. As he said to Schlemm, 'I like Burwash; he's a damn nice fellow, though we don't seem to find a lot to talk about. I hope this silly business is going to stop now. It's made enough bad feeling in the station, and we all know what happens in a station when you've got bad feeling. It's a case of everybody's poison getting into everybody's meat.

When, on the next morning, he was cut by Mrs. Pratt on the town road, he became melancholy. Judy, seeing him alone on his verandah, drinking gin, at half-past five, asked him if it was not against his principles to drink alone. He answered that it was, but he was getting into practice. That night there was no Scotch club. The traders drank by themselves; and, to judge by the noise they made, drank too much. Burwash and Fisk were busy in the office till a late hour. Carphew went to the Pratts'. Dryas and Rackham played tennis together, with Judy for umpire, and then had a very good dinner together in Rackham's house.

It was a parting dinner. Rackham had been called to headquarters, which wanted to hear his version of the assault. He was leaving at four in the morning to catch his train, forty miles away, by car, and would not be back for a week; if at all. Dryas was going in two days to Kaduna, where she was to stay with business friends of her brother. This was Dick's order, but she obeyed willingly. She said that Rimi didn't suit her. It was too stuffy in the river valley.

All appeared to be in the highest spirits. Rackham had been in uproarious spirits ever since the fight. As Rubin said of him, 'You'd think Jock had won that sweep at last—or the Grand National.' He swaggered about the station all day, usually with both his women, and every night he was drinking at the Hides. Not that he drank too much, because he could not. Nothing made Rackham drunk. But he was making a feast.

He spent his afternoons in the gym with Dryas. This was the only time he was alone with her; and it seemed to the curious observers in the station that it was understood among the three that Judy should not intrude upon the gym and Dryas should not come to the club, the new club at Mrs. Pratt's.

'And it's just as well,' said Mrs. Pratt, 'for when I went to the gym yesterday to get my racket back from the orderly, they were quarrelling, and when people begin quarrelling one knows that they're pretty far gone.'

But when Rackham and Judy came to the club they behaved in a most affectionate manner, as if to refute Mrs. Pratt; and now, at dinner, all three were affectionate and hilarious, as if to refute each other.

Rackham described his future career as a bookie; Judy showed how she would manage, as his clerk, to swindle the backers. Dryas laughed at them both until she complained that they had made her throat sore.

After dinner Rackham and Dryas went out to identify Aldebaran, and then walked up the hill to see if the Southern Cross had risen yet. Dryas was not yet tired of that 'cockeyed constellation,' as Rackham called it. They walked slowly, their arms touching, and they were both very grave. It seemed to Dryas that they had escaped from something unpleasant, and she said, 'I don't know what we've been laughing at.'

'Judy was amusing. She could have made a fortune on the stage.'

'I hate this place.'

'So do I.'

'You needn't.'

'You're not still worrying about that ape?'

'No, it's the whole thing out here. I feel somehow wrong.'

But this did not succeed in avoiding the man's irritation. Rackham seemed to be in high spirits, but his temper was short, and he would not allow Dryas to talk what he called cant. He said angrily that she was giving way to nerves. There was nothing essentially wrong in colonial government, especially the Nigerian variety, which secured local freedom and peace at the same time, etc., etc. When he had finished his lecture, the girl, who had listened apparently with close attention, said, 'You must have hit him frightfully hard. There was blood on my dress.'

Rackham threw up his head as if to say, 'My God! these women—they're all mad,' then took her arm. This was the first time that she had permitted him to take her arm. She even seemed to press against him.

They had reached the top of the hill, a favourite outlook. From this height the Niger appeared like a sickle-shaped cut in the solid black of the ground, backing on the concave slope of Rimi hill. The moon, perhaps a week old, seemed to give no light to the sky, which was dark steel-grey, like Damascus-work on a sword blade, oiled for storage; and the river reflecting it was the same colour. Though it was darker, the darkness of the ground made it seem quite as bright; so the effect was that of a scissors-cut through a thin black material into sky behind; and the faint stars reflected in the river seemed like real ones under the floating island of the earth.

The earth seemed to shrink under her feet. How small it was after all, a mere speck falling through this huge darkness. The upriver night breeze, lifting her hair, was like the wind of motion through space. Now her eyes were used to the dark, and she could see that the station was full of lights and shadows. Somebody was walking on the road.

Two lanterns bobbed up from the river. A hyena howled somewhere near the barracks; and a boy shouted close by in the bush.

In the town a drum began to tap—then two more—out of time. She heard now the murmur of a great many people like wind in grass. Thirty thousand people. The whole dark earth was full of creeping, murmuring. The speck of dirt was crawling with life.

A fourth drum, a big one, louder, deeper, rumbled with a steady beat which, though muffled, seemed to vibrate through the whole ground, as if it were buried in it. This drum and its heavy shaking beat at once gave centre and measure to all the other sounds—the deep, urgent murmur of voices, the erratic tapping of the smaller drums, a sudden shout of laughter from the barracks, and even the distant yowl of a hyena on the other side of the hill.

It was like a heart beating through the murmur of blood; the workings of a body; the amusement and sharp, unexpected pain of a living creature; and now it seemed to be frightened. It was a stupid savage heart, like that of a beast.

Rackham stood with the girl on his arm. He was not conscious of the drums, and he did not notice views in Africa. His ideal was the English meadows, with well-timbered hedges; or sometimes, when he went visiting, an Irish landscape with little crooked fields and wide banks, reminiscent of furious riding. He felt the girl shiver, and said, 'Are you cold?'

She did not answer. The drum had got into her now by its vibration, like an organ felt in a floor. She could not move. She was rooted in earth and the earth's heart beat in her, driving her blood. It was a frightened heart; as strange to her as her own pulse when she was taking gas at the dentist's. Its stupid violence threatened to choke her.

'You're shivering. Take my coat,' said Rackham.

'No, I'm not cold. It's these beastly drums.' Her voice was irritable. The man had never heard her use that tone before, and he said, 'They're getting on your nerves. Some people out here can't stand the night-drumming.'

The girl sighed and said, 'The poor things don't get much fun, I suppose.'

'Plenty. They haven't taken to thinking, and they don't suffer too much in their consciences, if they have any. But I suppose you couldn't understand that state of being.'

'Me? I haven't much conscience, or I wouldn't be here.'

'I brought you here.'

'I wanted to come.'

'I'm glad about that.' He began to put his arm round her waist. She slipped away from him and said, 'We ought to go back. Judy's all alone.'

He was annoyed by this putting off, and said, 'Judy would have come if she'd wanted to.'

'She didn't come because she thought she wasn't wanted.'

'Oh, Judy is always thinking things, and I wish she wouldn't.'

'So do I—but she does. She's like that.'

Since Rackham would not move, she took his elbow and turned him down the hill. They walked back at a yard apart—their usual distance.

When they reached the house, Judy had gone. Dryas was frightened; Rackham more disgusted. Judy's lantern-boy was found in the compound, and he had not seen his mistress leave the house. Rackham sent him to look for her; but Dryas insisted on going with him.

She had not gone twenty yards before Rackham came running after her with a paper in his hand.

'She's broken it off. I've just found this in my room.'

'Poor Judy—but she's right.'

'Where are you off to?'

'I'm going to look for her.'

'Why go?'

The girl looked at him, and even in the lantern-light the change of her expression could be seen—like that of a kept-in schoolgirl who sees the door open at the end of her hour. 'No, I don't see why. It might be rather the wrong thing.'

'It isn't *really* too soon,' she said, after another minute's reflection.

'Not for me.'

'Not for me, in that way. I was thinking about Judy.'

'What a cool fish you are.'

She shook her head, smiling faintly. 'I'm afraid not—that's the trouble. It's you that are pre-war.'

'Ach!' An indescribable Irish guttural, not spoken in joke, but impatience.

Doctor Schlemm had dined with Rubin and Carphew. Rubin was once more in spirits. His scheme for a competition in Corinthian bagatelle; entrance fee, half a crown; handicapping by a committee, was launched.

Rubin had a bagatelle board on which most of the station had tried their skill at one time or another.

'It will bring people together,' said Rubin. 'Nothing like the competitive spirit for bringing people together.'

'Dat is a fery interesting thought,' said Doctor Schlemm, 'fery interesting'; and he began to talk about Hegel. Neither of the soldiers had read Hegel, so that the doctor was obliged to begin with a little sketch of dialectic idealism.

Afterwards Rubin saw his guest home. Rubin always saw his guests home. He hated the end of any kind of party.

While they were walking home towards the hospital rest-house, Carphew explained how he himself had come to be interested in philosophy from seeing an advertisement in an evening paper. He asked Doctor Schlemm, as an expert, what he thought about the problem of the lost tribes of Israel.

It was at this moment that they all saw Miss Coote, in a green evening dress, turn the corner from the fort road in front of them, come to a stop. Obviously she did not like the meeting. But she was in the light of their lanterns, and she could not turn back without betraying her wish to escape. She had to advance or openly run away.

She advanced, and enabled them to see the reason of her hesitation. Her eyelids were swollen so much that her eyes had almost disappeared; her nose wanted powder. Rubin was panic-stricken. He could not even say good evening. Carphew, the man of the world, said, 'Getting rather chilly, Miss Coote. Wouldn't you like a coat? My boy can get one in a second.'

Miss Coote thanked him in a husky voice, and said that it was chilly. She believed she had caught a cold already. But she was going home to take a hot bath.

They wished her good night; she passed them. Rubin said, 'That girl oughtn't to be alone. She's got it badly.'

'She seemed all right,' said Carphew.

'I don't like it. She looked queer.'

'What!' Doctor Schlemm awoke from some private meditation about Hegel or the chimerical Coker, and said, 'You think Miss Coote would do herself some harm. No, I can't think so.'

'She's got it badly,' said Rubin.

'But vy you don't stop her?' Doctor Schlemm began to trot down the road at an extraordinary pace, calling, 'Miss Coote.'

The soldiers saw the girl, whose green dress under the bright moon made her seem like a wraith, begin to move quickly away, as if a ghost were gliding over the earth. She was running from the doctor.

'By Jove,' said Rubin, 'the river.' At once, both he and Carphew, though the distance between themselves and Judy was at least a hundred yards, began also to run. Carphew went off at a great speed.

But about that moment Judy was seen to stop and turn round. Her white face, like a minute piece of moonlight, was turned towards them.

They stopped running abruptly, and stood about ten yards apart on the road, in very awkward positions.

The doctor came up with the girl and took off his hat twice, with a long interval between the movements. He was probably blown.

They walked on together towards the Hides bungalow. The next morning it was known that Judy had accepted an invitation to visit the Kifi mission. She was leaving that day.

The Resident tried at the last minute to prevent this journey. Coker might be making trouble.

Would they wait until Mr. Sangster returned and could accompany them with an escort?

Doctor Schlemm was shocked by the suggestion of an escort, and indignant that anyone should suppose his pupils at Kifi capable of being perverted by a man like Coker: certainly not Coker.

The Resident was too much worried by his own affairs to press the point. He had just been asked by Makurdi to hold an inquest on the Emir. Apparently Makurdi was prepared to charge Salé with murder—a political move, no doubt, but an awkward one. Aladai had sent another ultimatum, even more absurd and threatening than the last; and the Treasury department had queried to know from what source 'the sum of nineteen shillings and $4\frac{3}{10}$ pence has been credited to court receipts miscellaneous in April ult.'

On the whole the last problem was the most troublesome. In his experience, everything blew over in time except a Treasury query.

These are the various reasons why Schlemm and Judy made the trip to Kifi on the Friday morning.

XXVI

KIFI MISSION is on a plateau beside the Kifi rapids. It is well laid out. The buildings, though chiefly of mud, are well built, and form a square with one open side towards the river. The chapel stands at one inner corner, the missioner's house opposite. The staff, at full strength, was Schlemm, a married assistant called Fortt, a doctor, two native teachers, and a native dispensary assistant; but at this time the doctor was on sick leave. There were over a hundred pupils in the different classes at Kifi, and about three hundred communicants in the neighbouring village. But several thousand came to the mission for medicine and advice, and of these many considered themselves Christians, or part Christians—that is to say, they had added to their *ju-jus* some object connected with the mission—a cross, a bottle, a prayer-book or a piece of one.

When Coker was chased out of Rimi, he went to the nearest mission, which was Kifi, because he was sure of a welcome there. Kifi was on his rounds. He used to visit it regularly every two or three months, to preach and make a collection.

His services were held in a clearing about a mile from the mission, among high jungle. This place had been a *ju-ju* house dedicated to the crocodile *ju-ju*. The crocodiles had lived in a deep narrow swamp which passed along one side of the clearing. It was probably an arm of the river. Certainly the crocodiles came there to be fed—either with chickens and goats, or human sacrifices. The last reported sacrifice was in 1920, when a pagan from Kifi complained that his wife had been taken. The woman's body was found in the *ju-ju* place, split open, and laid on the banks of the swamp. But, as human sacrifice was not officially known in Rimi, the inquest found murder against persons unknown.

But the *ju-ju* priest had run away, and the place was deserted; soon it was grown over and forgotten. It was impossible to reach it by the old tracks, closed by an undergrowth thicker even than that of the old jungle on both sides.

Coker opened a new track from the north side in 1925, and took possession of the *ju-ju* place. He preached at any time when there was a quorum—even to one person he would preach. But when he came to Kifi on the Wednesday night, and the news went round that he was in the *ju-ju* place, hundreds made their way there. Most of these were villagers, but at least half the communicants, and even some of the senior pupils from the mission itself, went to hear him. They liked Coker's preaching far better than any white man's. It gave them pleasure. As the educated pupils agreed among themselves, it went to the heart.

When, now, Coker returned to Kifi, his audiences increased quickly. Soon nearly all the mission attended—even the young boys.

The news of the Rimi war and the Emir's death had gone through the whole country. The mission pupils, like the rest, were at tension. They did not sleep much now. They spent all day and night talking, and all this talk was of war, danger; of old wars and old massacres. It produced a kind of excitement which made the people crowd together. Nobody could bear to be alone. Everywhere one saw groups with their heads together, their lips moving, their eyes and eyebrows working.

At night the people went in single file through the winding alley of the *ju-ju* path. They held to each other because they were terrified of the darkness and the spirits of the place—spirits of victims, spirits of gods. They could hear them rustling and breathing softly among the leaves. At each sigh they felt themselves weak with fear, and this satisfied them.

In the opening they could see more clearly—the glitter of the moon on polished heads; shining liquid eyes, like china under water. Nobody spoke. The black stream trickled out of the black wound of the path, and slowly spread upon the bare trodden ground of the *ju-ju* place.

It was shaped like a very tall oubliette, narrowing towards the top, with one flat side. This was where the muddy stream flowed through the swamp.

The drops continued to fall from the black slit of the path until the ground was covered and no more could come out. But the path was still crowded.

In the middle of the clearing there was a ring of broken wall, where the chief *ju-ju* hut had stood. Here Coker, dressed in his tight blue suit, high collar, yellow boots, was sitting in a camp-chair, beside a table with a lamp, a Bible, and some papers in a spring clip. He always carried these papers. Probably he had noticed that the officials used spring clips for their papers. It was a symbol of authority.

He was not reading. He seemed vacant, half asleep. His face, as he sat sideways in the lamplight, gazing in front of him with his eyebrows raised high, a wrinkled forehead, a dropped under-lip, was like that of an imbecile. In fact, he was not thinking of anything. His mind was as completely vacant as if his body were inhabited only by a collection of organs. Like other negroes, he was capable of falling into this condition at any time, and passed long hours during which he was unaware of the passage of time. His body informed him when it was time to feed or sleep. He had, then, no personality, only his body had physical idio-syncrasies. Coker's astonishing vitality was probably due to this power of repose—more profound than any white man's. A black man's sleep is like death. He is out of the world. A carrier with a hundred pounds on his head walks in a waking swoon. Coker was for the greater part of his life in a similar condition.

His blank eyes, like pieces of yellow glass, sometimes turned towards the mass of his followers, whose heads shone close together over the whole ground, like shot in a tray. Eyes, fixed upon him with awe, glittered here and there like flecks of new-cut lead among the shot. Although no one spoke or moved, there was sound in the air character-istic of gathered people. A faint vibration rather than a sound, like a distant ship almost heard through water. It was probably the noise of hundreds of lungs opening and closing, hearts beating. In the forest there was the incessant mysterious movement of an African forest at night—sighs, moans, quick whispering speech, and then the squawk of a bird or the cough of a leopard.

Coker sat for a long time gazing at the crowd. He did not seem to know what to do with it. At last he stirred, opened the Bible, and looked at it in silence. Coker liked to begin a sermon with a text, but any text would do, because his sermons were always the same, and had no logical construction.

He read out now in Rimi, in a voice so weak that few could hear it, 'God said, surely the blood of your lives I will require.'

He remained staring at the book, and then repeated the text in a louder voice. He was waiting for inspiration. Coker was not a mountebank. He was a sincere believer and disciple, according to the rule that he had learnt, to wait for God to speak within. Then he would obey.

Within was the key word for those who taught him. Guidance was from within a man. Coker waited for his inside to speak.

Again he repeated the text in a louder voice; and now at the word 'blood,' usually an efficacious word, something came into his mind, came from the dark, like the crocodile out of its swamp. It was not, however, an idea. It was an impulse. Coker never had ideas for a sermon, he preached with the voice of his God.

Now he was on his feet, shouting the words of the text; and, in the silence that followed, it seemed that the vibration of the approaching ship was a little stronger. It could be heard. All the hearts were quickened.

The Fortts, placid Swiss, were not even surprised by the disappearance of their whole congregation for the night. They said, 'Poor things, it's their nature to get crazes now and then. It's no good expecting any serious work here until they get tired of all this political nonsense, which will take at least a week.'

They were, however, anxious for political news, and eagerly looked forward to Schlemm's arrival, promised for the next morning.

But they were waked up early the next morning, by a terrified assistant teacher called Jonathan, to see the school house on fire. A crowd of naked savages was running in and out of the other houses, apparently looting.

Fortt thought at first that the mission had been attacked by pagans. He ran to tell his wife to dress. He found her being dragged out of the back door by a crowd, in which he recognized several of his own pupils in the school. She was making no protest. She seemed to have fainted. On the floor a body was lying, without a head. A man was taking off its shoes. Fortt had barely time to wonder who it was, and to recognize one of Jacob's patent-leather shoes in the stranger's hand, when he received a blow on the head, from behind, which knocked the sense out of him.

XXVII

When Doctor Schlemm had called to Judy, and said, 'Miss Coote—Miss Coote—stop, please,' she ran because she couldn't bear the thought of company—least of all Schlemm's. To be treated with sympathy—this would be bad enough; but to be offered religious consolation would be intolerable.

She wanted nobody to tell her how to think and feel. She understood her situation perfectly. She had enjoyed, by a piece of extraordinary luck, great happiness, the greatest personal happiness—a communion of feelings and spirit and mind in a relation which was a new kind of existence. It had lasted only a few months; but anybody who had lived so, even for an hour, was changed—like a converted person who had looked into Paradise.

Now she had lost her happiness, and for ever. It had had its weak place in one difference with Jerry—a thin crack, which had proved to go through the whole substance, so that at a slight shake the whole mass had fallen apart, with the more violence because of its weight. Old maids and barely solvent men don't commit suicide; that is for jilted lovers and bankrupt millionaires. Judy had despised suicides, but now they seemed to her very reasonable people.

Schlemm's voice made her run quicker towards the river. She had only to step over the edge in the dark. It would look like an accident. Religious consolation would be unnecessary torture. Why should she bear any more? The very thought of the man with his stooping shoulders, his grotesque hat and walk, his ridiculous nose, covered with lint and plaster, his thick amiable spectacles, revolted her. He was like something soft and lukewarm, spongy and slimy, touched unexpectedly in the dark. But, when he called the fourth time, his voice stopped her. It pulled some string in her broken will which worked the signal—something which had responded often before to a voice asking her to stop and behave herself.

She was stopped, but she was only a broken will. She did not know how to speak when the doctor came up to her and took off his hat, panting, bowed, put it on again, and then after another attempt to get his breath, and another failure, took it off again and made another bow, as if to say, 'Please don't run away yet—give me a moment.'

'Miss Coote,' he burst out, at last, 'I wanted—so much—to ask

255

you something. Excuse me, please—I haf to run—I fear you go to bed.'

These words, and Doctor Schlemm's manner in saying them, removed the whole situation from the sphere of despair, broken hearts, and religious consolation to that of daily courtesy and social obligations.

Of course, Judy knew perfectly well why the man had run after her. She had seen those two stupid soldiers running too; in spite of their quick stop.

But it was not going to be admitted between them—not then, anyhow. There was not going to be any religious consolation. The great advantage that Doctor Schlemm possessed, as a missionary and Christian, was his breeding. He had been brought up in good society. Judy looked at Schlemm, smiling; and tried to answer in the same polite manner. 'Anything I can do, Doctor Schlemm, of course I'd be only too pleased,' but she could not speak.

However, that did not matter in the least. The doctor knew his way about in the drawing-room as well as any attaché. He put on his hat, and said, in serious urgent tones, 'No, no, wait and let me tell you—it iss about Mrs. Vowls. She iss not well. She tell me she iss quite well—but she is quite wrong. But she insists that she must come to do some work for me in Kifi. It is some writing work—for an appeal to my American friends. I wonder would you be so good as to come instead—so that I can say to Mrs. Vowls that she will not be yet needed—but perhaps you think it rather imbertinent of me to ask you so much?'

Judy, now finding her voice, said that she did not think so. She was greatly honoured. She would pack at once.

Doctor Schlemm was profuse in his thanks, and, when he said good night, pressed her hand, and said, 'You must allow me to say, "Got bless you," my dear Miss Coote, because I want Him to bless you.'

He then took off his hat and shuffled away.

Judy, therefore, did not escape religious consolation in the form of Doctor Schlemm's prayer.

She did not believe in a god to whom one prays for benefits. She was familiar, of course, with the theory of communication. To pray is to get in touch with the spirit of God, of Christ, of the Saints.

But Doctor Schlemm's prayer was instantly and powerfully effective. It left her once more speechless, but full of new purpose and the power of love.

She perceived, when she was capable of reflection, that the spirit does not always work by communion. It can be projected. This interested her very much.

It was said, after the Rimi troubles, that no one but a lunatic would have behaved like Coker. The military argument was that when he had the game in his hands he sat down and did nothing. But soldiers do not understand mystics, especially primitive mystics. It was quite logical for Coker, having raised his army and won his first victory, to go into mental coma again. He was, in fact, asleep all the next day.

His village followers, meanwhile, returned to rake the embers of the mission for loot, and the older mission boys wandered about with wretched bewildered faces, like men waked out of a drunken dream to find themselves with bloody knives in their hands.

Many of them took off their mission jumpers and ran away into the bush.

Schlemm's well-known dug-out was seen approaching at a little before five in the evening. At a quarter past it stopped at the village, about half a mile above the mission. On journeys down river the dug-out usually stopped at the village to bring down stores to the mission. This was a quicker and cheaper journey than land carriage. There were two passengers on board—Schlemm and another. Schlemm and the other, a small woman, whom none had seen before, lame in the left leg, walked towards the mission.

They were talking with animation, and presently the woman took Schlemm's arm. Both of them were laughing. Schlemm was describing something. He took off his hat several times, and made vigorous gestures with it.

When they reached the mission they stopped laughing, and looked with surprise at the burnt-out buildings. Doctor Schlemm's look of amazement, his open mouth and eyes, caused some of the village people who were watching, in spite of their warlike tension, to laugh.

Schlemm then ran into his own house. As soon as he left the woman's side, she was caught, gagged to prevent her screaming, and carried, as a prisoner, to the *ju-ju* place.

Schlemm was taken by another party in his house, while he was gazing at his empty bookshelves. Coker had ordered the capture of Schlemm, but not of the woman, whom no one expected.

Judy had been gagged so thoroughly that she was nearly suffocated. She became faint, but this was discovered, and the rags were pulled out of her mouth. Some raw gin was poured into her mouth, and she found herself gazing at foggy darkness—like that seen by a person who is recovering from an anæsthetic.

She was lying on wet earth at the edge of a bank, cramped but not tied. She could move, but, when she tried to get up. a tenor voice said something in Rimi, and pushed her with a broad flat foot. The touch

257

disgusted her so much that she contented herself with staying where she was.

It was dark, but the moon was rising. It could not be seen, because of the great height of the trees surrounding the tube or wall of forest in which she lay, but its rays fell on the upper leaves, a hundred and fifty feet above, with the effect of floodlight on the pinnacles of a tower. These glittering pinnacles of silver made the sky seem as black as the forest below, but an intense living black, as if it were making blackness. The forest was dead black, sucking life out of the air, blackness out of the sky. The few stars were as bright as sparks from the moon.

Below she could see these stars reflected—perhaps ten feet below—in water, and also, more dimly, on slimy mud. They made tangled threads of blue-grey steel on the water, but fainter, shorter spots on the mud, like dim phosphorescence.

The water was moving; the threads were in continual motion, as if being woven on a machine. Sometimes one or other of them, or several together, were wiped out by some dark long object, like a dug-out, which moved very slowly, and rather up and down than forwards and back. The water was seen as a surface of coke-grey darkness between the cavern-black shades, vague and hollow, of the banks; and this dark object appeared on its surface, first as a narrow broken line, which then gradually widened into a long oblong or oval, perhaps twenty feet in length. This lay on her right hand. On her left she could see, twenty yards away, a table, with a book and a lantern on it, and a tall thin man, with a pale brown face, apparently in deep black, sitting at it. He seemed to be asleep. He was surrounded by people, squatting on the ground, closely packed. She could see eyes among the trees, and, even twenty and thirty feet from the ground, faces, yellow in the lamplight, hung like swollen fruits from the huge trunks, sweating their sap in the hot motionless dark.

The yellow man was getting up. She recognized Coker. He began to speak. At first he muttered, shutting his eyes, opening his mouth a little, and curling back his lips like a fish. Then he began to shout. He still made no gestures, kept his eyes closed. But he opened his mouth to an enormous size, and, turning slowly from side to side, uttered his sentences in quick panting yells and roars which made Judy's own heart jump. Each yell seemed to hit her nerves like a plectrum on tight strings. This was specially so when it was delivered straight towards her.

The crowd was yelling. The blast of its yells terrified her. But she still stared at Coker. He turned, and began to walk slowly towards the bank. He still bellowed; his eyes still appeared to be shut; he still carried himself stiffly; he looked like a sleep-walker. A boy had snatched the lantern and book from the table. He walked beside the preacher, with the book under his arm. He held up the lantern so that its light fell full on the ground in front of him.

When he reached the bank, Judy saw that the dark object in the water was an immense crocodile, now lying half upon the black mud, half in the water. When the light flashed in its eyes, it lifted its head and tail, scuttled into the water, and disappeared.

Coker knelt down on the bank and began to pray. Some of the people also knelt down, others threw themselves on their faces; many stood by the bank, gazing at the water with imbecile expressions, their eyes bulging, their mouths hanging open. Behind them a great many seemed to be dancing.

The crocodile was rising; the serrated knobs of his backbone broke the water.

The yells had changed their character. The waves of noise were broken by furious cries. Some of the dancers continued to jerk and gyrate in their dance; others rushed here and there, waving their arms. The confusion increased. Suddenly the crowd broke in the middle, and three tall figures were seen walking towards the bank. The first was plainly Aladai. He was dressed in the famous coat, put on over a blue kilt. His legs were bare, and there was a small white skull-cap on his shaved head. He looked like the cannibal chief in the comic papers, in his old school blazer. The white patch sewn round the spear-hole in the pocket made a good imitation of a school shield.

He was carrying a long spear in his hand—no doubt the *ju-ju* spear. The two following him were a man and woman Judy had not seen before. The woman was young, and, as she walked through the crowd, she looked at them with smiling disdain. She had the air of being on holiday. The man was an old black pagan, almost naked, also with a long spear. He was obviously terrified. He kept shouting at the crowd with the gestures of a man surrounded by fierce angry dogs.

The yellow man did not get up until Aladai was within a yard of him. Aladai shouted at him in English, 'What you do, you damn fool?'

The other answered in Rimi. Aladai, shaking spear and fist in the air, and making a leap, howled, 'You spoil everything—do you want the soldiers to come and shoot you? You damn fool beast!'

Coker, who had seemed too much surprised to answer, now also began to yell; the crowd yelled. And now no voice could dominate the uproar of three or four hundred shouting voices, because they had no order or coherence—they were a continuous fluctuating roar.

Judy could not hear what Aladai or Coker was saying. Often she could not see them, because now the whole mob was on its feet. But suddenly she was surrounded and seized. Excited voices jabbered in Rimi. Somebody said, in English, 'Doan call, missy. We do you good.'

She was pushed into the darkness and stood against a tree. The jabbering became frantic. Somebody hit another person a sharp blow in the face. A machete whizzed past her face and cut into wood. Cut tie-tie fell across her shoulder; caught her by the feet. She stumbled up, and at once powerful arms grasped her by the waist and lifted her into the air. She was sitting on a shoulder, with her right fingers tangled in the wool of a negro head. The skin of the head jerked in time with the rapid speech of its owner, who never stopped talking for a minute.

Now a dozen machete were at work, slashing through the tie-tie, chopping into the thick stems of creeper. Sometimes the heavy blade struck a tree with a heavy dull sound—a clop, and then the owner could be heard cursing while he jerked at his blade. Judy's steed moved slowly forward, talking all the time.

XXVIII

AMONG THE TRAVELLERS held up by the women during the Rimi war was a forester, whom they treated very well; a Gold Coast clerk, whom they beat and robbed; two white prospectors looking for blue clay, whom they imprisoned for five days in a hut less than eight feet in diameter; Rackham; a new M.O. called Fathers, coming to relieve Pratt; and Dryas Honeywood.

She was found at the railway rest-house. Her boys bolted at the first warning about tea-time, and the women walked in and helped themselves to her kit. Luckily the girl had the sense not to resist. They pushed her about and jeered at her, but they did not hurt her; and they left her the clothes she was wearing and a topee.

The next day all these whites except the prospectors were brought together at a place about twelve miles from Kifi. This was done apparently by some of Coker's followers, but not by his orders.

Fathers was a plump young man, at once dogmatic and shy. He retired into a hut and was not seen except at meals, which, by agreement, were held in mess at the rest-house. At meals he either made all the talk, lecturing everybody, or none at all. The forester was also young, but taciturn. He smoked a foul pipe and sulked about his misfortune, especially the loss of his books. 'What good,' he asked, 'is P. G. Wodehouse to these——' He swallowed the word in deference to the lady. He was very polite.

Dryas and Rackham's engagement had not been announced; but both these men treated them as engaged. Their mutual excitement was very plain. They protested against being left alone, but they were glad to hide their embarrassing happiness and still more embarrassing passion from the unhappy and depressed young men lamenting their lost property. The more Rackham knew Dryas, the more she excited him. He had realized that, for all her control, she was nothing of a prude; but he was surprised by the frankness of her love.

It was delightful to watch this girl handle anything, from her own love-affair to a rebellious, sulky servant or a teapot. She had always the same power, concentration, and neatness.

They had agreed to leave Nigeria. Rackham would not withdraw his resignation. Dryas hated the country; hated the dirt, the insects, the heat which made her skin sticky, and especially Aladai.

Rackham protested against this last; he had forgiven Aladai now that the man was at a distance from his life. When news arrived by the forester's assistant, who brought him a razor and some tinned army rations, that the soldiers were coming by the railway to cut off Aladai and Coker's escape north, their only road of escape, he said, 'Poor devil, that's the end of him.'

'I suppose they'll shoot him.'

'If he is fool enough to fight.'

'I don't really care if he is killed.'

'I will rather. That nig's got guts. The way he came up for punishment. I had to push him in the river to get rid of him.'

'Yes, there was blood on my dress.'

' "Out, out, damned spot." '

'I suppose they'll ask him to surrender first?'

'I don't believe in the soldiers. Burwash won't allow any shooting; it would be too dangerous.'

'They'd murder us. That would be certain.'

'I meant for his career.'

'I hope they'll hurry, whatever they do. This is hell.'

'Which of us is the Devil and which is the lost soul?'

The girl coloured; but she did not smile as usual. She said, 'I'm not a devil. Even this place is too hot.'

Rackham was alarmed by her looks, and said, 'Did you take your quinine this morning?'

She admitted that she had not. It made her head ache. But he gave her ten grains.

The next morning her head was aching, and he prescribed aspirin. Luckily, the doctor had some with him. But she did her usual day's work, washing and ironing her single change of clothes, and cooking for the whole party; she was still silent and preoccupied.

Rackham could not go away from her. He did not know why he was so anxious about a trifling illness. He fussed about her like a nurse, though he could see that she wished him away.

In the evening, after their supper, when she was mending the doctor's shirt (he had only one, and he had gone to bed while it was mended), he hitched up his chair to her till his knees touched hers, and said in the Irish accent which usually pleased her, 'Do you know what's wrong with you at all?'

'I wish you hadn't told me about the soldiers.'

'About what?'

'The soldiers.'

'I thought you were tired of washing your underclothes every day.'

'No, it's that man.'

Rackham turned red with anger. He might defend Aladai himself; he did not allow her to do so. He said now in his sharpest tone, 'You're sentimental.'

She looked at him blankly, and her stupid, obstinate expression, setting upon her face like a mask upon living flesh, angered him. She muttered, 'It's only a feeling.'

'Of course, it's only a feeling. It's the kind of feeling that makes flappers everywhere *schwärm* on the nationalist hero—especially a nigger, because there's an extra thrill.'

Dryas thought how she had recoiled from the touch of Aladai's hand, and her face became still more obstinate. Her under-lip was thrust out. She looked like a naughty child. She was not going to quarrel with Jerry or tell him that he was talking nonsense—that, so far from *schwärm*-ing on Aladai, she loathed him. It was no good; he would not understand.

How could she explain to Jerry the sensation that had kept her awake all night; of fear and guilt. What had she done? Why shouldn't she go away from Africa? Why shouldn't she enjoy her happiness now that she had it.

She lay in a trance deeper than fear under the darkness which pressed upon her like a secret law; a law of nature; crushing her down; into the African earth which she hated.

That had been a nightmare, she supposed. She must have been dozing. It had gone when, by a strong effort, she jumped out of bed.

But she could not expect Jerry to understand that she was terrified by Aladai's danger; because she had secretly recoiled from him; from his blackness. She didn't understand it herself.

'Your politics are all in your feelings,' he said to her. 'Haven't you heard Judy on that subject?'

It was a mistake to mention Judy, as he saw at once by the girl's heightened colour and quickened breathing. But Rackham did not care. He was too angry; and also he was frightened. The thought jumped up in his brain, 'This is going to spoil our happiness, this absurd complex about that damn nigger'; and another thought at once followed, even more disturbing and unexpected: 'It's a punishment exactly fitting to my crime—a perfect fit.'

He instantly drove both intruders into whatever recess of his brain from which they had sprung, and turned furiously on the girl.

'Look here, hadn't you better pull yourself together?'

He abused her for three or four minutes, telling her that she was suffering from a morbid conscience; that if anyone was to blame for the Aladai affair, it was Judy and himself, not she.

She answered, 'We're all to blame.'

'Not you. How can you be?'

'I mean everybody.'

Rackham controlled his temper. Wild notions came to his mind. Did he know the truth about Aladai? What had really happened in the bush? He exclaimed, 'Did he make love to you?'

'No, of course not.'

'Then why——? He stared at her. He thought, 'No, it's impossible. She's as straight as they make them—as clear as glass. Then why——?'

He caught her looking at him with a peculiar expression of defiance. He felt a shock of alarm; smiled at her in an embarrassed manner. He seldom felt embarrassed, and he did not like the sensation. He thought, while he held this absurd grin to reassure the girl: 'No foundations, that's the trouble. She'll never break, never go to bits. But she might sink bodily into the mud.'

She was sewing again, bending her head over her work; a charming domestic scene. But Rackham's uneasiness increased, and he felt angry with the girl. He thought, 'Yes, that's what it floats on, all that sentimental sixth-form culture. Slush, a crocodile swamp,' He exclaimed sharply, 'You'll ruin your eyes sewing by that candle-light.'

'I promised the shirt for to-morrow.'

Rackham jumped up and prowled across the hut and back. He exclaimed suddenly, 'You seem to forget that you disliked the man at first sight. It was you who said you hated black men.'

She got up to escape, and made this incomprehensible remark: 'But don't you see that's why I feel so awful now?'

At night they sat opposite each other for two hours without speaking a word. He did not know what to say; and she had nothing to say. But when she got up and said good night, he exclaimed, 'For God's sake, when we were so happy, you're not going to let this stupid thing spoil us now?'

Her mouth trembled again and her under-lids became red. 'I don't want to—that's it. Oh, how I wish I'd never seen that man!'

Rackham did not go to bed. He walked up and down in the moonlight until he was tired. Then he wrapped himself in his warm and lay down in his chair. He could not bear the thought of the stuffy, narrow hut. He would not be able to breathe in there.

He was full of uneasiness. It puzzled him. Why had he been so angry with the girl, and what was worrying him? How absurd this was! He was like a new married boy, all nerves and doubts.

Suddenly the uneasiness came to a head, and formed in his brain the single word, 'Vowls.'

'Vowls.' He stared at the black bush. 'What am I thinking of? She's nothing like—quite a different type.' He got up slowly and looked behind him at the hut, as if he could see Dryas's athletic, strong body through the walls.

'The athletes aren't immune—anything but——'

He fell back again in his chair. 'No, no, it's this bloody hole getting on your nerves. All the same'—his nose wrinkled—'Mrs. Vowls—there's a taste of her there.'

He reflected, and a kind of groan came out of him. 'Why did I do it?' And then again, aloud, 'Who did it to me, or what?'

XXIX

JUDY WAS TAKEN to Kifi village, where she spent the rest of the night in her own bed. Most of her property had already been gathered, and what was missing and necessary was supplemented from the mission loot.

Aladai came the next evening to apologize for the attack upon her. He was curt, almost rude; blaming her for coming to Kifi at such a time. Schlemm was lucky to escape, he said.

'They wouldn't hurt Schlemm, would they? Not here at Kifi?'

'Coker would murder him if he caught him.'

'But where is he, then?'

'In the bush somewhere, I suppose. He'll find his way to Rimi all right. He used to shoot big game before he was a missionary.'

The boy seemed gloomy and ill-tempered. 'You too are lucky to be alive.'

'I suppose I have to thank you for that, Louis.'

'I'm afraid you had a bad time.'

'It may have been at the time, but now I am very glad I had it. It was *really* exciting.'

She began to ask him questions about crocodiles, Coker, local Christianity. This was not all from policy—to draw the boy out of his depression and make him chatter and instruct, as he loved to do—but because she was exhilarated and full of new curiosities and ideas. Had Aladai ever attended one of Coker's meetings? Was that crocodile a *ju-ju* beast?

He lounged in a chair, gazing at the floor. He had not gone to Coker's meetings. Coker was a lunatic. No doubt the crocodile was a *ju-ju*, but, if so, he would shoot it as soon as this war was over.

'Not exactly a war, Louis.'

'The killing hasn't begun. But it is a war.'

'But, Louis, no one is dreaming of a war. Unless Elizabeth is, and you could easily settle her.'

'Elizabeth.' He shrugged with his whole frame, making the chair creak. 'I haven't seen Elizabeth for a week. I don't know what she's up to. She's hiding from me—that's a woman's trick.'

'Why don't you go to Rimi and see the Resident?'

'This is the danger-point.'

'Then leave it before the trouble begins. I'm sure the Resident would be very glad to see you.'

'The Resident knows what I stand for.' The boy jumped up in excitement. He was in native dress, with the grey coat. 'Why didn't he answer my letter?'

'You don't want a real war, Louis.'

The boy made a gesture, as if to say, 'So be it.'

'And then a lot of people will be killed for nothing.'

'Perhaps it would be the best thing.'

Judy was indignant, and said that she did not think it would be a good thing for anybody. What Rimi people wanted was peace, and more money to buy themselves food, clothes, and health; and they could not spare anybody capable of giving them intelligent leadership.

Aladai stood looking down on her. Then he said, speaking coolly enough, 'You think me a hot-air merchant, Miss Coote, but I am not so unreasonable. If people are killed, the Government—I mean your real Government at home'—Aladai, like Jamesu, called England home —'will take notice, and perhaps they will realize that it is a crime in this country to let a whole nation—a loyal and peaceful people, who only want to be good citizens of the commonwealth—live and die like their own pie-dogs who starve on every rubbish heap.'

Judy, frightened by this fierceness in the boy's look and speech, said, more sharply than she intended, 'War never did anyone any good.'

He smiled and answered, 'I'm sure you know better. What would England or France or Rome have been without wars? No, don't laugh. I'm not thinking that we Rimi can conquer empires. We don't want to. But we can be a nation, a real nation with a soul, with freedom. There are a million of us, you know, and our rulers say, "You people are too stupid to think, to learn. You are only fit to be slaves; *ju-ju* worshippers." '

'That simply isn't true, Louis. There aren't any slaves in Rimi.'

'They are all slaves—the worst kind—slaves to ignorance and *ju-ju*. And do you think anything will be done for them unless they fight?'

'Louis——'

But Aladai, thinking of the wrongs of his people, could not stop for argument. 'You think we do not dare. You think we are afraid. But the Rimi are afraid of nothing. It is all they have—their courage—and they know this, that even if they are defeated——'

'They must be, Louis.'

'It would not be a defeat if your English Government were frightened; if somebody in England said, "Why were these people killed?" and it was answered, "Because they fought for books, for teaching, for an escape out of their helpless misery." '

The boy's voice had not risen; but it had the effect in emotional force of a shouting army, trumpets. It made Judy's heart beat quickly and her cheeks flush. But she said mildly, 'I like you in native dress, Louis.'

He did not answer, but he slightly changed his position to a more becoming pose. Then he turned to her, struggling to catch his breath, and said, 'Forgive me, but it makes me angry to think how stupid they are.'

'Why not write to the Resident and tell him so?'

'Because it is his turn to write to me.'

'I shouldn't stand on ceremony, if it will prevent a war.'

'I don't stand on ceremony, but why should Rimi crawl to a foreigner?'

'Oh, no, I didn't mean that. I should put your case strongly—it is a very strong case.'

Aladai stood breathing quickly, with savage anger in his mouth and eyes. But they were fading. He looked again at Judy—doubtfully, as if saying to himself, 'She's playing with me—making a fool of me.'

She said to him, 'Your great strength with the Resident is that he knows you are an educated man, that you won't be carried away by slogans, and I'm sure he's your friend. Salé has been unpopular since the strike began. They even accuse him of poisoning the poor old Emir.'

Aladai was now calm, the European. He answered, 'Yes, but suppose he makes me Emir and does nothing—no development, no education— what will I be able to do? He will say, "Slow and sure," and put it all off for a hundred years—for ever. And if I make trouble, I will be got rid of.'

Judy could not deny the possibilities of this, and she was too honest to attempt it with Louis, who was honest too. She said only, 'I suppose one has to trust somebody, Louis, or nothing would ever be done, and when you are Emir you *will* be able to do something. You will have an official position. You can go straight to Downing Street.'

Aladai was looking at the wall, and, seeing his expression at once dreamy and exasperated, she wondered if he were so confident as he seemed; if he were not hiding indecision by his brave tone.

He turned, caught her eye, and said, 'I only ask now, What does Rimi need? I must do what she tells me.'

Judy did not like this use of the word 'she'; it was, she thought, one thing to speak of Britannia or France or Italia as 'she,' and another of Rimi.

She said nothing. She was afraid of hurting the boy's excited feelings. But he, more sensitive even than usual to the criticism of a friend, had already withdrawn from her. He said politely, 'You do not feel like that? But, then, this is not your country,' and he added with a faint smile, 'Your slogans are not my slogans.'

He shook hands with her, thanked her for her friendship, and went out, leaving her in what she admitted was a sentimental but anxious mood.

Half an hour later, when the drummers began for the night, and the crowds began to pour into the village, she saw him walking among them, spear in hand, and they fell at his feet, crying, 'King, lord, Master, save us!'

She could understand then that he had some excuse for nervous exaltation. In spite of the grey coat, wrinkled across the shoulders and split under the arms, he looked more royal, more the leader and king, than any ruler she had seen.

XXX

I BU WAS LEFT ALONE in the bush *ju-ju* with the old cook. She was a bad-tempered old woman, like many cooks, and she did not like children. She had driven Ibu out of her kitchen a hundred times.

But the child returned again in two minutes, like a fly to treacle. She could not keep away from the cook, who was exactly like a dozen old women that she had been brought up with—dirty, fat, perpetually in a fluster, grumbling to herself all day.

When Elizabeth failed to return, the cook was frightened, and she did not drive the child away when she came to the door. She continued to cook and sweat and grumble, as if she had not seen her. Ibu, with the discreet face of a child disobeying its elders, walked round to the back of the fire.

'Now then,' shrieked the old woman. 'What are you doing?'

But she did not shout, 'Go away,' or throw her pot-stick. Ibu, scared but resolute, sat down.

'Just one word,' the old woman said, waving her pot-stick. 'One word.'

Ibu drew herself together; her eyes rounded, she sat silent.

'Slipping away like that,' grumbled the old woman, 'and all these evil spirits about.'

'Granny,' said Ibu thoughtfully.

'But it's always the same,' said the woman. 'She doesn't think of anyone but herself.'

'Did you ever go to the palace?'

'And what am I going to do now?'

'*I* went to the palace with Musa.'

'But this is the last time. That's what I say.'

'You don't know who Musa is; he's got one eye.'

'No yams left.'

'Granny?'

'No consideration.'

'What's a judgie, granny?'

The old woman gave a shriek which caused Ibu to shrink up like a hedgehog; her eyes grew huge. But the old woman was only screaming her own thoughts. 'I'll clear out—yes—I won't stand it.'

Ibu at once uncoiled. 'Granny, do horses eat people?'

'What are you talking about? Hold your tongue. No, you little fool.

What about horses? Where's your cloth? If you've lost that cloth, I'll give you something.'

'Granny.'

'And the pepper nearly finished.'

'Do you like cigarettes, Granny? I don't—they make me cough.'

'What did you touch them for, then?' said the old woman.

'Fanta gave me one.'

'Fanta—Fanta—who's Fanta? You little silly—there are hundreds of Fantas. It's all lies; I can see that. Oh dear, oh dear! What a day! I'll give you a smack in a moment, if you tell lies.'

But Ibu was extremely happy. Nothing that the old woman could say could crush her or frighten her; she was used to old women like this one. She continued her chatter.

After two days the cook lost her nerve, and came into Rimi, bringing the child with her. But no one in the cannon *ju-ju* had heard from Elizabeth.

In the evening the cook sat in the cookhouse with the other old hag the doorkeeper. They grumbled together. 'What did I tell you? She never thinks of anyone—never tells you anything.'

Ibu sat between them, with her face in the smoke. Her eyes were watering, and she sneezed when the fumes went up her nostrils; but she would not have been anywhere else. This was the same delicious smoke that had made her eyes water in her own kitchen.

'Granny, do you know what Musa said?'

She had already found the gang on the waste land. She had been playing with Musa that morning.

'It's *ju-ju* business, I suppose?'

'He said that camels——'

'Be quiet, you pest.—But she'd have told me then.' This was the doorkeeper.

'Granny, do you know what Oya calls her baby?'

But the hag from the door suddenly caught her and threw her into a corner. 'Lie still, you pest, or I'll give you a whipping.'

'But, Granny——'

The hag, with the cook's approval, then smacked her, and put her to bed in the corner. Ibu did not cry. She was not frightened, but she knew that the doorkeeper was less patient than the cook. She lay still and tried to go to sleep. But she was wide awake, and her body did not want to lie still. It wanted her to scratch it; to move its legs and arms; to roll it over; to get up and run it about. She tried to hold it still; and then suddenly she felt as if somebody wanted her.

The impression was so strong that she said, 'Granny, did you call?'

'You pest; do you want another smack?'

Ibu, since this time she had not been talking about her own affairs, was wounded in her feelings. She considered herself justified in crying; and cried herself to sleep. But at night she woke up suddenly, got out of bed, and walked into the yard. It was empty. The old mortar, with one side chipped and split half-way down, stood by itself in the moonlight, full of blackness. Ibu did not like the look of it; she made a circle round it on her way to the porch.

The gate was closed by a bar, to which three or four old tins were hung as a warning bell. When Ibu, in the dark of the porch, tried to lift the bar, the tins rattled, and the old porter, who at night guarded the outer door, started up with an angry yell.

Ibu was frightened. She shrank down. The old woman pounced on her. 'Running away! Where's my whip?'

Ibu, who had been whipped once already, by Lisbet, for being stupid, began to weep. 'But I was only going to Lisbet,' she cried. She had not any hope of escaping the whip by this statement, but it had a surprising effect. The old woman, hobbling at her with a bamboo-stick already shaking in her hand, stopped and exclaimed, 'Lisbet—you heard her?'

'She called me.'

The old woman threw down the stick and opened the door. But the lane was empty. This, however, did not seem to disconcert her. She ran back into the yard, shouting names. In two minutes Ibu was surrounded by the whole staff of the place, talking to her at once. They wanted to know where Lisbet was.

Ibu gazed at them. She was much alarmed.

'Where is she, child?'

Ibu reflected. 'I don't know now.'

The porter took her by the arm and shook her. 'Now then, do you want a whipping?'

'I've forgotten,' said Ibu. She began to shake and weep. 'I've forgotten.'

Obishala took charge. She sent the others away, gave Ibu a honeycake, and took her back to bed. Ibu fell asleep again. But she turned and moaned in her sleep. In half an hour she sat up, with wide-open eyes; then jumped down and ran towards the gate. It was open. She ran into the alley, and turned towards the market-place.

She hesitated there, afraid of the huge shining place in which she could be seen from all sides.

But Obishala stood beside her, smiling. She took her hand, without speaking a word. Ibu knew at once that she was doing the right thing. She said, 'Lisbet is in a hole—in a wood down there.'

'Let's go that way.'

They went, hand in hand, through the town to the west gate, which

270

is, at Rimi, only a gap in the old wall, and then turned into a bush path.

Ibu stopped here, and said, 'It isn't this wood—I don't know what wood it is. I've forgotten.'

'Don't cry,' said Obishala. 'Sit down and rest.' She made Ibu sit down in her lap, and soon the child was asleep again. She slept for nearly two hours, and waked up cross and stiff and hungry.

But Obishala said, 'Now, can you hear Lisbet? When we find Lisbet, we'll all go home to chop.'

Ibu sat still and listened with her mind, with her whole body, but she did not hear anything. Only it seemed to her that Lisbet was in the direction of her left shoulder. She pointed, and said sleepily, 'The wood is somewhere there.'

Obishala took her by the hand, and they went towards the river. Half an hour later they came to the thick jungle on the river-shore.

But Ibu was now so tired and sleepy that she could scarcely walk. She began to weep, and the cheerful, impudent Obishala looked at her as if she would like to slap her. This made Ibu cry loudly. Obishala took her to a hunters' village at the edge of the wood, brought her some gruel, and put her to bed.

Three hours later Ibu woke up again, and took a party, consisting of Obishala and three of the hunters, straight to Elizabeth, who was lying scarcely half a mile away. She had vomited, but she appeared to be dead. Her body, patched with dirt and sweat, swollen and twisted, frightened Ibu so much that she ran away and would not come near it. Obishala poured water over her mistress, and in a little while she opened her eyes and whispered to the girl, who went into the bush, and gathered some leaves, which she pounded in a corn-mortar and boiled. Meanwhile Elizabeth had been brought to the hunters' village on a stretcher made of blankets, thrown over two canoe-poles.

Obishala gave her the medicine and she vomited; then she shivered, and the sweat poured out of her as if she had been a water-skin punctured all over with thorns. But she continued to drink the medicine.

At night they brought her to the cannon *ju-ju* and put her into her own room; she drank some medicine, and Obishala washed her in very hot water. But at two o'clock Obishala left her, because she was about to bear her baby. In Rimi, a mother is left alone to bear her child, in case the child should be a witch.

At six in the morning, when everyone, even the porter, exhausted by the night's work, was asleep, Elizabeth came out into the compound, washed herself into a hole in the ground, which she carefully filled in; and then, in a strong loud voice, called her people. They came running, to admire the baby and to congratulate their mistress.

271

But Elizabeth was in a bad temper. 'Where is Akande Tom?' she said. 'Bring me my whip—my big manatee whip.'

Obishala answered with her most impudent voice and look—'Your Tom went away yesterday from the palace with two loads of presents, and a small boy to carry his pot, and he bought two more boxes full at your Uncle Makurdi's. They say that Salé gave him ten pounds.'

'And why did you let him go?'

Elizabeth was in a rage. She made a practice of raging, now and then, usually for no cause. Nothing better supports the distinction of a despot. But now she was really angry. Not even the news of the Master's death, who had died that morning, could appease her, though, as Obishala declared, he had swelled up like a dead crocodile and screamed without stopping from sunset to morning.

'And so will you. All of you,' she screamed; she shook her fists in the air.

She tore off her cloth, tossed up her arms, rolled her eyes, bounced up and down, and uttered such shrieks and bellows and curses that one would have said, 'She will choke herself at that rate.' But she did not stop. She grew louder and angrier every moment. She was deliberately going mad; and mad people have superhuman powers of endurance.

'I know how it is when I go away,' she shrieked. 'Nobody does anything—all you lazy bitches go to sleep—and here I am—that had a baby this morning—but I'll beat you—I'll kill you!' She flew at them, murderous; and they scattered. She had taken care to go into her rage while standing in the outer door, so that they had not been able to escape. She required their blood.

For an hour, naked, she charged through the yards like a mad bush cow, which is much more dangerous than a bull, for she looks where she is going. When the shrieking girls tried to dodge her, she whisked aside, and put out a long arm, to grab them by the arm or hair. With the other fist she pounded them in the face and body till they fell limp, pretending to faint.

This was not a certain escape from Elizabeth's rage, but it was the only one possible, Obishala, with bleeding nose, torn lips, and one eye almost knocked out, was seen at the town dresser's about four o'clock. But the swelling of her nose even improved her ability to look as if she did not care for anybody in the world.

When the bellows and screams had ceased to come from the *ju-ju* house, about six o'clock, she returned.

Elizabeth was in the inner compound, making medicine to bring Akande Tom back; and already the other two girls, scratched, covered with blue bruises and the dusty marks of weals, were spreading the news in the town. They took care that all the porters and boatmen heard it. It excited much attention. Elizabeth's reputation had gone up since the Master's death.

The old cook and the porter had remained in their kitchen throughout this house-cleaning. Elizabeth did not beat them, because they were looking after the baby.

They showed not the slightest interest in either the Master's death, Tom's disappearance, or the mistress's irritation. They both loved babies, and they were rejoicing in this strong, beautiful boy. They took it in turns to dandle him and give him his medicine—especially a purge of the strongest kind, pushed down his throat with their crooked, knotty fingers.

XXXI

To quote the official report on the Rimi women's strike: 'It differed from the dancing-women's war of 1925, the spirit-women's war of 1927, or the Calabar women's war of 1929, in being slower in development, and also less destructive. The people of Rimi have had less emotional religious propaganda than the south, and are, therefore, not so subject to popular hysteria. Also they are less closely organized than the Calabar women. It appears that the Rimi women's clubs were started in 1926, and, though they spread with great speed, like all organizations of the kind among primitive people, where nothing opposes, they were, at the time of the strike, not strong in the outlying villages.

'Above all, the moderating control of the woman Elizabeth, or Lisbet, deservedly commended in Appendix A, far exceeded that of the southern leaders; and prevented, until her unfortunate absence, the extraordinary violence and obscene brutality which marked the other risings almost from their beginning.'

In fact, it was not till the sixth day of the strike, when the first news of the burning and looting began to trickle through the blockade of Rimi district, that anything like a riot occurred in the station. On that day about four or five hundred women suddenly gathered at the Hides Store and demanded presents. It was noticed at once that their manners had worsened. They used bad language, jeered at the whites, and threatened to loot the store. This riot was stopped only by a quarrel among the women themselves. The older ones, who belonged to a separate club, attacked some of the young girls and beat them so severely that Pratt had six in hospital.

In this sudden crisis, Burwash kept his head. As he pointed out to Fisk, it is fatal in an official to lose his head in a crisis. 'What one has to remember is that after a really serious crisis—that is, the very kind that is most likely to cause an inexperienced officer to lose his head—there is bound to be an enquiry; and nothing makes a worse effect in an enquiry than evidence showing that heads have been lost.'

Mr. Burwash kept his head and his deportment right through the crisis. But he was greatly disturbed by the violence. Violence almost always leads to enquiries—perhaps even to a commission of enquiry, which is the worst thing that can happen to a Resident.

He sent off at once a runner to recall Sangster, if he could be found; and he wrote also a personal letter to the only leader of the strike whose name and power were certainly known to him—Aladai. He pointed out to Aladai 'the inevitability of a serious deterioration in any political situation due to a policy of drift.'

'I need not point out to you that this situation is not to anybody's advantage. It will, if persistent, compel the Government to take steps to put an end to an intolerable position.

'I have already reported to the Governor your very strong claims to the succession, and only the precipitate action of the irresponsible elements among the hill pagans has prevented my receiving a reply which would, I believe, be not unfavourable to your pretensions.

'I should be glad to meet and discuss the whole question with you, without prejudice, at your very earliest convenience.'

This was sent off by runner that night to Rimi, where Aladai was supposed to be. The next morning Burwash informed Salé, who had proposed to visit him, that the time was inopportune. He explained this move to Fisk.

'One has always to *think into* the psychology of these people. Now why do you suppose it might be dangerous for me to see too much of Salé?'

'They might think you were going to choose him.'

This was the answer Burwash had been going to give; so he had to find another. He said: 'They may think that he has influence with us. *That's* the way their minds work. And it's very important to avoid raising that assumption. It would greatly damage—ah—our usefulness in any sudden crisis. So I'm going to keep Mister Salé at arm's length for a week or two.'

'Has H. E. plunged for Aladai?'

But this was too sudden and direct a question from the young man. Burwash said that nobody had plunged for anybody. He then discussed the whole situation from every point of view, and concluded that the

274

best man for the emirate, other things being equal, was almost certainly Aladai.

He was in noticeably good spirits. Fisk put this down to his letter to Aladai. He noticed that the Resident was always in good spirits when at last he had taken a decisive step.

Fisk therefore had no hesitation in reminding his chief that there was to be a meeting of the Scotch club at Rubin's, under the kuka-tree.

'The Scotch club? I thought it was dead.'

'Captain Rubin sent a note that it was going to meet under his tree.'

'Oh, yes—Rubin. I think I got a note too.'

'Everyone got a note.'

Burwash smiled and said, 'Poor old Rubin.'

Fisk answered the smile, but briskly, carefully avoiding anything like an impertinent gaiety. He did not, of course, echo the remark. Rubin was his senior. He said instead, 'And he asked me to bring my own cue, if any.'

'Cue, cue. What does he mean?'

'I think it's bagatelle, sir.'

'Yes, of course, bagatelle. Ha, ha. I suppose the soldiers were playing bagatelle in India on the day the Mutiny broke out.'

'It's nearly six now, sir.'

'Yes, yes. I suppose we mustn't disappoint him'; and Burwash, who loved the Scotch club, set out at once for the kuka-tree.

'I hope,' he said, 'that somebody else has turned up.'

'I don't suppose many will.'

In fact, Rubin was found alone with Sergeant Root. They rose to receive the Resident. The sergeant insisted on dusting the seat of his chair. It was obvious that they were welcome.

As soon as they sat down, Fisk exactly thirty seconds after his chief, a boy stood on each side of them offering them small chop—expensive French small chop on real toast. And Rubin exclaimed, 'Drinks are on me.'

They saw that this was a party, a reunion party. Bottles stood in ranks on the three large tables brought from the company office; two dozen of beer stood in jars full of water.

Another table in the middle of the ground supported a Corinthian bagatelle board, complete with balls and cue. The board was split from end to end, twisted up at one corner, and patched in two places with tin. Also a good many of the pins were missing. But it was the only board in the station.

'Is that the board?' said Burwash.

'Yès, sir. That's the board for the competition.'

'How many entries have you?'

'Everybody has entered. I put 'em all down, so they had to.'

'Are they all playing to-night?'

'That was the idea.' Rubin looked a little disconcerted. 'But there's time enough. It's only just past the hour.'

However, in ten minutes his nerve began to fail. He remarked that Rimi station, as a station, was going to pot. You could hardly call it a station.

Finally he called his orderly, scribbled a note, and sent the man off. Within ten minutes Pratt and Sangster had both arrived. Five minutes later, Honeywood, Prince, MacNeil, and two marines came up together.

Honeywood was very angry. 'What do you mean,' he shouted, 'about me owing you five bob?'

Rubin was on his feet directing his boys in his usual dignified manner. He turned his stomach and imperial nose towards the newcomers and said, 'That's for a walk-over in the first round.'

'What d'you mean, the first round? First round of what?'

'Of the Rimi bagatelle season. Entrance fee, half-a-crown; stake money half-a-crown. Makes five bob. Pay up, Dick. You'll get it back to-night.'

A storm burst. MacNeil, who had never been known to open his mouth before, declared that the thing was 'naething but a do.'

'You put your names down,' said Rubin, 'and the opening game was last night.'

'What happened last night? Nobody was here.'

'I was here, and played,' said Rubin; and as the storm broke out again he raised his voice. 'It wasn't a walk-over. I played my qualifying round first—five hundred. Gentlemen, gentlemen, allow me. The committee of the Rimi Bagatelle Club has decided the rules and handicaps.'

'Who is the committee?'

Rubin held out a large piece of foolscap at arm's length and read gravely: 'President, Mr. J. O. Burwash; vice-presidents, Sergeant Root and myself. Gentlemen——'

The Resident opened his mouth to protest that he had never heard of the committee, but Rubin was already reading the handicaps: O. F. Honeywood, minus fifty; A. L. Prince, minus ten; Mr. A. D. O. Fisk, scratch; ending with Miss J. Coote, plus two hundred; Captain Rubin, plus two hundred and fifty; Sergeant Root, plus three hundred and fifty.'

A short silence followed. Then Mr. MacNeil spoke again. He said, 'Ah'm damned.'

Honeywood had turned upon Burwash. 'But it's his board. And he changes it every day. I've seen him knocking out the pins.

276

'I wasn't there,' said Burwash.

'In the unfortunate absence of the President,' Rubin beamed, 'the handicap committee was obliged to sit alone; and may I add, gentlemen, that time waits for no man. The competition for to-night ends at half-past seven sharp, and everyone who has not then completed his score will forfeit his entrance fee, green fee, cue fee, and drinks to the Scotch club. It's in the rules—it's in the rules. As passed by the committee. Dick, you play first.'

Bagatelle on Rubin's board was a special game. Those who have played it at all will remember some of the shots, such as the water-jump, over the first bit of tin, for fifty or the floor; the canyon, down the crack for hundred, or, if the board had been much in the sun that day, again to the floor; the dry ditch, over the crack with a powerful push, for seventy-five in the pig-pen, if there were enough pins standing to hold the ball; the cut-and-come-again or maiden's kiss, up the hill to Tattenham Corner and back again to fifty, the starting-post, or the knot-hole protecting the hundred pocket, which counted a fine of drinks all round.

Rubin himself was an expert at all these shots; but even an expert could be defeated by a board which changed its shape from day to day; sometimes in the course of a game or the roll of a ball. This could shake the nerve of the coolest player.

Rimi bagatelle is an exciting game. On this evening, with money at stake and handicaps to beat, even the Resident was heard to say, 'Dash it all!'

Nevertheless, the Resident won the singles in so short a time that the Vice-president Captain Rubin proposed a match; the sides to be Soldiers and the Resident against the Rest.

'I think that would be about fair.'

The club did not agree. Honeywood was so angry that he threatened to resign. He was in his touchiest mood on account of the strike, and also the loss of the former game.

The sides were therefore fixed at Soldiers and Fisk against the Rest. Fisk had knocked more balls out of the ground than any other player. But he had also made a hundred by a miscue which had made the ball jump out of the runway.

This division made a close match. At eight o'clock, past dinner-time, the whole party was closely crowded round the board, watching Honeywood play the last ten balls for the Rest. The scores were: Soldiers, 1,475; the Rest, 1,210.

Honeywood was the only bagatelle player present who could be described as having style. His shots took at least three minutes. For, having first stooped down until his eye was level with the board in order to see if any new mountain had risen since his last shot, and then

277

bent his whole long body over it and carefully examined its surface from above, stooped to blow away any cigarette-ash or press down the corner of the tin-field at the mouth of the upper right-hand fifty, he was still only at the point of taking his range. This he did by holding out the cue at arm's length, like a conductor about to give the signal for a symphony, shutting one eye, and gradually bringing down his nose till it lay about a foot behind the ball.

If anybody coughed at this moment, he began all over again.

His first shot after three periods of range-finding, conducting, eye-shutting, and argument with Rubin, whom he accused of coughing, then of breathing at him, ran three inches up the runway and fell back again.

'Ah!' he said. 'I see it wants a little more wrist.'

The second shot, after hovering on the edge of the runway for several seconds, trickled on to the board and slowly wobbled the whole length into the hundred pocket. The cheers of the Rest, including the Resident, brought some of the women out of the surrounding darkness.

These women were now always prowling in the station. Nobody paid any attention to them any more, even when, as they often did, they stood outside a bungalow watching the occupant at his meals and making loud comments on the manners of whites. Now twenty or thirty of them gathered closely round the bagatelle players, peering between them, talking to each other in their harsh voices.

Voices and looks were those of grown-ups visiting a nursery or standing round the monkeys' cage at the Zoo.

They gazed about them with the same wide-open, contemptuous eyes that monkeys see from their cages; at the white men, laughing, shouting, arguing round their foreign and therefore foolish game.

Honeywood, after seven or eight violent disputes with the committee, represented by Rubin, and some astonishing flukes, made 250 with nine balls. He had one ball left.

The Rest had to make fifteen for a tie. There was great excitement.

Honeywood waved his cue for three minutes before, on second thoughts, he laid it down, took his coat off, rolled up his sleeves, blew his nose, and asked Rubin to leave the end of the table, because, he said, he kept on looking at him.

Rubin with great dignity moved to the side of the table; and Honeywood once more took range.

The ball went less than an inch—a mere tremor. Honeywood, startled by this result from so much preparation, made a quick jab at it as it rolled back. It flew up the run, up the hill, skidded over the tin, and flew straight at the pig-pen, which, owing to the loss of two pins knocked out by Sergeant Root with his elbow during the first round, stood wide open.

278

Prince and the Resident uttered exclamations of joy; MacNeil was heard to say very quickly, 'I'll tak that half-croon on it, Rooty.'

But at this moment, when the ball was actually within the mouth—or, rather, the side—of the pig-pen, shooting across it like a bullet, the whole board, before the eyes of everybody, was seen to open up from end to end. The side on the left of the crack rose; the right-hand side sank down, leaving a gap of more than two inches, through which the winning ball shot into space.

Honeywood stared; the Resident laughed; MacNeil said, 'Ye missed your chance, Rooty—ah thenk ye were late.'

But now Honeywood turned upon Rubin—the whole party turned upon him. 'You leaned on the table!'

'And look at the table,' said Prince, giving it a push.

It was true that the table was flexible. It was Rubin's folding-table, which had seen almost as much service as himself. All its legs, eaten by ants, chipped by hard earth, were of different lengths; all its hinges had free motion in all directions. As Rubin's boys said, 'It walked.'

'Look here,' cried Prince. He pressed the table and the board closed; pushed and it opened, pivoted on the nails in the rim.

Rubin, surrounded by the tumult, stood smiling and unperturbed, with one hand raised. His voice was heard between the outcries of the beaten side: 'Gentlemen—natural hazards—umpire's ruling final—see rule 2—no disputes—rule 3—vice-president is umpire *ex officio*—gentlemen, as English sportsmen——'

Honeywood was extremely angry. It was probably lucky for the bagatelle club's future that the scene was interrupted. A young woman, with a manner noticeably cheeky even for a Rimi woman at that time, walked up to the Resident and poked him in the ribs.

This conduct startled even the Resident; the other members of the club, except Honeywood, stopped abusing Rubin to stare or smile at the intruder. Prince glared; Rubin smiled.

But, before anyone could remonstrate or compliment her, Miss Coote was seen approaching out of the dark. She was accompanied by a very tall and powerful negress and a small lantern-girl. The negress carried an enormous whip, like a wand of office.

Miss Coote had come from Kifi, and she had a message for the Resident. Everyone now pressed round her. It was suddenly perceived, as if by a public announcement, that she was a popular person. Rubin offered her a cold beer; Fisk a chair. But she waved them aside and beckoned the negress. 'You know Elizabeth, Mr. Burwash.'

The Resident, surprised, said, 'I don't think we've met.'

Miss Coote was also surprised. She looked at him for a moment, and then said, 'She has a certain position among the women here. I think she would like to talk to you.'

The Resident at once accompanied the three women and the little girl to the office. His plan was to leave the negress in the office and take Miss Coote to dinner. But she insisted that she did not want dinner until they had discussed their business.

In the office, the big negress took a chair. The office sentry, who had appointed himself, with negro sympathy, orderly and chief clerk, made indignant ejaculation. Elizabeth looked at the man with majestic anger. Judy said hastily, 'My friend has just had a baby.'

There are advantages as well as disadvantages in a diplomatic bent. Burwash smiled and said, 'I hope she is as well as she seems.'

Elizabeth turned upon him the same glance with which she had already sought to crush the policeman. Probably she thought that Burwash was trying to make fun of her; her chin went up and her lips curled back. Judy said still more quickly, 'My friend is at the head of the cannon *ju-ju*.'

'The cannon *ju-ju*.' Burwash was delighted at last to have a chance, an opening. He at once got up and shook hands with Elizabeth. He said how glad he was to hear that the cannon *ju-ju* still survived—it would give him great pleasure to see it. He had been reporting about it only last week, and was obliged to say that it could not be traced. Everybody supposed that it had been lost during the troubles of 1908. He must beg Elizabeth, if her cannon was really a Portuguese relic, as described in the old accounts, to take particular care of it, as it was now one of the most ancient monuments in the province.

'I think it's still in use,' said Judy.

'Really? I must get the particulars of this.'

'It is the chief woman's *ju-ju* in Rimi. My friend Elizabeth wanted to see you about the riots.'

'I tell dese women dey no fit make palaver,' said Elizabeth. 'Den I sick—I no fit stop dem. Dey do fool ting. Now I say dey stop one time.'

'I can assure you, Miss Elizabeth, that the Governor is always glad to co-operate with the religious leaders in Rimi in anything that furthers the general advantage of the Rimi people.'

Burwash had not forgotten the absence of his interpreter. But he always talked to natives, especially important ones, as to officials, because he knew from experience that they appreciated it, and resented pidgin.

Elizabeth quite understood what he meant, and answered promptly, 'You do wat I say, war done stop one time.'

Burwash stooped forward, put his hands between his knees, turned his head slightly to one side, in the pose of one Governor consulting with another at the club, and said, 'I should be very glad to have your suggestions.'

'You go tell my brudder Aladai he come back from Kifi you make him king.'

'Ah!' Burwash leant back again in his chair. 'I'm afraid I could hardly——'

'Perhaps you'd like to see his letter,' Judy suggested. 'I've got his answer to yours.'

'I think that is our next step.'

Judy brought out the letter, sealed in three places with seals rather larger than half-crowns, impressed with the initials L.A. upon what looked like the design of a Maria Theresa dollar.

Judy quaked as the letter was opened. She feared that it would be like the seals. But it was a most sensible letter. It proposed a meeting at Duchi, on neutral ground, alone.

Burwash was startled by this proviso.

'Quite Napoleonic,' he said, meaning, 'Really, that's damn cheek.'

'It is rather like Tilsit, isn't it?' said Judy. 'But does it matter?'

'Not at all, not at all. If the situation demanded it, I would go to Kifi.'

Elizabeth said, 'No, no, not Kifi; very bad mans at Kifi. You say to my brudder he no stay at Kifi no more.'

'I think Elizabeth is right,' said Judy. 'All the hooligans in the province seem to be collected at Kifi, and the atmosphere is rather strained. Is it true that the troops are coming?'

'Not that I've heard of. I should be greatly surprised if they did.'

'I'm glad about that.' The woman, who looked white and thin—almost all-in, as Burwash reflected—gave a deep sigh of relief. 'Somebody told him there was going to be shooting, and of course that made him feel worried, really almost desperate. I mean, he doesn't find it very easy to keep his people quiet, Coker's crowd specially.'

'How is Schlemm? There was a rumour that the mission had been attacked.'

'It's burnt out. But that's not Aladai's fault. It was the local people did it. In fact, Aladai probably saved all our lives.

'Schlemm is with you?'

'No. Isn't he here? Coker swore that he had sent him back here.'

'I hope nothing has happened to our good doctor. I need not point out how much that would aggravate the position. I hope Mr. Aladai understands that.'

Judy assured him again how much Aladai hated bloodshed; how eagerly he sought peace; how important it was to come to some agreement with him before his people got out of hand.

Burwash, of course, warmly agreed with her about everything. It was impossible to know what the man thought. Yet he seemed to be sincere when he declared with great force, 'I believe that he is the only man who can prevent the position from becoming something very like an impasse.'

But Judy suspected that he was only quoting from his last report.

Elizabeth, who had listened to the conference with attention, now said, 'If judge go to Duchi—I send Obishala—den none make trouble for him.'

'But can't you go yourself, Elizabeth?' Judy asked her. 'You ought to see Louis.'

Elizabeth shook her head, 'I no fit to go from my own place—I wait for somebody.'

It was therefore agreed that the Resident should meet Aladai the next afternoon at Duchi. Burwash would drive himself there in his car, with the young woman for passenger. The woman would carry a pass to take the car through the pickets. He would take no guard or weapon. 'Not even a pistol,' said Judy, looking at the man with her brown eyes which did not see him clearly, but seemed to him to have the penetration of bradawls. 'It wouldn't be safe. They're certain to hear of it in the station, and that means the town and the *ju-ju*.'

Burwash cheerfully gave his promise; and Elizabeth then got up and held out her hand. She was about the same height as the Resident, but she seemed to condescend to him from a different level.

'I gree for you,' she said, as the Resident politely shook hands. 'But dem women play too much—dey no fit catch sense—dey mad—dey spoil all ting. You fit to shoot 'em one time—shoot 'em plenty—I tell you now.'

'Now that we are working together, Miss Elizabeth, I think we may be confident that there will be no need for shooting. And you may be sure that when I report to the Governor in due course, I shall not forget to mention your name for special consideration.'

Elizabeth answered carelessly, 'I go write to Governor about dem dues—dem *ju-ju* house. You no fit break my *ju-ju* house. Good-bye.'

The two potentates shook hands, and Elizabeth moved slowly away, like a monument on wheels, with the little girl bearing her lantern. The other, the impudent one, remained, and when Burwash and Judy mounted to the second floor, where dinner had been laid for them, followed.

Burwash was saying in a tone of some concern, 'Do you suppose she has really been sending letters to H.E.?' when Obishala strolled from the stair-head. She paid no attention to the whites. Her walk, nevertheless, was that of a pretty girl who challenges the world to put her down; with breasts thrown forward, shoulders loosely bent, hips swaying, buttocks lazily sliding up and down, and knees jerked back at every step. She looked round her with detached and scornful curiosity, despising the white man even in his things, hitched up her cloth, and scratched herself on the belly.

'This is your guide,' said Judy, and added a few words in Rimi.

Obishala grinned, and took a leafy twig out of her breast, where it hung from a string. She then looked round for a seat. Judy said in Rimi. 'You needn't stay now.'

Obishala made a face at her and sat down in Burwash's chair. She was on guard.

Judy looked uncertainly at the Resident. But he again rose to a diplomatic situation. He smiled, inclined, and waved his hand. 'I hope the lady will consider herself my guest.'

'There'll be no difficulty,' said Judy.

She left within an hour for Kifi. She had promised Aladai to return personally with her answer; and no persuasion was needed to make Burwash agree that time was valuable while the situation was showing such plain signs of deterioration. But he gave her his own official barge, with two cabins and a spring bed, so that her journey downriver should be quick and easy.

XXXII

ALADAI WAS SLEEPING in the mission store. The roof had disappeared, but the three tin walls were sound, and he wanted to be separated from the people. The fourth wall, facing the river, had been stripped of its metal by looters, and let in the river night breeze and the river view which Aladai loved also.

He had furnished the room as far as possible like an English official's camp, with folding-table, long chair, gramophone, even a black tin office-box.

At night he went to bed in pyjamas, like an official. The girl Osi slept on a mat beside the bed. But he was sleepless with anxiety. Why did not Elizabeth send to him? Where was she? Would the Resident answer his letter? Would the women let Miss Coote return to Kifi with an answer?

It was certainly no good asking or worrying. He turned up the flame of the lantern, which stood on a box just outside the bed net, and took a book from the pile lying within it, ready to his hand. Osi lay still, flat on her back; but her eyes were open. He could see the lamp-flame shining in them beneath the thick lids.

She was now again beautiful; from the waist up. It was astounding to see how her body and face had put on their beauty again, in spite of the terror which had made her almost insane, almost dumb.

He had accepted Osi for a guard, but not for a wife. She was too savage, and her legs were spoilt. He had taken her sometimes to give her comfort, and himself sleep; but she remained silent, trembling in his arms, and he was left more wakeful than before—more uneasy, as if he had caught from her some of her fear.

Her eyes were watching him now. He felt irritation. What could he do for Osi, who, when he reasoned with her, gazed at his lips and trembled, and, when he caressed her, still trembled? She was a trouble to h⬩⬦—another burden, another complication.

What burdens Rimi had brought upon him because he loved her! He could not sleep or eat for anxiety. And what loneliness! To carry burdens made a man lonely; but not to see his way clearly—this was what made him feel his loneliness.

But it was no good worrying. He must watch Coker and wait. There was no other policy until Elizabeth came out of hiding. He had no control over the women. Elizabeth had beaten him there. His turn must wait until he was Emir. Then there would be no more *ju-ju* in Rimi.

He said to Osi, 'Go to sleep now; nothing can hurt you.'

Her lips moved. She was saying the word 'lord.' The whisper did not reach him, but he knew the motion of her lips.

He sighed noiselessly, and opened the book. It was one of Schlemm's books—*The Historical Christ*, by Schweitzer. Schlemm had an English copy, though he had annotated it in German. Aladai had already read half of Schlemm's English library—anthropology, poetry, theology. He did not understand much of it, but he had nothing to do but read. It passed the time while he waited. For what? He put down the book and pulled up the net. Osi was lying flat on her back. Her face was like a carving, calm and beautiful as marble. She had closed her eyes. He stepped over her carefully, and went into the moonlight.

He gazed about him at the sky, filled with moonlight like the smooth energy of unstopped light flying through space; at the Niger, like a silver snake whose lighted scales threw little blue-black shadows on its coils—wrinkling, it slowly twisted through the broad ditch of the dark. The high forest was like grass to it, feathered with light. He felt like an insect in this giant landscape; lost in the grass.

He walked through the ruined station, not looking at the roofless huts and the skeleton chapel, but the enormous trees behind them—wall and ambush at the same time.

Aladai often went walking at night, when books had failed to make him sleepy; and sometimes he made his rounds through the village, to make sure that none of Coker's people were up to new mischief. The

284

old mischief he could control. Coker's preaching was stupid, savage; but it kept his party quiet. While he did not go beyond talk, he was not dangerous; and, if he did, Aladai was a match for him. He had proved it.

A distant bugle sounded. Aladai jumped, and stood holding his breath. The bugle sounded again; it was not a bugle, but a man's tenor call in the forest behind, deflected by his hut.

Aladai exhaled in a deep sigh. Then he laughed, and said, 'What a fool you are. The soldiers are still at Rimi—you know that; and there are no others to trouble you. How could soldiers be there yet?'

He went back to bed, stepping over Osi, and opened his book. But he heard the bugle, quite clear. He snatched up a pistol, and ran into the compound. But the sound was not repeated. Aladai, in a rage, returned, threw the pistol on the bed and drew on a sweater. Then he sat down and reopened the book.

For a long time he read, sitting upright, and still in his chair. Then, while he turned the page, he caught once again the lamplight in Osi's eyes. She was not asleep. She was watching him. He looked again at the book, but he had forgotten the beginning of the sentence; and then he perceived that he had forgotten what the book was about. He had not been reading at all, and suddenly he felt such terror and loneliness that he wanted to beat his head on the wall. He sat still, but his body trembled with the effort. He was no longer looking at the book, but over it, into Osi's eyes, which catching his, turned nervously aside. She was frightened of him too. There was nothing she did not fear. She was a living fear; and it seemed to him that the terror which existed in the room, like an atmosphere, apart from himself, was breathed from Osi.

He felt hatred for her, and fear. But at once he remembered that these were savage foolish emotions. Trembling, he got up and went out, stealing away as if from an enemy—from fear.

He walked towards the village. At once he heard the noise of feet behind him. Osi was following. He turned, and said to her, 'Go back and go to sleep—you must sleep, or you will never be well.'

The girl, shortened by her twisted legs so that her body now seemed much too long, crossed her hands on her breasts and stooped towards him, like a suppliant. He took her hand, and drew it towards him. 'What are you afraid of, Osi? You are safe now.'

She dared not look at him; she did not believe him.

'No one will dare to touch you.'

She began to tremble, as if the word touch had reminded her of the arrest, the fire, the inexplicable things that had suddenly happened to her. Aladai was sorry for her, but he felt impatient. 'No *ju-ju* can hurt you now—not as long as you don't believe in them.'

She raised her eyes to him; but not in enquiry or hope, only in wonder. She always looked at him so, when he argued with her fears, as if to say, 'What does he mean? Has this anything to do with me?'

But Aladai knew that there was no way of taking away Osi's fear; she was beyond argument, as she had always been outside reason.

Accused witches generally went mad or killed themselves. Osi would probably go mad.

He drew her with him as he walked, more slowly to keep pace with her shambling gait. He began to explain that *ju-ju* was a false thing—a fear in the mind; a fear put into the mind to make people suffer—but he knew that his words had no effect on the girl's brain. She clung tightly to his hand, and once she whispered, 'Pardon, lord.'

She seemed to understand that she was a nuisance, that she oppressed Aladai with a sense of his heavy burden, his loneliness. But he said to her, 'Don't be afraid. No one shall touch you.'

At the turn of the village road, in the thick high jungle which grew on both sides of the crocodile swamp, he heard a peculiar sound, rhythmic and metallic, which gradually increased till it was a loud murmur. It was Coker speaking, and, as he spoke, turning towards the road.

'What mischief is he up to now?' said Aladai, aloud.

But his motive was not so much to see Coker as to be with his Rimi; to cure his loneliness. He turned into the well-known *ju-ju* path. In three minutes he stood at the mouth of the clearing.

It had been greatly enlarged in the last few days. It was twice the size; and on the trunks of cut-down trees hundreds perched, as if in the circles of a theatre.

Aladai was not satisfied to be at the edge of the crowd, which, at the outskirts, was standing. He pushed through it. The people gave way quickly when they recognized their chief. Soon he was in the thick of the crowd, closely pressed on all sides, warm and already amused, interested. Osi stood close beside him. She looked about her in surprise, with round eyes.

They were now within five or six rows from the edge of the crowd which formed a semi-circle round the preacher's table. The chord of this semi-circle was the edge of the crocodile-hole, which appeared now as a bar of deep shadow.

Coker had just begun speaking, in a sleepy manner, but Aladai did not listen to him. He was much interested by some of the congregation: half the Kifi old mission, Schlemm's most faithful pupils, were in the first rows, and the rest were Aladai's own men.

The most prominent among the audience was Akande Tom. He was dressed in a new white suit, white helmet, tortoiseshell spectacles, blue shirt, red tie, and enormous yellow boots; and he carried a huge book open in front of him, possibly a Bible. He was looking from the book to Coker and back again, like the judge in court who reads out a man's evidence to him for his verification. Now and then he coughed, took off his spectacles, looked at them, and put them on again. He could not wipe them with one hand.

Once he turned the book round, glanced at the back, frowned, looked indignantly round him, and then opened the book again, the other way up, at a different place. But upon second thoughts, after another indignant look round, he reverted to the former arrangement.

The crowd paid no attention to Akande Tom. Their eyes were fixed on Coker; already their mouths were opening and shutting, unconsciously following his motions, and faint sighs, hisses, and inarticulate murmurs came from their throats.

Coker was now at full steam. 'And He gave His blood,' he yelled in one gasp, 'to save all men—not the white man alone—not the Jew alone—not the black man alone—but for all men—He gave His blood— His holy blood.'

Coker was a savage, Aladai reflected. He did not know anything, or want to know anything. Probably he could not know anything now, his brain was dead. He was only the noise of a body, of a spite.

But the crowd was swaying and jerking to the noise; at each blast they moaned and swayed. The moans broke out of them like the puffs of steam and dirt from a crater crack before an eruption. Each was louder and bigger, coming from a wider surface.

Aladai was swayed with them, amused; and suddenly he, too, wanted to moan. The moan was gathering in him until he felt that it would burst his throat; it pressed on his brain, and especially on the backs of his eyes, as if his veins were bursting, and all the blood in his body was swelling, thrusting.

Akande Tom was on his knees; his eyes were closed, and the spectacles dangled from one ear; he was holding the big book in front of him, between his two hands, and swinging it to and fro, up and down, in syncopated time with his swaying, jerking body. He was dancing with the book.

Aladai, even while he himself swayed and moaned, gazed in surprise at Akande Tom. He was still more surprised to see Osi close behind the man. How had she dragged herself there? She pulled herself forward with her arms; so that she was now within three yards of the preacher's feet. Her twisted legs were coiled under her. Her round face and big stupid eyes were raised towards him with the concentrated look of a starving animal, at food held out behind the bars. Her eyelids never winked; her cheeks quivered; her great lips were pushed out as if they sought to reach his words and taste them in the air.

Other women behind were screaming. Coker picked up some round

287

object in a bag, and held it at arm's length. His mouth was like a crater, and his voice panted, 'He gave His blood—not for white man alone—not for black men alone—and——'

The object was Schlemm's head. Aladai had known for three days that Coker had a great *ju-ju* in the forest. That was why the people were pouring in to him. He had known also that Schlemm was dead; that Coker had lied to him. A moan broke out of him. He had known perfectly well that Coker's *ju-ju* was Schlemm's head, but he had not wanted to admit it. What was a man to do? And why did Schlemm go and get killed? He had asked for it. It was his job. His job to die. It was good to give one's life.

He swayed, and the moans tore him like giant hiccoughs; he couldn't stop them. But his brain was working. It kept time with Coker, but it worked like a good clockwork, wound up and balanced to go in any position. You could check it for a moment, but it would go on again as soon as you released the pressure.

'And we must die—we must give our blood,' Coker yelled. 'And he that is first—shall be for a sacrifice.'

'Why must we die?' said his brain. 'Coker is a fool—it's quite unnecessary—all this talk of blood is disgusting nonsense—it is what—you—call it—the unconscious—speaking—the lower brain—the beast blood.'

Osi was kneeling at Coker's feet, and he was touching her with his *ju-ju*. It was a baptism. He was shrieking, 'Our sister is for de Lawd—she is coming to de Lawd.'

Aladai knew quite well that Coker had been baptising for the Lawd during the last week—sometimes four and five a night; sending them straight to heaven, washed clean of their sins.

'Giving up the sins of the world,' Coker shouted. 'Where all must die—and he that is first—shall be the sacrifice—the blood of the lamb.'

'When all must die,' moaned the crowd. 'We all must die.'

'We all must die,' moaned Aladai. 'He that is first—must be the sacrifice. It is very odd, all this,' said the brain, in a European voice. 'I shall speak to Miss Judy about this. Why this lust for death? It does not seem natural. Nature wants to live—not to die. Why should the beast blood want to pour itself out? Why does the blood love pain as well as joy? What is this spite and jealousy in flesh? Why do people cut themselves for the *ju-ju?* What is the god of nature—this reasoning of blood soaked for a million years in the agony of beasts?' Coker was moving towards the swamp; he swung the bag in time to his shouts. At each shout Aladai swayed, jerked, wobbled; his moans were cries of pain, and he, too, was moved towards the swamp. He did not know what he wanted, but his body moved towards the swamp. It was wet with fear.

288

'Schlemm was dead for Christ—and that would mean war—and he, too, must die—for Rimi'—a moan broke out of him in the word—'he must give his blood for Rimi.'

'But what nonsense,' said the brain briskly, like a tutor, but less polite. 'That won't do Rimi any good—What Rimi wants is peace, trade—schools——'

'Rimi,' he moaned. 'Rimi, my country—I give my life—for love of Rimi.'

'Rimi,' said the brain, 'is a *ju-ju* for the herd—the religion of the blood, the race, the old crocodile——'

'Rimi,' he shrieked. 'For Rimi——'

Coker stopped shouting. The effect was not to relax pressure, but to increase it. Aladai could not breathe. He stood staring, clutching his chest. He saw Osi rising slowly on her crooked legs towards Coker's hand which swung the head. He swung it towards the swamp, and she staggered, in her crab-like gait, to the edge. The crowd was silent, and the woman did not make a sound. She walked over the edge and disappeared.

At once the air was torn by shrieks so piercing and loud, so quickly repeated, that they seemed incredible. Aladai stood thrilling. What was that? What beast? What agony? The shrieks grew louder, quicker; they stabbed the ear; then broke and fell downwards in sobs, cut off suddenly with a bubbling noise.

Aladai's brain said, 'The *ju-ju* croc. has got his victim for to-night.'

Coker had ceased to shout. He was kneeling at the edge of the swamp. Aladai looked round in surprise, and all about him he saw others turning their heads and eyes round them with the comical expressions of awakened sleepers.

The pressure had gone. He felt, indeed, an extraordinary peace and lightness. He saw the people's eyes, awakening, fix on him, on his pyjamas, on the *ju-ju* coat. They recognized him.

Akande Tom came up to him with outstretched hand. He was excited. 'Good night, Looiss,' he cried. 'I leff dem Lisbet—you go tell her I no care for her fool *ju-ju*.'

'You've left her?' Aladai felt exhausted; he gazed at the boy.

'I leff her,' Akande Tom shouted. 'Now dey say she make *ju-ju* call me back—I no hear *ju-ju*. I Christin man now. Christin man no fear *ju-ju*. You tell her, Loo-iss.'

'I'll tell her.'

Akande Tom turned his face towards the west, in the direction of Rimi, and exclaimed, 'You tell her dem *ju-ju* no good—she stop him.' His voice rose to a shout; he raised his chin, and bawled over the trees towards Rimi, 'She fool woman, Lisbet—I no fear dem fool *ju-ju*—

she stop 'em now—dey no good—dey no hurt me—I no savage mans no more—you tell her, Looiss.'

'I'll tell her,' said Aladai, moving away. But Akande Tom was still shouting at the tree-tops. 'Dem Master—he rotten—everybody know him rotten—dem *ju-ju* no kill Master—he rotten long time.'

Aladai was so tired that he could scarcely drag his legs, and he remembered that he had not slept for two nights. What should he do now? About Schlemm—about Osi—about Coker? But he was too tired. Why had Schlemm come back to be killed? It was madness; or had he done it on purpose? Had he wanted to die? Or had he been guided—the blood of martyrs is the seed of the Church—the blood of the Russian nihilists—the blood of the Irish nationalists. 'Go to bed,' said Aladai's brain. 'You're too tired—too worried. You'll be as mad as Coker, if you're not careful.'

He fell on his bed and slept. But dawn was breaking; in less than half an hour he was awakened by the noises of the camp. There was a great deal of noise. He shouted angrily, and then jumped up. Somebody said, 'Aladai, the white woman.'

The words brought such relief and comfort as he had not known since he had first swayed in the *ju-ju* crowd; it was as if he once more found himself among his own kind, but this time English people, sensible people. Miss Judy was always sensible.

He pulled on his trousers over his pyjamas, and the *ju-ju* coat; strolled out with a smile. In the middle of the shouting crowd he saw Dryas Honeywood, in a dirty crumpled dress, and close behind her, tightly held by both arms, Captain Rackham.

The people knew that Rackham was his enemy. They were laughing with joy, flourishing their machetes over his head.

Rackham was speaking to them, and, as Aladai lifted up his hand to silence the shouters, he heard the man say. 'I know I need a shave, old chap, but I prefer a safety-razor.'

Aladai hated Rackham as much as a sensitive young man can hate another who has humiliated him in front of a woman. He had often devised elaborate methods of putting him to death. But just now he was English. He was even dressed as an Englishman. He therefore said to the people, in severe tones, 'What are you doing? These people are my friends.'

The crowd, surprised, fell back. Aladai walked up to Rackham, and offered his hand.

Rackham hesitated for a moment, and then shook the hand. He said, 'You must excuse an early call. The fact is it's really not my visit. But when I got up this morning, I found that Miss Honeywood had left in this direction.'

Aladai had paid no attention to Dryas, who had been standing to one

290

side with a confused and slightly ironical look, like a prefect waiting for two young creatures to finish some childish ritual.

Aladai turned to her with the same grand air and theatrical magnificence, which made Rackham, staring at the man with clear bright eyes, feel such disgust that he could not keep it out of his face. His nose wrinkled over the wings; his lips twisted. Rackham himself would have behaved with much the same swagger, in the same position.

Dryas gave her hand, hot and dry, to Aladai, who shook it in a formal manner.

'The pose is now the prophet who can scarcely be bothered with human beings,' said Rackham, to himself.

Dryas said that she had come to warn him that the soldiers were going to attack him.

Aladai made a proud gesture, and said that he had expected it. 'The Resident has betrayed me. I trusted him, because, as you say, he seemed to be a white man.'

'But that's why *you* can't trust him,' said Dryas, in a common-sense tone. 'Don't trust anybody—but just escape as soon as you can.'

Rackham then became angry. He called the girl a fool, and asked Aladai not to listen to her. Aladai made a signal, and he was dragged away.

'I hope you won't let them kill him,' said Dryas. 'I didn't mean him to come, but he found the way I was going, and came after me.'

Aladai did not seem to hear her. He said gravely, 'It is fate.'

'But you could get away now. They won't stop you.'

'And my people here?'—raising his brows with a dramatic air.

'They haven't a chance against soldiers; but perhaps you could tell them to go away too—hide in the bush.'

'The Rimi are not cowards, Miss Honeywood. What would *you* think of a people that ran away from battle?'

'But you haven't a chance, Mr. Aladai.'

He answered, 'The greatest chance—to die for Rimi.'

Miss Honeywood did not seem to be so sympathetic as he had expected. She said only, 'If you think that's the right thing; but I've warned you'; and then she asked to be sent back to the rest-camp, with Rackham.

Aladai said that was impossible. 'You would be killed on the road. They're all Coker's people on that side. You are safer here, as long as I am here. And when the shooting begins, I shall see that you are put into a place of safety.'

But the girl seemed more anxious about Captain Rackham.

Judy arrived at eight o'clock, and found the camp in a turmoil. Coker was speaking in the middle of the mission square, and, when he

291

saw her, he pointed at her, and shouted, 'Here is another of those who must die.'

She struggled, with difficulty, through the crowd to Aladai's house, and found him there with Dryas. When she told him of the Resident's promise, and the meeting arranged at Duchi, he answered that he had been betrayed already; he was not going to Duchi. 'I will give my life here. It belongs already to Rimi.'

Judy argued for an hour, until she was exhausted. She knew that she was dealing with one of those obsessions which seize upon every brain at times, but especially the half-educated, and the negroes, and she fought it with the only weapons she had—sense, ridicule, abuse.

She turned upon Dryas, suspecting some bad influence. But when she said, 'You know that there's no idea of catching Louis,' the girl answered, 'I don't know—but I'm sure there might be.'

'What on earth do you mean, might be? What awful nonsense, Dryas.'

Dryas, who looked her usual self, calm and confident, answered, 'Look at the Indians and the Irish.'

'What on earth does that mean? "The Indians and the Irish." What have they got to do with Rimi?'

Judy almost screamed in her disgust and anger; but she saw that she had even less chance with Dryas than with Aladai, because Dryas was at once stupider and stronger. The girl had a fine character. That no doubt was one of the reasons of her influence over Aladai. Character always made itself *felt*. Dogs knew it.

She turned on Aladai again. 'Why do you believe Miss Honeywood? She hasn't been near Rimi for a fortnight; and I was there only last night,' she cried.

The man made a gesture. 'You do not understand, it is not what anyone says—but what Rimi needs.'

But when a few minutes later, Coker's people, raised to frenzy by the story that the soldiers were coming, swarmed into Aladai's hut, she was still arguing.

Aladai left her there while he went out to subdue Coker. When she tried to follow him, protesting that all this was stupid, the mob at once intercepted her. But, as they dragged her away, she shrieked at the top of her voice, 'It's so stu-pid.' She was furious with the stupidity of everybody. They knocked her on the head to prevent Aladai from hearing her, and threw her into Coker's *ju-ju* house, which alone was out of Aladai's reach.

Burwash went to Duchi, and spent a very uncomfortable day there. In the evening he was attacked by a mob of women, who smashed the car with pestles, and would have murdered him had he not jumped

into the river. He was rescued by a couple of villagers in a dug-out, who brought him back to Rimi that night. He made immediate proclamation, through the native administration, that the market dues would be revised, as from that date; but the war had already begun. The Hides store was attacked and looted at six o'clock next morning. Two of Honeywood's clerks, who tried to defend it, were promptly beaten to death. By seven, Makurdi's was burning, and all the lower bungalows, the hospital medical store, and clerks' quarters were in the mob's hands. No appeals to the women had any effect. They murdered one of the clerk's wives, a young girl from the south, apparently for amusement. The women seemed suddenly to have gone mad.

Rubin had his troops standing by from dawn, and Sangster came in with the police after a forced all-night march of thirty miles. But the Resident wished to avoid further bloodshed. He went alone down the hill to make a personal appeal. He was instantly knocked down and overrun by a mass of yelling, shrieking women.

Sangster, now holding himself in charge of the station, at once turned out the police and prison guard, on his own responsibility, and fired a volley over the heads of the mob.

This had no effect. The women charged, screaming with rage. One round of ball did not stop them; and for a moment it looked as if the twenty policemen were going to be torn in pieces by three thousand frantic women. But the latter were charging uphill, and the police, all veteran soldiers, stood their ground. They just had time to reload, and the last discharge of the carbines literally blew the front rank of the enemy backwards. Probably this front rank included some leaders, or at least some of the more violent and energetic of the rioters. The rest stopped, and, when the police took aim again, broke. No more shooting was needed. In ten minutes there was not a townswoman in the station, except nineteen wounded and eight dead.

Burwash was found under a bush, with a large lump on his head. He had escaped being murdered while his captors were rushing the police. He at once took charge, to use his own phrase, of the situation, and made it known in the town that further violence of any kind would incur severe penalties.

As for the other section of the Rimi war—what was called the 'Coker end'—that was settled by troops from Dubo, and Rubin's company. The rebels made a poor fight. There was only one action. Coker and Aladai, leading a large body of spearmen, charged the troops on the Kifi road, but they chose the worst possible place for an attack, without cover. Their followers began to scatter at the first volley, and the second cleared the field, with the exception of Aladai himself and three more. These four came within twenty yards before they were disposed of.

Aladai, just before he went down, waved his arm, and shouted something about Rimi, but no one could distinguish what it was. Coker had been killed by the first volley.

There was no further resistance. The casualties were small; three men wounded in the Dubo company; and, among the rebels in the Kifi fight, six killed and sixteen wounded. There was no more fighting, and Burwash prevented village-burning.

There was no trace of Miss Honeywood. The rumour was that she had been murdered, by some of Coker's fanatics, just before the Kifi fight.

Rackham had escaped within an hour of his imprisonment. He picked a hole in a two-foot mud wall with his knife, which was fitted with a leather borer, and jumped down the bank of the crocodile swamp. According to his own tale, he landed on the *ju-ju* crocodile's back, and got such a fright that he jumped twenty feet into the air again and landed on the other side. But this is an Irish story. He tells it in English clubs, when he has leisure from his training-stable on the Berkshire downs. But he has little leisure, as he is already doing very well. He doesn't run horses for himself, and he doesn't bet.

XXXIII

Judy Coote and the Fortts, lying in the huts next Rackham's, were found two days later when the troops went through the place. The Fortts, except for dirt and discomfort, were well and fat. Some faithful converts had been taking care of them. Judy Coote's left leg was broken in two places, and she had been starved. She was so nearly dead that Pratt despaired of her, and even Fathers, now come to take over from him—a keen and confident young man, fresh from the hospitals—admitted that her chances were poor.

But, like other people whose physique seems to have suffered at the profit of their brains and nerves, she turned out to be very tenacious of life. A week later she was still alive, and within three weeks Pratt admitted that the leg might be saved. But it was two months before she was allowed to see her friends. They found her changed. She was not only shrunken to half the size, so that, as Rubin said, she reminded him of a famine baby, but she was listless.

Fathers complained that she did not do him justice. She made no effort to get well; and she would not fight against the depression natural to the sick in Africa, where it is the most mortal of tropical diseases.

She had an obsession about Dryas Honeywood. She believed that she had caused the girl's death, and no argument could persuade her that it had been due chiefly to bad luck.

'But I left her in the bush with him,' she answered.

'It was the only thing to do,' they told her. 'She couldn't have looked after Mrs. Vowls.'

No one liked this subject, because the case of Miss Honeywood had already made quarrels in the station. Honeywood had blamed the Government, Rackham, Burwash, and finally the troops. His chief quarrel with the troops was that they did not kill enough Rimi. The objection that they could not find them to kill, since they were all up the trees, merely enraged him.

Honeywood was supported by his clerks and Makurdi, who, lamenting Aladai with public cries and tears, declared it was not he, but those bad pagan men, who had caused all the trouble.

Makurdi's tears for Louis were mixed with moans for his store. For a week he wept every day in the provincial office, crying sometimes 'My poor boy,' sometimes 'My poor store.' But after he had obtained in compensation about three times what his store was worth, he became more composed. He has built a new store entirely of tin; Jamesu, if he can survive, will be the richest man in Rimi.

The opposition party to Honeywood was led by Mrs. Pratt, who declared that the Honeywood girl had caused all the trouble by encouraging 'that black man.' Everybody was extremely glad when the Pratts went home by one boat and Honeywood by the next. They were glad to forget the quarrel, and Dryas herself, for her death had hurt them more than Schlemm's. Schlemm, they argued, had died on duty; and therefore well. But the poor Honeywood girl had died by accident; and therefore badly.

They did not like Miss Coote saying, 'I killed her—it was my fault,' because it reminded them of tragedy.

But Judy's body grew stronger in spite of her depression, her listlessness; and her brain was always alive, as if it carried on a private existence. Fathers said that when she was almost at her worst, and he supposed her unconscious, she had whispered, apparently referring to the disinfectant he was using, 'Is that a mercury compound?'

She was carried out of hospital for the first time on the day of Salé's inauguration as Emir, but not to see it. She took no interest in Salé. Rubin had persuaded her to visit the bagatelle club in the evening; and she had consented because it was easier to agree than to refuse.

Rubin, arriving at the hospital just after five, with a fatigue of maxim-gun carriers and a hammock, was almost fussy. He was greatly put about when the hammock was stopped on the road by a tall negro in a blue shirt, much crumpled, and a white helmet.

The man was much excited, and neither Judy nor Rubin could make sense of a long speech which he gibbered at them in the worst English. But, as it contained the name Loo-iss, Judy listened to it, and Captain Rubin did not care, for the lady's sake, to interrupt it.

But every time she said, 'Yes, Louis Aladai—you knew him,' the young man became more excited and much more incoherent.

It was about half-past five. The police were already putting out the club chairs under the kuka-tree; and, in the middle, the Rimi bagatelle board, already protected by special by-laws and in charge of a real committee.

Just below, Carphew, perfectly booted and breeched, was knocking about a ball on the polo ground with Fisk. On the other side of the road the doctor was beating the Resident in a second game of tennis; in the absence of back nets, four small boys were kept extremely busy, by a police orderly, chasing the balls.

In the distance the new District Officer's wife could be seen taking a late tea with Mrs. Fathers on the latter's stoop. It was the fifth week of the rains; all the flower-beds were filled with zinnias; and the air, after rain that afternoon, was itself as clear and bright as a raindrop.

In this sparkling air, voices travelled with sharp definition, like bubbles in champagne.

'Forty—love.'

'In India they bar a chap who——'

'You want whipping, do you, you rascals!' This was the orderly to the ball-boys. He felt the importance of his task while the Resident played. The boys got no rest.

'At least in a cavalry regiment'—Carphew's high voice.

'Too good for me, doctor. I can see that you are a real acquisition to the station.'

The tall young negro in the blue shirt, flourishing his arms, streaming with sweat, and pouring from his loose, twisting lips a stream of broken words, appeared out of place. Judy and Rubin were growing tired of him.

But Judy was still unhappy for her friend Louis, and still hoped sometimes that Dryas might be alive somewhere in the bush. So she was patient, and repeated again, 'Yes, you knew Mister Aladai—at Kifi?'

'Take it easy, old chap,' said Rubin, 'The more spit, you know, the less grace.'

'Try Rimi,' said Judy.

The young man gave a deep sigh and said in Rimi that he was a friend of Aladai, and a Christian; that he had done with *ju-jus*. But he felt a little sick for belly and he wanted some medicine. And he had

296

come to Missy Coote because she too was a friend of Loo-iss and an enemy of *ju-jus*, and because he wanted to be her boy.'

'So you teach me book,' he concluded, breaking into English.

'I don't need a boy in hospital,' said Judy.

But, seeing the despair on the boy's face, and remembering her friend Louis, she said, 'Why do you want to read?'

'So I be clerk. *Ju-ju* no fit touch me no more.'

Judy reflected, and said, 'I'll ask the doctor if you can come.'

'Oh, missy, you save my life for dis poor boy, go' bless you.' He took off his hat and went down on his knees in the dust. He began to sob loudly.

'Easy, old chap,' said Rubin, who had not at all approved of this arrangement. But he was confident that the doctor wouldn't allow it. Judy could barely lift a finger. He gave the signal to the bored hammock-carriers.

But his evening was spoilt. Judy talked of nothing but her new pupil; the proper education of negroes. Towards seven o'clock she was trying to get Burwash's consent to start a class in Rimi town.

'It is a very good idea,' said Burwash. 'I'll think it over. But I hardly think the political situation, at present, would allow of popular education on a large scale.'

'You'll get newspapers before you know where you are,' said Rubin, who had been away on company business for half an hour.

'Communism,' Carphew suggested.

But Judy, who was suddenly revived, who had for the first time in two months colour in her cheeks and a light in her eyes, exclaimed that perhaps Communism would be more dangerous if the people did not know anything. They could still hear propaganda. And what would happen when they got richer, and bought wireless sets capable of hearing Moscow?

Burwash, sitting high above her on his special *rhoorkee*, remarked that the situation was more complicated than it appeared.

Judy looked up and fluted at him, 'But, Mr. Burwash, don't you think this Government could stand an experiment? It must be one of the strongest in the world.'

The Resident was in a very good humour. The Court of Enquiry on the Rimi troubles had lately reported, exonerating everybody from blame except 'the irresponsible agitators who made political capital out of local grievances due to the recent disturbances of trade routes,' and 'Mr. D. O. Sangster, whose firing on an unarmed crowd in Rimi station was unjustifiable.' The Resident's action in preventing further bloodshed by his prompt warning to the rioters that violence could not be tolerated was strongly commended. In fact, the whole affair had probably done Burwash a great deal of good, in the right places.

He therefore smiled on Miss Coote, when she praised the Nigerian Government, with even more than his usual benevolence. He raised his eyebrows and said, 'That's very nice of you, Miss Coote.'

'But don't you think so? It's federal, isn't it, and it's national—evreybody has home rule—and you could really say'—she deferred to the Resident with her eyes—'couldn't you say, Mr. Burwash, that it was international too? I mean, as far as the police and army and currency and foreign policy go. You control that.'

'Me,' said Burwash, amused. 'You mean the British Government.'

'Yes, don't you think Nigeria is rather like a baby world-state—just like it, in fact—and so it's rather interesting to see it working.'

'You think our system works well?'

'It's very *strong*,' said Judy, 'and, of course, I am rather Conservative myself, so I don't mind its being rather Conservative, though I think, in the world-state, that will be the danger. A real world-state might be a wee bit too Conservative.'

But, seeing a slight shade pass over Burwash's good humour, she added quickly, 'Though it will be a very nice State to live in—like this.' She looked round at the fire, the recumbent club members stretched out in their long chairs, the glittering tumblers, the pipes, the attentive servants, moving round the circle with plates of savouries. 'I wish I could live to see it.'

'Do you think they'll play polo?' said Fisk, who had hit his first goal on the day before, 'or will that be considered a bourgeois game?'

'I'm sure they'll play all the most expensive games—there'll be nothing else to do except amuse themselves with a little voluntary work. And the ponies will be free, of course.'

Rubin, who was in high spirits, rubbing his knees and curling his moustache, glanced at the company store over his left shoulder, gave a chuckle, and asked when the free ponies would start to be given way.

'Some people say quite soon—they think the world-state has started already.'

'I belong to the League of Nations myself,' said Fisk.

'I know, and I think you're quite right'—with a glance at Fisk which seemed to include him in a private understanding. 'But I wasn't thinking of the League, but more of international finances and the different Treasuries. Some people think that they will do it much sooner—to keep everybody from being ruined, and themselves from being murdered.'

'Not a hope,' said Prince, now in temporary charge at Hides Store. 'Do you know what I'm getting for hides, f.o.b. Forcados?'

But he was interrupted by the arrival of a soldier in fatigue khaki and a green wool cap, carrying a large sheet of white paper. The paper

was printed with six two-inch hieroglyphics, sharply and clearly defined in blue-black ink.

'What do you think of that?' said Rubin, springing up and handing. the paper to Judy. Judy blushed with surprise and gazed at the paper.

Rubin pushed out his stomach to its most dignified. He said, 'Let me introduce Company Quarter-master Sergeant Suli Bouchi.'

The soldier, a hideous little man, middle-aged, with a deeply-wrinkled face, stood stiffly at attention, except for his right hand, which held the paper like a sword at an officer's salute. Rubin took the paper, and held it up so that both the party and the sergeant could see it.

He pointed at the first of the hieroglyphics: ᗺ
'What's that, sergy?'

The sergeant, still rigidly at attention, compressed his lips and then burst them open in a loud explosion: 'Beee.'

Rubin swelled a fraction; his chest was perceptibly larger. 'And this, sergy?' He pointed at ⴼ

'Eff,' said the sergeant.

'And this?' ꓵ
'Issss,' hissed the sergeant.

'And this?' ꓭ
'F-f-four.'

But Burwash interrupted, 'Ask him the one at the end, Rubin.'

Rubin quickly pointed at ꓤ; but Burwash said, 'No, not the gibbet': and the whole party began to call at him together, 'The one at the bottom.'

'The one you've got your thumb over.'

'No, no, the gibbet,' said Judy.

But Rubin was not at all disconcerted; he shifted his thumb, and exposed this ꓜ. He said in his most dignified voice, 'Do you mean——'

'No, no,' they shouted at him. 'Ask the sergeant.'

'Double-yuuu,' sang the sergeant.

Rubin beamed upon him. 'Splendid, sergeant. As double as you like. Now if you could go and make a shot at the rest, I'll come along to the store in half an hour and see about the printing.'

The sergeant saluted and right-about-ed. Rubin said loudly, as soon as the man turned his back, 'That's the cleverest man in Nigeria, bar none.'

This was his method of congratulating the sergeant without injuring his respect for white prestige. He sat down, still holding the paper, and smiled at the party. 'Of course, cutting 'em out of an old tyre was my own idea. Rather a brain-wave, I think.'

The party congratulated him, and he said thoughtfully, 'But I've got other ideas for using old tyres.'

Judy interrupted, 'But, Captain Rubin, what does the sergeant read?'

'Ammunition boxes and signals. He's a dab at figures, too, any side up'; and he told a long story about the astonishing skill of his company signallers in taking down and sending messages in a language they did not understand. At the end of it Judy declared suddenly and forcefully that people had a right to learn reading, it was an elementary right.

Everybody had forgotten her fad, and her remark produced a lively argument. Nobody took her seriously, because they knew that she had been a don, but all desired to refute her, even Fisk; who, having lately been educated, and not yet having experience, was inclined to doubt the value of all education. The air was full of the clichés of a thousand years.

'What would they do with it?'

'Making them discontented.'

'Shakespeare for a lot of apes.'

'Slow but sure is the secret.'

'Give me the real old bush pagan.'

'The worst horse-boy I ever had was from the mission school.'

'But *not* mission schools,' cried Judy, 'and *not* Shakespeare, and *not* everybody, and *not* in English unless they're going to be clerks. It isn't slow and sure nowadays, it's slow and dangerous.'

'I know *exactly* what you mean, Mr. Fisk. I feel *just* like that myself.'

'You're *absolutely* right, Mr. Burwash—an out-of-work intelligentsia is a *frightful* danger and nuisance, and it would be *awfully* wrong to take them from their farms. But, Captain Rubin, English soldiers are quite *well* educated nowadays, and they didn't run away in France.'

The doctor, who at eight o'clock arrived to rescue his patient, found her carrying on four different arguments and two flirtations at the same time.

She did not flirt with Rubin because she was too fond of the man. She was beginning to be critical of the manner in which he neglected his gifts and opportunities.

Fathers took her straight back to hospital and put her to bed. He was indignant.

He was still more indignant when the hospital boy called him at nine o'clock from his coffee and his young wife, and he found Miss Coote propped up in bed teaching the A B C to a blue-shirted negro sitting on the floor. Rubin, in his dirty white mess-jacket which was too short for him, so that his patched shirt appeared between it and his cummerband at the back, was sitting beside the bed. He was pointing out the letters with his polo-stick walking-cane on a sheet of paper spread on the floor before the pupil.

Miss Coote, in a brown silk pyjama jacket, with her hair in two pigtails tied with brown ribbon, held another sheet, and was explaining rapidly in mixed Rimi and English that A was like a new roof.

She was flushed; Fathers, as soon as he set eyes on her, said, 'This will put up the temperature again.'

He was firm; to Rubin he was short and almost rude. As a Nigerian doctor he was not going to stand any nonsense from anybody. Judy pleaded with him, 'Just for a few minutes, doctor. You know I don't ever go to sleep till twelve, anyhow.'

'I'm sorry, Miss Coote, but this is the hospital.'

'But you said I might?'

'To-morrow morning.'

'But the poor boy's so anxious. He was waiting when I came back. He's been here all the evening, and he says he must begin now.'

Fathers was a young man as well as a Nigerian doctor. Nothing could move him.

'I'm sorry, Miss Coote, but I'm responsible for you and the hospital.'

The boy on the floor began to make an outcry. He crawled at the doctor's feet. He said that he would die if he was not allowed to learn book that very night.'

'Just ten minutes, doctor,' Judy implored. She smiled her most charming smile; she was going to bewitch the doctor.

But he, just married and impervious to eyes, answered, 'One evening can't make much difference'; and to the boy, 'You have plenty time to learn book—it will take you a year at least.'

The boy stared at him with horror; his eyes rolled upwards; his jaw dropped.

'No, no,' said Judy. 'Tom's a clever boy, aren't you, Tom? He was Louis's friend. He'll learn in six months.'

'Six mont,' the boy gibbered, and then he gave a despairing cry. 'You say you teach me to-night.'

The doctor laughed and Judy smiled. She began to explain that reading could not be learnt, even by a clever boy, in one night. The boy got up slowly and caught himself by the belly. He gave a deep moan which seemed to be the exhalation of a whole body and mind in a last agony. Then he ran out of the hospital.

XXXIV

Down in the *ju-ju* house, about half-past nine, Elizabeth was sitting at the back of the outer yard in her long chair; the whip lay across her knees.

A crowd stood four deep round the yard; and behind them rows of heads could be seen overtopping the mat walls. Their eyes glittered in the lantern-light like those of wolves come to a feast.

From the *ju-ju* house two long lines of watchers, three, four, and five deep, reached up the lane and across the square and half-way up the main street leading towards the station. Here the two lines joined and bulged outwards into a large cluster, from which a loud noise came, of voices talking all at once, and bursts of high whinnying laughter; the laugh of those, all the world over, who expect to enjoy the humiliation or pain of others.

In the middle of this cluster Akande Tom, in full dress of shirt and hat, carrying in his hand a large sheet printed with A B C, was explaining why he did not mean to return to the *ju-ju* house.

'I not fit go dem *ju-ju*,' he shouted, raising his chin, pushing out his lips into the air, as if to aim, allowing for the trajectory, at the *ju-ju* house. 'I no fear dem Lisbet—I catch book—I Christin man—she no fit teach me——'

He moved incessantly; strutting round the circle of the crowd, running a few steps towards the *ju-ju* house to yell at it.

'I no go back dar—I no *gree* for dem *ju-ju* house'; and then running back again, and speaking over his shoulder: 'You leff dem *ju-ju* now, Lisbet. Dey no good. I go 'way—I catch book.' And he flourished the sheet with the A B C. 'I Christin man—I no savage man no more.'

He was pouring with sweat; his face worked in spasms; it seemed to be all in movement, soft and plastic, like a small baby's; and his expression was now one of fury, and then he seemed to be weeping.

'I no fear you, Lisbet,' he screamed.

But at every run to and fro he was a yard nearer the *ju-ju* house.

The people were shrieking and dancing with laughter; they staggered about like drunkards with their loads of joy, the nervous convulsions of the intoxicated. They were not drunk only with cruelty and its stimulation; but something much deeper and richer, full of

302

their own pain; full of spite against humanity itself and their own weakness.

They delighted in Tom's misery and terror, not only because he tried to escape from the herd, but because they were sunk in fear themselves; and also because some fragment of spirit in them, which knew freedom and had pride, was enslaved inside them, blind and helpless, and forced to eat humiliation every day.

When Tom came to the door of the *ju-ju* house, the screams of hysterical laughter suddenly ceased. The people held their breath, standing with open mouths and shining eyes.

Tom was looking through the porch door. He could see, twenty feet away, Elizabeth sitting in her chair. The lanterns hung on each side of the yard showed her in strong light and shadow; and exaggerated her size, her huge shoulders, the wide flamboyant curl of nostrils, lip, and jaw. She looked like a Rimi idol, carved by one of their own craftsmen and polished with oil and blood offerings; enlarged to the size of a giant. She was as still as wood. The enormous whip across her knees made a tapering line of gold in the lantern-light; a horizontal base for the mounting curves of muscle.

Tom was stooping forward with his eyes turned up, fixed upon Elizabeth. He could be heard muttering to himself very fast, like a man with a chill whose teeth chatter while he is trying to talk.

He did not know what he was saying, and his gibbering lips clipped off the words in the middle.

He shuffled slowly through the porch, one step in half a minute; his stoop grew lower; his mouth looser; his arms hung down; his body and face were changing before the eyes of the people, watching the spray fly from his flabby, jerking lips.

He seemed like a baboon, shuffling to and fro, stooping down; and his meaningless speech was like monkey chatter: 'No gree—Lisbet—catch book—leff *ju-ju*—gree—ju—boo—lisboo—booju——'

But nobody laughed. They stared, fascinated, to see the witch's work on the man; to watch him change from man to beast, with a beast's stupid brain.

Obishala strolled out from some corner with a cigarette in her mouth and Elizabeth's baby in her arms; she placed herself beside Elizabeth, and looked at the people with a bored, condescending air. The baby seemed to stare at Tom, but it was probably too young to see anything except the blue of his shirt.

He was leaning gradually further out of the perpendicular. His hat fell off. At last he fell suddenly on all fours. He began to creep along the yard, still muttering. But his arms seemed to grow shorter; his head and blue shirt became lower, flatter, as if they wanted to sink back into the dirt; until he was creeping like a lizard, with his elbows above his back, and his legs doubled under him. He moved like a lizard; stopping for five minutes in one place without motion except in his head and eyes, gazing and blinking upwards, then rushing off with a loud scraping of his knees and hands.

After two lizard rushes which carried him about eight feet, his chest and chin were on the ground; his legs, spread out like a frog's, trailed behind him. His arms were under him, and he no longer used them; he was wriggling, jerking; tremors passed through his back and thighs from his neck to his feet. He was now silent. In this silence a low mumbling sound was heard; a door opened somewhere, and a child's voice, full of excitement and energy, exclaimed, 'But, granny, do you know that——'

An old woman, grumbling to herself, carrying by a string handle a kerosene tin full of hot water, pushed through the crowd and waddled across the yard. She was followed by Ibu, who, breaking off her question, looked round at the crowd, at Elizabeth and Tom, and, finding nothing to interest her, ran after the cook, grumbling still more loudly at the crowd, which was impeding her work. No one paid any attention to these intruders. But the people, even while they stared, fascinated, at the bewitched man, moved hastily out of Ibu's way. She was known to have a witch's power and to be Elizabeth's pupil.

Ibu, accustomed already to crowds and ceremonies, and indifferent to them as any little princess, was chatting again: 'Granny, granny. But you aren't listening. I said——'

Their voices diminished into the next compound and were cut off, no doubt, as they entered the kitchen hut.

Tom's body was still wriggling, as if by itself; and, though his arms and legs were limp and dragging, it was seen that by some action of his jerking, working muscles he was moving forward inch by inch. It was as if, in becoming like a snake, he had acquired a snake's power to move without limbs. But it was ten minutes or more before he had wormed his way across the last three yards and his face touched Elizabeth's feet.

Obishala, holding her head crooked to keep the cigarette smoke out of her eyes, stepped forward and with a lazy gesture pulled the blue shirt over the boy's head. Elizabeth kicked away his face and got up; she smiled at the crowd, but nobody dared to answer even with a smile. They dared not even meet the look of a person so terrible in power.

Tom lay motionless and soft. His tense muscles had relaxed; his thighs bulged against the earth. As he lay with his head under the blue shirt he seemed to have lost shape; to be spreading like a flattened, boneless mass—a black jelly, protoplasm.

Elizabeth disappointed her admirers. She did not use half her strength. The boy was walking in a week. Her explanation was that she had not wished to spoil him too much.

It is agreed in the town that a whipping was what Tom needed. He swaggers more than ever; but even the little boys laugh at him; and he no longer tries to be a white man, or to learn book.

He therefore gets plenty of pocket-money, and plenty of smuggled gin from Makurdi's new store. His figure is going. Obishala gives him six months.

Prefatory Essay by Joyce Cary
written especially for the Carfax Edition of
THE AFRICAN WITCH

THE AFRICAN WITCH

*a prefatory essay by the author specially
written for this edition*

THIS book began in a sketch, made sometime in the middle twenties, of an African nationalist. I called him the Black Prince, and he was, as far as I can remember, a much more violent and hysterical man than Aladai.

For some reason, having got so far as notes on possible plots and a few descriptions, I put all the papers into one of the canvas bags which I had used in Africa to carry manuscripts. Later I added to the same bag some notes on the watch-tower movement in Africa, and other primitive sects derived from various sources. I remember a newspaper cutting about a prophet who, when he baptized converts, at night, in a deep river, also drowned them, so that, being cleansed of sin, and having no time to sin again, they went straight to Paradise.

I opened that bag from time to time and was always excited by this rich material. What can be more fascinating than the work of the religious imagination, for good or evil, on men's minds and so upon history. James' *Varieties of Religious Experience* is one of the most absorbing books in the world. For the fundamental question, the root of all politics, all arts, is what do men live by? What makes them tick and keeps them ticking; and if you answer love and hate, curiosity, ambition, duty and pride, you are already deep, whether you like it or not, in metaphysics, in the science of the soul, or whatever synonym you may choose for that central activity.

The oddest thing in this odd world is to see the violence

of people who think of themselves as atheists and mechanists, in argument about questions which are purely metaphysical, questions of right and wrong, duty, social justice, and truth. It is a revelation of character to see how angrily good-natured men, who regard themselves as completely reasonable beings, will fight about some question of politics (the materialist dialectic) or science (just now it has been once more evolution) upon premises which ignore the ground of the whole discussion—in politics, human nature, or in evolution, the will to live (and to win arguments at all costs)—that is, upon a tacit understanding to fight according to a mechanist convention. And yet with what strong feeling and obstinate will, each defends a position taken up perhaps twenty or thirty years before, which has now become both fortress and prison. The argument itself, so far from being mechanist, is hardly rational. It is a bitter war to defend those dogmatic fortresses and prisons from which the warriors would no more venture their noses than primitive negroes dare to go out at night into a strange forest, full of were-beasts and demons.

And each is trying to persuade the other (as well as himself) that his creed is the only reasonable certain truth, and that outside it there is in fact nothing but darkness and devils.

The attraction of Africa is that it shows these wars of belief, and the powerful often subconscious motives which underlie them, in the greatest variety and also in very simple forms. Basic obsessions, which in Europe hide themselves under all sorts of decorous scientific or theological or political uniforms, are there seen naked in bold and dramatic action.

But though I often opened the green bag and added a note to it, even wrote parts of chapters, I always turned aside from the serious work of making a book about the Black Prince. And after I finished the *American Visitor* I decided to write no more books about Africa. I was actually planning Castle Corner, to cover a wider scene (and, above all, to avoid the African setting which, just because it is dramatic, demands a certain kind of story, a certain violence and coarseness of detail, almost a fabulous treatment, to keep it in its place), when my agents asked me for another African book, and I reflected that it would be easy to complete the Black Prince before I had finished the great amount of preparation needed for the *Castle Corner* monument.

In the event, it was not easy. I found that one difficulty which I had not faced (but perhaps an unconscious perception of it had discouraged me before) was the similarity between my nationalist spell-binder and the African priest. Both were hysterical enthusiasts. And the second, even greater problem, was the eternal one of limits, what to bring in, to give a fair picture, what must be left out, to avoid muddle and incoherence.

This is where a writer's responsibility is most pressing; to do justice and to give truth, in a medium which is at once the only vehicle of truth as an experience, and at the same time highly subjective and irrational; that is to say, the truth of art which is true because it conveys the feeling without which 'facts' are insignificant and delusive, but at the same time personal to each reader. So that the writer has continually to ask himself not only, is this a fair picture, but how far can it be misunderstood. In practice, as every writer knows, whatever he writes will be somewhere misunderstood. This book, for instance, was at once treated, even by serious officials, as an attack on their administration; by street corner politicians, as a work on the colour-bar. True, in 1936, political ideas and political arguments were a good deal more innocent than they are to-day. Most of the discussion was in the style of Reading without Tears. A cat is on the mat. The Empire is naughty. Primitive savages are good—but European civilization is corrupt. My book was meant to show certain men and their problems in the tragic background of a continent still little advanced from the Stone Age, and therefore exposed, like no other, to the impact of modern turmoil. An overcrowded raft manned by children who had never seen the sea would have a better chance in a typhoon.

What is startling to anyone who has done a real political job, is the naivety and cocksureness of popular slogans about government, which is the most difficult and uncertain job in the world. And comments on this book made me say I would never write another like it; they made me feel that I could not do so (knowing the actual difficulties of government) without the meanness of rousing prejudice and creating injustice.

For instance, the story of Tom who wants to 'learn book' was used to raise the cry that the Empire had failed to educate the African, and that this was the worst of its crimes. But the authorities had given plenty of thought to a problem which was full of difficulties. There were no teachers in Africa, no common language, no agreement between races on language, no text books. And there were as good arguments for starting with small numbers and giving picked minds a first class education in English as for general elementary teaching which would have to be of the lowest type.

What was behind this cry were two assumptions equally hollow. One was that education would abolish barbarity and violence. The contrary is true. Education would bring in more violence, more barbarities; it would break up what is left of tribal order, and open the whole country to the agitator.

The second was that education is a natural and 'obvious' right of mankind. But it is neither natural nor obvious. The demand, in fact, that anyone should be educated is purely ethical. It belongs to metaphysics, to a view of the world as the realm of spirit. The real reason why Africa should be educated is that it is the duty, the religious duty, if you like, for all of us to desire enlightenment for all men, for all God's souls. And this was the motive (even when they did not know it) of the 'atheists', rationalists, and so on who declared education a 'natural right'. What they meant by 'natural' and 'obvious' was that it was beyond argument, that they were absolutely sure of it. But they would find it very hard to justify such an assumption on any political or rational grounds.

The problem of education in Africa, like all the rest, is full of uncertainties and dangers. We must educate the Africans as fast as we can. And the Africans will take education because they eagerly desire it. They want it at any cost, not because it will give them peace and happiness, but for the same reason that they desire wealth (if only a reach-me-down suit of cotton and a Manchester cloth for their wives) to satisfy need, to create some glory and dignity for themselves and those they love.

J. C.

About the Author

Joyce Cary, who died in 1957, was born in 1888 in Donegal, Ireland, of a Devonshire family long settled in that part. He was given for first name, according to a common Anglo-Irish practice, his mother's surname of Joyce. He was educated at Clifton and Trinity, Oxford, and also studied art in Edinburgh and Paris. Afterward he went to the Near East and joined a Montenegrin battalion for the war of 1912-13, and was attached to a British Red Cross party at the front.

Subsequently Cary studied Irish Co-operation under Sir Horace Plunkett, and in 1913 joined the Nigerian political service. He fought in the Nigerian regiment during World War I and was wounded at Mora Mountain. On returning to political duty, as magistrate and executive officer, he was sent to Borgu, then a very remote district, where he made close acquaintance with primitive native life. His health, however, had never recovered from war service and he was advised to retire from tropical Africa. He then began to write, and his first novel, AISSA SAVED, was published in 1930.

In addition to many novels, Joyce Cary wrote books and pamphlets on political theory, and the film story of MEN OF TWO WORLDS with an African setting. Joyce Cary's last novel, THE CAPTIVE AND THE FREE, was published in 1959, his collected short stories, SPRING SONG AND OTHER STORIES, in 1960.